# The Hill of Dreams

*Volume 2 of the Guardians of Albion Series*

by

## Dolores Ashcroft-Nowicki

**Library and Archives Canada Cataloguing in Publication**

Title: The hill of dreams / Dolores Ashcroft-Nowicki.
Names: Ashcroft-Nowicki, Dolores, author.
Description: Series statement: Guardians of Albion ; 2
Identifiers: Canadiana 20200304380 | ISBN 9781896238258 (softcover)
Classification: LCC PR6101.S5d3 H55 2020 | DDC 823/.92—dc23

Twin Eagles Publishing
Box 2031
Sechelt BC
V0N 3A0

pblakey@telus.net

## Dedication

To Thomas my grandson with my love now and always.

The Singing Stones and Hill of Dreams were written for my grandson Thomas. He is now a grown man, but he is always close to my heart as the young boy he was. The real Thomas and the character have grown together. I hope there will always be room for the magical and the unexpected in his life as there has been in mine.

## Acknowledgements:

To Herbie Brennan who has always been an encouragement.

To Carol and Steven Lomax without whom this book would never have been written. Their encouragement and practical help in suggestions and the skilful editing has been my mainstay. Plus their emotional support for me and my family during a time of great personal stress kept us going. Thank you and bless you.

To Michelle Cowbourne for permission to use her photo of the Tor as the Cover.

To Chris Hill for the incidental drawings and the Fae Escutcheons.

# Chapter One

## Cambridge: The University Fencing Salon. 4:30pm

**The duellists circled**, sword tips just touching, each feeling out the strength of their opponent's grip. They exchanged a few minor passes, then came a flurry of action punctuated by the instructions of the taller of the two.

"Prima, tierce, quatro, secundo, lunge, advance, parry, advance. Lunge, riposte, retreat, retreat, running lunge and… strike!" The man acknowledged the solid hit saluting gracefully, then took off his mask and smiled at the perspiring girl in front of him.

"That was much better Becky, it was quicker and far more accurate, but your running lunge needs a bit more ferocity and intent behind it. Just because we don't fight duels for real anymore doesn't mean we can't fight with passion. Get it? Okay, off you go and get your shower." The girl nodded and departed glowing from his praise.

Left alone Thomas Carrick walked across to the mirror set into the wall of the fencing salon and stood for a moment just looking at his reflection. He was not a vain man, but every now and then he liked to take a good look at himself just to make sure he was still who he thought he was. The face that looked back at him still showed traces of the boy he had been nearly ten years ago when his life had changed so dramatically

Now, at 5'10" the mirror showed the same fine boned face and dark blonde hair, the same inborn grace of movement and ready grin and the same ocean deep-blue eyes. The only thing that might be remarked on was a slight point at the top of the ears! His friend Drew said it was his fairy blood showing through. He smiled at the thought and turned away unbuttoning his padded jacket and whistling as he walked to the men's changing room.

It would be Drew's birthday in a couple of days and he still hadn't decided what to give him as a present. That he was wealthy enough to give his friend anything, from his own island to a top class racehorse, was beside the point.

As a man of simple tastes, Drew appreciated the thought far more than the gift itself. Thomas turned different ideas over in his mind as he showered.

Later, dressed and on his way to dinner, he crossed the quadrangle still mulling over the problem. Halfway across he heard his name called and turned. Mullins, one of the porters, came trotting over the gravelled path waving an envelope in his hand.

"Sir Thomas, Sir Thomas Carrick, a message for you sir. Just been delivered."

"Thanks Mullins, much obliged to you." He pocketed the paper and went on to his meal still thinking over the knotty problem of Drew's present.

Dining in the University hall always thrilled him, the formality and the feel of centuries of tradition was something he appreciated more than most of his companions. As he took his accustomed place he exchanged greetings with tutors, friends and acquaintances alike. He was a popular figure with most of them. Not because he was wealthy, indeed many of them had no idea how much he was worth, but because he was pleasant, obliging and well-mannered. His tutors worked him hard and doted on him in private, grateful for work handed in on time that was readable and not covered with coffee stains.

In the last eight years Thomas had struggled to discipline himself to accept the studies selected for him. It had come as a pleasant surprise to find he'd inherited his great-grandfather's business acumen and his propensity to cope with wealth without letting it overpower him.

"Hey Tom, there's a party at Steven's place tonight, are you coming?" The freckled face of Robbie Gordon beamed with delight at the thought of an evening away from his books. Thomas shook his head smiling.

"I'm away home tonight, I've got a party of my own over the weekend. A friend of mine has a double celebration on Sunday. His forty-sixth birthday and his daughter's second. He's still in shock at being a father after all this time."

Amid the laughter that followed Charlie Naughton, a second year man still feeling his way into the group, asked rather shyly. "Er, Tom you live up in Derbyshire don't you?" Thomas nodded, his mouth full of Shepherd's pie.

"Maybe we could travel as far as Macclesfield together, unless of course you have other plans. I mean, I don't want to intrude or anything." His voice trailed off into an embarrassed silence.

Thomas was delighted. "That would be great, it's a long trip if you've no one to talk to. Are you packed and ready?" Charlie nodded eagerly. "So am I. I'll meet you outside the main gate in thirty minutes." Charlie hastily drank his tea and excused himself hardly able to credit the fact that he'd be travelling with someone as popular as Thomas. Perhaps things were beginning to look up for him in Cambridge.

Back in the dining room Robbie shook his head at Thomas. "What did you say that for? Now you'll be stuck with Chubby Charlie for hours. He'll bore you silly with stuff about the Roman invasion of Britain and how to dig broken bits of pottery out of holes in the ground with an old tooth-brush."

Thomas fixed him with eyes that had suddenly turned glacial. "Well I'll tell you Robbie, as it happens I'm very inter-ested in Roman Britain. Plus it's a damn sight more interest-ing than listening to you drone on about modern sociology. Besides, I remember what it was like to be new at Cambridge and not knowing a soul. For the first three weeks I never got so much as a Hello!"

He finished his tea and got up. "You're lucky Robbie. You come from a large family so you've never known what it's like to be lonely. I hope you never do. See you on Tuesday guys." And he was gone leaving the group with their mouths open and feeling rather foolish.

Charlie was waiting with a battered suitcase at his feet anxiously counting his money. He needed to get a taxi at the other end and it just occurred to him that Thomas might be travelling first class. He never seemed to worry much about money. Then Thomas himself spoke at his elbow making him jump.

"C'mon get in, it's starting to rain." Charlie was pro-pelled towards a top of the range Bentley saloon where a smiling middle-aged man in a well-cut grey suit was holding the door open. Before he could draw breath Charlie found himself sliding into a car that smelt of polished leather and had seats like armchairs.

The driver took his suitcase and stowed it away then climbed into the driver's seat as Thomas introduced him.

"Charlie this is Frank, Frank Jackson. His wife Betty is my housekeeper up in Deepdale. Frank meet Charlie Naughton, he's reading Archaeology, Medieval History and Middle English and we'll be seeing a lot more of him from now on. This was a great idea of yours Charlie I've been wanting to talk to you for a while now but you never stay around long enough for me to get hold of you."

Charlie tried to get his thoughts into focus. "Er is this a hire car?" he asked. "You see I usually catch the bus to the station." Thomas smiled. "Not this time Charlie, you're with me, and we'll take you right to your door, and pick you up early Tuesday morning. Is your first lecture in the afternoon like mine?"

"Er, yes it is. Thomas is this *your* car?"

Thomas sat back and laughed. "Don't look so worried Charlie I didn't nick it. Yes it's my car and Frank's going to drive us all the way home, nice and comfy and warm."

"It's really very kind of you, I feel awful asking to travel with you. I didn't know you see…!" His companion put a hand on his arm.

"No need to apologise, I'd have asked you before now only, as I say, you're a little hard to get hold of. I know what it's like in the first couple of years, no one seems to want to know you and there's so much going on that's new and bewildering it's like a bad dream."

"Yes," admitted Charlie beginning to relax. "Is that how it was for you?"

"It was for a while, then I learned to stand up for myself, and for others." He leaned forward. "Now, tell me about your studies, Roman Britain is your speciality isn't it?"

For the next two hours he listened with rapt attention as the young man the others called Chubby Charlie dazzled him with his expertise. He answered questions, and gave examples, quotes and references. Halfway they stopped in a lay-by and shared hot coffee and slices of homemade fruitcake that melted on the tongue. Then exhausted by excitement and enthusiasm Charlie fell asleep soon after they resumed their journey.

Frank nodded at Thomas in the driving mirror. "The lad surely knows what 'e's talking about don't he just?"

"Yes, he's a full scholarship man, which doesn't endear him to the playboys. I think I'll invite him to live at the town house. It'll give him more privacy, and companionship if and when he wants it and ease the money problem as well. I'll ask his tutor what books he needs and 'loan' them to him. He's a real find Frank. But now I think I'll follow his example and take a nap." Frank nodded smiling and drove on into the gathering darkness.

\* \* \*

Thomas shook Charlie's arm gently. "Wake up Charlie we're coming into Manchester and Frank needs your address." Charlie rubbed his eyes and tried to focus on his surroundings.

"Heavens, I must have slept for hours. You should have woken me up. That was so rude of me." He ran his fingers through a mop of brown curly hair. Thomas hastened to re-assure him.

"I've been asleep myself. Now, where do you live?"

"Oh, it's Farley Road in Newton Heath, number 26. But you don't have to take me all the way Mr. Jackson." He leaned over to the driver, "I can grab a bus from anywhere near here." But Frank was having none of it.

"Not at this time of night you won't lad. It's not safe when it gets past closing time, besides it's still raining hard. It's not but a few minutes to drive thee." Twenty minutes later he stopped outside a little terrace house and got Charlie's case from the boot.

"I don't know how to thank you, both of you. It was

9

a great trip, just sorry I spoilt it by falling asleep. Too many late nights I think."

"We'll pick you up on Tuesday morning, about 9:00. Will that be alright?" asked Thomas smiling. Charlie nodded, too overcome to speak. Then he grabbed his bag and ran up the neat little path pulling out his key. Frank and Thomas got back in the car and drove away.

Frank looked in the mirror at the back seat. "What's tha' thinkin' lad?" he asked. "There's summat goin' on in that head o'yourn."

Thomas smiled, there was not much that got past Frank. "I was wondering why Charlie Naughton has come into my life at this particular time. Who is he? What is he? Where does he fit in? Somehow I know he'll be important in the future, but why?" A faint pressure at the back of his head told him there was more to the meeting than coincidence. Content with that he lay back and drifted off again.

Forty minutes later they came in sight of the Dales. Frank stopped the car in a lay-by bordering the moors and woke Thomas from his sleep.

"I thought ye'd like a run lad. Yer usually do, I'll wait fer thee int' usual place." Thomas got out of the car and stretched, sniffing the clear Dales air.

"It's good to be back Frank, even for a few days. This will always be home." Quickly he stripped down screened by the open door of the car, while Frank kept watch. Naked to the cool air he shivered, then closed his eyes and let the Change flow over him. Frank looked away knowing the lad preferred it that way. A moment later he felt a touch on his cheek and turned to look into the velvet eyes of a huge stag. He rubbed a gentle hand over the soft muzzle.

"I'll be waiting fer thee lad, take care now." The stag sprang away leaping down the embankment and on to the heath beyond. Then he was away with a thunder of hooves.

Thomas was back where he belonged. He ran with every ounce of strength in him, leaping the gullies and racing the shadows cast by the clouds as they scudded across the sky. The moon was almost full, the air was sweet and filled with the scents of the night and he was free. The miles flowed beneath his hooves and at some indefinable point he switched from the world of the Real onto the world of The Second Road.

This was a Britain that never changed, a Britain that Charlie Naughton would have recognised. Thomas met with and passed others of his kind along the way. Greetings were exchanged with most, some he avoided, while others avoided him. The landscape began to change back as he drew nearer to home and as he passed through an invisible barrier he returned to the world in which he lived most of his time. He slowed and finally stopped in a stand of trees by the road where the car was waiting. He stepped out from concealment and flowed into his own form. Frank held out his clothes.

"That were a quick run lad, I've only bin 'ere a minute or two meself."

Thomas dressed and feeling warmer slid into the car. "It was wonderful, but then it always is. Let's get home Frank, Betty will be worrying by now."

Within minutes they were turning into the driveway of Carrick House, the gracious old Manor left to Thomas by his great-grandfather. The front door was flung open and light streamed out as the car drew to a halt. The woman who came down the steps to enfold Thomas in her arms carried faint scars on her pleasantly rounded face, scars of a battle that had changed many things for all three of them. Her welcome was warm, her voice anxious.

"You've been running again haven't you Thomas? I hope you've not got chilled. There's hot chocolate and a sandwich by your bed. Go get a shower, then to sleep. 'Tis nigh on midnight you young rascal." She ruffled his hair and shooed him inside, waving to her husband. "I'll just be a minute Frank."

Her husband nodded and turned the car round ready to drive back to the Gatehouse. He lit a cigarette and thought about the stag racing away into the night. Not many human beings could do that he told himself, but Thomas Greystone-Carrick was not altogether human, leastways, that was his opinion.

Upstairs, Thomas undressed for the second time that evening and found the unread message in his coat pocket. Frowning, he turned it over. It was certainly addressed to him but he didn't recognise the writing. He yawned and returned it to his pocket. Whatever it was it would keep until morning, but now he needed a shower and some sleep.

\* \* \*

He was dreaming, at least he thought he was dreaming, but it seemed very real. He was on top of the Tor locally called The Hill of Dreams and some sixty feet below stood the Singing Stones Circle. At the moment the Tor was occupied by a tall elegant figure with hair as black as Whitby jet and eyes of silver grey. He sat at his ease on the chair-shaped rock said to have magical powers and smiled winningly.

"The Luck of the Evening Star to you Thomas Carrick," said the stranger in a musical tenor that held the lilt of Erin in it. "Our meeting has been long in coming but 'tis all the more welcome for that." He rose to his feet in a fluid movement that set his black ankle length leather coat swirling around him. I bring you greetings from Avalon, especially from the one you knew as Grim." Thomas moved forward eagerly.

"You're from Avalon?" He asked.

"Not exactly, though our borders meet at certain places... and times. I am Cormac, son of Midir of Tyr nan Og and my race is that of the Sidhe though you would call us Faerie. A human term we never use when speaking of ourselves."

Thomas, used though he was to the unusual, shook his head in amused disbelief. "A Fairy! Do you by any chance have wings?" His companion smiled broadly.

"Only when there is a need for them. What you see as wings are simply extensions of the etheric matter of our normal form, as are our clothes. However, if you prefer it...!"

The coat melted away leaving him clad in a tunic of green and gold with high boots of scarlet leather. From his shoulders sprang two translucent fan shaped appendages that quivered in the night air. Delighted, Thomas threw back his head and laughed. "I think Prince Cormac, we would both prefer your former appearance as being more fitting for this time and place." They laughed together and the Sidhe resumed his modern dress.

"Why am I here?" asked Thomas. "If you've called me, and brought me greetings from Avalon, then there is a reason. I'd also hazard a guess that my physical body is still sleeping, is that true?" Cormac nodded.

"Merlyn said you would be easy to speak with, but will you be easy to teach, Thomas of Carrick?"

"Ah," said Thomas quietly. "So that's the way of it. I should've guessed. Though I think you should know that I have studies of a different kind to deal with at the moment. They are important to life in my world where many people depend on me."

"That is understood, what you will learn from me is not onerous, but it will affect your life in both worlds. You must learn to exist equally well in both and for that you need my help for your enemy is also a man of magical power.

13

Thomas was startled. "My enemy? But surely Mordred is now in Avalon with his father and an enemy no more?" Cormac walked to the very edge of the Tor and stood looking out over the moors.

"You are, or will be, the Arch-Mage of Britain so you will always have enemies Thomas. You will face challenges to your position in both your physical life and in those worlds that border your own. That is why Merlyn asked me to be your guide in these matters." Thomas went to stand at his side, unafraid of the drop below him.

"I am not unwise in the ways of those worlds, and I know that nothing is given without a return. What is your price Prince Cormac?"

"That is the second time you have addressed me as such, giving me no choice but to answer truthfully Sir Thomas. As you surmise, I intend to ask a price for my services."

"It is wise to be wary of the ways of the Sidhe," said Thomas. "At least so Father John once told me, so I ask you again Prince Cormac, what is your price?"

"When the time comes I ask you to name me Guardian of your eldest son."

Thomas turned, startled. "You would take my son from me? One as yet unborn?"

"No! By my blood and honour I would not ask such a price. I ask only that you name me his Guardian and mentor in my world. I give my word he will not be harmed in any way, only that he will know me and know my world, as will you, his father. Have we a bargain?"

Thomas looked out over the Dales he loved and thought, not for the first time, of having a son to follow him. "Are you so sure I will have a son?"

Cormac's presence behind him was like a pillar of power. "Yes, you will have two sons, and a daughter also. Will you meet my price Thomas?"

14

Thomas was silent for a long time. This was a question with many answers, none of them easy. Dealings with the Faerie world needed a cool head and a certain amount of cunning. Yet, there was a good feeling about this meeting and a noble of the Sidhe would be as good as his word if he in turn was treated with honour.

"If you ask for this there must be a reason and an important one. May I ask what that reason might be?"

Cormac was silent for a while, then said, "Yes there is a reason and, at least for me, a very good one. However I would ask that for the moment you do not press me on this. It might work against us both if you knew." He turned to face the young man beside him. "Give me your trust on this Thomas of Carrick and I swear by the Cauldron of Dagda you will have no cause to regret it." Thomas looked into his eyes and made his decision.

"Then yes, I will meet your price, on your word that you will not harm him in either of our worlds."

The tall Sidhe extended his hand, "My hand and my honour on it." Their hands met and clasped. Then Cormac took hold of a strand of Thomas' hair and with quick deft fingers wove it into a thin tight braid.

"This is called a Geas, a braid that binds you to your task and your word, it may not be broken in your world or mine, and cannot be undone until the task is completed." He shook his own sable mane back and Thomas saw that he too wore a Geas.

"Now we are both bound, by our tasks and by our destinies and they are closer than you realise. Goodbye until we meet again my friend, and that time will not be long in coming." Cormac pushed him and Thomas went over the edge and fell, plummeting through the air.

He woke sweating in his own bed, his heart pounding and his yell of fright echoing in his ears. He got up and went to the window to look across the lightening sky towards Circle Tor. He had no doubt his dream had been real and Cormac would be true to his word, they would meet again. As he turned to go back to bed he heard a scratch at the door and a soft whine. He opened it and an enthusiastic bundle of black and white fur leapt into his arms.

"Hi Grim little fellow, it's great to see you again." The Jack Russell leapt on to the bed and gave a soft whuff cocking his head to one side inquiringly. "Well it's just after four and I went to bed late, so you'll have to wait for your morning walk. But you're welcome to sleep on the bed until I get up." He got back into bed and the terrier curled up at his feet content to wait.

Thomas slept again, but dreamlessly this time and woke to a misty morning, a knock on his door and the impatient barking of Grim. Yawning, he turned, stretched and called out, "Come in Dad."

Steven Greystone had not changed a great deal over the last eight years. He now wore gold-rimmed glasses and stooped a little, but the same grin that lit his son's face was reflected in his own.

"Hi there Tombo, great to have you back son. Betty has your favourite breakfast on the go right now. You have ten minutes to shave, shower, and dress. So get to it. Grim, you come with me and have a quick run outside. I'll take you on the moor after breakfast." The dog padded after him and Thomas reluctantly got out of bed and headed for the bathroom.

As he showered and dressed the house slowly came alive around him. The sound of vacuuming, doors opening and closing, shouts and conversation from the staff as they went about their daily tasks were all reminders of home and he slowly relaxed into the dear familiarity of it all. He wandered into the kitchen just as Betty Jackson was filling his plate.

"Morning Tom," she beamed. "It's good to have someone with an appetite in the house. Your father seems to think one piece of toast and umpteen cups of coffee make a breakfast. I can't get him to understand that a good meal should begin the day." She put a plate of eggs, bacon, and fresh field mushrooms in front of him and stood back with a smile as Thomas fell on it like a young wolf.

Steven poured himself a third cup of coffee and sat back. "Well I seem to work better on an empty stomach. Reminds me of why I began to write in the first place... to pay the food bills."

"You did well dad, just keep doing what you do and we won't starve." Thomas' quip sent Betty Jackson off into gales of laughter.

"With two multi-millionaires in the same house I don't think we'll have trouble paying the milkman." She went off chuckling to herself.

"How's the new book coming along dad?" asked Thomas over a mouthful of mushrooms.

"Pretty well, I have to go down to London next week to do some research at the Imperial War Museum. Then I'm due in the States next month to run a three week course in Creative Writing at the University of Pennsylvania. I'll take some time after that to visit your mother."

For a moment the two men were silent, both thinking of Nora Greystone, now Nora Kowalski. The hurt and turmoil of the divorce had left its mark on both of them in different ways one of which was a mutual determination to protect each other. Thomas, sixteen at the time had leapt to his father's defence against the accusation of neglect and disinterest, pointing out that it was Steven's work that had given her everything she wanted including the man to whom she was now married.

Things had sorted themselves out eventually, but Thomas had drawn away from his mother, though she was welcome at the manor whenever she wished to come, providing she came alone. For his part Steven still loved her and would have taken her back at any time, but he understood the hurt Thomas had endured.

Betty came bustling back with the post with Wally the postman trailing after her. Wally was one of the Guardians of the Singing Stones and was looking forward to a well-earned retirement. He headed for the coffee pot as usual and settled into a chair to gossip with Betty. Thomas greeted him with affection and finished off his breakfast while they talked. His father had taken Grim for his promised walk so he took the post and went to his office.

As he entered he looked up at the portrait of his great-grandfather and greeted him with a cheery salute. "Morning, you old rogue. Let's see what's cooking in the mail." He'd fallen into the habit of talking to the portrait from the time they had moved in to the manor.

This had been the old man's study, with his desk and chair still in use. Thomas had wanted his father to have the gracious wood panelled room, but Steven pointed out that he worked better in a smaller and less ornate setting. His study was at the back of the house and looked out over the gardens lovingly restored by Posy Docker, another of the Stones' Guardians.

Most of the mail was bills, requests or complaints from tenants and invitations to parties and events both locally and elsewhere. He threw them into the IN tray and went to look out of the window. Thrusting his hands into his pockets he came across the letter he'd brought with him from Cambridge. The envelope was of expensive handmade paper and bore a return address to an exclusive London area. Thomas opened it with a feeling of uneasiness.

Dear Sir Thomas,

I trust you will forgive my foregoing a formal introduction. I have been hoping for some time to effect a
contact with you. I knew your grandmother and was
once a guest of your great-grandfather at the manor.

I have been out of England for some time and only re-
cently learned of the death of your grandmother and
of your accession to the title.

I understand you are studying at Cambridge, I was
an Oxford man myself. I will be in London until next
Friday and was hoping I might offer you dinner on
Thursday next. I can be reached at my Club, the address is below, any day after twelve or you can leave a
message with the desk.

If the time is not convenient to you please let me know
and hopefully we can arrange another day.

Assuring you of my best wishes,

Yours faithfully

*Justin Thorndyke Ph.D.*

Thomas refolded the letter and slipped it back into
the envelope. He'd learned over the past eight years to trust
his feelings, and this letter had warning signs written all over
it in big red letters.

Uneasily he recalled his recent conversation with
Cormac, to the effect that he would always have enemies.
He stood thinking for a while then put the letter in the IN
tray with the others and went to one of the floor to ceiling
bookcases that lined three of the four walls and took down
the latest edition of Who's Who.

Seating himself at the leather topped desk he began

to leaf through the pages looking for relevant information on Justin Thorndyke. Before he accepted any invitations to break bread with this Mr Thorndyke he wanted to know more about him. A lot more.

# Chapter Two

"**You should have** seen it mum," said Charlie eagerly, "…
all polished leather, with a little fridge, a Mobile, even a little
TV. Everything you could wish for right there in the car." He
reached for another piece of toast, and continued…

"…. and it wasn't him showing off or anything like
that, he was just… well ordinary I suppose. He knew a lot
about my kind of work too, and asked some pretty searching questions. Took me all my time to answer some of them.
You'll be able to meet him when he comes to pick me up on
Tuesday morning." His mother beamed at him proudly.

"Well, that'll be one in the eye for Mrs Barnes next
door, Our Charlie in a chauffeur driven car. Well I never,
what do you think of that dear?" She lifted her face for her
husband's morning kiss.

"I think we have a very lucky son and I hope he
knows that." James Naughton eased himself down into his
chair and carefully lifted his stiff leg under the table. "Sounds
like a nice lad this Thomas Carrick."

"Well he's really Sir Thomas, dad, Sir Thomas Greystone-Carrick, but you'd never know it to talk to him. I mean
he speaks nicely, but not, you know, snotty like. His father is
Steven Greystone, the writer. They've just made a film of his
latest book, '*Run for your Life*'. It'll be out just before Christmas. I'll buy a copy of the book and ask Thomas to get his
dad to sign it for you."

His mother leaned forward anxiously. "Ought you to call him by his name Charlie, I mean, him being a knight and all that?" Charlie grinned at her.

"He asked me to, said it got boring being 'sirred' all the time." His mother nodded, impressed by her son's status as the friend of a titled gentleman. Then his father brought them down to earth.

"Well now Charlie, since you're home, you can give me a hand up at the allotment. There's a fair bit of weeding to do and we need to get the spring cabbages in afore the first bite of cold weather. It's a fair Autumn we're having, but it'll not last." Charlie mopped up the last bit of egg with his toast and got to his feet.

"Right, dad, be with you in a jiffy," and went off to get his coat. His mother looked after him, a little worried.

"Jimmy do you think it's alright him being friendly with this young man. He seems nice, but well, you know some of these titled people are into… drugs and such like." Her husband laid a hand on her shoulder.

"We brought him up proper Maisie lass. He's got a good head on him, he'll know if he's been taken in soon enough. Besides, we'll get a look at this young man on Tuesday. Don't fret." His wife smiled, calmed by his words and helped him on with his coat.

"Got your bus pass and your pills?" she asked. Father and son laughed at her motherly fussing, kissed her and went off. She watched from the window, then grabbed her cardigan from the back of her chair and went next door to do a little boasting on her son's behalf.

* * *

"Thank you Professor, I'm pretty sure I have at least three or four of these titles in my own library, the others I'll order in. Thanks for your help."

Thomas put down the phone and with the list in hand went over to the bookshelves. He'd paid a couple of English Lit students during the Easter recess to catalogue the library, and they'd done a good job. It took him a mere fifteen minutes to put together a selection of books that would be of use to Charlie Naughton. Then he put them on the desk and went to find his father.

He found him surrounded by empty cups of coffee and munching a slice of apple pie. "Come in," he yelled, hearing the knock on the door. "It's open. Oh it's you Tom lad, wait a minute, just let me save this piece… There, what can I do for you?"

"Dad I have to go into Manchester to look for presents for Drew and Jessica. I wonder if you'd ring through to this publisher and order these books for me. When you have a minute will do. Get them posted to Cambridge, there's someone at the house all day. Anything you want from Town?"

"No, I've already got my presents. There's a hand knitted Aran Sweater for Drew, got it up in Orkney doing some research last month, and some shares in that new Chilean winery venture of yours for Jessica, plus some little toys for her to throw around. What are you going for?"

"Haven't a clue," said Thomas. "I'll know when I see it. See you at dinner."

The sleek Aston Martin cruised down the drive and Thomas hit the automatic Gate button but nothing happened. Surprised he stopped the car some yards short of the gate and got out to open them manually, then froze. Standing just beyond the gates was a figure he knew well.

"Mordred," he yelled and ran to open the gates. But when he got there he knew why they didn't open. He was at the edge of The Second Road, and Mordred was not in real time and space. He reached through the Gates.

"Mordred, I'm so glad to see you." His hand was taken in a firm warm grip. "As I am to see you little brother." They stood silent, both remembering a time eight years before when they had been enemies, and standing each side of these same gates.

"Thomas, I've come to warn you, there is a man coming into your life, and you must beware of him. He is charming and plausible." Mordred laughed a little self-consciously.

"As once was I, you may remember. But this man is dangerous to you. He seeks your death and your title as Arch-Mage. A title you have yet to claim fully. Beware Thomas. There is someone close who can help you." His form wavered, dimmed. "Look into the old records, look for the squire of Amicus Carrick he will be the one. Be well little brother." He was gone.

Thomas stood bereft for a few minutes then smiled, at least he knew Mordred was alive and well in Avalon, but that he had spent a lot of energy crossing time and space to warn him was worrying. The gates creaked belatedly and began to open so he went back to the car and drove out on to the Manchester road.

First things first. His shopping list and then some research when he got back. Things were beginning to move faster than he liked. He wondered where Cormac was and if he knew about these new developments. But at least he'd had eight years to get ready.

The Manchester offices of King-Stag Enterprises were newly built and boasted a large well-lit parking area. Thomas cruised into his private space and greeted the security man's salute with a wide grin. "Hi Pete, how's the missus, got over that last bout of bronchitis?"

"Yes Sir Thomas, thank you. She's well on the mend now. Will you be staying or is this a flying visit?"

"Just a bit of shopping, I'll be back about four. But

don't let upstairs know, or I'll be trapped into a meeting."
They both laughed and Thomas walked up the ramp and
into the street. He took out his phone as he headed into the
crowded streets and made a note to get Pete and his frail
wife off to one of the King-Stag hotels before the really cold
weather set in. The one in Madeira would be nice and not
too far to travel. Ten days in the sun would help her battle
through the bleak northern winter.

Whistling cheerfully he set off on his search for Drew's
present. Three exhausting hours later he saw just the thing.
A bronze statue of a rearing stallion and its Native American
rider. Fashioned with the attention to detail that only a man
who knew and loved horses could see. It was an original by
Frederick Remington, and Drew would love it. While they
packaged it he wandered around the small antique shop
and came across a Victorian coral and pearl necklace with
a matching bracelet, made for a child. Jessica was too young
for it now, but by the time she was three or four it would look
lovely with her dark hair and brown eyes. Satisfied he left the
shop with his purchases and headed back to the car park.

As he crossed Whitworth Park a flash of colour caught
his eye and he slowed his pace as he came up to a fountain
burbling quietly to itself. At first he thought it was a cloud of
late butterflies circling above the surface of the water. Then
he stopped and looked again. One of the small creatures
fluttered towards him and he found himself looking into a
tiny pointed face. It grinned mischievously and returned to
its companions now circling in an ascending spiral.

Thomas looked around him cautiously as the hair on
the back of his neck stood up. *He was on The Second Road.*
Between one breath and the next he had shifted levels. Panic
rose in him, how had this happened? He had always been
careful not to cross the boundaries unless he was alone. This
meant he'd been summoned.

He looked round and saw the everyday world in which he lived had become faint and hazy as if seen through a fog. Superimposed on it was another world, one with which he was familiar, but which had intruded without either his knowing or his permission.

The sound of hooves made him turn and he saw a black horse approaching. Its rider sat with easy grace in the saddle, the black cloak and hood masking the form and face completely. The voice was educated and held authority, its owner was obviously used to giving orders, and seeing them obeyed.

"Well met Thomas of Carrick. My apologies for the lack of warning but my time in the world of men grows short and the affair that lies between us must be settled quickly. When I have achieved my goal then time will no longer be my master."

"You have me at a disadvantage sir. You know my name and where and how to find me, but I know nothing of you, and little of the matter of which you speak. However, I was warned to expect something of this nature. But courtesy and the laws of Albion demand that I am given time to make my arrangements. Also that I am made aware of your title, status, and the nature of your claim."

Thomas was no longer a boy, his ancestry and breeding now came to the fore making him stand erect and proud before the stranger.

"Then allow me to introduce myself. On The Second Road I am Iorwyth ap Gryffdd, who I am in the world of men you will soon discover. My status? Let us say I am your Nemesis. My claim? The Position of Arch-Mage of Britain. You stand in my way Thomas of Carrick, step aside and I will let you live, maybe. Defy me and it will be a battle to the death. The choice is entirely yours."

Thomas was silent for a few moments then said

quietly, "I've never backed away from a challenge that was just and I don't intend to do so now."

"That is the answer I would expect from you Thomas, but first the rules must be laid out." The voice came from behind him. The black horse reared, its hooves flailing the air causing the rider to struggle to control it.

"Merlyn! And you also Cormac of the Sidhe. You have powerful allies Sir Thomas, but I repeat my claim, I am the one most suited to carry the title of Arch-Mage, and I issue a challenge with both of you as witnesses, this you cannot deny me." Merlyn nodded.

"That is true, but I named Thomas as my heir and you can only challenge him for the title when it is truly his. He has yet to undertake the Tests that will empower him. Once he has been named Arch-Mage and is your equal in power, then and then only may you challenge him to combat. Until that time you are forbidden to use your powers against him. To attack one weaker than yourself is the way of the coward and unworthy of your lineage Iorwyth ap Gryffdd. Leave us, and when the time is right the battle lines will be drawn."

The Stranger was silent for a moment then he snarled, "So be it Merlyn. Until then Thomas of Carrick I will obey the Law. But there are other things I can use against you, be vigilant." He wheeled the horse until it pawed the air, then took off down the track, the mist enclosing him as the sound of hooves died away.

Thomas turned and threw his arms about Merlyn. "It's great to see you Merlyn, you too Cormac. I was more than a little worried I can tell you." Merlyn gripped his shoulders.

"Listen well Thomas, I have little time, once in Avalon it is difficult to exist elsewhere even on The Second Road. That is why I have sent Cormac to you. He will explain the finer points of the challenge to you. In his hands I have placed your training for the Tests of the Elements. You also must abide by the ancient rules. However Ap Gryffdd can and will, cause trouble in your own world."

"What are these tests Merlyn, this is the first I've heard of them. I am up to my neck in studies and soon I'll be taking my finals. I could do without this. Who is this Iorwyth ap Gryffdd? How did he get me on to The Second Road without my knowing, I'm confused." He shook his head.

Merlyn's form faded into transparency, then returned, "I cannot hold the link, Cormac, you must tell him what to do. Thomas I must go..." He faded from sight, his eyes fixed on his young successor.

"Merlyn, don't go, try to stay... Oh damn." He turned to Cormac and found himself standing by the fountain in the park back in the real world but alone and in a state of shock. After a moment's hesitation he made his way back to the car, his mind whirling with the unexpected events of the afternoon.

As he drove home through the late Autumn twilight he tried to put together his conversations on the Tor with Cormac, Merlyn, and the Stranger on The Second Road. Why did everything have to come at once? But he knew the answer. The Stranger had seized a moment when he was distracted, his mind full of his studies and the responsibilities of his own world.

As he crested the hill overlooking Deepdale he stopped the car and got out. The cold air and fresh wind called to him. He longed to Change, to run and keep running, but he pushed the longing away, this was not the time to indulge himself.

"You have a remarkable amount of self-discipline... for a human." said the tall dark figure at his side. Thomas turned wearily. "Do you always creep up on us humans? What do you want now Cormac? I don't think I can take much more. It's been a weird day." He leaned against the sleek black car.

Cormac smiled. "Get used to it Thomas. Come, let us sit in the car, I find your world a little cold for my liking." He sank into the passenger seat and produced a silver vial on a chain from his pocket. "Let a little of this slide down your throat and you'll feel better. There's few in this world that have tasted the golden brew of Tyr nan Og."

"I'm driving," said Thomas shaking his head as he took the wheel. "But go ahead. God knows I could do with a drink, but only when it's safe to do so."

" 'Tis a grand chariot right enough," said Cormac, "though I prefer to use my own way of transport if you understand me." He watched Thomas' skilful handling of the powerful car. "In the olden days you would have been worthy of driving the chariot of Cuchulain himself." He was silent for a moment then spoke with more gravity than was usual for him. "Thomas we need to begin your training, and soon. Ap Gryffdd will not wait long. In this world he grows old and desires the long life and strength that is the prerogative of the Arch-Mage of Albion." He raised his hand as Thomas opened his mouth.

"I know, I know, you have other pressing duties but everything depends on the outcome of the Tests. Unless you take them, and successfully, Albion will fall under the hand of a Dark Mage. That would be disastrous." Thomas stopped the car outside the manor gates and turned to his passenger.

"I know how important it is Cormac, but it's like I am fighting on three fronts. Mental, physical and The Second Road. How can I do that without totally exhausting myself?"

Cormac put the silver vial into his hand. "First, you can take this, Thomas, **and keep it with you at all times.** It is much more than a brew, it is what keeps The Tuatha young and strong. But you need to use it sparingly. No more than a thimble full when you feel the need of strength. Secondly you need someone to help you, do research for you, and, most importantly, be with you when you take the tests. That someone must be able to guard your back and act as your squire would have done in the old days. You need to find such a person and take him into your confidence."

"Oh that won't be a problem… I'll just say to one of my Cambridge pals and say, 'Look here, I'm the future Arch-Mage of Britain and a shape shifter. I have a Fairy Prince for a teacher and I'm looking for someone to help me take on an evil wizard who's out to destroy me!! Please! I already have a name for being eccentric."

Cormac studied him with serious eyes. "The one you need is closer than you think. In ten days time it will be All Hallows Eve. Look for me then Thomas and we will begin your training."

"I'll be back in Cambridge," protested Thomas.

Cormac smiled. "I will come for you then. Farewell my friend." He opened the door and stepped out with fluid grace, then turned and bent down to look back at Thomas. "It is time to teach you a new Shape." He moved back into the shadow of the trees and vanished.

For a while Thomas sat in the car looking out at the lights in the village below. Down there was England, the place he loved most in the world, the place he had been born to defend against The Dark Powers. Ahead of him there was work to be done, a lot of it, and some of it would not be pleasant. He let in the clutch and drove on into the gathering darkness.

\* \* \*

The dinner table was laid only for one, his father was

locked in his study writing furiously and had requested no interruptions. It was Betty's night off but a meal had been left prepared for the microwave. Thomas ate quickly thinking about the events of the day, then stacked the plates in the dishwasher and headed for the library. Something Mordred had said was sticking in his mind...

*"Look for the squire of Amicus Carrick..."*

He got down the leather bound book of the Carrick family history and began to plough through it. A lot of it was either in mediaeval Latin or Old English. He needed someone to translate the early pages he thought, and made a mental note to ask around in Cambridge. There must be someone who could do it.

Turning the next page he came across a display of heraldic blazons. Not just those of his own family he noted, but also of those who had served them down the ages. The page showed a line of hand coloured shields, the Coats of Arms of the Squires. Most had come from noble families having been sent to other households to be trained in the Bearing of Arms and to prepare them for their own knighthood. An ancient form of boarding school his father had once called it. Intrigued by the colours and symbols Thomas turned the page and froze.

There was the name Norton bracketed with (Naughton) and below it a full blazon complete with motto and crest. His eyes lingered on the motto; *Serve with Honour, Live with Faith.* Charlie Naughton; that was why he had felt that shiver of excitement, the feeling of closeness during that long drive home, and the sense of everything falling into place.

Charlie was the one who would stand with him through the coming tests, who would watch his back and act as his squire. He was the ideal choice, and also the one who could translate the Latin and Old English as well. Thomas slammed the book shut with a whoop of delight and headed for the phone then paused.

Okay, perhaps Charlie had the right name, but then there were a lot of Naughtons... he may not be descended from that particular family, on the other hand did it matter? No, he decided, what mattered was the name, and above all the character of the person and in his heart of hearts Thomas knew Charlie was the right one. He sat down in his great-grandfather's chair and began to think things through. It must be done gradually, though something told Thomas that Charlie would catch on pretty quickly.

He needed to get to know him on many levels and the first thing was to get him into a place where they would be seeing each other every day. Getting him into the Town House was the first step as it was just a twenty minute walk away from Kings College. Plus, as good luck would have it, Rich Leaver had taken up an offer to do his last year of International Law at Harvard, so his room and study would be free by the end of the Michaelmas Term. Once Charlie was in the house there would be plenty of opportunities to bond with him.

He sat back in the chair and rested his head against the leather cushion. Although an only child he had never felt lonely until he had met Mordred and gained an insight into his tortured childhood. The upsurge of sympathy and the overwhelming desire to share what he had with his own father with this lost, misguided and desperately lonely man had taken him by surprise.

The bond that had grown between them and been so swiftly and tragically cut short had persisted on a higher level. Though they no longer shared a world, each knew in some finer dimension they would always be in touch.

Since the departure of Mordred for Avalon there had been times when Thomas had been lonely and longed for someone to talk to and share thoughts, ideas, and dreams with. Maybe, just maybe, Charlie Naughton would be such a person. But for now, that was in the future and there were more pressing things demanding his attention. With a sigh Thomas reached for his briefcase and took out the papers he needed to hand in on Tuesday.

He worked steadily until the grandfather clock in the hall struck 11:30 then groaned and pushed away from the desk. It had been a day of surprises both pleasant and unpleasant and he needed to clear his head. He crossed to a table holding a crystal Tantalus and poured a small brandy into a glass then he went to stand by the window and looked out into the darkness.

Out there was a whole different world that nine-tenths of this world knew nothing about. Thomas suddenly felt very old as if he had lived for hundreds of years and the weight of those years rested heavily on his shoulders. How would he ever have the strength to complete the tasks that now faced him. Both worlds demanded the best he could give, and both had their priorities.

It occurred to him there must have been many Arch-Magi between Merlyn and himself. He wondered who they were and where they had lived. Had they been famous or lived and worked quietly at their task. As he looked into the darkness, the window shimmered and became a mirror. In it he saw an elderly man in a monk's habit working at a desk, he raised his head and smiled at him. "Simon of Whitby," he said, and turned back to his writing. His place was taken by a shepherd with a rough wooden staff, a long beard and piercing eyes "Rhys ap Hoel," he said with the lilt of Wales in his voice and gave way to a tall man in a fur edged robe who stood with his arms folded and a grim expression. "Raymond, Lord of Heywood Manor and its Domains." One by one they gave their names and passed. Among them John of Gaunt, John Dee, Elias Ashmole and a priest who reminded him of Father John and a modern woman with a bunch of violets in her hand.

There were others whose names had never been known but who had guarded the Blessed Isles as its Arch-Mage. They had served their time, long or short taking inspiration from the original Merlyn. The last had been his grandfather. There had been times when Albion had been without a Mage, times of great danger, but they had always won through. Now it was his turn to serve. Thomas felt within him the sense of a test that had been passed and a new chapter of his life now opened before him.

The clock chimed the hour and Thomas realised more than two hours had passed. His brandy was untouched, but by his feet lay a bunch of violets. Shaking with the backlash of the experience he set the glass aside and taking the flowers he made his way upstairs to his room. Too drained to think of undressing he fell face down on the bed and into a deep and dreamless sleep.

The room filled with power and shapes gathered around his sleeping form. Each in turn passed to him a portion of their knowledge, power, and energy. Last came Merlyn to bless the boy Thomas had once been and acknowledge the Man he now was. On his brow Merlyn traced his own sigil of the Hawk. It would stay until his time was over and another Merlin took his place.

In the Court of Avalon Arthur, Guenevere, Mordred, and Barnaby sent their blessings across time and space. But in an elegant apartment in London a tall grey haired man brooded over his brandy. The title, powers, and sigil of the Arch-Mage of Britain should be and would be... HIS. Through it all Thomas slept deeply and dreamlessly as the sun rose over the ageless moors.

# Chapter Three

**Sunday dawned bright** and clear and Grim's demanding bark brought Thomas awake with a start. The events of the night before were clear in his mind, but he pushed them aside for a later time. Today was Drew's birthday and there was a party to organise. It was customary that the remaining Guardians celebrated birthdays, weddings and Christenings at the Manor. Drew and Posy had been married in the chapel and their daughter Jessica had been Christened there.

Today, although the weather threatened rain, the autumn colours were in their full glory. The Hollies and Mountain Ash were bright with berries and added a cheerful look to the front drive. Thomas let Grim out for a quick relief trip before heading for the kitchen where the tempting smell of breakfast filled the air. His father was already there with the inevitable cup of coffee sifting through a pile of yesterday's late mail. He looked up with a cheery grin and waved a handful at his son as he sat down and reached for the coffee pot.

"You're a popular boy, all these are for you and not a bill among them. You must be leading a very pure life. All mine have those little windows that tell me I owe somebody some money, I'll be a pauper at this rate."

Thomas nearly choked on his coffee and Betty giggled as she placed a heaped plate in front of him. "That'll be the day when you worry about a bill Dad." His father peered at him over his glasses and assumed a stern frown.

"There was a time when bills constituted a fair amount of stress in this family... don't ever forget that Thomas. Money has a nasty habit of drying up just when you need it."

"Sorry Dad, I can remember those times as well and I know what you mean, but you know, they were happy times as well. We always managed... just. Now about the party, the caterers are coming at 11:30 so the table will have to be set up by then. Betty I'm sure you already have all that in hand."

His housekeeper nodded, "Though I still think I could have done all the cooking." She sniffed and Thomas smiled at her.

"I know you could Betty, but you and Frank are guests and you can't cook and enjoy the party as well. This is a day to be waited on. Lunch is at 1:00 so if the drinks can be ready in the library by 12:00, the early birds can enjoy themselves while waiting. Don't forget to put out the high chair for Jessica. If you put it between yourself and Posy there'll be two of you to keep her amused and you can take it in turns to eat. The presents will come after lunch with the cake and coffee.

"Dad can you see to the drinks and act as host until about 12:30? I have some calls to make and its 9:30 already." He finished his coffee and stood up. "Thanks for breakfast Betty," he said kissing her cheek. "Now get out of the kitchen and enjoy yourself for the rest of the day."

Betty watched him go whistling out of the kitchen and wiped a tear away. "He never ever forgets to thank me, or kiss me goodbye, I don't know what I've done to deserve that boy." Steven rose and patted her shoulder affectionately. "You deserve his love and respect Betty, and mine, you always will. Now let's get these dishes cleared up and then you can go and get your glad rags on and doll yourself up for the festivities."

Thomas headed for his study letting Grim back in on the way, he wanted to get in touch with Charlie Naughton as soon as possible. But as he settled at his desk he paused and took a moment to examine something new within himself. He felt different, more assured, more in charge of things around him, in fact, more of everything. Puzzled, he got up and went to the antique Venetian mirror on the wall opposite and looked at himself. He thought he still looked the same so what was different. Then he saw it, faintly and only for a few brief seconds. Across his forehead stretched the head and wings of a Merlin Falcon. Then it was gone.

Returning to his desk Thomas sat with his head in his hands and gathered his thoughts, he took a deep breath and opened up to whatever was trying to get through. Slowly the memories of the night before came flooding back. He felt deep within himself the accumulated knowledge of every Merlin before him and knew himself to be one of their number. There was no longer any doubt in him at all, the title was justly his, but the power that came with the title still had to be won in order to be able to use it with good judgment.

Power. A word he disliked to use in connection with himself, but from the knowledge that had so lately been passed to him came a clear and concise subconscious message. *"Power is best used by those who do not seek it."* What power did he have? What power did any of the Merlins have? It was the first time he'd thought about the "magical" side of things. He accepted the power of shifting his form as something natural, unusual yes, but he had never questioned it. Even when the Great Battle was at its height he'd never thought of it as magical, just a sort of talent.

One of the past Merlins stirred within him. Raymond of Heywood.

*"Magic is a word for children Sir Thomas, the true name for it is the power of the life force within you. In your time it is simply called energy. When you link energy to emotion, and emotion to imagery, imagery to intent and intent to will, it becomes magical Power. But remember, magic is an energy obeying a natural Law that is not fully understood... yet!"*

Thomas came to with a start, what was he was going to do? Oh yes call Charlie. He reached for the phone, unconsciously judging the distance and weight of it. Quietly the phone lifted from its cradle and fitted into his hand. Without noticing what had happened Thomas called Charlie's number and waited for the connection.

"Hello." The voice was soft and a little anxious as if the person was not at ease with answering a phone.

"Good Morning, am I speaking with Mrs. Naughton?"

"Er yes, this is Mrs. Naughton, I mean yes... I am Mrs. Naughton," the voice sounded flustered and made Thomas smile.

"I'm sorry to bother you on a Sunday Mrs. Naughton my name is Thomas Carrick and I'm a friend of your son Charlie. Is he there? If possible I'd like to speak with him."

"Oh! Oh my goodness, yes, Charlie is here I'll get him now Mr. Carrick, I mean Sir Carrick... Sir Thomas.... Charlie, Charlie it's your friend from the university, come on dear, don't keep him waiting."

Thomas heard the scrape of a chair and the whispered conversation... "Oh my, I called him the wrong name... I hope he isn't offended, come along dear..." Charlie's voice came down the line his north country accent more pronounced than usual.

"Thomas, great to hear you, what can I do for you, if it's about Tuesday and you find you can't pick me up don't worry, I'll get the train…"

"No, it's nothing to do with that Charlie. Frank and I will pick you up as arranged. I wondered if you were free tomorrow to come over and look through the library here, I have some books that may be useful to you and you can borrow them for as long as you need. I'll drive over and collect you. There are a couple of things I'd like to talk over with you as well."

"Tomorrow, well to tell the truth I was going to take mum and dad out to tea and a film, but I dare say if it's important we can go another time, and I'd dearly love to see your library." Thomas thought for a moment.

"Tell you what Charlie, we'll combine the two, I'll send Frank over about two o'clock to pick you all up and bring you back here. Your mum and dad can look round the house and the gardens, Betty would love to show them round. You and I can talk books and other things, then we can have high tea together and Frank will take you back again. How about that?"

Charlie looked over at his parents with a grin as wide as a yard of ale and said, "Thomas has invited us over to Carrick Manor tomorrow afternoon for tea. He'll send the car for us would you like that?" Maisie Naughton clasped her hands together and gasped with delight.

"Oh yes, indeed, we would love that wouldn't we dear?" Her husband looked at her excited face and smiled, he could never refuse her a chance like this. He nodded to Charlie.

"Thank Sir Thomas for us and tell him we would be honoured to accept his invitation." Charlie turned back to the phone, "Mum and dad send their thanks and would love to come Thomas, we'll be ready for two o'clock and thank you, thank you so much. That'll make my mum's day. See you tomorrow."

Thomas sat back with a broad smile... things were falling into place. The next call was to his housekeeper in Cambridge to discuss setting up the rooms for Charlie in the New Year. Then he called Rich to see if he needed anything stored while he was away in the US. Having arranged things to his satisfaction he whistled to Grim and together they sneaked out of the house through the wood and out onto the moor where he stripped off and placed his clothes in a rucksack under a bush.

On an impulse he took from a pocket the silver vial and chain Cormac had given him and hung it round his neck. The Sidhe had impressed on him to keep it with him at all times. For a moment he stood and just looked, feeling the pull of this place where his ancestors had lived for generations. Then he looked down at the little terrier and said, "Let's go."

Grim leapt to his feet watching with excited yips as his beloved master slid into his stag form. The brushwood fence was no barrier to either of them, The stag cleared it in one graceful bound while Grim dived through his own specially made entry point and together they raced across the moors.

Steven Greystone watched them go from the window of his study. It never failed to fill him with wonder that it was his son who held this incredible power. It was his son who would soon take over the task of the Guardian of Albion. He longed to shout out to the world his pride and his joy but knew that could never be. Even Thomas' mother had never seen, would never see, that incredible transformation or understand the meaning and the magic that underlay it all. Even now after eight years he still had to pinch himself to believe it. Shaking his head he finished his coffee and went to help Betty and Frank prepare for their guests.

Thomas and Grim ran until the little terrier had had enough and sank panting to the ground. The great stag paused and gently touched noses with him and licked his ear in a gesture of affection before flowing back into his own form. Still warm from his race he sat with his back against a rock warmed by the weak October sun and gathered the dog into his side for extra heat.

His restlessness somewhat relieved by the run he recalled his memories of last night's events and sifted through them. There had passed before him a line of the past Merlins and each one had offered a name. A gesture of trust and respect, for the one who would take on the responsibility that had once been theirs. But there was more. During his sleep something had changed in him, deeply and forever. There was a new power building within him and instinctively he knew it came from his predecessors. Each one had left something of themselves with him. He knew that each had held a certain talent and a small part of that talent was now his to use. This thought brought an immediate response. In his mind's eye he saw John Dee and heard his thin and somewhat reedy voice.

*"Slowly young sir. True you have within yourself some part of our powers, but only a small part. No one Merlin can or should, hold complete power. There will be limitations. Also you must discover what those powers are and how to use them. Some will be of use during your Tests. Others will manifest as and when they are needed. Know also that every Merlin has a weak point. This is intentional. Without it they would become arrogant and too powerful to be humble before those whose powers are greater than theirs can ever be. From time to time we will offer aid or advice but do not count on such help entirely; you must develop your own talent and your own strength."*

The voice faded leaving Thomas with his mouth open and the start of a massive headache. While he appreciated the information he'd been given, he'd used a lot of energy on the run and with this new information it was time to get back to the house. But as he got to his feet everything changed and took a turn for the worse. A shadow loomed over him shutting out the light and bringing with it an unnatural chill. A voice he recognised rang through the air.

"So, Thomas of Carrick we meet again, this time without your Mentors to guard you." The figure of Iorwyth Ap Gryffdd stood before him. As he watched the form changed and became a huge timber wolf. Thomas backed away aware of his danger. Tired by a long run and the pain in his head, he was no match for a battle. Its eyes gleaming in anticipation of the easy kill facing him, the wolf crouched low on its belly and prepared to spring.

Then a furious bundle of black and white fur shot past Thomas and buried a set of razor sharp teeth in the wolf's hind leg. Grim clamped his jaws tight and hung on. The wolf howled and spun round seeking to tear the unexpected opponent apart. But Grim was not easy to dislodge. As the larger animal sought to snap at him the dog swung its body from side to side evading the lethal jaws.

Frantically, Thomas, looked round for something, anything to use as a weapon. There was nothing. What could one use against a wild animal on the rampage? Fire! No matches. For one wild moment Thomas regretted not smoking. A knife? He didn't carry one and the only thing he had was the small vial of liquid Cormac had given him. He remembered his words.

*"Use it sparingly, just a thimbleful when you have need."*

If ever there was a need it was now. The Wolf had succeeded in shaking off the little terrier and now had him by the scruff shaking him viciously and trying to break his neck. Thomas took advantage of the distraction to take a well-aimed kick at its ribs, then sprang back and took a quick sip from the vial. Its effect was immediate. Strength raced like fire through his veins and hit his brain with the force of a jack-hammer!

A bone deep fury erupted within him unleashing a side of himself he'd not known existed until this moment. With a roar he leapt forwards shifting as he did so and Wolf met Wolf in full combat. Snarling, his opponent dropped Grim and turned to face the new threat. As they clashed Thomas sent a clarion call for help ringing along The Second Road. Then it became a blur of speed, blood, pain and an overwhelming desire to rend, rip, tear, and kill.

The use of the wolf form had been instinctive, using like to battle like, but it was a form Thomas had never used before plus he was smaller and carried less weight than his opponent. He backed off a moment to give himself time to think up a plan but the larger animal refused to allow it and pressed him harder. Using his smaller size and quicker re-flexes he circled his enemy trying to dart in and attack flanks, legs and back. But his attacker circled with him and kept him at bay with the ease of long practice. Then with a roar he carried the battle into close quarters again tearing at the younger wolf's shoulder.

Thomas rolled and got to his feet, his shoulder was bleeding badly and the pain of a torn muscle was excruciat-ing, but he had no choice. He flung himself back into the fight determined to keep going as long as he could. In his mind he felt regret that he would not complete his destiny, but another part was determined that if necessary he would take his opponent with him into the darkness of death. He fought with every ounce of his strength, trusting that help would come if not soon enough to save him, then soon enough to destroy his enemy. Better that Albion should be left without a Mage, than one who served the Dark.

Back at the Manor Drew stopped in mid conversation, his head came up sharply. Ian Atkinson met his eyes across the room and conversation stopped as the urgent cry for help was picked up.

*Thomas, danger, moors, Second Road, hurry, hurry.*

Drew leapt for the glass doors that opened on to the lawn and flung them wide. Between one breath and the next he shifted and a huge stallion thundered across the lawn and cleared the wall dividing the woodland and moors from the landscaped gardens. Two sleek greyhounds followed close behind him.

Posy clutched Jessica close to her and breathed a prayer. The others gathered around her, joining their thoughts and energies and sending them winging along The Second Road. Nurse Pym anticipating trouble ran to fetch the doctor's medical bag from his car and her own bag for good measure. Frank urged by Betty went for the off-road Jeep used for heavy work. He picked up Nurse Pym and headed onto the moor following Drew as he raced flat out across the moors flanked by the fleet footed greyhounds and following the scent left by the stag.

Thomas was tiring quickly, losing blood and getting the worst of the fight. He could see Grim lying limp and motionless and feared the worst. The short burst of energy given him by the Life Water of the Sidhe was giving out. He'd had time for only a small sip and the effect was not strong enough to cope with the greater experience of his foe.

He realised he had to help himself and reaching deeper within than ever before, he no longer asked for help... he called it to him as his right, as The Merlin to Be. It came in the form of an enraged stallion and two sleek greyhounds as they came up over the rise. He threw his last bit of strength into a desperate attack to reach his enemy's throat but fell to the ground under the timber wolf's flashing teeth and claws.

44

Drew reared up over the black wolf his forelegs slashing down to cut deep into the shoulder. The wolf howled and threw itself to one side shifting form as it did so into a black stallion and turning to meet this new enemy. The two clashed together teeth and hooves becoming lethal weapons and the battle was renewed.

Ian flowed into human form and bent over Thomas while Marjory went to Grim, both were in need of their skills. As they worked to staunch the wounds Frank, driving flat out, skidded to a halt beside them. Nurse Pym jumped out to hand one medical bag to Ian and the other to Marjory. Behind them the battle was reaching its climax.

Every protective instinct in Drew's body both stallion and human was in full flood. Thomas had been placed under his protection by Father John and if anything happened to Steven he would take on the role of father as well. Thomas' safety was tied up with that of Albion's future and this coward had attacked without warning at a time he thought his prey would be unguarded.

Teeth bared he screamed defiance at his counterpart and reared to his full impressive height. Razor sharp hooves slammed down across back muscles ripping the skin open and cutting deep to the bone. Then he dropped down spun round and lashed out with his back legs. There was a sharp snap and a scream of pain and the black wolf had had enough.

Wounded, outnumbered, and thwarted in his attack Ap Gryffdd shifted into a buzzard form and took flight, leaving Drew panting, bleeding, but triumphant. He changed back to his own shape and went to where Thomas still in wolf-form lay bleeding heavily and in shock. His eyes flickered open and his thoughts touched Ian's... "Grim?"

"Marjory will see to him, you're the one who needs my attention." Ian set to work to stop the bleeding and ascertain the damage.

Marjory leaned down to comfort Thomas. She had wrapped the little terrier in her coat and was holding him close keeping him warm. "He's lost a lot of blood, needs some stitches and I think he may have a broken bone in a hind leg. We'll get him to the vet straight away dear. You're the one who got the worst of it."

Drew squatted down beside Thomas and laid a gentle hand on his front paw. "Thomas take some energy from me and change back, the change will help to heal the worst of the wounds that's the way it works, but you'll need some of my energy to do it. Do you understand?"

The young wolf licked his hand and relaxed, accepting the offered energy. For moment nothing happened then, the animal body shivered convulsively and slowly flowed into the change leaving a badly bruised, bloodied and exhausted Thomas lying naked on the ground. The bites and claw marks were deep and angry but had already begun to stop bleeding.

Drew carried him to the jeep and gently settled him in the back seat with Ian. Nurse Pym gave Drew enough energy to enable him to shift and get back to the Manor then she got into the front seat with Grim. The others in a convoy set off for the House though more slowly this time with Drew needing to recover.

On the way home Ian called Steven on his mobile to reassure him that though Thomas had been in a fight he would be OK. Thomas, still in shock, fretted over Grim's condition, but Frank promised he would get him to the vet as soon as they got home.

Once back at the manor Thomas was fussed over but successfully thwarted attempts to get him to bed. Steven and Betty shaken but determined to support him, persuaded the rest of them to eat the long delayed lunch while Frank took

Grim to the vet.

Over the meal Thomas relayed the events leading up to the battle and its outcome and at the end of the meal toasted not only the double birthday of Drew and Jessica, but also his rescuers timely arrival. He quietly added another drop of Cormac's elixir to his wine glass and with its restorative power was able to last long enough to see Drew's pleasure with his gift and get a kiss from his God-daughter for her present. Then between them Marjory and Betty quietly packed everyone off home and got a still protesting Thomas up to bed. Steven sat with him for a while talking over the plans for the following day. Then his father asked quietly.

"Tom, these tests you have to take, are they all going to be this life threatening?"

"I don't know dad, I only know they'll involve the elements in some way."

Steven thought this over then asked, "This Iorwyth fellow, he's after the whole lot isn't he, I mean like Mordred needing the regalia, this guy wants your place as the Arch-Mage?" Thomas leaned back against his pillows and gave a rather shaky laugh.

"Yes I guess he is, but unlike Mordred he doesn't intend to play by the rules of Chivalry. He did warn me he would try. He can't interfere with the Tests, but he can, and after today I believe he will, see if he can get to me in other ways. I'll just have to be on my guard 24/7. But I've learned some things today dad. I found I can use other shapes besides that of the stag. Cormac told me I'd have to learn to do that. Plus I learned that by changing from a Shift back to my own form I can heal more quickly, and there's something else, something even more important."

He told Steven about the meeting with the past Merlins and the information he had been given by John Dee. Then he added his own thoughts about Charlie Naughton

47

and how he might be the one to stand by his side. At the end of it all he leaned back against his pillows, exhausted by the day's events and smiled wanly at his attentive father.

"I'm sorry about all this Dad, I know it worries you and I'm really grateful that you just let me deal with it without making a fuss and getting protective, though I know that's what you long to do. As a dad, you're the best there is and I love you to bits."

Steven stood up and brushed the hair back from his forehead. "You're too old to be kissed goodnight Tom, but it doesn't mean I don't long to do that, but I'm proud of you and what you are doing and I'll do what I can to help you win through. Now rest up and I'll see you in the morning." He turned away to hide the tears that threatened and closed the door gently behind him.

For a moment he leaned his head against the wood and held on to his emotions. His boy, his son, was facing events, tests, dangers he could only imagine and he, his father, was helpless to do anything but let it happen. Betty met him at the top of the stairs with a mug of coffee smelling strongly of rum.

"Get this down you Steven Greystone, and remember this, that lad got his strength and his dedication from you, and from the way you brought him up. You're his rock, his foundation and don't you ever forget that." Then she went back to the kitchen wiping away her tears to prepare for the next day.

Miles away in London Ap Gryffdd nursed a battered, broken and bloodied body. He had badly underestimated Thomas Carrick. Young though he was the power in him held a trace of Angelic Help, something of which to be wary. Neither had he counted on the strength of the interference from his friends and their ability to work in unison. He needed to rethink his plans.

He had expected that with the ending of the Guardianship of the Singing Stones they would have lost their powers of Shifting. Obviously this was not the case so he would be facing a group made strong by their deep affection for each other and bound by the battles they had fought.

He cursed long and fluently, there had to be a way, something he could do to break that bond of love. Someway he could get at the boy without anyone interfering. He winced as his healing muscles and broken bones twinged. He must win, he must, everything he desired rested on it. He must look for help and for the kind he needed he would have to cross over to the Dark Side. He shuddered at the thought.

# Chapter Four

"**Oh dear, do you** think I should have worn something more dressy? Perhaps I should wear the blue dress I bought for Chrissy's wedding. It's only two years old and it goes better with this hat."

"Mum you're not going to Buckingham Palace or a fashion parade, you're going to a friend's house for tea." Charlie looked up from his notebook and grinned at his mother who was looking in the mirror for the fifteenth time that morning. He turned to his father, who was deep in the morning paper.

"Can't you calm her down dad this is the third outfit in two hours." His father looked up and stifled a laugh.

"Let her run on son, she'll quieten down in a minute when the car comes. This is the most exciting thing that's happened to her since her sister presented a bouquet to the Queen five years ago."

"Well it's too late now, Frank just parked outside so let's go mum."

He hustled his mother through the front door and down the path. The car had been polished to perfection and Frank spruced up in his official uniform grinned and swept off his hat. He gave a little bow and presented Mrs. Naughton with a single red rose.

"With the compliments of Sir Thomas madam."

Maisie Naughton went bright pink and her voice came out in a soft squeak. "Er, thank you I'm sure, it's beautiful, and in October too, it's so kind of Sir Thomas to invite us. Look Jimmy." She held the bloom out to her husband.

"Allow me to help you madam." Frank was enjoying himself no end and played the attentive chauffeur to the limit. "If you'll get in you'll find a rug on the seat if you feel cold, or I can adjust the heating if you wish."

Maisie settled in feeling like a queen and still blushing under all the attention. She giggled like a teenager as Mr Naughton got in beside her and gave a regal nod of her head at their neighbours' windows where the curtains were twitching as if in a gale. She smiled and waved towards them.

Charlie turned to Frank his smile filled with glee. "OK if I ride with you Frank, then mum can do the royal wave at the neighbours as she goes past?"

"Of course lad, settle yourself in while I make sure your mum and dad are buckled up." Having seen to their safety he got in beside Charlie and winked. "Yer mum's fair chuffed about this, I got strict instructions to do the 'chauffeur' thing and Betty's gone to town on setting up things up fer tea. Tom's a bit under the weather he took a fall yesterday and collected hisself a few bruises, but he's OK and lookin' forward ter showing you round. Plus 'e's cooking up a surprise fer you lad."

In the back of the car Maisie was chattering non-stop. "Oooh Jimmy look there's a tiny TV, and a little fridge, well I never did, and these seats, just like real leather."

"That's because they *are* leather Maisie love." Jim was having more fun watching his wife than driving in a top of the range car. Frank drove sedately past the neat row of houses to allow Maisie's friends to get a good look then turned onto the main road. Once on the motorway he opened up to give them an example of her speed, passing other cars with ease. At Stockport he swung off onto the A6 and headed for the Derbyshire moors. As they came into Whaley Bridge he changed to the smaller roads and slowed down to give them a view over the high moors.

"There be some rare views ter be seen up here when ye get a fine sunset," he told them. "You'll be seeing this road a lot from now on Charlie lad, Tom's says as 'ow yer'll be coming up wi' us regular like from now on. You're just what 'e's bin needin', some company of his own kind an' his own age. You'll do 'im a world o' good."

"Well he is very easy to talk to and good company. I think we can learn a lot from each other. I know he was disappointed about not being able to take the courses he wanted, so I'll be happy to fill him in on my stuff. Then he can show me how to cope with Cambridge politics and such like."

"Bin giving you a hard time 'ave they lad? They did the same to Tom when 'e started. Never seen 'im so down as 'e was in that first term. 'e'll be glad when the finals are over and can stay up here where 'e belongs. There's a sight more to Tom than can be seen at first. But tha'll soon find out fer the' sen I dare say. He's bin on about thee ever since we came back."

Charlie turned pink with pleasure at the implied compliment and his mother, unashamedly listening in nudged her husband in the ribs, her eyes brimming with pride in her son.

Half an hour later they turned into the Manor Gates and she gave a gasp as the house came into view. Autumn had gilded the trees lining the drive with reds and greens and golds. The Hollies already heavy with berries alternated with the Beeches to frame the gracious proportions of the house, presenting it to the eye like a Constable painting. Thomas was waiting on the steps to greet them but there was a noticeable limp as he came down the steps.

Charlie was out of the car first his face concerned as he reached for Thomas' hand. "Thomas, Frank said you'd had a fall, are you sure you're OK. You should have called we could've come another day."

"Not at all, I'm alright, just a bit shaken. Mrs. Naughton, I'm so delighted to meet you, you too Mr. Naughton. Please come in, it's getting chilly and there's a nice fire inside."

He ushered them inside where a maid waited to take their coats then opened the door into the drawing room. A log fire blazed on the hearth its flames highlighting the wood panelled room with its deep armchairs and thick carpet. Betty was waiting with a trolley loaded with hot buttered crumpets, sandwiches, tea and her famous "melt in the mouth" fruitcake. She beamed delightedly as Thomas made the introductions and bustled around making sure everything was to hand. Like Frank, Jim Naughton was aware of Charlie's need for friends of his own age and cast a curious eye over Thomas.

Maisie Naughton however was in heaven, filling her eyes and mind with everything around her so she could share it all with her neighbours the following day. Settled into a chair by the fire she was fussed over and made to feel very special. Her initial fear that she would find herself surrounded by "Toffs" and made to feel out of her depth was soon laid to rest. Betty's easy manner with Thomas and her gentle teasing of him as well as her unashamed north-country accent soon put her at ease.

She was even more astonished when Frank joined them. He and Betty were obviously very much a part of the Carrick family as well as being part of the staff. There was no class division in this house.

She sighed over the delicate porcelain china and silver service and won Betty's heart with her lavish praise for the fruitcake. Within a short time they were deep into family gossip as Betty filled her in on the history of the Carrick family, Steven's rise to fame as a writer and Thomas' unexpected accession to the title.

Then Steven himself wandered in and was introduced all round. He settled down next to Maisie with a big mug of coffee and to her amazed delight began to fill her in on all the latest Hollywood gossip. Open-mouthed that she was sitting beside an Oscar winning novelist who was friends with all her favourite film stars almost, but not quite, silenced her. Highly amused by this Betty kept the teapot filled and the cake sliced.

Frank was talking gardening and greyhound racing with Charlie's dad. They compared notes on the best kinds of potting earth and who was the favourite to win the title of Top Dog at the next meeting. Jim Naughton had run a greyhound for many years, but after the accident with his leg he had been unable to walk and train her so she had become a much-loved family pet until her death two years ago.

They talked about the upcoming Dog of the Year race at The Laurels stadium in Manchester and Frank, whose birthday gift from Thomas had been Box-seat season tickets, offered to take Jim with him to the coming event and would drive him there and back. Delighted Mr. Naughton accepted and when Frank produced a small silver flask of Jameson's to "freshen the tea"… he grinned and held out his cup.

Smiling, Thomas watched his guests settle in and relax, it would make it much easier to bring Charlie into his inner circle if the Naughtons were happy. He didn't want them to feel he was stealing their son away from them, but he knew that Charlie was destined to be part of his own future. He carefully divided his time between his guests while making sure Charlie was not left out. He waited for an opportune moment then got to his feet.

"Charlie come and have a look at the library, I've picked out some books for you and I have some more down in Cambridge. Ladies, Mr. Naughton, if you will excuse us." He winked at Betty and gave her a thumbs-up sign as he ushered Charlie out leaving the others to enjoy the afternoon.

The stained glass window with its hidden secrets at the top of the first landing caught his eye and to Thomas' amusement he began to point out the various pieces of the Arthurian royal regalia. He finally managed to drag him away and into the library.

The library with its floor to ceiling shelving, padded chairs and small reading tables with built-in lamps was a dream come true for Charlie. In one corner there was a computer with printer, scanner and copier to hand. It was in all respects a smaller but better edition of the one he used at the university. On one table was a small pile of books and Thomas drew him over to look at them.

"Here are the books I picked out for you to use. One of them is not even in the British Library, so that should give you an edge in the exams." Charlie looked at the titles and then at Thomas with his mouth open.

"Thomas, these are rare books, first editions, I can't just borrow these like library books. I'd have to have them in my digs and I don't have the security they need. Good Heavens they'd be pinched in a heartbeat. I'll just make notes from them when I come home and use those, if you don't mind me coming over and using the library here for a couple of hours each time."

"Ah, well, I was going to talk to you about that," said Thomas hitching a hip on the table. Rich Leaver is doing his final year at Harvard in the US, so his place in my town house will be vacant next term. So how would you like to have his rooms. It's much quieter than where you are now I would think. Are you in that place in Turner St?"

" 'Er yes, I have a bedsit there, it's close and there's a café round the corner," stammered Charlie, still bemused by the books.

"Well Rich's rooms will suit you much better. There's a bedroom with its own bathroom and a small study room so you don't have to clutter up where you sleep with papers and books. There's a large communal sitting room downstairs with a good sound system and a 50 inch TV and the dining room is next to it.

"The rooms are cleaned and the bed linen's changed every week and the housekeeper makes breakfast and an evening meal so there's no need to rely on takeaways and pizza. There's a laundry room we all use, and on the house-keeper's day off we cook our own dinner, but whoever cooks cleans up as well. The house is totally secure so the books can go down with us tomorrow and be safe. How about it? I'd really like to have you there Charlie, I think we'll get on well together." He looked eagerly at him.

"Well, it's really about money, you see my grant gives me an accommodation allowance and the place I'm in covers it, just."

"How much are you paying?"

"Er it's £500.00 a month."

"Good God, they have the cheek to charge you that much for one room and a shared a bathroom with six other guys, plus you feed yourself!" Thomas was outraged. "At my place you'll pay £300.00 have your own bathroom and study, the run of the house, and two meals a day. You'll find the bed a damn site more comfortable as well. There's only four of us in the house and I choose people carefully so we all get on.

"Come on Charlie, say you'll come and I can pick your brains about history and archaeology. You know how much I wanted to take those subjects, but the estate is so big I had to take Business Studies and Finance and Law, and just think... you'll get to drive both ways..."

Charlie stood there looking at him. He was a shrewd North country lad born and bred, and ripe plums like this did not fall into one's lap without some kind of cost. He stood straight and looked Thomas in the eye, risking everything on his need for honesty.

"Why Thomas, why me? I'm not of your class, my parents have gone without a lot of things to give me this chance. I don't belong in a house like this or in a big car with a driver. You are offering me things I've always dreamed about most of all your friendship. But I have to know why. I can just manage with the digs I'm in and I'm darned sure what you're offering me won't be covered by what you're asking for. I'm not thick, I know we get on well, but there's something more to all this. I can feel it. I would love to take up your offer. These books will give my end of term papers just the boost they need, and to work and study in a quiet place with no yelling and doors banging would be heaven, but Thomas, why me. What have I got that you want? What made you ask my parents and me here today?"

Thomas looked at him for a long time, then he got up and walked to the window and looked out, the sun had almost set and the whole sky looked as if it was on fire. Deep inside him the other Merlins stirred and spoke.

*"Sometimes you have to risk everything you have to get the one thing you need."*

He turned to face Charlie and spoke from the heart. "I need what you have just shown to me. Honesty, straight-forwardness, and the inner strength that comes from what you are deep inside. The ability to believe in something so completely that it overrides everything else. I need someone not afraid to tell me when I'm wrong but who will support me when they know I am right. I need someone I can trust literally with my life.

"Way back Charlie a knight had to trust his squire, and those squires often became a part of the knight's family, living with them, accepted by them completely as dependents. Many of them went on to achieve knighthood themselves. Your studies have told you all this. Look, look at this."

He took up the book of Heraldry and opened it at the page showing the Squires' Coats of Arms. "See this Charlie, this was your family's Coat of Arms back in the thirteen hundreds. One of your ancestors was the squire of Sir Ralph Carrick then. In 1298 a Naughton served with Sir Robert Carrick during the Crusades. I can give you at least five more examples like these.

"For better or worse Charlie, your life is bound up with mine. I know it. I didn't know my grandfather was a Baronet until I was fourteen. I wasn't born into all this, I had to grow into it. My whole life changed at fourteen and soon it will change again. Be with me when it does Charlie, I need you." He turned away to look out at the darkening sky.

Charlie stood stunned by the passion with which Thomas had spoken then he looked down at the brightly coloured Coat of Arms and spoke quietly. "When you were speaking something came alive inside me. Something that has always been there, It was that, that made me want to learn about the old ways and traditions, as if I knew it would one day be important. Then I met you and I knew you were different somehow. It's as if… you're bigger inside than you are outside. That sounds daft I know, but that's how it feels."

Thomas turned to face the man he needed to be his friend and companion. Time was not on his side and soon he would be facing trials that would test him to the utmost limits of his courage and strength. If he chose wrongly he would lose a friend and an ally, he might even make an enemy. But, if he chose well he would gain something more valuable than anything else he possessed. In those endless moments he weighed, estimated and risked. Standing there by the window with the sky on fire behind him and a prayer in his heart, he flowed into the change.

The blood left Charlie's face leaving him the colour of cheese curd. He stared into the velvet brown eyes of the great Stag and everything he had ever known, read, thought about and believed in came together in one great realisation. His legs went from under him and he fell to his knees but his eyes never left those of the stag.

"Oh, God," he said, his voice close to a sob. "Dear God, you're a Merlin!"

# Chapter Five

**The dark heavy scent** of Myrrh, Wolfsbane, and Opoponax filled the air and tendrils of smoke from the dark blue candles wreathed around the man standing at the altar. He lifted the crystal ball from its holder and held it high over his head.

> *"Dark of Moon and Depth of sea*
> *The Dark in me doth call to thee*
> *Ash of fire and gasp of fear.*
> *Tell me what I need to hear.*
> *From Below I summon Thee*
> *With my blood I pay the fee.*
> *Morgana gone from life and light*
> *Aid me in the coming fight.*
> *I seek a weakness in my foe*
> *Tell me what I need to know."*

He set the crystal down in its holder and picked up a dagger and with it slashed across the palm of his hand. The blood spurted, covering the crystal ball and dripping onto the dark blue cloth covering the altar. The man wrapped his hand in a cloth and bent over the bloodied scrying ball. For long moments he stared into it and then, slowly, it began to clear.

It showed a woman's face with a deep scar across her throat and long black hair that whipped about her head as if in a strong wind. Her voice was thin and weak but the hatred in her dark eyes was strong.

*"Who calls me from the depths of my long cold sleep. By what right do you summon me with blood and spell as in the days of old. To waken causes me pain and fills me with dread and despair. Tell me why I should not strike you down?"*

"Because you no longer have the power to act in this world Morgana. Your own greed was your downfall. But tell me how I can achieve my aim and I will give you a new body to inhabit here upon earth. With the power I will have at my command I can select a body, oust its inhabitant and give you access to it for your own use and, no doubt, nefarious aims. I think this offer would be of interest to you."

The crystal blazed with a dull green light and the face of Morgana displayed a savage glee.

*"You can do this? You do not deceive me with something you cannot deliver?"*

"Once I am the Arch-Mage of Albion I will have almost unlimited power at my command. Unfortunately I have to first dispose of another contender. I believe you know of Thomas Carrick."

Morgana's shriek of fury almost shattered the crystal.

*"That misbegotten little bastard. He warped the mind of my son and turned him against me. So many years wasted and nothing to show for it. What do you want of me? I'll do what I can to aid you and will take your offer as my reward."*

The Dark Mage smiled, he had caught his fish and must now bring it to shore. "I need to know Carrick's weakness. Every Merlin has one I know, though that is something I will rectify when the position is mine. He has powerful guardians. Merlyn himself selected him and Arthur upholds

61

his choice. They have given him into the care of Prince Cormac of the Sidhe one of the most powerful of Midir's people. I cannot issue a Mage challenge until he has completed his trials. But I can harass him in this world and will do so if I can find his weakness. For that I need your knowledge of him."

Morgana smiled slyly:

*"What guarantee do I have that you will honour your promise to me Ap Gryffdd. As yet you do not have the power or position you crave, so I must wait and trust your word until you do. I know of you, you have the tongue of a snake, split in two and always ready to turn coat. Swear to me by the blood on this crystal that you will give me the human body I desire, and be warned that if you play me false I will drag you down into this place to share my unending solitude."*

Ap Gryffdd hesitated then shrugged, he could deal with her threats at a later date, better to swear now and get what he wanted, then he could renege later. He saw no difficulty in thwarting Morgana once the power of the Arch-Mage was his. He laid his hand on the crystal. "I swear on my blood."

Morgana laughed and the eldritch sound rang round the small room until Ap Gryffdd clapped his hands over his ears to shut out the dreadful sound. When at last she stopped her face loomed in the crystal distorted by its shape and leered at him.

*"I will want a young body, full of life and promise and with many years ahead of it. With it I will hunt down everyone Carrick cares about and destroy them. Then... maybe I will come to you again, we would make a good partnership. His weakness lies in his love and concern for others. Strike at them and you will cripple him."*

The crystal suddenly shattered leaving a heap of bloodied shards on the blue cloth. The Mage slumped over the altar, drained of energy and the effort of keeping contact with such a malevolent disembodied spirit.

Slowly and carefully he cleaned and re-arranged the room, leaving no trace of his dark work to be seen.

Back in the comfort of his study, elated by the seeming success of his ritual he stood in front of a full-length mirror and imagined himself in the robes and accoutrements of a Merlin. Soon, all that immense power would be his and he meant to make the most of it. There were old scores to be settled and old rivals to destroy. He was going to enjoy that.

Morgana was right in one respect they shared a desire for revenge and power over those weaker than themselves. He went to his desk and began to draw up a list of people who were close to his rival.

\* \* \*

In the sitting room above the bar of The Carrick Arms Drew sat with his little daughter on his knee reading her a bedtime story. Posy sat by the fire with her seed catalogues in her lap making notes for her purchases for next year. Thomas had promised to enlarge the Herb Garden at the Manor so she could extend her Herbal Products to sell in her shop as well as making the herb pillows and sachets that had sold so well this year. She planned to start a world-wide mail order link but was half listening to her husband's voice as he growled his way through Goldilocks and the Three Bears then, suddenly his voice stopped and she looked up.

Drew's face was white. He stood up with Jessica in his arms and handed her to Posy. "Summat's wrong," he told her. "Finish the story love and get Jessie to bed there's a good lass." He left the room and made his way downstairs and out into the chill of the night where he looked around cautiously then shifted to the mental level and opened his Seer's sight.

He reeled as a sickening stench of evil filled the air around him. A dull red and black shadow towered over the inn reaching with its tendrils towards doors and windows, seeking out a way into the light and life energy that filled it. But even as it did so it was met by a blaze of light that speared up from the foundations of the inn and struck at the heart of the shadow. Linked as he was to the higher levels, Drew heard the scream of pain and frustration in his mind as the interloper shrank back from contact with the pure light.

Drew knew what it was that protected them. Eight years ago at the height of the Battle between Mordred, Morgana and The Guardians of the Singing Stones, for a short time the inn had housed the Coronation Sword of Arthur. The hilt of the sacred blade contained a holy relic, one of the nails of the Crucifixion. The power and influence of the relic still protected the building but Drew knew without a doubt that he and his family had now been marked by the same power that had attacked Thomas the day before.

He waited until the last of the menacing shadow had melted away then went back inside. Jessica was sleeping soundly but Posy was waiting anxiously to hear what was going on. Drew explained what he had seen but emphasised the fact that although the house was well protected, they needed to increase their personal protection.

He then rang the other Guardians to warn them that whatever it was that had attacked Thomas might well include them in its desire for revenge.

They all agreed they must all be on their guard from now on. Having done that he debated with himself whether he should also call Thomas, but decided to leave it until the next day when he could talk it out with him face to face. Then he went down to the Bar to take over from the afternoon staff and see if any other Guardians were there.

Posy went back to Jessica's room to make sure she was sleeping soundly. Sitting in an antique rocking chair that Thomas had found in the attics of the manor and passed on to her, she thought about what had happened. When it was just themselves and Thomas they had to worry about it had seemed easy to face up to the scary things. Now there was little Jess, the child she had given up hope of ever having. Jess, for whom she would give life itself with no hesitation. But, as Posy well knew, there were even greater demands on those who had once stood shoulder to shoulder with the angelic army of Michael, and defeated the hordes of the Undead called up by Morgana. She rocked and cried and watched over her beloved child.

Miles away The Dark Mage cursed and raged at having been defeated twice now by those who stood firm around the Carrick boy. He needed to find a way to separate them. Together they were too strong, but they could be toppled if taken one by one. Morgana was right, Thomas Carrick's weakness was to be found in his love and loyalty to his family and friends.

He would change his tactics, at least for a while and see if he could get Thomas on his own. He had already scouted the Manor house and found it warded to the hilt by angelic forces. There was no way in there, but once outside its protective aura Thomas would be vulnerable. But he must not be too confident, the boy had proven himself to be a powerful Mage... But, he was still green in power and not yet at the full height of his potential, he must use patience and bide his time, time that he could not really afford.

He walked over to a small table and poured himself a glass of aged whiskey savouring the peaty taste on his tongue... he had earned this. But tomorrow, yes, tomorrow he would begin to plan a new attack and this time he would make sure of his prize.

# Chapter Six

**Charlie slumped in the chair** and looked at the brandy sloshing around in his glass. "I can't seem to stop shaking," he said apologetically. "My hands won't keep still." He looked up at Thomas standing in front of him and frowned. "Your hands are OK." He sounded a little peeved at this. Thomas smiled and drew up a chair to sit beside him.

"It's no longer a shock to me," he pointed out. "You'll get used to seeing it happen. First things first, now you know why I want you to come and live in the town house. We need to be close together not just because I'll need to pick your brains about certain things, but it will be safer. You see we... at least... I, have enemies, one in particular who is determined to see me off... literally. Secondly before I can actually claim to be the Arch-Mage I have to go through trials, each involving one of the elements, there may also be a fifth one I'm not sure about."

He got to his feet and began to pace the floor, "All I know about them besides the elemental part is that they will involve certain aspects of ancient British traditions. That's where you come in, also... to be honest I want you to be with me when I go through them. You see I'll need someone to watch my back. There's always a chance I may... lose out."

Charlie gulped down a mouthful of brandy and squared his shoulders. "Not if I'm there you won't. I'll be right beside you, or in front or behind or wherever I'm supposed to be." He gave a nervous laugh and asked, "Are these trials all you have to do?"

"I don't know, I'll have to ask Cormac." Thomas sat down again resting his arms on his thighs and rolling the brandy glass between his hands.

"Cormac? Who is he?" asked Charlie raising his glass to his lips. Thomas grinned and said casually, "He's the one Merlyn sent to train me for the trials. He gave his name as 'Cormac of the House of Midir', he's one of the Sidhe, a sort of fairy prince. You'll enjoy talking to him, he's an immortal and can tell you everything you need to know about Roman Britain… he was there."

This time Charlie really did choke and Thomas had to thump him on the back a few times before he could speak again.

"You are joking," he said. "You are… aren't you?" Thomas shook his head his eyes alight with laughter.

"That's what I said when we first met. But no, I'm afraid he's real Charlie, a real fairy I mean. Though I wouldn't say that to his face and mean what you are thinking it means. He'd be a good man to have with you in a fight believe me."

Charlie put his head in his hands and moaned. "Please God no one at Uni ever gets to know about this. I'm sure I'm going to wake up in a minute and find myself back in my bed at home with a raging hangover."

Thomas sat down again, "There's a lot to explain Charlie, too much for the time we have today. But on the way back tomorrow I'll fill you in with how it all began eight years ago. Then you'll find everything falling into place."

"But how can we talk about things like this with Frank there… Oh… oh… he's part of it isn't he… and Betty too?"

Thomas nodded. "There are a few others as well,

you'll meet them all soon enough. I'm afraid that whatever or whoever is fighting me for the title may attack them as well. It's only a small band of people but when you meet them you'll understand how important they are to the whole story, and to me... and you.

"Once you know the story of what happened eight years ago you'll know how much help I need from you. That book I showed you with the Coats of Arms? A lot of the early stuff in it is in Latin and Middle English. Do you know anything of either of them because I need it translated?"

Charlie snorted and looked down his nose at him then stood up assuming an orator's stance and declaimed:

"*Communi fit vitio naturae, ut invisis, latitantibus atque incognitis rebus magis confidamus, vehementiusque exterreamur...* Or in other words; It happens by a common vice of nature that we trust most to, and are most seriously frightened at, things which are not seen, which are hidden away, and unknown..."

"Middle English won't be a problem either." He went on;

"Þis kyng lay at Camylot vpon Krystmasse
With mony luflych lorde, ledez of þe best,
Rekenly of þe Rounde Table alle þo rich breþer,
With rych reuel ory3t and rechles merþes.
Þer tournayed tulkes by tymez ful mony,
Justed ful jolilé þise gentyle kni3tes,
Syþen kayred to þe court caroles to make."

"Do I speak Latin and Middle English... Hah!" He drained the last of his brandy and looked Thomas belligerently in the eye. "I can translate any damn thing you can put in front of me." He sat down again shakily.

"I think," said Thomas, ringing through to the kitchen, "that we need some black coffee."

Half an hour later they re-joined the others who had been taken on a tour of the house by Steven. Betty meanwhile had made up a basket of apples from the Manor House orchard, some of her gooseberry and ginger jam, several packets of dried herbs from the garden including one of Posy's Lavender and Vervain pillows and a couple of bottles of choice wine from the cellar. Carefully resting on the top was one of her fruit cakes in a tin to keep fresh.

Maisie Naughton had fallen in love with the gracious old house and was full of praise for the way in which Thomas had kept the original style of the house. Jim who had gone round the greenhouses with Frank was going home with a box full of cuttings for his allotment and a bottle of Frank's special Elderberry cordial.

"It'll keep t' cold out while thee's weeding tha' knows."

At six the car was brought round and a bright eyed Maisie was tucked in with a woollen rug around her knees and her basket of goodies by her side.

"It's been a wonderful afternoon, thank you so much Sir Thomas."

Please Mrs. Naughton I would much rather you just called me Thomas, then perhaps I might be allowed to call you Maisie and Jim or James if you prefer."

"Jim'll do nicely lad, we can't thank you enough for all your kindness."

"The pleasure is mine and you must both think of this as an extra home. Charlie will be in and out of here from now on, he'll tell you all about his new digs in Cambridge on the way home. By the way we'll be having a bonfire and fireworks party in November so you must come along and stay overnight so you won't miss any of the fun by having to go home early."

Charlie paused on the steps and gripped his hand,

"Thomas Carrick, I'm your man, now and for as long as you have need of me. I'll see you tomorrow 9:00 on the dot. I don't think I'll get much sleep tonight but who cares, from now on I'll be living my dreams and my research for real." He got in beside Frank and surreptitiously wiped a trace of moisture from his cheek as the car drew away.

Steven and Betty joined Thomas on the steps and waved them off on their journey home. As they re-entered the warm hallway Steven placed a hand on his son's shoulder.

"You've chosen well and wisely Tom," he said. "That's a good man and a strong one with a wealth of common sense in his head. Good family too, I'd love to be there when Maisie tells her neighbours about her afternoon. She's a real card that one."

"It'll take Frank a good hour and a half, or more to get there and back," said Betty. "Will dinner at 8:00 be alright for you men?"

Father and son nodded and she went on, "I've got pork steaks, stuffed green peppers and mashed potatoes, with blackberry and apple crumble and cream to follow… Kitchen or Dining room Sir Thomas?" She winked at Steven. "Wouldn't want to lower the tone of the afternoon would we."

Thomas laughed and hugged her, kissing her cheek. "Kitchen every time Betty, its warmer and we don't have to go far for second helpings. I'm going to pack for tomorrow so I'll be upstairs if you need me." He ran up the stairs whistling.

As he approached the door of his room it opened quietly and allowed him to pass through. Still whistling he grabbed his holdall and began to pack a few things. He didn't need much for he kept a second wardrobe in Cambridge. But remembering that he needed to arrange a meeting with Justin Thorndyke he packed an evening suit along with a shirt, tie and decent shoes. He had learned long ago to dress down in Cambridge it made sense not to stand out too much. He changed his Patek Philippe watch for an Accurist, checked his wallet, cards, small change, then stopped as he suddenly remembered something unusual happening.

He turned and looked at the door, something was wrong... well not wrong exactly, but out of place. He thought back over the last few minutes. He'd come up the stairs, walked along the corridor to his room, opened the door, NO! He had not opened the door, he had no recollection of actually opening the door, but it had opened. A cold shiver ran down his back. He walked to the door, opened it and looked out. The corridor was empty. He closed it, then opened it again and walked to the top of the stairs.

For a moment he stood looking down on the landing, then he turned and walked back towards his room, on reaching it he went to put out his hand. The door opened. He stepped back and it closed, stepped forward and it opened again! Thomas rarely swore, he had not been brought up to use bad language, but his years in University had made him familiar with the usual expletives.

"Bloody Hell!"

How long had this been going on, had anyone else seen it happen, anyone at Uni? If so he was in deep trouble, telekinesis was not on his curriculum. He sat down on the bed to think. He went back over this last weekend. Quite a few extraordinary things had happened, things that might have triggered this new talent. Then it hit him.

The Merlins; each one had passed to him something of their own talent. Was this one of them? Somehow that didn't seem to fit. On the other hand one of them had spoken of him finding his own particular talent... maybe this was it. He sat quietly thinking about this new development and finding it hard to deal with. He would have to keep a close watch on himself, things like this could not be allowed to happen around other people. Cormac had said he would make contact on All Hallows Eve, he made a mental note to ask him about this new development, he also decided not to mention it to anyone else until he had it under control.

He finished his packing and spent some time putting together his work notes for the coming week, he would need to put in some real study time in the run up to the end of term. Not for the first time he wondered how he was going to cram everything in. He sighed and turned his attention to the question of the legalities of land ownership in the nineteenth century and the effect of the cotton industry on agriculture.

The sound of the dinner gong brought him back to earth. He was hungry and dinner sounded like a good idea. He finished up his notes zipped up the packed holdall and headed for the door then stopped. He and the door contemplated each other, then it opened and waited politely for him to pass through. He laughed, suddenly feeling at ease with everything. He patted the door as he went through and didn't even bother to look round, knowing that it would close of its own accord. Dinner smelt good.

As they sat around the table Frank recounted the return journey with the Naughtons. Maisie had fallen asleep but he and Jim had talked dog racing almost the whole way. Betty was delighted he had found someone who shared his enthusiasm as it was something that had never interested her.

Thomas asked about Charlie and was told he had hardly said a word during the entire journey. "He seemed a bit 'pixilated' but then I gather you had summat to do with that Tom. You spent quite a time together. He's a good lad that 'un."

Thomas nodded, his mouth full of food, "What time

do you want to leave tomorrow Frank, if we are picking him up at 9:00 we'll have to leave early."

"I'd like ter be on us way by 8:00 am lad, that'll give us time to cope wi' the traffic. After 9:30 we'll be out of the worst and can take it easy like. When will yer need picking up again?"

"On the 4th please Frank and can you arrange with the Naughtons to pick them up about 3:00 on the 5th. Betty will you get rooms ready for everyone. I'd like Drew and his family to stay overnight as well as Charlie and the Naughtons, then Jess can stay up a little later. Put Maisie and Jim in the Camelot room she'll love that Four Poster bed and the tapestries. Will you be with us dad or does that clash with your trip to the War Museum?"

"Ummm, I think it might, in fact I think I'll go straight on to the US from there. I'll visit your mother first, then fly back East to give that writing course in Philadelphia and be back here in time for Christmas."

"Sounds good dad. Is Frank taking you down to London?"

"No, I'll go by train then I can do some work on the way. Besides Frank will have his work cut out gearing up for the holidays here." Steven's eyes widened slightly as the sugar bowl slid across the table and then stopped abruptly as Thomas hurriedly picked it up. Betty and Frank deep in conversation had noticed nothing. Steven lifted an inquiring eyebrow at his son, who grinned, then drew a zip across his mouth. Steven nodded and went on as if nothing had happened.

"Anything you want me to say to your mother?"

"Just that I hope she's ok and look to see her sometime next year."

Steven hid his disappointment at the non-committal answer and poured another cup of tea. It was his dearest hope that Thomas would one day forgive his mother for what he saw as her betrayal of them both. But he knew it was a forlorn hope more especially with the Arch-Mage trials looming ahead of him. He needed all his strength both mental and physical to get through the next year. He finished his tea and stood up.

"I'll take another hour in the study and then head up for bed, going my way?"

Thomas stood with him. "Yes, thanks for the dinner Betty it was great as usual, Frank thank you for driving the Naughtons back and forth it was good of you to take the time. By the way what did the vet say about Grim?"

"I'm to fetch him on Wednesday. The leg was badly bruised but not broken, he's got twelve stitches along his neck and shoulder and he's lost the tip of one ear, a real 'war wound'. But he'll be up and running around when you get back. We'll take good care of him don't worry."

"Thanks for that, I'll not have to worry about him while I'm away. Goodnight both of you, I'll see you in the morning." He joined Steven and they walked together as far as the staircase where Steven paused and looked quizzically at his son.

"Since when have you been playing checkers with the china Tombo?"

"You were not supposed to notice that." Thomas sighed and kicked moodily at the first stair. "It's a new development and I have to learn to control it. At the moment it's pretty haphazard, doors mostly, they tend to open before I touch the door-handle. It gave me a bad few minutes before I figured it out. I'm turning into a freak dad. The sooner I can get the finals over the better, at the moment I am liable to get myself arrested. I'll be glad to see Cormac at All Hallows, maybe he can help. Though knowing him he's likely to laugh his head off."

Steven clapped him on the shoulder. "God I wish I could write you up as a character in a book. It would make the Exorcist look like a Marvel Comic. See you when I get back lad." He hugged him and went on to his study.

Thomas stared after him, wishing, not for the first time, that he could just stay here where he felt safe. Wishing he'd been born an ordinary human being who could have grown up into someone like Charlie. He started up the stairs and on the first landing came face to face with Cormac.

"I thought you said Halloween," he grumbled, pushing past the tall Sidhe and continuing up the stairs.

"I was… passing through and caught a stray thought or two about wishing you were someone else… am I right?" Thomas stopped at the top of the stairs and turned to face him.

"Yes, dammit. Too many things are happening at once. I came home for a quiet weekend and what happens? I get attacked and damn near killed along with my dog. A bunch of ex-Merlins arrive to give me advice and pass on … 'abilities' I don't know what to do with, such as doors opening before I get to them and sugar bowls offering themselves to my spoon. I get Charlie on board and find him kneeling at my feet. It's too much Cormac, I'm a freak in stag's clothing!" He strode down the corridor and stormed through the door that hastily opened for him. Cormac followed, his silver eyes amused and took a seat.

"That is why I came a little early. Calm down Thomas, everything is happening according to plan, well, almost everything. The ex-Merlins as you so quaintly describe them always pay a courtesy call to their new successor. The 'abilities' they offer are left deep within you. They will surface over time as and when they are needed and many will only be needed once or twice in your lifetime. It is more of a helping hand than an ability that will stay with you. Charles

Naughton knelt not to Thomas Carrick, but to The Merlin, the representative of the Spirit of your race and The Guardian of The Blessed Isles."

Thomas sighed and scrubbed his face with his hands. "I'm sorry Cormac, it's just that there is so much to do and to learn in both worlds. The telekinetic stuff was the last straw."

"Well that I can help you with *Deartháir.*"

"What does 'jarther' mean," queried Thomas

Cormac winced at the mangling of his native tongue. "When pronounced in the correct way it means Brother. What you humans call telekinesis has two actual causes. One is more acceptable to humans than the other. There is a magnetic field surrounding every manifested form, animal, vegetable and mineral and Fae included. This varies considerably in type and intensity from one to another. In some people the field attracts everyday objects that have a reciprocal rate of vibration. So things get attracted to them and they move towards them or sometimes away from them. In the distant past humans used it to attract game to them. Predators use it even now to do the same thing. In a different way and on a different level it also attracts male to female. Think about it."

Thomas thought about it, and was intrigued. "You said there was another cause for this ... attraction."

Cormac smiled. "Yes, the one less likely to be accepted... But nevertheless in your case it is the one to be considered. What do you know about Elementals?"

"Well there are four kinds, Gnomes, Sylphs, Salamanders, and Undines, Miss Pugh, Edna, taught me about them. She had a close connection with them. Posy has the same feeling for flowers and trees which I suppose is connected to the earth elements."

"Correct. You have a strong connection to this part

of the country, it is your birthplace, your native land. Your body is composed mainly of the minerals and earth elements of this place. As a Merlin you are its Guardian so the earth in all its forms responds to you. Wood, China, Clay, Stone are attracted to you. Everything, literally everything, has a certain amount of sentience, in other words it has a consciousness. So when recognised it responds to the best of its ability.

"As Grim responds to your caress with a lick of his tongue, so a wooden door responds to your desire to walk through it. It understands you would hurt yourself if you walk into it, so it prevents that by opening. The sugar bowl feels your attention to it and responds by offering its contents.

"You rightly named the Elementals as Gnomes, Sylphs, Salamanders and Undines... but Thomas, all these beings exist within you as well as outside of you. You are becoming more and more aware of your AT-ONE-NESS with everything around you and therefore everything is becoming more *aware of you as an awakened being*... in other words, a Merlin. It is a title and a position as well as a name.

"The earth minerals that make up your body also owe an allegiance to the earth, it is the 'gnome' within you so to speak. It is the same with the other elementals. With your heightened sense of awareness you are responding to the elements inside you and they in turn respond to their counterparts outside your body.

"Do you understand? There is no need to try and 'control' them. Just relax and be at ease and they will understand the need to conceal their presence from anyone who is not of your inner circle. As time goes on you may find some people close to you exhibiting the same kind of talents. In fact they may already do so but, like you, they are just not aware of it.

"The fact that this has happened will make my task much easier. Recognition of the internal elements will enable you to shift more easily. But you found that out when you were attacked. You reacted instinctively to the Wolf form. But now you must rest. I will come as promised on All Hallows and we will talk more on the subject of shifting, the time of your first trial draws near and you must prepare. Goodnight Thomas."

His form dissolved into a mist that drifted towards the window and paused: "Well…?" said Cormac's voice. Thomas laughed and reached out mentally to the wooden windows frames. The top one slid down and the mist flowed out into the night. Thomas closed the window again. More at ease now with the new development he showered and brushed his teeth then slid into bed and was asleep as his head touched the pillow.

Some miles away Cormac stood beside the bed of another sleeper. Charlie lay sprawled across a bed slightly too small for him now. His mouth was open and a gentle snore emerged from under the old fashioned eiderdown. Cormac smiled and gently began to manipulate his dreams.

*High above the white cliffs he watched the Roman legions come ashore. The first twenty spread out looking for a good campsite. The smiths urged the horses over the side of the boat and swam with them to the beach. Once there they rubbed them down with straw and ran them up and down to get the stiffness out of their legs. Others were wading ashore with baskets of provisions, tools, tents, and weapons.*

*Overall he thought there might be some fifty ships and maybe a thousand men. From the rough speech and many different accents he understood that the same thing was happening all along the coast for maybe a day's march. This was an invasion force.*

*Jars of wine, blacksmiths' tools, bars of rough iron for*

*horseshoes, dried rations followed. By nightfall the fires had been lit and the men were eating. Behind the trees further back crouched dark figures dressed in rough skins. Some were naked or streaked with a vivid dark blue dye in strange patterns. All were armed with clubs and flint headed spears. Suddenly there arose a howling like that of a wild animal. On the beachhead men leapt to their feet grabbing for their weapons, but many were clubbed to the ground before they could scream. Terror reigned all along the coast of what would one day be called The Blessed Isles.*

Charlie came awake with his dream vivid in his mind. He threw back the covers and switched on the light. Grabbing his battered PC he began to type furiously, trying to get down as much as he could before it faded. By the time the sun rose he had the first ten pages of his end of term paper. It was good he thought reading it back, in fact it was damned good. It might even get him top marks.

As he washed shaved and dressed, a fading image of someone tall and dark with an off-beat sense of humour nagged at the back of his mind, but he dismissed it as part of the dream. Thomas would soon be here and the thought of a warm comfortable drive down to Cambridge rather than a cold wet train journey lifted his spirits as he went down to breakfast. Next term he would have comfortable digs with a quiet place to study and congenial company when he wanted it. All thanks to The Merlin that he, Charles Naughton, now served as his ancestors had served long ago.

A few minutes after 9:00 Frank drew up outside the door and Thomas got out to greet the Naughtons with his usual courtesy. With his case stowed away Charlie kissed his mother, hugged his dad and got into the car. They waved as they left then settled back in comfort. A few pleasantries passed between them as Frank headed for the A628 to join up with the M1 heading south. As they began to cross over the Peak District Charlie turned to Thomas and said in his straightforward way.

"Alright Thomas, it's time to come clean. What did happen eight years ago?" Frank chuckled and shifted into touring gear. This was going to be an interesting journey.

# Chapter Seven

**Maisie Naughton turned** up the radio and sang along to the music as she washed up the breakfast dishes. A neat pile of freshly washed clothes sat waiting to be ironed. Her husband had taken out the bins and lit the fire in the sitting room and now came into the kitchen to put the kettle on.

"Fancy a cuppa Maisie?" he asked, "And perhaps a bit o' Betty's fruit cake?"

"Ooh that'd be great. I'll do the ironing at the same time." She dried her hands, set up the ironing board and plugged in the iron. "Wasn't it nice of Thomas to offer those rooms to our Charlie. It'll be nice and quiet and less money as well."

Her husband was quiet for a moment filling the teapot then he said, "As long as Charlie doesn't start gettin' ideas above his station. He'll be moving into a different class of people from now on and I hope he doesn't start lookin' down on his own folk."

Maisie took a sip of her tea and started ironing. "I don't think young Thomas is like that. Charlie did say as how he'd not been brought up to money. That he didn't know about the money and the house an' all until he was nigh on fourteen."

"Be that as it may old girl, I don't want our lad getting above himself. I don't say as how it won't do him a world of good later in life to 'ave such connections, but I don't want 'im ter look down on his beginnings."

Maisie gave her husband a bright smile. "You old fusspot, Charlie is so much like you, he'd never look down on us. He's as level headed as his dad. Though I must admit it the thought of spending a night in that place makes me think a bit. I'll nip into Marks and Spencer's tomorrow and buy a new nightie, and some pyjamas for you. You've almost worn through the seat of yours." She went on with her work happy and contented that her son would be well connected and looking forward to telling her neighbours about their afternoon at the Manor.

\* \* \*

Drew was frantic. Having failed to get hold of Thomas before he left, he rang the house in Cambridge and left a message to call him as soon as possible. He had called the others and they had agreed to meet and discuss the new threat that had come into their lives. Ian had been called away but the rest of them were now gathered together. Posy had asked her assistant to stand in for her at the shop and Jessica played with her dolls in the corner.

"But I don't understand why this is happening now and to us," said Posy tearfully. "It's not fair, we went through so much eight years ago." Drew took her hand in his and held it tightly.

"We got through it then and we will get through this as long as we stay close to each other and remain true to what we believe in."

"So far it seems to be concentrating on you Drew, maybe it's because you are the closest to Thomas. As he's away it's trying to see where there's a weak point. I wish Father John was here. This is something he would know how to deal with." Nurse Pym sighed and sat back in her chair. "Perhaps Thomas will have some ideas when he calls."

"And if he doesn't, what then," demanded Posy. "If this... this thing is after him, why are we involved? It's Jessica I'm worried about. I don't want her mixed up in this kind of thing. It was different eight years ago, we knew what we were fighting for and there was no child involved."

"Yes there was... there was Thomas. We fought for him then and we will fight for him now Posy." Drew spoke with conviction. "For better or worse we are bound to the future Merlin, and I for one won't let him down. If we allow ourselves to be divided, this evil, whatever it is, will win. Together we are strong, but if we give into fear we can be picked off one by one. Be with me on this Posy, please."

Her face streaked with tears Posy nodded but her eyes were on her daughter. The others spoke together and agreed to wait until Drew has talked to Thomas before they made any kind of decision on how to confront this new threat. Then they left.

Drew took Posy into his arms and held her close sharing his strength both physical and spiritual with her. "Sweetheart, do you think I would let anything happen to Jess or to you. You have to have faith in me darling girl. Whatever this is, we can fight it as we fought against Morgana. I swear to you I won't let anything happen to Jess, neither will Thomas, you know how he loves her."

Posy nodded hiding her face in his shoulder. Deep inside she knew with a mother's instinct that there was trouble to come, but more than that she knew that both she and Jess would be involved. She clung to her husband and fought a deep and terrible battle in her heart.

At a few minutes past 2:00 the phone rang.

"Drew, what is it? What's happened, is it Jess, Posy, You? For Heaven's sake tell me." Thomas was frantic.

"Thomas, it's OK... for the moment. We are alright, all of us, but I don't know for how long. We've had a bit of a scare and I'm pretty certain it links up with this guy who is after the Arch-Mage-ship. The one you told us about, the Wolf-Shifter. It happened last night..." Quickly and concisely Drew gave him the full details, putting on the speaker phone so Posy could listen in.

"That it happened at all I found worrying, it takes a lot of power to keep it on the astral level and unseen. You're going to have your hands full with this one Thomas."

"That's true but two attacks of such power within days of each other will have left him a lot weaker. He threatened to attack me in the real world, not on The Second Road, and he can do that in various ways, at Cambridge, at the Manor, or even through the Guardians as he has done already.

"Drew, I may have an idea. I don't know if I have the ability to do it, but I have to try. The focal point of the Manor's protection is the Chapel where Father John introduced me to the Archangels of the Quarters when he warded the whole estate. I might be able to call on them for help.

"I'm coming back to Deepdale right away. As it happens Frank is still here, we blew a tyre just outside Cambridge and had to stop and change the wheel. Frank went off to get a new spare, you know how he is about being prepared and came back to have lunch before setting off home. It's 2:30 now and we can be back by 6:00. Get Posy and Jess to the Manor while it's still daylight, and they can stay overnight. Then get as many of the Guardians as can manage it to the Manor for, say 7:30 tonight. I haven't a clue what or how to do it, but I'll trust to what is in the Chapel to help me."

"Thomas, you've just gotten down there, there's your lectures and such like. What will your teachers say?"

"I'll get someone to take notes for me and tell my

tutor I was called back home on urgent business… which is true. Nothing is more important to me than keeping you all safe, especially Posy and Jess. I'm on my way Drew." The phone went dead. Drew turned to Posy.

"See love, you mean so much to him he's turning right round and coming back. He may be only a young man but he is also The Merlin, or will be soon. He'll make things right. Now I'll just see if the Bar needs a hand."

Posy nodded brightly. "I'll pack a few things to take with us and call Judy at the shop and let her know she's on her own for a day or two." She swung Jess up into her arms and pressed her face into the soft curls. "Nothing's going to hurt you darling, I'll see to that. Merlin or no Merlin Mummy will keep you safe." She went upstairs to pack.

Deep in the Underworld where her black soul was imprisoned Morgana smiled. The seed of doubt in Thomas's ability to protect them had taken root. A mother's love could be potently strong, but also a fatal weakness.

Back in Cambridge Thomas filled Frank and Charlie in on the new developments. Without a word Frank went to get the car and Charlie picked up his case.

"I'm coming with you," he said calmly, "if nothing else I can watch your back. Don't argue Tom, I've told you I'm your man now and I meant it. I can hardly back out the first time something crops up."

Thomas looked at him, then shook his head and spread his hands, he knew better than to talk such a man out of something he had set his heart on.

"I'll call Drew on the car phone and tell him there'll be an extra one on the team, and get Betty to prepare a room. If we are very lucky, and we get this sorted, we can be back in Cambridge later tomorrow. We'll call your tutor on the way as well. Leave your case here, I can loan you anything you might need. But you won't be able to bring your mum and dad in on this… the last thing I want it for them to be put in danger of any kind."

Charlie nodded. "Understood and seconded Boss." He grinned as Thomas's head came up. "You are you know, the Boss I mean, you're one of those people who go straight to the heart of things and get things done. Come on, here's Frank."

Within minutes they were on their way and Thomas was talking first to Drew and then to the Atkinsons. He followed this up with calls to both of their tutors and then to fellow students to take notes during the lectures they were both missing. That done he turned to Charlie and told him about the warding of the Manor by Father John and how the four Archangels had manifested in the chapel.

"My plan is to see if I can call them again and ask for their help. I've never done anything like this before, Father John was a priest, I'm not, so they may not answer me, after all The Merlin is, was, Pagan… sort of. But Cormac told me I would have to learn to do things on my own, and those who went before me would help as and when they could. I'm scared stiff Charlie, scared for my people, my friends and family. I have to protect them at all costs." His voice trailed off uncertainly.

Charlie, sitting beside him and listening to the desperation in his voice felt an answering emotion rise up in him. He could feel the loneliness in this man and began to understand what is must be like to hold this kind of power and know he was responsible not just for his own family, but for the racial soul of Britain. He had never been religiously inclined, attending church only when required to do so, but now something deep within him fought free and came to the surface and he spoke with an utter conviction.

"They'll answer Thomas, I know they will and they will bring something with them that will help us all. I don't know how I know but it will happen. Don't think about how, just concentrate on 'feeling and knowing' and it will come to you."

Thomas looked at him, at the fresh-faced, chubby-cheeked young man beside him and realised that he was no longer so "chubby". In the last few weeks he had become leaner, stronger, and in some indefinable way more assured of himself. He had begun the change from the ordinary into the extraordinary. As he had done eight years ago, as the Guardians had done for over a thousand years, now it was happening to Charlie. He smiled and leaned back in the seat.

"You're right, I'll let it come to me. Thanks Charlie you've put my mind at ease. I'll sleep a while and rest up for whatever is going to happen." He closed his eyes wearily. Frank eyed Charlie in the driving mirror.

"That were well said lad, Tom always has doubts about his own ability ter do things. He can and he does do 'em, but he worries. Now, wi' you beside him he'll do even better. It sort of spreads the load like. Now then you follow 'is lead and get some rest while yer can. I'm thinking this'll be a long day and a troublesome one."

Charlie nodded and looked across at the young Merlin beside him and a fierce protectiveness rose up in him. He tucked the car rug around him and pulled down the window blind then he settled down in the opposite corner to sleep. The dream slid quietly into his mind and eased its way down into the sub-conscious levels and began to impart its message.

*He was standing in a small village street outside a shop with an old fashioned mullioned window filled with bric-a-brac. A small SALE NOW ON sign was propped up against the glass. Ships in bottles and Toby jugs vied for space with faded watercolours and horse brasses. Tucked to one side and half hidden by a Victorian doll he could see a small horn with a tarnished silver mouthpiece and a silver rim. He looked up at the sign over the shop. 'Angela's Antiques'. A subtle command was placed in his head.*

"Wake up lads, it's time we got ourselves summat ter drink. Thee's bin asleep best part of an hour."

Frank had parked the car outside a public house in a small village and opened the door letting in a blast of cold air. Thomas opened his eyes and yawned then got out and stretched. "Great, coffee and a sandwich, I'll order it up for us." He headed towards the pub.

Frank locked the car and prepared to follow him when Charlie, getting out on the other side saw across the narrow High street an antique shop. *"Angela's Antiques"* it said. SALE NOW ON. His dream snapped into place.

"I'll be over in a minute Frank," he said. "There's something I have to do."

He headed across the street dodging a delivery van and a couple of boys on mountain bikes. Outside the shop he paused and looked in the window and there half hidden by a Victorian Doll was the horn he had seen in his dream. He chuckled to himself and pushed open the door. A bell tinkled as he entered and a bright-eyed middle-aged woman looked up from a wooden rocking chair and smiled.

"Good afternoon sir, can I help you?"

"Er… yes please, you have a horn in the window and I'd like to buy it."

Getting up from her chair the woman went to the window and peered in. She picked up the horn and turned to offer it to him. There was something about her gesture as if she was offering something very precious. As he touched it, it grew warm and a tingle ran up his arm from wrist to shoulder. He was holding something very powerful. He knew without doubt that it was meant for the work Thomas had to do that night.

"I'll take it... er... how much is it?" he asked, suddenly afraid he would not have enough money.

"Well the mouthpiece and the rim are silver and embossed by hand and it is very old." Charlie's heart sank.

"But we do have a sale on so I think I can let it go for fifteen pounds."

Charlie turned out his pockets and laid out the money on the counter. "Er... five... ten... and four pound coins..." He reached for his change purse, "... 50... 60... 70..." He rummaged around and found a twenty pence piece in another pocket then searched frantically for the final ten pence. After going through every pocket he found it deep in his pants pocket and heaved a sigh.

"Fifteen pounds... just," he said handing it over. "I'll have to borrow the money for my lunch now," and he laughed self-consciously.

"It was all the money you had," said the woman smiling. "But to give all you have for someone else opens the way to heaven they say." She wrapped the horn in a piece of violet coloured tissue paper and handed it over. Then she accompanied him to the door and opened it. "God bless you Charlie."

Stammering his thanks Charlie headed over the road again and looked back to wave. For one startling moment all he could see was a tall radiant, winged figure in a violet and silver robe. Then there was just a middle-aged woman smiling as she closed the shop door.

Charlie was about to bite into his sandwich when he remembered a curious fact. The old lady had called him Charlie, as if she knew him. In his pocket, lying against his side the horn grew warm.

# Chapter Eight

**Betty had turned** on the heating in the chapel and dressed the altar with a white lace cloth and a bowl of Holly, white Calla Lilies, and Autumn foliage. Two tall candles in silver holders stood at each side. Three golden candles in the East, three red in the South, three green in the North but in the West and just before the door stood one tall blue candle in a waist high holder. Everything was as ready as she could make it.

In the Great Hall Steven and the Guardians, along with Frank and Charlie, who had had his first meeting with them, stood waiting for Thomas. He had spent some time talking with Posy trying to convince her that while she and Jess were in the manor house they would be safe. Drew was beside himself, torn between his trust in Thomas and his concern for his wife and child.

Thomas knew he was skating on thin ice as far as Posy was concerned and was both puzzled and hurt she could not trust his word that he would keep them safe. Now it was time to prove his words, he called them together and they prepared to face their challenge. The small procession made its silent way along the path towards the little wood where the chapel awaited them.

Charlie walked beside Thomas, the horn tucked into his pocket. He was trusting that he would know the right time to give it to him. In his heart of hearts he had given himself entirely to the demands of the moment. As they had waited for Thomas to join them he had felt the call of ancient blood ties linking him to this group of people. This was his place, his time, and his destiny as much as it was that of The Merlin.

The air was frosty and the ground crackled beneath their feet. Drew carried his sleeping daughter close to his heart. But Posy, though she walked beside him seemed to be miles away. Betty waited at the door with a small votive candle for each person. They accepted it and lit it from the Western candle as they entered and proceeded to their seats. Drew laid Jess down on one of the pews on a thick folded blanket with a small pillow under her head with Posy and himself on either side of her. Thomas came last. He walked to the altar and turned to face them, he was silent for a few minutes, then he spoke.

"Eight years ago I stood here with Father John when he warded the Manor and made it a safe haven for all of us. Since then we have celebrated Christmas Eve Communion every year. Drew and Posy were married, and Jess was Christened here. We have come together to celebrate every Beltane, Midsummer, and Harvest Festivals. Many of us simply come here to be quiet and spend time thinking of those we love and who have left us.

"When Father John brought me here that day so many years ago, I had no idea what was before me. In some ways I still don't know, there are many trials ahead of me and there is always the possibility that I may fail. But of one thing I am sure, I will protect those who have come to mean so much to me. In the past few days we have come under attack from someone who wishes to take my place as the Arch-Mage of Albion. He cannot issue a full challenge until I have taken the trials ordained for every Merlin. But he has stated that he will, attack me and mine in this world to weaken my resolve.

"But, he is one and we are many. If we pool our strengths we can protect ourselves and even carry the fight to him. I have the power I was born with, and I have been promised the help of the Merlins of the Past. I have been offered help from the Race of the Sidhe and have accepted it and its cost. But I cannot fight alone. I need you, all of you, to fight with me and to lend me your strengths as you did eight years ago.

"We are under attack and our enemy has shown that he is not above threatening our most precious member, Jessica. That I will not allow. In this sacred place I give you my word that whatever it takes I will stand between you and this danger. I have no idea what to do here this evening... I am trusting that the powers that were placed here will come again and show me what I must do. I ask you to join with me in praying for guidance."

The small company bowed their heads in prayer and Thomas turned to the altar and stood straight and tall with his arms out. He did not kneel in supplication but asked as was his right as the future Merlin for the help he so desperately needed.

"Father John, beloved friend and mentor help me to call upon those you set to guard this place, for we are in need of their powers.

"Raphael, do you remember me? I stood with you in the East and wondered at the feeling of love and peace that came with you into this place. I ask for your Presence once again that we may be aided in our battle against the Darkness." He turned to the South.

"Michael, Father John called you The Sword Bearer of the Most High. I have no sword or shield to use against what threatens us, so I ask for the loan of your sword and your shield that I may guard those who mean so much to me. We called on you before when Betty was attacked, and you answered, please, answer us now." He turned to the West.

"Gabriel, we laughed together you and I. I asked you if you really did have a silver trumpet and you said yes. When Morgana held me prisoner under Ragnock Tor and I couldn't wake Mordred, you drew my attention to the horn that finally woke him. I need your trumpet now to awaken within myself the power that lies sleeping." He turned to the North.

"Uriel, You are the Guardian of this Earth, this Albion. I cannot, will not, allow it to be misused by one who serves the Dark. I offer my life if that is the price to be paid (he took no notice of the agitation this caused among the Guardians). Give me the means to fight and fight I will to the death if it is needed." He turned to the East again and knelt with head bowed. "Please, answer me, let me know we are not alone. Hear me as I call to you."

He felt a hand on his shoulder and looked up into Charlie's face. He held out a small hunting horn bound with silver and with a silver mouthpiece.

"Gabriel sent you this," he said and went back to his seat.

Thomas stood up with the horn in his hand, and everyone stood with him. He turned and looked at Charlie with his heart in his eyes then he faced the West, lifted the horn to his mouth and blew.

The pure note reached out and filled every heart in the chapel. Then burst into the world outside filling the night with a joy and blessedness that reached far and wide. In a cottage five miles away a newborn baby drew the sound in with its first breath and its destiny became a fact. An old man drew his last breath in the arms of his son, drew it in and left joyfully with its sound in his ears. The village of Deepdale and the surrounding farms were blessed by it as were their animals. Sleeping children dreamed deep and true, and in the priory of St Edward, the Abbot kneeling at his prie-dieu saw his small room filled with a light that was not of this world.

In the chapel four great Pillars of Power streamed through the stained glass windows behind the altar and gathered about Thomas as he stood with the horn in his hand. The others had been sent to their knees by the sheer pressure of the Angelic Presences. But Jessica woke up and slipped down from her makeshift bed and toddled towards the Powers, drawn by the colours and the beautiful faces that she, with her child's innocence and purity could see quite clearly. Posy tried to rise, to follow her, but could not. Like Drew she was held to the spot.

Thomas picked up the child and held her out to the Eastern Pillar. It received her spoke to her and blessed her and handed her on.

Cooing, she reached out to pat the Pillar of the South and made contact with Michael's face as he smiled at her. Taken up by the Pillar of the West she was held close and treasured as Gabriel remembered another child 2,000 years before playing in the dust of a carpenter's yard. The Pillar of the North held her, played with her, blessed her then returned her to her God-father. Thomas walked to Drew and placed her in his arms, then returned to surrender to the Will of the Four Great Powers.

They surrounded and enclosed him, his clothes fell away leaving him naked and vulnerable. They laid their burning hands upon him and seared his flesh. Michael's sword rose over him and pierced his heart. Gabriel's Chalice poured salt in the wounds until he screamed with the pain of it. Raphael pierced his hands and feet and Uriel thrust a crown of thorns down onto his head. They took him into themselves and filled him with the powers of their elements both good and bad, but leaving him with the Grace of Choice.

Betty fought to get to him, Drew bellowed as he tried to share his pain, Steven pleaded, begged and offered himself in place of his son. Guardians cried, begged, pleaded, offered and were refused.

But it was Charlie Naughton who came. He walked into the very centre of the searing light and knelt to take Thomas' broken and tortured body into his arms and lift him on to the altar. He placed the candles at his head and feet and tore the flowers to pieces sprinkling them over his ravaged body then wrapped him in the altar cloth. That done he sat on the altar step with one of Thomas' hands in his, and wept.

Slowly the Four Powers dimmed their radiance. Then Raphael spoke gently to those listening:

*"Great strength comes from great endurance. To know endurance demands first that you know pain. Knowing pain means understanding the pain of others. The pain he has endured will be his Shield and yours."*

Michael spoke:

*"Every Sword must drink Heart's Blood before it can bestow its protection. Few can withstand the pain of the pierced heart. But when the offer is made, the trial must be undertaken. The Pain of the Heart's Piercing becomes his Sword and your Defence."*

Now Gabriel, his incredible eyes filled with tears, added his silver voice:

*"Each Merlin is of his or her own time with all its misunderstandings, dangers, and burgeoning knowledge. This Merlin will be different. He will unite the belief systems of the Ancient world to those of the world as it is now. I am the Messenger of the Most High in the spiritual world. This Merlin will be a Messenger of Humankind in this world. The magic of the original Word lies within Him."*

Lastly came Uriel:

*"His pain was an offering, made from the heart and without any thought of self. The willing sacrifice wields great magic and the cost demanded is not always physical death but a willingness to LIVE to the utmost and to bring to that life all the goodness within that person. He asked on your behalf for our help. That means you had to watch his pain as he had to bear it. Thus you are bound together in the coming battle. Yes there will be more pain to be borne, but we have provided the power to overcome both the pain and the Darkness that threatens you. But you will not understand it until the time comes upon you."*

The voices of the Four blended into one voice.

*"There is a blessing on all who serve."*

The radiance dimmed and the four became a single Pillar of Coloured Fire that flowed through the door that opened to allow it passage then closed again leaving behind a silence that would be imprinted upon their hearts and minds forever.

Jess was fast asleep in her mother's arms. It was Drew and Steven who came to the altar to care for Thomas only to find him sleeping peacefully with no mark of his ordeal upon his body. Drew took off his overcoat and wrapped him in it and with Steven following carried him to the house. Frank and Betty went ahead to prepare hot tea and food and to see to those who would be staying the night. The rest followed, too stunned to do more than talk in muted whispers. Ian and Marjory and Nurse Pym left as both had early appointments the next day. The others followed soon after.

Charlie stayed in the chapel to douse the candles, shut off the heating and lock the doors. As he worked there came upon him a profound sense of peace. It seemed to him that he had become a lay brother serving in a great Abbey.

He moved quietly and with purpose and genuflected each time he passed the altar. When all was done he went to the door, turned to bow to the Altar and saw standing before it, a man he knew from a photograph Thomas had shown him. He smiled and lifted his hand in salute.

"Good night Father John, I'll give Thomas your love in the morning."

# Chapter Nine

**The pale October** sunlight filtered through the closed curtains and slowly filled the room. Thomas stirred and rolled over stretching limbs that seemed strangely cramped. He opened his eyes, yawned and lifted his head. His father was sitting hunched up in an armchair by the bed, a light blanket over his legs.

He sat up cautiously not wanting to disturb him and saw Charlie on the other side curled up on a pile of cushions under a blanket snoring gently. For a moment, still dazed with sleep he wondered what they were doing in his bedroom. Then fragments of memory returned and he gently shook his father's shoulder.

"Dad, dad, come on wake up, you're going to have one hell of a stiff neck sleeping like that."

Steven groaned opened his eyes and struggled into an upright position to peer blearily at his son, then came fully awake with a jerk.

"Thomas, Tom. Are you alright lad, how are you feeling... Charlie, Charlie wake up, Tom's back with us."

A tousled head, badly in need of a shave appeared above the other side of the bed. "Wha... wa... timzit?"

Thomas roared with laughter. "What in earth were you two thinking of sleeping like this, did you think I was going to fall out of bed?"

"When we got you to bed you were almost hypothermic, unconscious, with a low pulse rate and looked as if you wouldn't last the night. Ian gave you a shot of something and said he'd be round this morning to look you over. We honestly thought we might lose you Tom." His father kept touching him as if to make sure he was still breathing. Charlie, looking like a badly rumpled teddy-bear, chimed in.

"Yeah, if you intend doing things like this on a regular basis I'm changing my Archaeology major to Medicine."

"How are you feeling Tom," asked his father. "Seriously you gave us all a fright in the chapel. Do you remember anything of it, you were really out of it when we got you back last night."

Thomas grabbed his towelling robe and headed for the bathroom, "I'm fine dad honest. In fact I feel better than I have since all this started. I'm hungry too, can you ask Betty to make a big breakfast?"

Charlie headed for the door. "It's more likely to be a big lunch, it's gone eleven and I'd like to bet there's a pile of messages on the answer phone and a fair few on your email." He headed downstairs to the kitchen.

Steven stared after Thomas as he started the shower going and began to brush his teeth then, shaking his head he left for his own room to shower and dress.

Half an hour later all three were wading into eggs, bacon, sausage and field mushrooms and consuming endless cups of coffee. In between mouthfuls Thomas called Drew and the others to re-assure them that he was alive and well. Drew said Jessica had slept through the night and remembered nothing of what she had experienced. Posy seemed to have accepted things as well, though he said she was much quieter than usual.

Ian Atkinson arrived to give Thomas a once over and declared him fit, though it amazed him that there were

99

no visible signs of the harrowing initiation of power he had gone through. He took one look at Steven's pale face and shaky hands and took his blood pressure as a precaution. It was somewhat elevated so he packed him off to bed with a sedative and instructions to stay there until the following day.

Despite the protestations of both Betty and Steven, Thomas and Charlie were on the road back to Cambridge by two thirty, having made a detour to check on Grim. The little terrier was recovering well and the vet promised to have him back at the Manor within a few days.

On the way Charlie and Frank explained what had happened and what they had seen while he, Thomas, had been out of things. Charlie then added the fact that he had seen Father John as he had locked the chapel door. Thomas turned his head away, unwilling to let his companions see him close to tears. The loss of his friend and teacher still affected him after eight years. Then a thought struck him and he turned back.

"Charlie, that little horn, where did you find it and how did you know it would be needed?"

"Well, while we were driving back to Deepdale yesterday I fell asleep and I dreamed I was in an antique shop buying a horn with a silver mouthpiece.

"Then Frank decided to stop for something to drink and woke us up. That was when I saw the very same shop over the road with the horn in the window just like the dream. There was this little old lady, only she wasn't one... if you know what I mean and she sold me the horn. After that I went back to the car but when I looked back at the shop she'd changed into Gabriel. I recognised Him or It, or whatever, when they all appeared last night.

"I think whatever you have Tom, it's catching. I never used to dream like this. A few days ago I dreamed I saw the first landing of the Romans in Britain. It was so vivid that I got up early and wrote it all down. The detail was really amazing. It will make my tutor drool." He paused then shook his head, "I wonder if you can dream to order, I think I'd like to see and hear Chaucer reading his Canterbury Tales next time. It's like watching a DVD while you're asleep." They laughed together as the car sped on towards Cambridge.

\* \* \*

In the space where the world of Avalon and that of Tir nan Og overlap there exists a twilight place of shadows entwined with the Light of many different worlds. It is held in awe by those whose lands border it for it has neither a name nor a reality of form as they understand it. But there are occasions when it is used as a meeting place between the inhabitants of those worlds, where advice, exchanges of opinions and plans can be discussed.

Into this place of peace and harmony came four beings, all of stature and importance in their own worlds. Merlyn, the original Guardian of Albion and Arthur Pendragon stepped forward to greet Midir Lord of the Fianna Sidhe and his son and second in command Prince Cormac.

In the centre of the woodland glade four carved chairs had been placed about a table of veined marble. Four goblets of silver and a flagon of Avalon wine were set before the chairs. Here Men and Fae sat together to confer under trees of a kind the earth has never seen. Merlyn inclined his grey head to the Lord of the Sidhe.

"I bid you welcome Midir of the Sidhe, it is many an age since we last met, then it was you who welcomed me and my weary little band to Albion.

"We were still mourning the loss of the Temple of the Sun and the City of the Golden Gates. The kindness of you and your people in that woeful time has never been forgotten."

The Lordly One greeted him with affection, his seeming youthfulness belied by the age old wisdom that lay in his eyes.

"12,000 years and more have passed since the loss of Atlantis the Beautiful, Merlyn, but still its legends and traditions persist in the land you have come to love as your own. The very reason we have come together is to preserve and protect it and to aid the one you have chosen to be its Guardian. It is because of my respect for your work that I have offered the help of my grandson Cormac to train your young protégé. But it seems you need more from me."

Merlyn sighed and for a moment rested his head in his hands, then he looked up. Thomas's family and friends are being attacked by a powerful Mage who wants to become The Merlin of Albion. He cannot attack Thomas himself unless he issues a formal challenge and he cannot do that until Thomas takes his trials and becomes The Merlin. But he can attack those closest to the lad's heart, hoping to make him fail the trials or freely offer the Guardianship to him to halt the attacks."

"But surely," said Midir leaning forward, "surely the boy has power of his own and can protect them."

"Power he has and more than I had expected, but he is inexperienced and has yet to realise the full extent of his ability. He cannot stand against Dark magic until he has earned access to the fourfold powers of the Arch-Mage, for his enemy has access to the power of The Dark Sidhe."

Midir drew in a sharp breath and Cormac sprang to his feet. "That cannot be I saw this opponent and had he been of the Sidhe I would have known."

Merlyn shook his head. "It gets worse Midir, he is of your own bloodline."

Arthur laid a gloved hand over that of Midir. "He speaks the truth old friend. Do you remember your sister Eithne of the Golden Tresses? At the time of the wars between the Magi and the Fae she was taken captive by the Army of the Dark and disappeared into the void between the worlds. You mourned her during the siege of Tir nan Og, and thought she was lost forever in the darkness beyond Chaos.

"But she did not die. Better it would have been that she did, for the Darkness overcame her and she took one of The Dark Lords as her husband. Her son killed her with his birthing and took her powers into himself. With them and those of his father he forged a way back into Albion and took human form. Iorwyth ap Gryffdd is the name he goes by, and he is your nephew." Merlyn took up the tale again.

"He holds within himself three kinds of power. That of the Sidhe from his mother's side, those inherited from the World of Chaos, and the power his studies in the human world have given him. This makes him very powerful. I am powerless to help Thomas, locked as I am into the world of Avalon.

"Having passed my Guardianship to Thomas I must stand back and let him find the strength he will need within himself." Cormac leapt to his feet and paced about the airy meeting place angry at his failure to recognise the danger that now surrounded Thomas.

"I had intended to wait until All Hallows when the Power of the Sidhe is at its greatest to begin his training but now I fear I must begin before that," he raged. Midir raised his hand.

"Wait Cormac, I feel a change in the Winds of Chance. Something has come about since the time we have been here. I bid you call Fohla the Seeress to this place, we must consult her." Cormac's cloak swirled about him as he returned into the World of the Sidhe on his errand. Midir turned back to Merlyn and Arthur.

"A great change in power has come about and from a most unexpected source. Even as we spoke of these things I discerned an event in the human world that will change many things. An event that has its origin in a world to which neither you nor I have access. A world that lies beyond the mystery humankind call Death." He turned as Cormac reappeared escorting on his arm Fohla of the Leanan Sidhe, the fairest woman of the Faerie world.

Fohla walked with the grace of a willow tree in a spring breeze, her black hair reached to her knees and was bound with silver ribbons and hung with silver bells. Her dress of green velvet matched the colour of her eyes and her scarlet slippers echoed the colour of her lips. But great as her beauty was it was nothing to the beauty of her voice. She curtseyed to Midir and accepted his kiss on her hand. Then turning to Merlyn and Arthur she bowed her head in deference to both age and royalty.

"My Lords I give you greeting, Cormac tells me you have need of my skills such as they are." Arthur rose and offered her his seat.

"Please be seated Lady Fohla. We do indeed have need of your help but I will leave your Liege-Lord to explain the problem." Midir took her hand in his and spoke quietly.

"Lady, an event has occurred in the human world that will affect the outcome of the accession of the next Merlin of Albion. There is a young man chosen by Merlyn to ascend to the Arch-Mage-ship who is soon to undergo his trials. He is coming into his power but slowly. There is one from the realm of Chaos who would challenge him, and seeks to attack those close to him. But I sense he has called upon a power far beyond our knowing. This power does not come from our world, yet it is part of that which encompasses all worlds. I ask you to look beyond what is, to what may be, and tell us what power it is that he has called upon in his world."

Fohla stood up and took a small mirror from a chain about her waist and breathed on it three times then laid it on the grass and began to chant.

> *"Air of Air I call to thee*
> *Hasten now and come to me*
> *Make my vision true and clear*
> *What was hidden now bring near."*

The mirror began to grow and continued until it was the height of a man and as wide as three men standing together.

> *"Air of Water flowing free*
> *Show us what we need to see*
> *Name the power and its source*
> *Let the vision run its course."*

Within its depths the mirror now began to show the inside of a chapel filled with people listening to a young man who stood before the altar.

> *"Air of Fire now l flame*
> *I bid thee by the secret name*
> *Create within a circle bright*
> *The calling that was made this night."*

With the vision came sound, and the events of the calling of the Angelic Powers began to play out in full in the mirror.

*"Air of Earth the breath of life*
*Aid us now to harness strife*
*On this day and in this hour*
*Give a name unto this power."*

At the appearance of the Archangels and their initiation of Thomas into his power Arthur sank to his knees
and crossed himself, the others bowed their heads in silent
homage. The last image showed Father John before the altar,
then all faded as the mirror reduced to its normal size. Silence reigned in the group as the meaning of what they had
seen sank in. Midir spoke quietly...

"Lady Fohla, we thank you for your help in this matter. I need hardly remind you that this is to be kept within
your heart." The lady curtseyed. "That is understood My
Lord, I will take my leave. My Lords, I bid you farewell. Nay,
Cormac, I can make my own way, your presence is required
here." She stepped into the shadows and was gone. Midir
turned to Merlyn.

"... and this is the young man we are supposed protect? A human being who, with little or no experience calls
up four of the greatest Powers known throughout the Multi-
worlds? I was born when this world had yet to feel the imprint of a human foot and even I would not contemplate
doing what I just watched that young man do." But Merlyn
brushed aside his protestations.

"Did you not hear what they said Midir? There is
more to come, more tests more trials and they will be harder
than this. They gave him the strength and the power but
they hid it deep within him. It will still need to be understood
and reached for, before he can use it. The outcome is still in
doubt. They left him with the Grace of Choice, Free Will,
but he could lose it all if he makes the wrong choice. Cormac
your help will still be needed, tho' this power is of a different

kind to what he will need for the tests."

Cormac nodded. "This much I know and I will do as you ask. But being near to him, touching someone who has been touched BY those powers will not be easy for a Fae. How in the name of the Dagda did he know what to do?"

"He was thinking of John Foxton, a man he revered and loved, a man he has always thought of as his teacher, and beloved friend. Moreover a man who offered himself as a willing sacrifice, as we saw Thomas do just now. I think that this lad will face a test in the near future that will demand all he has to give and more. Albion faces that test with him. It will either rise up with him, or go down with him." Merlyn sighed, "I feel so helpless."

Arthur placed his hands on his shoulders. "Do not feel so, old friend. He made contact with Powers far beyond our own and though there is Darkness to face, it will find none in him. I am no prophet, nor do I have the gift of sight, but I know his heart and mind are true and clear."

"I know Arthur, it is not Thomas that worries me but those around him. I feel a weakness in the group. It is not evil, but obeys an instinct that draws strength from what it is. It lies below the surface of one who does not know it is there. You know from experience Arthur, a mother's love is both protective, or a desire for revenge, with many levels between them. Cormac, stay close to Thomas, he walks with danger and betrayal as his shadow."

Cormac bowed. "We are friends and have an agreement between us. My father gave me permission to come and go between worlds as I wish. Should the need arise I will bring him to Tir nan Og for ease of mind and spirit."

Merlyn turned to Midir and bowed. "For this grace I give thanks Midir. Few humans have entered the Halls of the Fae since the worlds were sundered. An hour or so there and he would heal and rest." Cormac fingered his Geasan braid and smiled. Thomas might come to know the world of the Sidhe sooner than expected, but that Midir need not know about yet!

Midir stood. "Time grows short, our worlds draw apart. Farewell Merlyn, you also Arthur Pendragon. Call if you have need, my ear is open to you and my son is at your disposal. Together we will prevail as we did long ago." The meeting place became shadowed, the table cracked in two and slowly the worlds pulled apart to show the void between them, each returning to its rightful dimension. .

# Chapter Ten

**"Sir Greystone-Carrick** sir," announced the butler with an unctuousness that made Thomas want to laugh. But remembering his manners he crossed the inches thick carpet to shake the hand of his host.

Justin Thorndyke was a few inches taller than his guest with a wealth of grey hair swept back from a wide forehead. Thick bushy eyebrows arched over deep set hooded eyes of an almost metallic grey. At the touch of his hand every nerve in Thomas' body went on alert. Whoever this man was, make that (whatever) this man was, he was no friend despite his warm greeting

"Ah, Sir Thomas, we meet at last. Do sit down here beside the fire. Such a cheering sight on a cold night I always think. May I offer you a pre-dinner drink? I have a very good Fino, or a Manzanilla but I can also offer Gin and Tonic, or Bourbon if you prefer."

"A glass of Fino if you please." Thomas settled into the chair and accepted the glass, politely raising it to his host with a murmured, "Your health sir."

"And to yours my young friend." They sipped and eyed each other warily. Thomas pretending to relax into what he realised was a carefully prepared atmosphere. With a newly acquired expertise he raised a shield of angelic protection around himself. As it snapped into place Thorndyke's eyes sharpened and flicked to both sides as if to see how far it went and how strong it was. But his words were calm and steady.

"The paths of your great-grand-father and I crossed a few times years ago, both in business and in similar interests. He bested me at an auction in 1952 snatching a Picasso from under my nose. I still mourn its loss."

"I know the one," answered Thomas, "the receipt and its certificate of authenticity were among his papers. The picture is now on permanent loan to the Manchester Art Gallery."

"A generous gift considering the price he paid for it." He sipped his sherry and probed gently at the shield, which gave not an inch, but in retaliation, sent out a pulse of Light that momentarily made its opponent draw in a quick breath.

"It was not to my liking personally," Thomas shrugged, "I much prefer something a little less edgy. I find Turner and Constable more restful to have on my walls. Do you still collect Mr. Thorndyke?"

"Yes, but in a different direction. I sold off most of my Art Collection and have now turned my attention to, shall we say, more ambitious aims. What of your own plans Sir Thomas, do you intend to carry on your ancestor's business empire? He had wide ranging interests as you know, some of which were quite *arcane* I believe. I have a passing interest that way myself. I thought we might discuss a 'merger' of some kind." Thomas smiled politely though he felt like baring his teeth at the sheer audacity of the man.

"At the moment I leave most of the estate business to my lawyers and managers. With my finals drawing near I have little time to spend on anything beyond gaining my degree with a reasonable mark. After that I will take some time for myself, there are places to see, things to do, and avenues to explore."

"Ah, the enthusiasm of youth. How I wish I had that time again, in fact I would do anything, anything (he paused momentarily) to have the chance to do so."

The emphasis was not lost on Thomas, and he could not resist the chance to throw out a challenge of his own. By this time he was perfectly aware that he was sitting and drinking with the wolf that had attacked him; his opponent for the coming battle for Albion.

He reached out mentally to the past Merlins and called on Rhys ap Hoel the gaunt shepherd who had once served as a Guardian of Albion on the hills above Llanberis. Rhys responded at once, his words coming easily from Thomas's lips.

"Mae'n rhaid i ni i gyd yn marw, Iorwyth ap Gryffdd." (...*we all have to die eventually...!*)

The effect on the man sitting opposite him was electric. He leapt to his feet and threw his glass into the fire. A torrent of Welsh spewed out of his mouth, and Rhys, still linked to Thomas, gleefully translated the curses and obscenities. Thomas waited calmly still sipping his sherry until his opponent had regained his control.

The butler hearing the commotion re-appeared looking both anxious at the noise and shocked at his employer's loss of temper. Having satisfied himself that no one had been murdered he returned to the kitchen. Ap Gryffdd fought down his anger and poured himself another glass of sherry. He was back in control, but his true nature showed in the icy tone of his voice.

"It would appear you have gained in strength and ability since we last met Thomas of Carrick. So you know me, you know who I am and what I want. What you don't know is how much power I can call upon. My mother was of the Sidhe and my father a Master of Chaos. I hold both

111

powers plus my own knowledge. I am more worthy to guide the destiny of Albion than a man-child barely old enough to drive a car. Under my hand Albion can be great again." Thomas considered the outburst for a moment then said.

"But at what cost to its people? Your Chaos blood would destroy what has been built over centuries. The Fate of Atlantis would happen again. I will stop you Ap Gryffdd. Stop you for good. I was once told by a warrior of royal blood, that in ancient days before a battle the opponents would eat and drink together with a sword on the table between them. Let this be our concession to the ancient laws of chivalry, or, we can part company now." He drained his glass, set it on the table and stood up to adjust the tie of his evening suit. For a moment he thought his enemy would throw him out, then the traumatized butler re-appeared. He cleared his throat nervously and after two false starts announced that dinner was served.

Ap Gryffdd laughed harshly and indicated to Thomas to lead the way into the dining room. "Come Sir Thomas, let us behave in a civilised manner by all means. The battle will begin soon enough and you will know and feel the extent of my powers. Until then, let us eat."

For the next two hours they dined amid silver cutlery, fine china and rare wines in crystal glasses, with a silver hilted poniard between them. They spoke of stocks and shares, art and business and ended the dinner with a fine aged port and Stilton. At 11:20 Thomas thanked his host but refrained from shaking hands. At the door they stood regarding each other and in that moment Ap Gryffdd knew his prize was not as safe as he had thought. The angelic shield had held fast throughout the evening, try as he might to break it. This stripling was not the weakling he had anticipated at their first meeting and he had powerful friends, but it was Thomas' own as yet untapped power that, for the first time gave his opponent cause to fear.

He watched his guest depart then dismissed his servant and made his way to a smaller room on the next floor. Carefully locking the door behind him he stripped off his evening suit and took a dark red velvet robe from a closet. Barefooted he approached the altar that dominated the centre of the room and lit five red candles. Taking up an ornate dagger he slashed across his right palm and let the blood drip into a shallow bowl. Lifting the bowl above his head he began to chant in a language that was old before the pyramids were built.

It was time to seek help from those more powerful than himself. Far away in a dimension beyond Chaos itself The Dark Ones stirred and turned their attention to the puny being who had dared to disturb their chaotic dreams. They listened, first with amusement and then with increasing interest to what was being offered.

# Chapter Eleven

**Once free of** the stifling atmosphere that had persisted the whole evening Thomas began to take stock. First things first. He directed his thoughts towards Rhys ap Hoel, thanking him for his help and added a blessing. Both were accepted and the ancient Merlin faded from contact. He debated if he should call Drew, but decided it was too late to disturb him with his account of the dinner with his enemy.

Back at the house he showered, using Posy's cleansing herbal soap to get rid of any trace of his opponent. He returned to the bedroom rubbing his damp hair to find Cormac lying at his ease on the bed. He grinned and flung the towel at him, "Shouldn't you be sleeping in a flower head, covered with a rose petal sheet like any other self-respecting fairy?"

Cormac threw the towel back and asked, "How did the evening with Justin Thorndyke go?"

Thomas looked up in surprise, "How did you know where I was?"

Cormac shrugged "I talked to Charles, and he said you had gone to dinner with a Justin Thorndyke. The name seemed familiar so I decided to find out about him."

"… and what did you find out Mr Sherlock Fairy Holmes?" asked Thomas, pulling on a pair of grey silk pyjama pants.

"Justin is an ancient Roman name. Thorn is a magical Rune and Thorndyke is the family name of an old and respected family long connected to the Craft of the Wise. He uses the name for his own purpose but has no blood tie to them. They would be horrified to know a Dark Mage is using their name. I asked acquaintances on The Second Road about him and was concerned by their words. I came hoping to warn you but you had already left. So I went to Charles Naughton. He was quite surprised to see me."

"I can imagine," said Thomas dryly… and now Cormac of the House of Midir, it's been a long day and I'd like to get into MY bed." Cormac stood up and looked as sheepish as a high ranking Sidhe could manage.

"I was rather hoping we could go somewhere."

"Go somewhere, as in what, to a pub, to the opera, both of which will now be closed, by the way."

"A nightclub, a casino." Thomas propped himself up against his pillows, then stopped and looked at him.

"You're serious aren't you. Dear God in Heaven Cormac, what on earth do you want in those places. You're a Fairy Prince who has the whole of the Otherworld to play about in, what can you possibly want with…"

He broke off, got out of bed and went to stand in front of the tall Sidhe. "Come on… out with it, what's going on in that weird Fae mind of yours." Cormac gave him his most winning smile.

"Well you know how Midir dislikes us having too close a relationship with this world. We get so few chances to really see and know it and… and… well… to join in with the things you do for fun."

"Like…" prompted Thomas trying to suppress the apprehension filling his stomach.

"Well like cinemas, nightclubs, casinos… and things like that," admitted Cormac. "It's as exciting to us as a visit to

Tir nan Og would be to you." Eagerness filled his voice, "It could be fun Thomas and I've got some friends lined up."

"WHAT!!!" Thomas was outraged, amused, and terrified all at the same time. "You want me to take a posse of male Fairies, I mean Sidhe, for a night on the town?" Cormac nodded and pointed over his shoulder.

Thomas turned and found himself facing three of Tir nan Og's princelings, all outrageously tall and good looking and wearing normal Sidhe clothing.

"I'll get them dressed to fit in," promised Cormac and spoke to his companions in their own tongue. They nodded enthusiastically and within minutes Thomas was looking at the denim and leather clad version.

"Look guys, if you want to go out on the town, jeans are not going to do it," he sighed. You need evening clothes for a casino or a nightclub. Look…" he opened his wardrobe and took out the Tuxedo he'd worn to dinner. "Something like this."

The Sidhe crowded round as excited as school boys and after pointing out that a Tee shirt did not go well with a Tux and Red leather knee boots were not a good fashion statement for evening wear, he had all four looking like male Models. As it would be a long night he felt the need for support and called Charlie to come over.

The look on Charlie's face when he saw the four Sidhe princes was something Thomas would remember for a lifetime. Having only just held it together when Cormac had appeared in his tiny bedsit, coming face to face with four of them left him speechless. Thomas looked at his off the peg suit, shook his head and took him upstairs. Rich Leaver was more his size and his evening suit would fit him well enough.

Since six of them would not fit into his coupé he called a taxi, having refused Cormac's offer to transport them all directly to London. The sudden unexplained appearance of four outrageously handsome and well-built males was hard enough to explain as it was.

Luckily he kept a fair amount of money in the house safe so he filled his wallet and Charlie's and doled out some more to each of the excited Fae. Once in the taxi with all of them talking at the same time he took a moment to wonder how he had gotten himself into this situation.

Charlie was still gawping as the taxi driver who, elated at the thought of a long drive and a big fare, let out the clutch and put his foot down. Later the next day he tried to remember how he managed to drive from Cambridge to London in thirty minutes and what route he had taken. But as Cormac said to Charlie, distances on The Second Road could be very deceptive!

They started out at the 100 Club where the entire female clientèle found excuses to walk past their table. The Sidhe were fascinated by the eager to please ladies and were soon paired off. Dancing the human way was a problem at first, but they caught on remarkably quickly. Human alcohol however was something they could not cope with. Cormac solved this by producing bottles of Sidhe wine, then the headwaiter objected to them bringing in their own drinks and they ended up outside.

Undaunted they set out for Ronnie Scott's where they acquired a new batch of ladies. Having sussed out the alcohol problem they ordered Coke and changed it into Sidhe wine, while the "ladies" drank champagne by the bottle. Charlie, who had never had more than beer and the occasional sherry or red wine found in himself an amazing ability to stay on his feet. Thomas stayed dry, explaining he was the driver.

At one point they began to run out of money but Cormac simply doubled what they had and it all started again. Thomas wanted to draw more money from a cash point but Cormac waved the suggestion aside. "After all," he said slapping him on the shoulder, "fairy money turns to leaves in the morning here on earth." For some reason this information amused Charlie who laughed himself silly.

It was almost three am when Logan, Cormac's younger brother decided he wanted to learn to play poker and insisted they try a casino. Thomas knew little about cards, but Charlie surprised him with his knowledge of the game. As they walked to the casino he gave Cormac and Logan a quick rundown on how to play, emphasising the need to give nothing away about the cards you held.

The group were marked by the professionals as soon as they walked in the door and within minutes had been asked to join a group of players. Thomas tried to warn them but Logan, Charlie and Cormac sat down to play while Liam and Rhodri looked on. Thomas crossed his fingers, held his breath and prepared to write a cheque when they all got fleeced. An hour later the pile of counters in front of the two brothers had reached startling proportions while the professionals were beginning to look grim. Thomas sent a warning thought to Cormac. '*They think you are cheating.*'

'*I thought that was the whole idea,*' was the answer. Thomas sent another image of them all being set on by professional muggers as they left, and got back another image that more or less said… '*let them try.*'

By this time Charlie was asleep and Thomas was wilting, so the brothers said goodnight and cashed in their winnings to the tune of £40,000. They left the casino and began to look for a taxi when Thomas' fear came true. Out of a nearby alley came a gang of four men armed with knives, bludgeons and knuckle-dusters, intent on getting their employer's money back from these young upstarts with their good looks and smart clothes.

Thomas had seen the Sidhe fight before, and he held Charlie back pressing him into a doorway out of sight. The four princelings suddenly became four very mean fighting machines. Knives met swords, bludgeons met fighting staves, and knuckle-dusters met magic that melted the steel into their fingers. It was all over in a short space of time, and the losers were carefully laid in a neat row side by side and left for the morning to find them. The Sidhe however had not even a bruise between them and were actually elated by the exertion.

By now dawn was lighting the east and the Sidhe decided it was time to go home. Scorning the idea of a taxi they took their human companions onto The Second Road with a Sidhe on each side of them and within minutes they were back in Cambridge. Charlie stumbled up to Rich's room and managed to mostly undress before falling asleep in his underpants, one shoe and a bow tie.

Thomas said goodbye to his Fairy guests as they left for their own world and sank down on his bed as he was and slept dreamlessly until noon the next day. When he did wake up it was to find a neat pile of real world money on his pillow with a note in Cormac's hand telling him to replace what he had given them and put the rest to good use. They had no need of it in Tir nan Og. Thomas smiled and put it in a padded envelope and on his way to College passed it on to the local Salvation Army hostel as an anonymous donation. The £30,000 gift made the headlines later in the day when the anonymous donor was publically thanked.

There was a side to the Sidhe Thomas had never thought of before. It seemed they were as curious about the human world as that world was about them. Looking back he found he had enjoyed helping them to see a little of his way of life by showing them things unknown in their own.

"We must do it again," he thought. "It's time the two

worlds got to know about each other. As he walked to his tutorial he reflected on the vast difference between the two incidents of the past 24 hours. The dark brooding enmity of Iorwyth's violent outburst stood in contrast to the light-hearted and slightly drunken revels of the Fae. The only link between them being the ferocity with which the young Sidhe had despatched their attackers.

His thoughts turned to Charlie upstairs. He'd had one hell of an introduction to the Otherworld. It would be fun to hear his reaction over dinner.

# Chapter Twelve

**Thomas stopped** with a roast potato halfway to his mouth, his eyes wide, "What do you mean you always knew about 'fairies'?"

Charlie smirked and refilled both mugs with coffee. "My mum taught me to look for them when I was a kid. She's always been able to see them. She got it from her mother who was Irish. Mind you the ones we saw then, and she still sees them occasionally, are a hell of a lot smaller... sort of 'flower fairy' like. But I reckon they're all of the same basic stuff... you know, the there but not there, kind of thing."

Thomas nodded, his dinner forgotten as he listened. "So, if your mother still sees them, do you?"

"Well yeah, but very seldom, sort of quick flashes. They like gardens and wild places and we've only got a tiny lawn at the back. But dad's allotment is full of a different kind, small and dark, not nasty dark, just sort of brownish, with beards... no wings. They like being under the earth and growing things.

"When I was little we had a fairly big garden that looked out over fields and woods. But when dad had his accident the firm reneged on his compensation and we had to sell the house and move to Newton Heath. It broke mum's heart."

"What about your dad? Does he see them?"

"No, though I think he knows about the ones at the allotment, he jokes about the 'gnomes' stealing his tools. They do tend to borrow them but they do a lot of the weeding. We get better crops than the others and dad sells quite a bit to local grocers. That's where my college fees came from before I got the scholarship to Cambridge. Now it tops up my living expenses and I help out by getting a job in the holidays and at half term."

Thomas jumped in… "Yes I've been thinking about that. You know you said you could translate those books of mine?"

Charlie nodded, "Yeah, I can do that with no trouble."

"Well you can't do it for nothing. I have a dozen or more of them and it takes time, time when you would be working in the holidays. Also you're going to have to come around with me a lot so you won't have time for a job. So you are going on the payroll as of this month."

Charlie choked on his coffee. "No, I can't do that, you're my friend. I can do the translations you need, I'll find a way. You're doing a lot for me. These new digs and the chance to use your library."

Thomas waved aside his protests. "Friends need to eat and have money in their pockets. There are other things as well, you need your own Tux, Rich will be taking his with him. On Saturday we'll go up to town and see my tailor in Jermyne St and get you set up. Don't argue Charlie. I won't use your skills or personal time for nothing. You'll need a car too, do you drive?"

Charlie went red. "Er… no actually. There's never been any need, or the money."

"Then I'll get Frank to teach you. He taught me and he's good. There will be times when I'm too whacked to drive, so you will have to do it." Charlie sat with his ears pink with embarrassment, caught between chagrin and excitement.

"Oh Charlie, I'm so sorry. I'm rushing you into things I've dealt with for eight years. I'm not giving you time to think or even say yes or no. Forgive me. I'm just so glad you're here, that I've now got someone to talk to and confide in. Drew is married now and he has Posy and Jess to look after. Frank and Betty are great but they have their own lives as do the other Guardians. Dad is wrapped up in his writing and... and I miss Mordred a lot." He pushed his plate away and leaned across the table.

"I need you Charlie, please accept my offer. It isn't done to make you feel obliged or beholden, but to allow you to be with me as an equal. Money is just something I can use to help those close to me. Have you any idea how much I'm worth?"

Charlie shook his head.

"I inherited over 250 million pounds, plus Farms, Paintings, Art work, a chain of Hotels, and other businesses, plus a title. All thanks to my great grandfather. I gave the farms to the families who had worked them for generations. The paintings are worth millions, but I put them on free loan or gave them to Galleries and Museums. I have properties all over the world, a hotel chain that extends over five countries. I can send you and your parents on holiday anywhere you can name. I'm one of the richest people on the planet, and... I'm lonely... and I'm scared.

"I fight battles with my own inner darkness that no one knows about. Soon I must take the greatest tests I have ever faced and I'm terrified. I can't do it without a special kind of back up. It will be dangerous, for both of us, but I promise, whatever happens, your parents will be taken care of."

He rose and began to pace the room agitatedly. "I'm scared of failing, of not being up to what's ahead of me. I'm afraid of the money I've inherited in case it takes me over and turns me into something I don't want to be. I need someone who can keep my feet on the ground. I love this land with a passion, its traditions, its people, its past and I need to learn how to protect its spiritual future. I can't do it on my own.

"I have all this money and it gives me pleasure to help those who depend on me. I'm not offering you charity Charlie I'm sharing what I have too much of with you, and not just you. Everyone in this house is on a full scholarship from an unknown donor. Richard, Heather, Carl, Dean all of them. It gives me pleasure to make them comfortable, share their lives and make believe I'm an ordinary run of the mill person who just happens to be rich. You said you would serve The Merlin. Well The Merlin is me, Thomas William Greystone-Carrick, who at this moment is in dire need of a good friend." He ran out of steam and dropped his head in his hands.

Charlie sat stunned by the passion with which Thomas had poured out his fears and hopes. He was filled with compassion for someone his own age, bearing an ancient burden. He also felt inner joy and a soul deep recognition of his own destiny. All this had been planned long ago. This friendship was much more than it seemed. Suddenly the past snapped into memory, detailed, accurate, clear and very real.

With a touch as tender as a woman's and as strong as a man's he brushed back a lock of Thomas's hair and spoke with a knowledge covering many lifetimes and now recalled, "In all the lives, in all the battles we have been together this will be the most important and after this there may be no need to return."

Thomas raised his head and spoke as if in a dream, "Thermopylae, and Crecy, the sieges of Acre and Jerusalem."

"Aye, Constantinople, and Montsegur and the fires of Templar Martrydom."

"Finding ourselves on opposite sides in the Civil War," Charlie shuddered.

"The Field of the Cloth of Gold, The Armada, Waterloo. We've always been brothers in arms. Now we're together for a final battle. One to be fought in different worlds but it will be the most important." He picked up a knife and drew it across his palm, and held it out to Thomas who did the same. Their blood came together:

"For Merlin."

"For Pendragon."

"For the Crown and Albion."

In a place and a time far from them, four great Pillars of Light flared into dazzling radiance. "He chose well," said Michael to his companions.

# Chapter Thirteen

**The next week** and a half passed quickly for everyone. There were essays to be handed in, extra tutorials to be taken, and a lot of hard studying to do. Thomas invited Charlie to share his quiet study during their clear periods in the evenings. As both were serious about their work and able to concentrate they worked well together.

They ate studied, argued, laughed and slowly deepened the bond between them, each one leaning on the other's expertise in areas not their own. It had been tacitly agreed that for the moment their school work came first and what little spare time they had was spent with friends who knew nothing of their other life. It was for them a time to just enjoy the Cambridge lifestyle.

On the eve of Halloween just as they decided to call it a day a shimmer of light in the corner of the room heralded the arrival of Cormac. Thomas, used to his sudden appearances simply cleared a space for him to sit. Charlie choked on his can of lager and coughed until his eyes ran, then offered a muffled Hi to the leather clad figure lounging in the armchair.

"Er, I'll go and let you two get on with whatever it is you need to get on with," he said, edging towards the door. Thomas stopped him.

"Stay here Charlie. Heavens knows you've seen this

guy at his best and worst." Cormac raised an elegant eyebrow. "You'll have to get used to him being around."

"But it might be private stuff Thomas, and I have to phone mum and dad tonight. When do we leave for Deepdale I'll have to let them know."

"Don't worry, it's all arranged, Frank is picking them up on Wednesday evening and taking them to the Manor. Then he'll fetch us on Thursday afternoon about 2:00. We'll stay Friday, Saturday, Sunday and be back here by 1 pm on Monday, in time for our first lectures. Oh and I've told Gieves & Hawkes to deliver your suits to the Manor by Wednesday morning, the other stuff will be here tomorrow. Don't forget to bring your papers with you, you'll need them in the morning. See you at lunch tomorrow."

"Yes, of course, goodnight Prince Cormac. Go mbogfaidh an réalta tráthnóna do bhrionglóidí." (*May the Evening Star shine upon your dreams*).

Thomas' jaw dropped as Cormac came swiftly to his feet and swept a bow in Charlie's direction. "May your feet find their way to Tir nan Og my friend, and please Charlie, use my name and forget the title." Charlie made a slightly awkward bow in return, and left flushed with pleasure.

"Where does he get all this stuff from?" Thomas asked as Cormac settled back into his seat.

"He has amazing linguistic skills and has been studying the history of The Tuatha de Danaan. I have often dropped in on him, without his knowing of course. He is as much a surprise to us as he is to you Thomas. Even Merlyn and Midir knew nothing of his background. We think it has been arranged by a higher power than ours, one over which we have no control. But, that is not why I am here. Your first test has been set for the 29th of January."

Thomas turned to him his eyes wide with apprehension, "That is only a few weeks after the Finals. It doesn't give me a lot of time to prepare. What is the test element? Where and what do I have to do?"

"All of them are hard Thomas, that is why I am here, to train you to deal with what you have to face. The first test is that of AIR." He produced a map and spread it out on the desk. "Here," his finger rested on a pinpoint of land. Thomas stared then raised horrified eyes to his.

"Cormac, that's The Needles, it's high, it's going to be freezing in January, and the winds are likely to blow me off. What do I have to do there?"

"You have to find a place to stand and stay there from sunset to sunrise. You cannot sleep or move more than an inch of two, you cannot bind yourself to anything, you must rely on your own strengths, physical, mental, and spiritual. But you can ask for help from those who belong to the element."

"This is crazy," whispered Thomas shaken to the core. "No one can do this."

"They can, if they are trained and prepared for it. First you must learn the way of the birds. They are the masters of the use of air. There will be work for Charlie also. Someone must take you to the Lighthouse at the point of the formation. From there you will climb to a place midway. Charlie must wait below until you return."

"If I return," muttered Thomas.

"You will *Dearthái*," came the reply. Thomas looked at him, "That's the second time you've called me brother. If I really was your brother I could sprout wings when I need them."

"The time to worry is when I call you *An Mac*," said the Sidhe slyly. But Thomas was looking at the map again.

"Is it possible to have a reccy at this place?" he asked.

"Of course, but I think you should try it in the form

of a shift. That means you have to learn the shift first. The bird form is difficult at first, there is a natural fear of falling but once acquired it can be very useful." His form shimmered and a falcon sat perched on the arm of Thomas' chair.

Thomas grabbed his scarf and wound it round his arm and held it away from his body. The falcon hopped on to it, its claws gripping tightly, its thoughts reached out to him. *'Study my form and memorise them.'* It spread a wing and allowed Thomas to inspect the delicate bone structure and the arrangement of feathers, both pinions and flight. He explored the feathered legs and the way the joint bent backwards.

"When a bird settles on a branch, the tendons of the leg as it bends cause the claws to tighten the grip. That is how a bird holds on to its perch in a high wind. But a seabird needs a different kind of foot. It has a much greater blood flow to insulate it from cold water. Look at my beak. It is meant for tearing flesh, but again each type has adapted to the kind of food it needs. My advice it to try first for a seabird, for that will be of most use to you in this trial." The Falcon hopped to the floor and Cormac resumed his own form. "Now you try."

For the next three hours he did try and the results, though they reduced Cormac to helpless laughter brought about a towering rage in Thomas. Failure to achieve any sort of result brought his rarely seen temper to the surface. By the time Cormac called a halt the room was in disarray. China smashed, books flung around, one chair beyond repair and his laptop only in one piece because Cormac rescued it in mid-air. Now he stood quiet and serious and regarded his distraught pupil.

"You are trying too hard, you know how the stag form flows, this is the same, only the mental image is different."

"I can't fail, this is too important, too much is at stake.

Merlyn made a mistake, I'm not the one he should have chosen. Maybe Charlie is the true Merlin." He paced the floor biting his fingernails. "My enemy is strong, he knows so much more than I do, has more experience. But he really is the pits. I mean Albion would go under if he won this battle. What can I do? How can I fight him if I can't cope with a simple shift."

The Sidhe stopped him in mid flow, "Rest Thomas, you are trying too hard, you need to set this aside for a while. There is time yet. Let me ease that headache building up inside you." He laid his hands either side of Thomas' head and slowly the throbbing ache subsided. "You need to sleep and tomorrow we will try again. I'll see you soon." His form shimmered and was gone leaving a weary young man who fell into bed and slept deeply and dreamlessly.

But though they tried, the next few days only brought the same lack of success. It was a silent and morose Thomas that sat with Charlie as they drove up to Deepdale on the Thursday. Charlie knew better than to chivvy him out of his self-imposed sulk, and busied himself making notes on a translation for the Finals. Frank was also concerned at the unaccustomed silence but kept his thoughts to himself.

Thomas roused himself when they arrived and greeted his guests with his usual charm but soon left Charlie to entertain his parents while he slipped off. First on his list was Grim now recovered and once more his exuberant self. The two of them walked in the grounds and inspected the bonfire ready and waiting to be lit.

The gardeners had ringed it with wire netting to make sure no unsuspecting animal was using it for a nest. In another area the fireworks had been set up, rockets primed and ready, and with wooden benches for the children to sit and watch in safety. The Marquee with tables and chairs lacked only the food and drink that Betty and her village helpers would be setting out tomorrow. The Manor gates would be opened and all were welcome.

But at the moment the young Lord of the Manor stood and looked back at the house and wondered how it had looked 2/3 hundred years ago, if children had played here and what they thought about. The task of The Merlin passed from family to family the length and breadth of the land, but now it had returned to where it all began as far as his family was concerned. Then the dinner gong sounded and he sighed, time to take up his duties again and he had guests to entertain.

* * *

As usual Betty had pulled out all the stops. First came a rich vegetable broth topped with a spoonful of cream followed by venison pie, roast potatoes, with diced carrots and swede. All rounded off with pears from the orchard served in frosted glasses in a syrup spiced with Cointreau. They all helped to clear away and then sat down in the drawing room to coffee and brandy. Betty, warned by Frank, had kept an eye on Thomas and when the hall clock reached 10:30 she sent them all off to bed.

"It's going to be a long day tomorrow with village folk in and out all day. Best we prepare for it with a good night's sleep. Besides, the lads have been hard at work with their studies. Breakfast is at 8 am on the dot. Maisie and Jim, yours will be sent up at 8:30, the kitchen will be full of people so take your time. I'll send a girl to bring the tray down later. You're here to be spoiled for a change.

Everyone made their goodnights and drifted off to their rooms. Charlie to unpack a pair of new suitcases filled with clothes he'd never dreamed of owning. Tucked into a corner were two boxes. The smaller contained gold cufflinks with the initials CN engraved on them. The other held a watch, not a flashy Rolex, but a Longine with a simple gold face and leather strap. On the back were the words:

*To Charlie: "After many lives we come together again". Thomas.*

He sat and looked at it for a long time, then set it by his bedside while he showered and got ready for bed. He hesitated for a moment, then did something he had not done since childhood. He knelt and placed his hands together and prayed.

*"Lord, help me to be worthy of the task that lies before me. Give me the strength of character I will need and the grace to know when to help and when to stand back."* Then he got into bed and slept deeply.

Thomas however remained awake for some time, drained of energy he wandered through the house coming at last to the big Hall with its vast fireplace. Above it was the mantelpiece behind which Drew and he had found Excalibur hidden.

But now he looked at the top where a line of silver figures stood like the Guardians they were. He touched each in turn, the two greyhounds, a cat and a ram, a horse rearing up. A deer, a ferret and a boar, a badger with a cub, a hare and an owl. Last of all a hawk, its wings outspread to catch the wind. Each held a memory, and two of them a deep sadness. Thomas made a mental note to take flowers to the graves before he returned to Cambridge. Now at last he felt he could sleep.

\* \* \*

The bonfire and fireworks were a great success. Most of the village turned up at one time or another. The children oohed and aaaaahed and raced around with sparklers and ate far too much ice cream and cake. Their parents enjoyed meeting up with friends, stuffed themselves with Betty's cooking, drank cider and beer and wine and generally had a good time. The vicar won a bottle of brandy in the Raffle and the local OAP's each got a hamper of goodies.

Drew and Posy kept tight hold of Jessica until finally she fell asleep in her father's arms. As they were staying the night Posy took her upstairs and put her to bed in what had once been the night nursery. By 11:30 people were going home and the bonfire had died down enough for it to be finally doused. When the gates closed after the last car Thomas thanked the helpers and the extra caterers and sent Betty and Frank off to bed. The clearers would come in the morning to take down the marquee, clear the remains of the bonfire and store the tables and chair until their next time. The burned-out fireworks and rubbish would be taken care of by the gardeners and by lunch time things would be back to normal. Though Thomas was always relieved that such events only happened four times a year.

As always after a Village Event he felt restless and out of sorts. Today in addition, he was worried about the combined burden of Finals and The Trial that lay before him. He called Grim and the two of them took off for the high moors. Thomas was more at home here in his stag form and made for The Singing Stones where he felt closest to those he had lost.

Standing in the middle of the circle he took his own form and looked around, recalling the events that has taken place there eight years ago. He went to the recumbent Mage stone and sat there with Grim at his feet as Barney had once sat and let his memories and his tears flow freely, unashamed of them. His thoughts took form in words.

"Father John, if you can hear me, tell me what to

do. I can't seem to find what is needed inside myself. I'm confused and angry and afraid. Cormac tries his best but there are things I can't do, things I must do if I'm to be The Merlin. I may not be what everyone thinks I am. Please, if you are able, tell me what to do." But there was no answer.

Restless he stood up and began to climb up the Tor to the stone Dream Chair where he had first met Cormac. As he hauled himself up the last few feet he saw someone was already there. He hesitated not wanting to intrude when the figure stood and turned to face him. His heart leapt.

"Father John, Father John," he went forward arms outstretched but the figure held up a hand and stopped him. "Wait Thomas, do not touch me or you will disrupt the particles of the form I am using and it will disappear. Sit down and listen to me."

Disappointed, but eager to hear what he had to say Thomas sat down on the Dream Chair and looked at his friend and mentor. He seemed just the same as when he had last seen him except for the faint outline of light around his form. He stood in front of him and spoke with the quiet authority Thomas remembered so well.

"Much is being asked of you Thomas, perhaps too much at this time with your work in the real world also demanding attention. But you must use all your strength to fit the two together. It will not be easy. The Powers of Darkness know this and that is why Ap Gryffdd chose his time well. But, he does not know how much strength you have within you, and you do have strength Thomas, you may not think so at this moment but it is there.

"I was proud of you when you called the Four Who Stand Before The Throne to the chapel. You opened up a well of strength within you then and you can do so again whenever you have the need. There are powers gathering around you that as yet you cannot see or feel, but they are there. In fact they are there for everyone, but only a few understand that and even fewer learn to use it. Do you remember my 'shift form' Thomas?"

"Yes sir, it was a Hawk."

"Try that shift with me now. Remember how I held out my arms and pushed my head forward? Lean into the wind and let it lift you, fall into it and trust to it and soar Thomas... soar." Thomas stood and copied his actions. The wind blew into his face and his nose lengthened into a beak, feathers emerged along his arms and over his body as it diminished into the small compact form of a Merlin Hawk. He soared into the sky with the larger hawk flying close beside him.

"That's it Thomas, keep the wings slightly curved, spread the tail feathers, bank to the left... now the right... fly Thomas, fly... fly... fly..."

With the wind, carrying him Thomas felt the full impact of the Element of Air, the freedom, the grace, the power and strength. He dived with wings tucked into his sides and flattened out close to the ground. He rose on the night wind and twisted and turned on its eddies. He was free of the skies, free to discover the joy of that freedom. Remembering his struggle to use the seagull form he wondered if he could shift from one form to another in flight... and did so effortlessly, and back again.

"I've done it!" The Merlin gave out a scream of delight and banked to fly back to Father John... but he was no longer there. Devastated, Thomas landed on the Dream Chair and flowed back into his own form. His face was wet with tears but his heart was filled with the strength and the determination to succeed. He collected Grim and descended the Tor. He was now ready to face the trial of the Element of Air. It was time to start claiming his Full Power.

# Chapter Fourteen

**The gaunt black horse** thundered along The Second Road eating up the miles that led to the Meeting Place of The Dark Lords. Iorwyth Ap Gryffdd bent low over his mount's head urging it on to even greater speed. His night black cloak billowed out behind him and his grey hair whipped about his head.

The small beings that inhabited this hidden part of Albion scattered at his coming. When the black-horned horses of The Dark Lords were abroad it took courage to stay on the Road. On that long dark ride only once did the horned stallion slow and shy away from a lone Radiant Being who walked there unafraid.

At last the green woodlands, hollow hills, dense forests and hidden castles of the Fae gave way to silent fens where bitter waters ran black and no birds sang. The obsidian tower of The Dark Masters rose up out of the bleak landscape with a single beacon burning on the topmost battlement to guide him.

He rode into a deserted courtyard and looked around. Out of the shadows came a hooded, faceless figure to take his horse and direct him to a door at the base of the tallest tower. He climbed an endless twisting stairway to the very top and was met by another servant who opened a door into a small circular room.

A brazier in the centre provided the only light, and gave off a sickly scent that caught in his throat. The dark tapestries and black wood of the sparse furniture combined with the scent and semi darkness was oppressive and suggestive of hidden dangers. Used though he was to such things, He felt ill at ease and lacking his usual confidence as he waited for What or Whoever, would meet with him. Had it not been that he found himself in need of allies he would not have asked for help from The Dark Ones. So he stood, waiting and sweating.

There came the sound of scrabbling at the casement window and his skin crawled as feelers like the antenna of a large beetle felt their way through the opening. He turned away, not wishing to see what lurked outside some sixty feet above the ground. A sudden draught stirred the tapestries and made the flames of the brazier flicker. He turned slowly.

The man and woman who now stood watching him were, to all intents and purposes, human. But he was not fooled. Whatever they were at this moment, it was not and never had been human. Both were tall and slender and possessed a beauty that was unearthly. The angular bone structure spoke of a distant relationship with the Fae, but there the resemblance ended. The beauty of the Fae was the beauty of Light.

This was the beauty of Chaos at its most destructive. Sharply angled cheek bones and tilted eyes with pupils of vertical black slits in a circle of golden amber. The ears were elongated and flicked back and forth like those of an animal.

The man's skin was an unhealthy white like that of bleached bone and the hair that hung almost to his waist was as white as his skin. But his clothes were black, with a blackness that echoed the inside of a cave that had never known the light of day.

Her skin was also white but with a sheen to it as if she had been out in the rain. Her hair, even longer than his, was as black as his was white. Her dress of midnight blue silk floated about her as if stirred in a breeze not of this world or indeed of any other. He knew with no doubt in his mind that what he was looking at was not their true form, something he had been spared for which he thanked his ancient Gods.

The woman took her seat and waved him to one opposite her. The man remained standing his long seven fingered hand resting on the back of her chair. The woman's voice was like molten silver that touched every nerve in his body with something almost painful.

"You have asked for our help, but have yet not heard or agreed to our price." She was stating a fact and he knew it. Faced with this kind of power to refuse would result in something far worse than death could ever be.

"Do sit down sir, we have much to discuss before dawn comes and we must be gone." He obeyed without question and sat. Briefly he wished with all his heart he had never contacted the Dark but it was too late now, much much too late.

\* \* \*

Saturday at the Manor passed in a gentle dream with Thomas more relaxed than he had been in weeks. Charlie spent most of it in the Library, drooling over books rarely seen outside the British Library. Frank and Jim Naughton played chess by the fire in the great hall while Betty took Maisie down to the village to meet her friends over tea and cream cakes in The Barleycorn Tea Room.

Thomas, left to his own devices took Grim up on to the moor and practiced his new shift aided with a book on birds. He soon found that he was limited to a certain size, nothing smaller than a Merlin Hawk, but nothing bigger than a Buzzard. He tried for a Golden Eagle and ended up with a mixture it took an hour or so to sort out. He finally managed a sleek graceful seagull and was perched on a rock preening when Cormac appeared.

"A fine example," he commented as Thomas flowed back into his own form. "I recommend you spend a day or two flying with a flock, preferably close to where you will be taking the trial. They are a species that stay close together and support each other. You may find yourself in need of their help at that time.

"Do it slowly and carefully, approach the head of the flock and be respectful. Catch a fish and present it as a gift. Allow them to preen you and even peck you a little, try to establish a place for yourself that is not too low but not high enough to present a challenge. Listen to their calls and imitate them, there are calls that sound alarm, calls that indicate food, calls that offer comfort and support, or, that ask for it. These are important things to learn in all the trials."

Thomas stood and stretched and walked around thinking, then he asked, "What happens after the trial, assuming I get through it?"

Cormac laughed, "Oh you will get through *Dearthair*, with some trouble maybe, but you will get through."

"I hope you are right *Dearthái.*" The answer came with its correct pronunciation. Cormac came to his feet in one smooth movement.

"Since when do you speak the ancient tongue of the Sidhe," he demanded his eyes alight with interest.

"Since I met up with the knot headed, smooth talking son of a Sidhe King who cheats at cards, drinks whiskey like water and fights like a Spartan at Thermopylae," came the answer. "Plus a little help from an Irish speaking student at

Cambridge."

Cormac placed his hands on Thomas' shoulders and looked down at him. "You are indeed like a younger brother to me Thomas and I will train you as I would a Sidhe warrior. For I tell you now, these trials are but the beginning. They will certainly make you a true Merlin. But there is one task that as yet no Merlin has achieved. All have tried, but none, as yet, have succeeded. You may be the one who will do so." Intrigued Thomas picked up his jacket and whistled to Grim, "Just what is this unfulfilled task?" Cormac paced alongside him as they made their way back.

"It began in Atlantis when the first of the rebellions began. Using the skill of the Fae, the ingenuity of the Human mind, and the knowledge of Those who were before Humanity and from whom certain lines still descend, Lucanor the Master of all Atlantean Metal Workers, created twelve Swords of Power. Six he gave to those who ruled the Great Council of Atlantis. Two were given to the Fae, Aengus Og and Midir of the Radiant Brow. Four were given to the Representatives of the Elements, you refer to them as Paralda, Djinn, Nixsa, and Ghob, though their true names only they know and use.

"Each sword was empowered and named as it was christened in its final cooling. Each power is different but can only be used if the holder discovers the true name. The first six were carried from Atlantis on the last boat to escape and since then they have passed from hand to hand, often disappearing for centuries. Some of the world's greatest warriors have found and used them and lost them again. A few, a very few, have discovered the true names and used their power, but seldom for good. Now they are scattered and no one knows where they may be. Those held by the Fae are safely hidden. Those held by the Four Powers have been used rarely, and always returned to the Hidden Realm when their task has been accomplished.

"BUT, unknown to all but a rare few, of which you Thomas are now one… Lucanor made not 12 swords… but thirteen. The thirteenth sword holds the combined power of all of them, it rules them, but only when they all come together can that power manifest and then only for a short time. It has happened rarely for those who can contain those few moments of power are seldom born and even then they must have its name.

"The Swords became spoils of war and over many centuries a few were found and used by Heroes and some-times Heroines. They became legendary and were sought by those desiring power. Great kings and warriors used them some wisely others not. Charlemagne had one, so did Arthur Pendragon, Galahad, Yamata, Beowulf, and many others. Each sword has its own name that it gives only to the one it chooses. Sadly they were often used against each other. But when they come together the Thirteenth will absorb the power of them all and be supreme.

"These swords have changed the world. Some were wielded for good, others for evil. Most have been lost. It has been said that if they were brought together under a great Ruler, the Dark Lords would be banished from earth for a thousand years. Many have sought them, but though some were found, most remain lost.

"Every land has its 'Merlin' or spiritual protector, often seen as part of a legendary cycle. Through the ages many have known of the Thirteenth but none have achieved it. The hardest part would be to get each sword to agree to a common good."

"If each sword has a 'spirit' what kind of spirit?" asked Thomas.

"When a sword is created by a Master Swordsmith it is brought to life with the aid of the Four Elemental Kings.

Ghob provides the ore for its physical body. Djinn gives the power of his element of fire to smelt the ore and heat it into metal. Paralda's sylphs provide the air for the bellows to keep the fire at the right temperature and the heated metal is cooled and tempered by the waters of Nixsa. The Smith adds his strength, expertise and creativity. He 'sees' the finished sword in his mind and bring it to birth through his labour. As he works he calls to it to give him its name that it may be christened as he cools it for the last time. If he has worked well the sword will awaken and know itself to be a child of five fathers, the Elemental Kings and the Smith. They alone know its secret name. To safeguard it the smith usually gives it a lesser name to be used by its owner.

"When the human owner dies, the sword is free to choose its next master, if it is taken in fairly battle it may stay, if stolen it may destroy the thief. It can hide itself from view for hundreds of years and emerge only when the right hand grasps its hilt. Swords have a life of their own Thomas, and not all of them take kindly to the hand that holds them. But for the moment, this does not concern you."

"There are many swords in the Manor," said Thomas, "I wonder if they have spirits. They seem very quiet to me."

"They are swords made just for battle and not magically created for a purpose or for a particular person. Which is just as well. You would not want them fighting among themselves at night, especially when you have guests." Cormac laughed and slapped Thomas on the shoulder. "Go back now and be with your friends, I will come again soon mo Deartháir." He stepped sideways into his own world. Thomas continued home as it began to rain.

\* \* \*

Betty was serving tea and cake in the Drawing room. "There you are. Charlie's been looking for you. Seems he's found summat in those old books of yours that has his eyes shining like stars. You'd best see what he's on about and I'll bring your tea into the library."

Charlie, half hidden by piles of books, was scribbling furiously on a large pad and muttering to himself in a mixture of mediaeval Latin and English. He looked up as Thomas entered then leaned back in his chair and said, "You've been with Cormac."

"How on earth did you know that?"

"When you've been with him for an hour or so you take on some if his… well… glow I suppose you'd call it. It kind of rubs off on you, like Tinkerbell's fairy dust." He laughed and ducked as Thomas feinted a blow to his head.

"Look what I found in one of your books. It's addressed to you and I've seen that handwriting before, I think it is Father John's." He held out an envelope addressed to Thomas in a fine copperplate hand that he remembered well.

Betty entered then with mugs of tea and chocolate cake, "Eat up boys, dinner will be sharp at 7:30," and disappeared again. Charlie rose and took one of the mugs and a piece of cake. "You'll want to read that alone I know so I'll take this up to my room. I'll see you at dinner."

After he'd gone Thomas sat with the envelope in his hand. How long had it been there he wondered, when had he hidden it and why? It held a faint trace of incense and felt as if something more than a letter had been placed inside. Part of him wanted to open it and part of him wanted to keep it until the time was right.

He cast his mind back to the last time he had seen him alive. Weary to the bone as they had all been after the battle. Edna had been taken home by Stan already in the throes of the pneumonia that had taken her from them. Thomas had begged Father John to stay with them overnight, but he had refused.

"I have done things tonight that no priest should do, I have taken lives. I must make my peace with God and confess."

"But who to, Father, who can you tell," Thomas had asked him. He had smiled that wonderful loving smile of his and simply said, "The Ultimate Confessor, Thomas and only to Him."

Steven had offered to drive him back to the Priory and he had accepted. He took Thomas' head in his hands and kissed his forehead and blessed him. He had watched the car out of sight and then climbed wearily into bed. At some quiet hour of the night his greatest friend and mentor had passed from one life into another and greater one. Now this had come into his hands as if he had known that there would be a time in the future when he would need what only he could give. Charlie had seen him in the Chapel, he had seen him when he showed him how to shift into bird form. He had not gone completely, perhaps in this envelope lay the answer to a question as yet unasked. He replaced it in the book and put it back on the shelf. He must wait for the right time then he would open it.

\* \* \*

**The Dark Tower**

An icy sweat ran down Iorwyth's face and soaked into his shirt. His eyes shifted desperately from side to side. "I-I-I don't think I can do that," he whispered hoarsely. "I have sort… of promised it to someone else already."

The brother and sister looked at each other, and then

144

back at him. The woman smiled. It was a smile that almost loosened the bowels of the man facing her. "And to whom have you promised this prize?" she inquired still smiling. Iorwyth groaned and wished himself a thousand miles away.

"To Morgana Le Fay," he whispered. "I called her back from the Underworld, I needed her help to find my enemies weakness. She wanted to return to earth with a new body and... I offered her the child. We have, we had... a bargain."

"How disappointing... for Morgana. You will of course inform her that you were mistaken and a new arrangement has been made. The child will be my new host, and the new Merlin will host my brother." Iorwyth came to his feet with an oath, his fear forgotten in his rage.

"No," he roared. "No, that title is mine, mine, I have spent years looking for the one appointed and I intend to challenge him once he has passed the trials. It was always meant to be me as the next Merlin. You cannot take this from me."

"Oh you will still have a part to play. I believe there is a companion who is close to this new Merlin... you can have him."

"No," snarled Iorwyth. "There is no power to be had there, I will not be a chattel to pick up leavings. I have planned and waited too long. You cannot ask this of me."

"Oh you will find we can." Their forms flickered, morphing into their true shape for a few moment of time. Powerful as they were, in this dimension they could not holds them for more than a second or two. But it was long enough to send Iorwyth to his knees. He screamed and tore at his face trying to cover his eyes, curling into a ball, so as not to see what was before him. He sobbed, begged, pleaded and finally lost consciousness for a few blessed moments. When he opened his eyes again they had resumed human forms and sat smiling and waiting. He crawled to his chair and painfully drew himself up to sit in it.

"What can I tell Morgana?" he asked.

"The truth. That we have taken over the plan. She will comply, as you did. We have waited for this moment since Atlantis destroyed itself rather than allow us to rule. We waited as each Merlin came and went. Some were strong, most were weak, but the strongest of all has come again. To defeat him and rule the land he loved will be a sweet victory. But the dawn comes and we must leave." She turned to the man cowering in his chair, "Make the trials real we need to know his true strength. He will be The Merlin, for just a short while. Our victory will be complete. With human bodies we can commence our rule of this land. After that there is the rest of the world." They moved to the window and the woman looked over her shoulder, "Since our true form upsets you, you had best turn away as we depart."

He put his hands over his face. When he looked up light filled an empty room. He staggered down the stairway and into the courtyard where his horse waited. He hauled himself into the saddle and rode away passing like a wraith through the dark lands. He did not fail to notice that those he met turned away from him, for he carried the touch and the stench of The Dark Ones and none could abide his presence.

# Chapter Fifteen

"**Sunday, sweet Sunday** with nothing to do… " carolled Betty as she prepared breakfast. Thomas always insisted that he and his father could look after themselves on Sundays, but with guests in the house he was grateful for her help.

As she moved around the spacious kitchen she cast her mind back eight years and wondered, not for the first time, how she had come through all the trauma. The faint scars she bore were barely noticeable but they served as a reminder of what might have been if it were not for Thomas and Father John and the Guardians. She was secure and happy in her place as housekeeper at the Manor and next year she and Frank would celebrate their Silver Wedding. Steven and Thomas had promised them a Round the World cruise as a present and she was the envy of her friends.

Thomas wandered in and headed for the steaming coffee pot. Charlie close behind him picked up on Betty's morning karaoke. He grabbed her and waltzed her round the big wooden kitchen table. His baritone slightly off key, "… lazy and loving, my one day with you…" Frank emerged from behind his Sunday paper and grinned. "I don't think Hollywood will be calling anytime soon. Meanwhile us men-folk is waiting fer breakfast… I'm starving."

Betty, pink-faced and laughing headed for the stove to dish up scrambled eggs, mushrooms, sausages and toast.

While they tucked in she took a breakfast tray up to the Naughtons. They had become good friends and she delighted in spoiling them during their visits.

The November sky was grey and dull and the only colour was provided by the Hollies and Copper Beeches lining the driveway. But not even the leaden clouds promising rain could dampen Thomas' spirits. He talked with his father over the computer video link for over an hour sharing what he had learned from Cormac and the brief time with Father John. He was less pleased to hear his mother would be returning with Steven and bringing her husband with her. Steven hurriedly assured him that they would be staying at the Carrick Arms and not at the Manor.

The morning was spent reading papers, while Frank gave Charlie his first driving lesson. Thomas read up on rock climbing and planned out what would be needed for the coming trial. The clearing up after the Bonfire Party had been done and Betty was now planning the Christmas Dinner.

Aware of a sudden quietness Thomas looked round and to his amusement found himself to be the only one awake in the room. Outside a few stray flakes of snow drifted past the window heralding the onset of winter. Soon, he thought, the Dales would be covered with a blanket of snow and the holly trees would be filled with birds feasting on the berries. On a sudden impulse he got up and went out into the hall where he shrugged into a warm fleece coat and, selecting a key from a rack hidden under a wall hanging he went out into the cold air.

He walked into the wooded area where the Chapel stood. As he unlocked the door he felt an inner warmth filling the sacred space; it should be cold, for the heating had been turned off, but, it was warm and welcoming. The winter light filtered through the stained glass behind the altar and rested

on the Cross. He sat in the family pew and remembered occasions both sad and happy. The look on Drew's face as Posy
walked towards him on Steven's arm on their wedding day.
Her dress sewn with tiny flowers, and dew fresh roses holding
her veil in place. He recalled holding Jessica in his arms, her
tiny hands catching the Jordan water as she was Christened.

He remembered Edna Pugh's casket resting all night
before the altar, the Guardians keeping watch over her. The
Memorial service for Father John and how he had cried in
his father's arms that night. He remembered the small casket
Stan had made with his own hands for the worn out body
of Grim when Barney's indwelling spirit had left it after the
battle. That had also rested here through the night and was
laid to rest in the centre of The Singing Stones. So many
memories, so many smiles and tears.

"Memory is the gift given to us by that which created
all life. We should treasure each and every one of them and
give thanks for them." Thomas raised his head, "Cormac,
what are you doing in this place? I thought... I thought..."

"That only humans had the right to worship something greater than themselves? No *mo Deartháir,* All life has
the right to that and the Sidhe are no different. This place
is not barred to us, just as our sacred places are open to you
and all who stand in the Light. You were called to this place
because you will have need of its strength in the near future.
There is news from Avalon. Ap Gryffdd has made an alli-
ance with The Dark Lords. An unwilling one it is true, but
he put himself into a position of great spiritual danger and
he did not have the courage to back away.

"Thomas go and stand before the Altar. You need
to align yourself with its power and strength." Thomas rose
and went to stand as directed. Cormac knelt behind him, his
head bowed, his sword drawn and laid before him in supplication. The light coming from the window intensified and

149

spread out encompassing both Human and Fae in its radiance. A portion of it bled into a deep red pillar of flame that solidified into the form of Michael, not robed, but in armour, sword in hand.

His voice rolled through the chapel like muted thunder, his face no longer warm and welcoming, but holding the promise of retribution.

*"Thomas of Carrick, The Battle Horn of Heaven has been sounded. From this moment you are a Champion of Light. I place in your hands the spiritual form of one of the lost Swords of Power. It was used by Flavius Cassius to divide the robe of Yeheshua at the foot of the cross. He was forgiven with the word REMISSIO, which became the name of the sword. Use it with this in mind. When its earthly form is needed, call its name and it will manifest for the time needed."*

The angelic form placed the sword in his hand. For a heart stopping moment it was real, weighty and powerful and burning hot, then in a burst of light it vanished and became one with the Champion. Michael raised his hand in blessing and vanished in the way he had arrived. Thomas looked at his hand and saw the imprint of a sword impressed in his palm, then it became one with his flesh.

Cormac took his own sword in his hands and knelt before him to offer it. "I too offer my service to you as a Champion of Light, Fae Friend, and Merlin of the Blessed Isles." Thomas touched the offered sword in acceptance and in silence they left the Chapel. Cormac returned to his own world and a subdued Thomas went back to the house and to his study. He took out the letter Father John had left him and sat for a time with it in his hands, then he broke the seal and read the letter.

*My Dear Thomas,*

*When you read this, I will no longer be with you in body, but always in spirit. Over the past few days I have spent much time looking at what lies before you. There will be, in the years to come, a task that will daunt you, but have courage. You were born for this, and if you approach it with a pure heart you will win though. Never doubt your own inner strength. When the moment comes to strike, remember this, No matter what the 'wrong' The Power of Forgiveness is always offered.*

*In Light and love*

*Frater John*

He read it several times then replaced it in the envelope and put it in his safe. With a lighter heart he re-joined the others downstairs. Charlie and Frank came in and treated everyone to a hilarious version of Charlie's first driving lesson. Jim wandered in with Grim and they all sat down to homemade tomato soup, roast lamb, Yorkshire pudding and roast potatoes and finished with baked apple drenched with a honey sauce spiked with brandy. Then Frank drove Charlie and his parents home so they could have some time together before he picked Charlie up early on Monday morning.

Thomas spent the rest of the day preparing for the next round of lectures and catching up on work set out by his tutor. Betty and Frank went back to the Gatehouse having left his supper ready to put into the Microwave. By 10:30 the house was in darkness and only the shimmer of the angelic wards gave any sign that this was a place where the Dark held no power.

Monday saw both Thomas and Charlie on the road

with Charlie sitting in the front seat so Frank could explain what he was doing and why and explaining the various road signs as they drove past. After a hasty lunch they reached Cambridge with barely an hour to get to their separate lectures, and were soon engulfed once more into the life of the university. If Thomas's colleagues were surprised by the sudden friendship between Charlie Naughton and himself they kept quiet about it. However, much to his surprise and delight he found a rock-climbers club in the town and went along to see what he could learn about the sport.

On inquiring about climbing the Needles he soon found out it would not be an easy task and set about practising on the climbing wall set up on the club premises. For the first week he spent more time falling off and dangling in the harness than he did climbing. He told everyone he had foolishly made a bet that he could do this climb and was now trying to get into shape, a story that, given the usual pranks played by university students was accepted without comment.

Ron Moulton the trainer let it be known that he didn't think much of bets that could end in a serious accident or worse. But finding his pupil adamant about the climb he set about making as sure as he could in the time available, that Thomas would have enough know how to get to the top. From there, he told him, he could abseil down. What he didn't know and what Thomas had no intention of telling him was that he planned to climb at sunset and spend the night up there.

Ron went with him to buy the footwear, climbing gear and rope he would need and made him memorise the easiest, though not the quickest route to the top. Getting to the Lighthouse was not a problem as he had friends with boats of all shapes and sizes in and around Cowes. Though not an expert he had sailed often enough to feel confident he could get the boat close enough to the Lighthouse steps to lash a line to them. Charlie would stay with the boat in the lee of the structure and wait until sunrise then they'd get back to the harbour in time to have breakfast. Hopefully, nothing would go wrong. And, although this Thomas fully expected, his Opponent didn't try any dirty tricks, they could be back in Cambridge by lunchtime, with the first of the Tests behind them.

It all sounded so simple when they talked about it thought Thomas gloomily as he fell off the practice wall for the fourth time in a row. At this rate he'd be lucky to get back in one piece. To top it off Charlie proved to be a bad sailor. They went down to Cowes at the weekend and took out a small launch with a miniscule cabin where he could spend the night. But they got just a hundred yards out before Charlie was over the side as green as an unripe apple. After stuffing him with anti-seasick pills they tried again the following day and managed to get fairly close to their target, but strong winds and high seas defeated them.

In the hotel later that night Thomas lay awake worrying over how they could overcome the combination of wind, sea, and weather when Charlie sat up in the other bed and said with some asperity, "Why don't you ask the Sidhe for help, I don't think you're meant to do it all by yourself Tom. Merlyn sent Cormac to train you so that ought to tell you something. You're trying to do it all single-handed and you can't. Even this Welsh Wizard guy has gone to others for help. The Sidhe traditionally are part elemental, so ask for their help with the weather and don't be so toffee nosed about wanting to do it all alone." He pulled the covers up round his ears and curled up on his side.

Thomas was stupefied. Charlie had never spoken so crossly, or criticised him so harshly but it made sense. He had thought it was his job to do it alone, but Charlie's outburst made him see that sometimes you needed to ask for help. Merlyn, Arthur, Mordred and Cormac were waiting to be asked, because it had to be his decision. If he was too proud to ask for help he could fail. To ask did not mean being weak, just that he needed the kind of help they could supply.

"Thanks Charlie," he said. Charlie grunted and snuggled deeper into his pillow. "Just thought you needed to know a few home truths."

In his own dimension Cormac heaved a sigh of relief and turned to the misty wind-tossed being at his side and bowed. "Paralda, King of the Element of Air, tomorrow the future Merlin of Albion will be presented to you."

# Chapter Sixteen

**Just before dawn** the next day Thomas and Charlie stood on a headland overlooking the harbour. They'd been summoned by Cormac who now stood tall and dark beside them, his customary leather coat lifting in the wind from the sea. However his human companions were wrapped up against the cold and stamping their feet to keep warm, as he prepared them for their meeting with Paralda.

"Paralda is neither Fae nor Angel but like all the Elemental Kings he is ensouled. In this he is not unlike yourselves. His power is great and extends from the lightest breeze to a tornado of devastating force. He cannot be fully controlled except by that which created him, none of them can. But they can be asked for help and if they see fit to do so they will grant their aid."

Charlie stirred a little uneasily and asked, "Cormac, you say they are ensouled and so rather like us humans, but does that mean you and your people are not gifted with a soul? That seems so unfair to me."

"Your concern and compassion for my race warms my heart Charlie, but do not fear for us. We were created for a different purpose in a time so distant even we cannot remember it. Our substance is not of this world but is a part of a dimension humanity has yet to discover. This is why we can appear and disappear at will. Why we can adapt the outer layer of our bodies to appear as clothes or to add what you see as wings that enable us to ride the solar winds coming from your sun. Our destiny is as spiritual as your own, but it lies in a different direction. You think of us as immortal but when we reach a time when there is no longer a joy in being what we are, we ask for release and it is granted." He turned to the sun that had just cleared the horizon. "Paralda comes."

Thomas and Charlie turned and saw coming out of the East a swiftly moving figure that seemed to be made entirely of movement. It was a mist but a mist that moved continuously. A figure and a face that was never the same two seconds together. Hair of the pale blue of an early summer morning, eyes as brilliant as stars. But neither could describe exactly what they were seeing. Warned by an inner voice they bowed their heads in respect.

"Paralda, King of the Element of Air and Guardian of the Winds, I present Thomas Greystone-Carrick the chosen Merlin, and Charles Naughton his companion and a Fae Friend." A musical voice like a high wind on a mountaintop bade them look up. "The People of the Sidhe speak highly of you both and Cormac has told me you have need of my help. Tell me what you need and why, and I will make a decision."

Cormac spoke to the Elemental in his own language and Paralda laughed. The moving form stilled and took a shape similar to that of the Sidhe. "Cormac says this will make it easier for you. My own form is hard for humans to endure for long."

Charlie, who was beginning to feel a little queasy bowed and murmured a heartfelt thank you. The courtesy drew a nod of approval from the Elemental. Thomas then set out the nature and location of the Trial and asked for help with both the wind and the weather. "I need to stay in one small space for the whole night, so a strong wind would be difficult to fight against for so long. Also there is the effect of a high wind on the sea. The boat is small and the approach is not easy. Charlie has to spend the night either on the boat or at the base of the rocks. I realise this is a trial and I cannot ask for too much help. But what can be offered, we will gladly accept."

Paralda went and stood at the edge of the cliff his head bowed in thought. After several minutes of silence he turned back to them. "As you rightly say, I cannot offer you too much help, a test must be a true test.

"At the time and place of your trial I must obey certain conditions even though Air is my element I must conform to the seasons and their patterns. But this much I can and will do. I will give you three periods of time when the high wind that normally buffets that area will lessen to a degree that will give you a space of rest when you can re-gather your strength. During those times my winds will also calm the sea. You however, must choose those times. I will give you Words of Power to do this. You must use your own discretion when to use them and then only for those three times. After that they will cease to be effective. Is this acceptable to you?"

Thomas bowed. "Your help is most generous King Paralda and we accept it with heartfelt thanks. I fully understand the conditions laid down and will obey them to the letter." A memory from eight years earlier surfaced in his mind and he added, "May you and the elementals under your care be blessed to the amount you are able to receive." A shaft of sunlight illuminated the Elemental King making his form into a pillar of pure light. Both humans shielded their eyes against it, then Paralda had gone, only his voice hung in the early morning air.

*"For this blessing I, and those in my care, give thanks. Here are the words you will need young Merlin, use them exactly as they are given to you."*

The three word phrase seared its way into Thomas' brain, causing him to cry out against the pain and Charlie caught him in his arms as he crumpled to the hoar frosted ground. Cormac knelt beside them. "He will be alright, it lasted but a few seconds, words of power always carry a cost." Thomas stirred and sat up shaking his head. "What hit me. Oh, yes, Paralda's Words of Power. Damn, that hurt. Has he gone?" Charlie nodded and helped him to his feet. "Can you drive?"

"Yes, I'm OK. Let's get back. Cormac, many thanks for your help. *Slan Aval Mo Deartháir.*" Cormac grinned, "Your Gaelic is getting better, though your pronunciation could be tighter. *Slan Aval.*" He moved sideways into his own world and disappeared.

Charlie and Thomas returned to the car and made their way back first to the hotel for breakfast, and later back to Cambridge. On the way they planned a more extended visit in January with a partial climb to time the ascent and get Charlie used to helping Drew with the boat.

The weather had turned wintery over the past week and worsened as they came to the end of term. Both now concentrated fully on their studies. Charlie spent most of his time with Thomas in his study returning to his own room only to sleep. Any spare time he spent on his driving lessons. Frank came down every Saturday and they spent the day driving around. Steven returned from his USA tour with a contract for three new books and was followed a week later by Thomas' mother and her second husband.

Thomas used End of Term exams as an excuse to stay away until the last moment. On the tenth he took some friends to dinner, and arranged with Frank to pick them both up after lunch the following Monday. They dropped Charlie off at his parents and stayed for tea and hot mince pies, and arranged for Frank to pick the three of them up on Christmas morning for dinner.

Christmas Eve was always a quiet time before the excitement of Christmas Day with just Steven, Thomas, Frank, Betty and Adam. Charlie and his parents would come for Christmas dinner. But Boxing Day was when the Guardians came together in the Great Hall and the old house rang with merriment. There were three Trees, one outside the front door, and one at the entrance to the drive. The biggest was in the Hall and the Manor always provided one for the village square which everyone helped to decorate. Thomas had never outgrown the magic of Christmas and threw himself into it.

Now as they headed for home Thomas got a call from his father. "Tom I don't know how to tell you this but your mother's here. I'd arranged for her to come on Wednesday but she turned up an hour ago saying she couldn't wait to see you."

"Don't fret dad, we'll have dinner, then call it a day about 10:30."

Steven's voice got grimmer. "You don't know half of it lad. She's brought Greg with her and his teenage son. I'm sorry Tom but they barged straight in. Nora said it was time you met your step-brother. I was so taken aback I just let them in."

"Then I'll have the pleasure of letting them out again," said Thomas with clenched teeth. "I made it clear to my mother, that I would not have her new husband in my house, and I do not have a step-brother."

Steven tried again, "I know lad, but they're here now and they won't stay over Christmas. Greg wants to spend it in Rome. It seems he was born Catholic though I doubt he's been to church in years. I thought we'd get dinner over tonight, lunch on Wednesday and see them off on Thursday."

"Okay dad, I'll do it for you but don't expect me to make them feel welcome." He ended the call and sank back in his seat. Frank gave him a sympathetic look in the mirror. "Never mind Tom don't let it spoil Christmas. It's only a few days."

"A few days of hell, I'll not put them up, they can go down to the Carrick Arms. I'll not have that man sleep under my roof." He stared out of the window. As if he didn't have enough on his plate he now had this as well. He put a call through to Drew.

"Hello Drew, my mother has arrived at the house, can you tell me if she's booked rooms with you? No! I thought not. She's hoping to cajole me into putting them up. I'll book on their behalf, one double and one single as they've brought his son with them. Thanks Drew, bill me for the rooms OK?"

His mood darkened as they came in sight of the house and he saw the big four by four parked before the house. He got out and kicked the rear tyre. "Frank, when you've parked our car have this moved to the back of the house will you."

Normally he would have carried in his own bags, but he was well into his Lord of the Manor mood tonight. Frank grinned, opened the trunk and got out the cases. Betty would be in a fighting mood as well. He almost felt sorry for Nora Kowalski, almost, but not quite.

# Chapter Seventeen

**Morgana's shade writhed**, trapped in the triangle of manifestation, beating at it with her fists. Her screams of rage thankfully diminished by her incarceration.

*"You promised, you promised. The child should be mine. I need to get back. I'll see you in hell Ap Gryffdd. You lying cheat. You betrayed me."*

"I had no choice Morgana. You of all people should know what it means to defy The Dark Ones. There will be others. Be patient." Morgana glowered at him.

*"But not as close to The Merlin. I could have destroyed the whole lot of them from the inside. Find me another form, and do it quickly."*

She shifted into smoke and returned to the Underworld. Iorwyth wiped the sweat from his face and set about closing down the triangle and clearing all traces of his work.

Later, showered and dressed, he sat down and began to plan his next move. The trials would begin soon he knew, but exactly when, and which would come first? He could not touch the mind of The Merlin himself, but maybe his new companion would be easier to subvert. The thought of turning Charlie Naughton from friend to betrayer made him smile. Yes, that would be amusing. He finished his coffee and he went to get his coat and hat. As he passed the potted plant in the hall he twisted one of its delicate leaves. He enjoyed tormenting it because his butler liked it and tended it carefully.

The nature spirit within the plant set about healing its leaf and sent out a call of complaint to its own kind. It also passed on what it had sensed in its tormentor's mind. The message flowed via root and leaf, bloom and bud. Birds picked it up and carried it on and a small breeze bustling through a park heard and relayed it to Paralda. The spirit of the plant nursed its broken leaf satisfied its message had been heard and passed on. The greatest plans can be undone by the smallest mistake.

\* \* \*

Thomas hardly recognised the woman who threw herself into his arms. The overdressed, highlighted blonde with lips a vampire would be proud to own was surely not his mother. Where, he wondered, had Nora Greystone gone? Was she still there under all this Hollywood glitter?

"Tommy," she cried enveloping him in a cloud of Chanel. "My little Tommy, so grown up and so handsome." (and so rich, thought Thomas). He disengaged himself and kissed her cheek, that being preferable to being covered in lipstick.

"How are you mother, well I hope. Did you have a good journey over?"

"Of course darling, we always fly first class, Greg honey, come and say hello to your stepson. It's been nearly five years since you've seen each other." *(and it's not long enough... Thomas thought, with as much of a smile as he could manage).*

"Yeah, too long, good to see you, great place you have here, plenty of room to move around." Greg Kowalski was a stocky red-faced man who liked to think of himself as "self-made". He was however no fool and was well aware of Thomas' opinion of him. The fact his stepson could buy him out fifty times over and have enough change to keep him in luxury for life rankled with him, plus there was "The Title". Nora trotted this out every time she met someone new.

Steven stepped into a gap in the conversation with a tray of drinks and everyone sat down. Thomas at ease and sure of himself in his own home, Steven longing to get back to his study, the guests began to understand their surprise visit had not been well received. Then Betty appeared and Thomas nearly choked on his drink. Instead of her usual skirt jumper and trousers if it was cold, she stood in the doorway in a neat but severe navy dress with a white lace collar. "Sir Thomas," she inquired in formal tones, "at what time would you like dinner served?"

For one wild moment Thomas thought he had landed in a badly written farce. Then he caught on and decided to play the game. He looked at his watch, "Eight o'clock if you please Mrs. Jackson."

"Certainly Sir Thomas, I will see to it." She gathered up the used glasses and swept out of the room. Thomas sighed and wondered what else she was cooking besides dinner. Minutes later the door re-opened and Frank, in what he called his "funeral suit", announced another guest, "Mr. Adam Kowalski, Sir Thomas."

Thomas looked into a pair of bemused eyes as blue as his own, but behind a pair of horn rimmed glasses and a shock of dark hair. Even at seventeen it was clear that Adam Kowalski was never going to be like his father. Smaller than Thomas, slender in build and plainly ill at ease in these surroundings, he hovered in the doorway blinking and holding tightly to a pile of books.

"Fer Chrissakes don't just stand there like an idiot," barked his father impatiently. "Get over here and say hello can't you."

In that instant Thomas saw himself as he could have been if he'd not had Steven Greystone for a father. He sensed the bruised spirit of the young man and walked over to him holding out his hand, "Pleased to meet you Adam."

"Er pleased to meet you too Sir Thomas."

"To you Adam, it's just Thomas, you look as if you like books, do you?"

"Too damn much he likes books," interrupted his father. "Always got his fool head in one instead of playing baseball or football like a real man." The accent was heavy on the last two words and Adam coloured up.

Thomas turned a steely look on him, "There's nothing wrong in liking books Mr. Kowalski (correct pronunciation of the surname). Some of the greatest men of your country and of your ancestral country have valued what books have to offer," he paused just long enough to make a point then continued, "it takes a discerning mind to appreciate a book."

He guided Adam to a seat next to him and began to sound him out. Steven took the hint and with a sigh set himself to entertain his ex-wife and her husband. After several futile attempts to break up the rapport building between Thomas and Adam, Greg Kowalski sulked in a corner and kept re-filling his glass.

Prompt at eight Frank announced dinner and Thomas escorted his mother into the dining room knowing that Betty would have set out the silverware and the gold edged porcelain service, along with the Venetian crystal glassware. Seen against the snowy whiteness of Irish linen edged with handmade lace it made Nora well aware of what she'd thrown away. She headed for the chair opposite that of Thomas as the host, only to be guided to the chair on his right, with his father on his left.

Greg and his son faced each other across the table. Two village girls, hand-picked by Betty and dressed in black with snowy aprons, began serving a creamy vegetable soup. Frank saw to the wine, ostentatiously offering Thomas the taster and the cork. Thomas played it to the hilt planning to have a good laugh with them later on. Making the best of a bad situation Nora raised a pencilled eyebrow.

"Have you any plans for choosing a Lady Greystone-Carrick?" she asked archly.

Thomas sipped his wine, "No, I'm content to wait for the right person to come along. There will be only one marriage in my family." An edgy silence prevailed as that remark was digested. Then Nora tried again.

"By the way, I noticed our bags are still in the hall dear, perhaps they could be taken up later."

"No mother, they will be put into your car and taken to The Carrick Arms where I have booked rooms for you. As my treat of course."

"But Thomas I thought as we haven't seen each other for so long it would be nice to stay here. The Master Suite has a lovely view over the moors."

"The Master Suite will remain unused until I am ready to bring my bride home to Carrick Manor. I think mother, you have forgotten the rules I laid down when you left my house." Nora coloured and took a hasty sip of wine. Greg was already on his third glass. "I thought it was time to let the past be forgotten," she said. Thomas answered her quietly, "That remains to be seen."

The first course was cleared and the second arrived promptly. Thinly sliced roast lamb with Duchesse potatoes, fresh vegetables and a sauce spiked with a vintage Merlot. Thomas turned his attention to Adam asking about what career he might have in mind.

"Well he won't be following in my footsteps that's for

sure," said his father using a desert spoon to scoop up his fresh garden peas (Frank appeared at his side and replaced the used spoon with a clean one, sniffed, and resumed his place behind Thomas' chair). "Young jackass wants to paint. I ask you, what kind of fool job is that. He'll go to business school and like it, or he'll have my boot up his ass."

"Greg dear, language," murmured Nora. "I call it as I see," said her husband waving his empty wine glass at Frank. "Great vino Tom, good stuff."

"Are you looking forward to Rome Adam?" asked Thomas, ignoring the interruption. "You'll be spoilt for choice with all the art galleries and museums there."

"He ain't coming with us, he's goin' back to L.A. I'll be doing business in Rome and Nora'll be shopping fit to bust. He won't know what to do with himself so he's goin' back next week." With perfect timing Thomas dropped a bombshell that had been building up in his mind for the last hour and a half...

"That's a pity, I was hoping he could spend Christmas here with us. I would take it as a personal favour if you would allow him to do so. You could collect him on the way back, after New Year." He cut into his roast lamb with delicate precision. Three pairs of eyes looked at him. One with suspicion, one with stupefaction, and one with a glimmer of hope.

Steven raised his eyebrows, but said nothing. Nora took a breath and was about to say something when Thomas speared an artichoke heart and looked at her. She closed her mouth and her eyes and thought for a moment. When she looked up again there was the faint sheen of tears.

"I think that would be a lovely idea," she said quietly. "Thank you Thomas." Greg began to bluster, feeling that somehow he had lost a battle, but not understanding how or when.

"Well I think we should ask Adam if he wants to do that, after all he's only just met… his step-brother. Yes I know, all the more reason why he should stay and get to know me." He turned to Adam and said with a grin, "We could take a run down to London to see The Tate Gallery and the Victoria and Albert museum. I have some paintings on permanent loan to the Tate and I also have a controlling interest in several art galleries, you might enjoy seeing them."

Adam's eyes shone star bright. "I'd love that, but Dad always said…" his voice tailed off, but Thomas took up the challenge.

"I believe Mr Kowalski that you are looking for backers for your new film. Perhaps before you leave we might talk about that." He could not have made it clearer. Kowalski grunted, belched and pushed his empty plate away.

"Well I guess it wouldn't be a bad idea at that."

"Good," said Thomas, "Now you must try Mrs. Jackson's Apple Charlotte, the cream is from our own Jersey herd. Frank tell Mrs Jackson we will have coffee and brandy in the drawing room in 30 minutes. The '59 Armagnac if you please." Frank grinned and left.

A few hours later their guests left for the Carrick Arms in the Bentley with Frank at the wheel. Greg was well over the limit for driving. A jubilant Adam left with a pile of art books and a fervent case of hero worship for his new step-brother. Greg nursed a bottle of French brandy and the promise of a substantial backing for his new film. But Nora was quiet and kept touching the string of pearls around her neck with caressing fingers. For the first time in seven years she dared to hope her son might one day forgive her. She wept quietly.

Back at the Manor they gathered in the kitchen to discuss the evening. Thomas complimented Betty and Frank on their "playacting". "You were so good I'm thinking of making it permanent," he joked. Frank roared with laughter. "Couldn't keep a straight face more than a few minutes, I had to sneak out to the kitchen."

Steven wiped his streaming eyes, "… and when he ate his peas off the desert spoon, your face!!" Then he sobered up and asked Thomas, "What's all this about young Adam. You were blasting off about him before you met? Now you've taken him under your wing."

"The boy needs rescuing. He's been battered down because he's not a bully like his father. I'll take pleasure in fostering his ambitions and getting him out of his father's clutches." He was quiet for a moment then turned to his father, "She's not as happy as she pretends is she?"

"No," said Steven, "she's put on a brave face for years now. I've seen the odd bruise, and there are rumours of other women. You made her very happy tonight Thomas, Those were your Grandma's pearls weren't they?"

"Yes, she needs to have them for a while, but they will go eventually to my wife if and when I choose one." As he spoke he caught the faint echo of a dream he often had of a windswept seashore over looked by an ancient castle and a woman looking out to sea. She looks over her shoulder and smiles, *"We'll meet when the time is right Thomas."*

# Chapter Eighteen

**During the rest** of their stay a battle was fought over Adam, and Thomas won! Greg Kowalski reluctant to lose the promised backing, gave in and allowed Adam to stay over Christmas and fly back to the USA in the New Year. The day they left, the car was hardly out of sight before Thomas was on the phone.

The following day he drove Adam down to London to stay in the Stag Hotel in Hampstead, leaving Charlie to work in the Library preparing for his Finals. For the next three days Adam lived a life he had only dreamed about. They explored Galleries, Museums, and Private Collections. He talked to people about his hopes and dreams, showed them his Sketch Book and was breath-taken at their comments and praise. He heard stories of their own early days, and listened to advice and recommendations, but knowing in his heart he was doomed to follow his father's plans. He grieved quietly over his lost hopes.

For his part on the drive back home, Thomas mentally gave thanks for a good memory and the ability to keep to strict study times. The Finals loomed high in his timetable but he was far more worried about the Trial of Air to come than about his university studies.

As they drew up outside the house Adam turned to him and almost in tears, thanked him for a time he would never forget. "When I'm trying to understand business studies... I'll think back to these three days and it won't seem so bad."

Thomas placed a hand on his shoulder. "I'm glad you enjoyed it, Adam, but we never know what Fate has in store for us, so take things as they come and we still have a week before Christmas. Now let's see what Betty has for dinner."

For the next few days life at the Manor was a whirl of activity. Betty practically lived in the kitchen, Steven worked on his book, and Thomas honed his shifting skills spending precious time studying the gulls, their calls, behaviour and habits. Charlie to his surprise and joy got several visits from Cormac who passed on details and information for him to use in his papers. It was a house full of hopes, desires, dreams and in Adam's case, silent tears of "what might have been". In the middle was a two day battle between Thomas, Steven, Greg Kowalski and two sets of somewhat bemused lawyers with the Atlantic Ocean between them. Things Thomas had learned, been told and found out in London were about to cause some unexpected changes in the Kowalski household.

Christmas Day dawned looking like a traditional greeting card. Snow garlanded the trees and evergreens and flurried round the chimneys, and frost turned the windows into lace curtains. The glow of the wood fire in the ancient hearth reflected itself in the mirrors, and the Spirit of the House basked in memories of past Christmases and hoped for their return in the future.

Thomas paused and looked out of his window, filling his eyes and heart with the sight. This was what Christmas meant to him, light, warmth, log fires and the sound of laughter throughout the house. On Christmas Eve he always visited the farms that had once belonged to him. Some years ago, after a tussle with his accountants, he had gifted each farmer with the deeds to their homes and land. "You have earned this," he told them. "For generations you have sweated blood over this land and my ancestors have benefitted from your work. It is time for a change."

He had handed the deeds to each family and enjoyed seeing their faces go from disbelief, to hope and finally to overwhelming joy. The moment had stayed with him and he re-lived it each Christmastide. He always visited each farm to wish them joy and share a Christmas drink.

The effects of those five small drinks had not quite dissipated as he came down to breakfast but he was looking forward to the day. Charlie and his parents would come later in the afternoon. Then on Boxing Day the Guardians came together for lunch. But Christmas Dinner was just for family. Steven, Betty, Frank, himself and Adam.

During the last five days, armed with information gleaned from art dealers, lawyers, hospital records and some clandestine inquiries, he had spent hours on the phone with Greg Kowalski, shamelessly drawing on The Merlin Powers available to him. It had taken guile, determination, ruthlessness and the unexpected help of his mother, but the result had been worth it, and would change Adam's life forever.

In the kitchen Steven was regaling Adam with his personal viewpoint on the Hollywood elite and their lifestyle and his audience were laughing their heads off.

"... it had taken all morning to get the set just right and then, just as the cameras started to roll, one of the extras let off this really loud fart. We all froze, then with a straight face the Director said. 'We'll keep in the sound effect, and if the person responsible will give his or her name to my secretary I will personally see they are given full credit on the titles, under the heading of 'Farts supplied by...' Strangely... no-one came forward, I can't think why."

Thomas sat down and reached for the coffee, "I'm surprised they let you back into Hollywood Dad... they must know you spread all the gossip around." Betty put a heaped plate in front of him.

"Eat up Thomas there's a long day ahead. Frank will fetch Charlie and the Naughtons for High Tea at four thirty and there's a pile of presents under the tree waiting to be opened, so hurry up." Thomas ate with his usual appetite and joined in the table banter while Adam went to add his presents to the pile.

While he was away everyone at the table pretended not to notice when the coffee pot kept filling Thomas' cup. Then it got over enthusiastic and started filling them all. It paused and stood for a moment as if thinking it over, then quietly replaced itself on the hob. Thomas sent it a small pulse of energy as a thank you, and was rewarded with a little puff of steam from the spout.

A call was made to Charlie and his parents to wish them Happy Christmas, then they moved into the Hall where the fire blazed in the hearth, its flames reflected in the decorations on the Tree surrounded by parcels. Adam re-appeared to add more presents to the pile, while Frank poured glasses of wine for everyone.

They toasted absent friends and loved ones and in silence remembered past Christmases. As always Thomas thought of his grandmother, of Father John, and Edna and held them in his heart. He sent a mental blessing to the past Merlins, to Cormac and his people, to Merlyn, Mordred, and Barney who had once been called Grim. In a lighter mood they toasted the coming year, soon to be with them. To new friends, Charlie, Jim and Maisie and now Adam, Then it was time for the presents.

Steven and Thomas had joined forces to give Betty and Frank a matched set of luggage for their cruise later in the year. two Cashmere Sweaters, one in rose pink and one in blue, the annual renewal of Frank's four seater Box for the

Greyhound Derby, and this year's Special, a Quarter Share in the ownership of the top greyhound of the year. Adam gave Betty a silver charm bracelet with tiny charms of kitchen items, and to Frank a sketch of Betty in a silver frame. All were received with laughter, tears, and kisses.

Thomas, notoriously difficult to buy for, had from Steven a Donation to an animal charity he supported in memory of Grim. While Betty with a giggle, gave him four pairs of emerald green pure silk underwear on each of which she had embroidered his name. He refused her suggestion to try them for size, but loved the ancient Fossil encased in a chunk of Baltic Amber on a silver mount that Adam had found in an antique shop in London, plus a sketch of Grim in a silver frame.

Steven's present was a combined one from his family. A set of his own books, first editions, BUT bound in hand tooled black leather with gold lettering. From Adam a sketch of Thomas in a similar frame to the others. He also got a giant coffee mug locally made and inscribed with the words *'From one Mug to another.'*

Thomas was deeply moved by the effort and skill that had gone into all of the sketches and could hardly wait to see the lad's reaction to his own presents. From Betty and Frank a hand knitted Aran sweater, as a native Californian he had a hard time coping with cold weather, and Betty worried over his health. But Thomas and Steven had something special for him, and wondered how he would respond. They sat him down and handed him three envelopes.

In the first was a letter accepting him as a student to a famous School of Art in Paris. All fees had been paid for and the first term began in the middle of January. The Second letter held the lease of a small apartment, close to the College. The Third confirmed an account had been opened for him with an international bank, for the duration of his studies.

Stunned Adam looked at them, then, unashamedly he cried. Cried for the life that now opened before him. Cried for the gift of love, caring, and understanding he'd never had from Greg, or the mother who had died giving him birth. Cried for what was now offered with no strings attached.

"But my father insisted I do a business course, how did you get him to this. Tom, Steven, you don't know what this means to me, to be able to paint, to know Paris. I'll never be able to thank you. For the first time I know what it is to have a family."

Frank poured a glass of wine and put it in Adam's hand. "Drink up lad, you're going to need it, there's more to come." Betty came to sit beside him and took his hand in hers. Steven drew up a chair and said quietly:

"The truth is Adam, Greg is NOT your father. Your mother fell in love with a young French artist many years ago, but Greg would not give her a divorce. When you were born, your mother died a few days later, so Greg decided to bring you up as his own. Your real father had no money at that time, he was a struggling artist and couldn't bring you up on his own, so very reluctantly he allowed Greg to claim fatherhood so you would be taken care of.

"You see Greg is unable to have children, he is infertile, and he doesn't want it known... we used this to make him agree to you studying Art. Also, you are seventeen, in a year you will be legally free from him. He never told you this?"

"No, he never talked about my mother. How did you find it out?"

"When you were in London one of the artists you met got the shock of his life... you are the image of your real father at your age. It's from him that you get your talent."

"Does my step-mother know? She did her best and stood up for me. She misses you Thomas and I kind of took your place."

Thomas put a hand in his shoulder, "This has been healing for me as well. She helped us persuade Greg to let you go, that and the fact he doesn't want his image as a man's man to be damaged."

"Is my real father still alive?'

"Yes, he is part owner of the school where you will study. At the moment he is in Russia at an International Arts Conference. But he'll be there to greet you when you arrive. My mother has left for the US and will help you get your things together. I don't think you'll see Greg for some time... it's up to you. But your real father is overjoyed at the thought of finally being with his son. We emailed him some of your sketches and he is so proud of them and you." Thomas stood up and went to the tree where the last parcel was waiting and gave it to Adam. "He sent you this, the first gift he has been able to give his son."

With shaking hands Adam opened it to reveal a set of pencils, brushes, palette and watercolours. A card held a single sentence, *'To my Son, after so many years I can finally say those words. I cannot wait to hold you. Emile de Beaufort. (your Father)'*.

"I think I'll go and collect the Naughtons," said Frank blowing his nose hard.

"And I think," said Betty in her no nonsense voice... "what we all need now is a good Christmas Dinner inside us. It will get us back on an even keel. The table's laid and every-thing's prepared. You men fill your glasses and go and sit down. I'll start serving as soon as the rest of them get here." She headed for the kitchen wiping her eyes on her apron as she went.

# Chapter Nineteen

### Evening: Christmas Day

"**Why do we always** eat too much on Christmas Day? You'd think we'd learned a lesson after all this time." Steven eased himself into a fireside chair and sipped at the antacid concoction Betty had thoughtfully left on the sideboard, and continued his mental self-abasement.

"I swear this is the last time, next year it's beans on toast and a chocolate digestive. No turkey, no roast potatoes no sprouts, no plum pudding and brandy sauce, and definitely no alcohol." He eased the top button of his waistband and gave an audible sigh of relief. Frank, and Jim Naughton had long since lost the fight to stay awake as the occasional soft snore from the sofa attested.

Betty and Maisie had left their menfolk to themselves and, having stacked the dishwasher to full capacity, retired to Betty's parlour behind the kitchen to watch the current "weepie" on the TV. Adam, after a private and emotional meeting with his father via Skype, borrowed a heavy coat and took Grim for a walk on the moors, to clear his head and think of his future.

Of the jubilant, and slightly bucolic group that had worked their way through Christmas Dinner, then High Tea, only Thomas had remained unscathed. A "mental" request to his plate and glass, kept both "apparently" full so it seemed as if he, like his guests, had wined and dined well. But he had other things on his mind.

Leaving Charlie gloating over his new Apple Mac Laptop in the library, he slipped away through the back door into the Herb Garden. The flow of the Change, was a matter of seconds. The hawk rose into the air and headed for the Hill of Dreams, below he could see Adam and Grim heading for the same place. He raced ahead sending out a call to Cormac as he did so, and landed on the tallest of the Standing Stones. Moments later another Hawk landed on the stone next to him.

"The Luck of the Evening Star to you Thomas."

"... And to you also Cormac. To you and to your people I offer the blessing of the Season. May we live in Harmony together."

"This Blessing I accept on their behalf and my own. You are held high in their esteem Thomas. What do you need from me?"

"Some answers Cormac, why has Adam come into my life at this time? Is he, or will he become in the future, a part of what is happening to me and to Albion."

"Sidhe I may be, but I am not a Seer. But I can tell you this. As the Arch-Mage of Albion many will come to you in the future, for reasons big and small. How you deal with them will define your time in that position. The title is not always hereditary and since Merlyn held the title many changes have occurred in your world and you are a part of that change. Being human you are subject to the demands, and ills, of the human race, as will be those around you."

He paused as Adam and Grim reached the Stones and began to climb. "Adam carries within him the seed of renown but that is well into the future. Concern yourself with your own trials at the moment, in both worlds, and now I must go, Farewell."

As Adam and Grim reached the top of the Hill of Dreams he saw two hawks fly off in different directions and wished he could have sketched the moment. He sat on the rough stone seat and thought about his future. Maybe, just maybe, one day he would paint a masterpiece!

\* \* \*

Frank tucked the car rug around a sleepy Maisie still clutching her basket of goodies, and a slightly unsteady Jim who kept thanking everyone for a... faba... fabu-lucy, a wunnerful day!

Charlie packed a lightweight G-Tech cleaner and his father's new pride and joy, an electric hedge-trimmer into the boot and climbed in beside him.

"It's been an amazing day Frank, I can't remember when I've laughed so much, eaten so much, or seen my parents have such a good time. Usually my aunt and her husband and son come down from Northumberland, but he's hard-line Church and they spend the time either in prayer or reading chapters from the Bible. They don't drink, and don't eat Christmas pudding because of the sherry and the brandy sauce. Christmas presents tend to be hand knitted socks and scarves, or something from the Charity shop. I have a drawer full of socks I've never worn because they're all too small."

A slight snore from the back made them look at each other with knowing grins. "You might have to carry your Mum inside lad. Hope the neighbours won't think this will be a given thing from now on."

"So do I. I'm sure I'll be getting my own breakfast tomorrow morning, or even tomorrow afternoon." They drove into the night laughing.

Ap Gryffdd covered the crystal ball with a velvet cloth and went to stand by the window. He looked out over the London skyline ablaze with Christmas lights and scowled at the sound of revelry drifting up from below. His plan to increase the division between Thomas and his mother and cause trouble between him and Adam had not been successful. He would have to rely on the planned party on the 26th. He was wary of Drew... his link to Thomas was very strong, but when it came to love for his wife and daughter that was where he could hope to score.

He cursed himself for calling on The Dark Lords for aid which had lost him the coveted position of Arch-Mage. He would have to be content with the lesser power wielded by Naughton. He consoled himself with the thought that nothing major could happen until Thomas achieved the Four Elemental Trials. If, by a stroke of good luck... he could deal a fatal blow to Thomas in that fleeting moment before he could, assume the Title and its Power he might be able to wrest it from him and with it draw on the Power of Albion itself.

With this he could defy The Dark Lords and rule as heir to the Power once held by Atlantis. A power no human had ever been able to use. A remnant of the Power of Universal Creation. Few knew of its existence. He poured a glass of wine and sat back to dream how he would deal with those who thwarted him; the list was long.

In the corner of the room and hidden from sight by the butler, the little plant Gryffdd liked to torture, tuned into his thoughts and plans. It repeated them via its link to other plants in the apartments throughout the building and on to the trees in the surrounding area. The wind picked it up and passed it to the birds and anyone who would listen. A city fox told it to a feral cat who in turn passed it to the ancient Troll living beneath Blackfriars Bridge. Within days the news had spread throughout the Hidden Soul of Albion and even to Avalon.

*"The New Merlin will soon be taking the Four Trials... but a Dark Opponent plans a magical assassination. Be Aware. The New Merlin must be guarded."*

The plant snuggled down into its roots and nursed its damaged leaves. Its news has been received and understood. Revenge was sweet.

# Chapter Twenty

**The Day after Christmas**, traditionally called Boxing Day in Britain, was always kept for the Guardians. It was accepted that families came first, but on the day after Christmas they came together. Instead of exchanging presents, each gave a donation to a Charity each year. This year it was Guide Dogs for the Blind.

The dinner was for the Guardians only, so the food was laid out ready and Thomas served them himself. It was something he enjoyed doing, seeing it as means of saying Thank You for their friendship and dedication. Betty, Frank, Steven, and Adam ate in the cosy kitchen and watched TV.

After the meal they discussed dates for their meetings at the Stones and, as always there was a hand written message read out from the "One" who, in the aftermath of the never to be forgotten battle, had received Arthur's Crown from Thomas' hand. When everyone had a glass in their hand, Thomas revealed the Four Trials he had to face to win the title of Merlin, and where the Trial of Air would take place.

For the first time they realised the spiritual Fate of Albion had been placed on the shoulders of a Merlin younger than any before him. Success depended on his mental and physical stability and his spiritual fitness to hold and use the Power of an Arch-Mage.

They were also made aware of the part they had to play in the days ahead. Once before they had stood together, fought a battle, and won. But now they faced the Powers of Darkness and must put their trust in someone only a few years into his second decade. Stan Simonite laid a gnarled hand on his shoulder. His emotions showing in the increase of his Derbyshire accent, "Whatever thee has to face lad, we'll be with thee, never fear. We'll be at yer back ready ter fight."

They gathered round him in a circle of love and trust that blazed with light on the Inner Levels. "It goes without saying Thomas, count on us." Nurse Pym kissed his cheek. The Atkinsons joined in. Drew nodded as one by one they let him know they would be with him in the coming battle. Then Drew drained his glass and careless of its worth smashed it into the fire. The others followed suit.

Only Posy playing with Jess by the fire was silent. If there was danger ahead for Thomas, it would touch them all in some way. That meant Jess would also be in danger. Maybe she needed to keep her family away from Thomas and cut ties with him. Whatever he was involved with must not touch her family. These thoughts, so unnatural to her, had haunted her for days and kept filling her thoughts with doubts about Thomas and the work before him. She needed to think about this as he allowed her to use the Manor gardens to grow her Herbs, and was also the landlord of her Village shop.

* * *

The week of the Finals found both Thomas and Charlie in a state of calm that irritated their fellow students and livened the conversation of the Faculty. They arrived early each day and took their places. When the starting Bell sounded they opened their papers and began to write. There was no muttering, no heavy sighs, no frantic chewing of finger nails, just a quiet, steady attention to the work before them.

Though they were in separate Halls, their studies quite different, the intense, totally focussed attention that both displayed in oral and written work drew the fascinated attention of their Tutors and the irritation of their fellow students. Also it did not go unnoticed that those who shared lodgings with them showed a similar lack of examination nerves. Charlie was in his element. His talks with Cormac and the freedom of Thomas' library had given him an insight into his papers far above his fellow students. His command of Latin and Middle English and his clarity of insight into the medieval mind drove his tutor into raptures of delight.

Oral or written it was the same. It was as if the answers, information, and details were in front of them. Essays, points of view, references pertaining to dates and events seemed to flow from the head to the hand and onto the paper. Charlie's essay on the first invasion of Britain by the Roman Army was passed from hand to hand and judged one of the best ever received. It was a foregone conclusion he would pass with ease.

At the end of each day instead of joining the usual pub crawl to celebrate or commiserate they both went back to the house to relax, and look up anything untoward that might show up in their papers the following day. Both knew they had done their best to prepare despite everything else going on in their lives. What happened now was in the lap of the Gods, or, whichever way the Examiners got out of bed.

Each day took all their mental and physical strength. For Thomas this was a blessing. It took his mind off what lay ahead and he slept deeply without dreaming. Cormac kept out of sight. But he kept close watch on their opponent. This had an unforeseen effect. A closeness between of the Sidhe and the Angelic, something that had not happened since the Earth was young and named Eden. Both worlds watched with interest and hoped it would continue. It was Cormac's hope that this might be one of Thomas' tasks as a Merlin, but it must wait until he had won his "magical spurs".

As each day dawned, silence hung over the ancient buildings. Young hopefuls strove to achieve their goals with every ounce of their abilities. Some would make it well, or scrape through. A few would lose their dreams and hopes and settle for less. A few would try again. But in the halls where Thomas and Charlie worked, an air of purpose prevailed. The calmness and sense of purpose surrounding them covered the whole room. Tutors had seen this in Thomas' work, but Charlie had also changed and displayed a confidence he'd lacked before. He approached his subject with a skill that had left them speechless.

His closeness to Thomas and Cormac opened unused areas both mental and spiritual. In his future lay the possibility of academic honours, and even a knighthood. But now he was just Charlie Naughton biting a pencil and trying to recall how to spell circumnavigate. When the week ended the entire university, students and Tutors alike heaved a sigh of relief. The town of Cambridge braced itself for the usual twenty four hours of celebration and inebriation.

Thomas and Charlie allowed themselves one party then slipped away knowing they would not be missed. Frank drove them home, both sleeping all the way. What lay ahead would demand all their courage and faith.

# Chapter Twenty-One

"**Getting there is** no problem this time of year. The holiday flats are empty and the Attractions closed. Problems begin once you ARE there. All the boats are battened down for the winter. It's going to be bloody cold out there Thomas, you'll need thermals and the kind of gear they wear to climb Everest." Charlie sorted through a pile of photos and papers on his desk.

Thomas grinned at him, "You sound like Betty. I have thermals, but I'll need the heavy duty kind for this jaunt. Plus climbing boots, gloves and a helmet. I've studied the way up, there's a map of the climb made by Nick Fowler. He was the first to climb to the top but Cormac said I don't need to do that. There's a space big enough for me to use about the 3rd or 4th point. Fowler marked out areas he called 'Points" where climbers can rest. One of those will do.

"I'll do a 'reccy' later to see which one to aim for. Cormac said it has to be small, to make the test a true one, but to be sure I had a firm backrest to lean against when the wind gets strong. But you'll be warm in the boat."

"I don't like it Thomas, what happens if things go wrong? What could I do. I can't just sit in the boat and watch you fall."

"You worry too much Charlie, I'm not going to fall..."

"What about this Gryffdd guy? He won't miss a chance like this to get at you."

"I have three periods of calm Paralda gave me and I can call on the powers of the other Merlins, plus I can use the Gull form, there's nothing to say I can't do that... I'll be OK, stop worrying, it makes me nervous."

"So it should."

There was silence for a while then Charlie asked... "Thomas, what's it like when you shift? Does it hurt or feel strange or does it just... happen." Thomas leant back in his chair and cast back in his memory.

"The first time it did hurt, but I was not expecting it. It was a totally new experience. But it happened so quickly it was over before I had time to react. It was hard to walk with four feet instead of two, but the antlers were worse, I kept forgetting they were there and got caught up in the branches that stuck out. It hurt when I changed back, but that was because I'd been running on four legs instead of two and I felt bruised all over. But by the time I'd done it two or three times it was just a sort of... flowing feeling… like diving into deep water. Odd, but not unpleasant. It's better if I strip off, but I can keep clothing if I need to but sometimes a bit gets left behind. I lose a lot of shoes that way, but thank God I've always managed to keep my pants."

Charlie grinned, "That would certainly make the front page. I can see it now. Multi-millionaire appears naked in Soho."

Thomas laughed. "I'd end up in jail. Now I'm going to buy the rest of my gear. It's just a week now. I've borrowed a boat with a cabin, and Drew's coming down to take charge of getting us there and back. He knows about boats, so you'll have company and there are bunks in the cabin."

"Yeah... like I'm going to snore my head off while you're out there facing God knows what. Forget it! At least there'll be two of us if there's trouble. When will you do the reccy?"

"Tomorrow about an hour before sunset, so I'll be able to judge the place in daylight and in darkness. Also, I need to judge how long I can keep a 'shift'. I've never kept one for longer than a few hours."

"What about clothing, will it come back when you shift again?"

"Still worrying about me keeping my pants on? Don't, I got some advice from the past Merlins. I'm off, I'll see you at the hotel." He went off whistling, But Charlie sat and worried some more.

The day of the Trial dawned wet and windy and Charlie was up at dawn looking at weather reports on his iPad while Thomas slept peacefully in the next bed. They'd spent the week looking at videos of The Needles climb. Thomas memorised it and was confident he could manage it. He also found a place he felt was suitable to stand on and that was as safe as could be hoped for.

He had climbed up to it three times. Each time Charlie and Drew watched with bated breath as he pulled himself from one handhold to another. Now the day of the trial had arrived and no one, least of all Thomas, had any idea of what to expect.

Cormac had been noticeable for his absence. Something Charlie was vocal about, but Thomas knew was deliberate, so as not to take his mind off the Trial. Every day he shifted to his Gull form and spent much of the day with the resident flock. He went to the fish market each day and bought a supply of small fish to spread on the rocks directly below where he would stand. He also took care to approach the Leader with a succulent gift each day. In Gull form he practised the calls, Food, Danger and Flock Summons, until he was reasonably sure they would answer.

Charlie was fascinated by the change and watched with amazement and more than a little envy. He had seen Drew and the Guardians shift into their "Stone" forms, but they had just the one. Thomas' ability to use any form he needed was above the norm it seemed. Now the waiting was over, and at this time tomorrow the trial would be behind them. Or, thought Charlie with a sinking heart, there was the other possibility. He went and woke Thomas with a gentle hand.

"Time to wake up Tom." He rarely used the shorter form of his name. That he used it now showed the depths of his concern. "It's 7:30. You'll need a good breakfast to start the day."

Thomas opened his eyes and stretched, "Morning Charlie, and yes, Today's the Day." Charlie went to answer a knock on the door and a maid wheeled in their breakfast.

"I ordered a full English for all of us, we'll need it. Drew will be in soon. I woke him early, as he wanted to get the boat ready. With luck we can get off by 9:30. It depends on the weather, reports say it will be wet and windy. So you'll have to take it slowly and make sure of each hold before you let go of the one you have."

Thomas headed for the shower, "You are sounding more like Betty every day. It's going to be alright Charlie. Merlyn would not have chosen me if he didn't think I could manage the Trials." He shut the door and the sound of the shower clashed with a full throated tenor belting out the latest top hit.

"Sounds like he's raring to go," said Drew closing the door behind him and heading for the breakfast table.

"He's not taking the risks seriously," argued Charlie pouring a large mug of coffee. "He thinks he's invulnerable, the silly sod!"

"Maybe he is," said Drew adding eggs to his plate.

188

"He wouldn't have been chosen if they didn't think he could do it."

"He said those very words to me just now," grumbled Charlie.

"Then believe him son, he's got a lot of people behind him, including 99 percent of the Sidhe nation. This time tomorrow I'll remind you of your worries. By the way," he added with a broad smile, "have you thought that this is just the FIRST Trial. There are three more to come."

Charlie stared at him wide-eyed. "Oh dear God, I'd forgotten that. You're right there's another three to come. I'll resign, I can't take another week like this."

"Yes you can Charlie, because you promised you'd be with me and Naughtons don't break their promises." Thomas sat down in his towelling robe and reached for the coffee. "Let's eat... I'm starving."

## 11.30 am

Charlie swallowed another anti-seasick pill and washed it down with water. "I swear I'll never get in another boat as long as I live. Why can't the damn thing stand still."

Drew put down his binoculars and looked at him with sympathy. "Because they're meant to move Charlie, move on water, and the water moves as well. The two moving parts don't always agree. Some people don't notice it, others like you find it difficult. If you were on a boat for several days your stomach would adjust to the movement and you'd be eating bacon and eggs again."

"Please don't, don't mention food, I shouldn't have had the egg and bacon. Not that they're with me anymore, in fact I think I've lost most of my innards!" He belched, turned white, and rushed to the side of the boat. Drew continued to watch Thomas as he slowly inched up the towering slope of the rock. A few weeks of practise on the climbing wall at the gym had not turned him into an expert.

Thomas paused to catch his breath and looked back at the boat below and saw Charlie dash for the side. He looked up and estimated how far he still had to go and felt a bit squeamish himself. Then, suddenly, he felt within himself a familiar presence. Startled, he tightened his grip on the rock. "Mordred, I'm a little busy right now..."

"Of that I'm well aware my brother in arms, that is why I am going to share my strength with you. As you have not yet begun the Trial, such help is permissible."

It began as warmth in his numbed hands and grew into a flow of heat and energy that began at his feet and rose to fill his whole body. Physical strength flowed into his shoulders, arms, and hands and he used it to haul himself up to the next hold, and the next, until he was well over halfway to his goal.

Then it suddenly left him. He felt Mordred collapse and called out to him, "Mordred, Mordred, you gave me too much, for the love of God are you alright..." Merlyn's voice spoke soothingly in his head, "Fear not Thomas, he gave all the strength he had at that moment. He sleeps and will heal in a few days."

"Merlyn, are you sure he'll be alright? It helped me so much and I'm now in sight of the Trial Stand. Another thirty minutes and I'll be there, then I can begin to prepare myself. Pass my thanks to Mordred. One day I may be able to repay him."

"You have already done that Thomas, when you brought father and son together. They can never thank you enough for that. Now be strong, be aware of your goal and remember."

He shook himself and came back to the reason for which he was here. He turned his attention away from the brilliant reds, golds and oranges, of the dying day... (did days die???)

8:30 brought the wind. Vicious chilling gusts that bit through his already soaked clothing and chilled him to the bone. At first it slammed him against the rock-face, then changed direction and caught him sideways threatening to blow him off into the sea below. He clung to the pitons he had hammered into the stone and gritted his teeth. This attack was using natural forces, so he dared not use his powers yet. There would be stronger attacks than this, and far more deadly, of that he was certain.

At 9:00 the wind dropped and the rain shrank to a drizzle. Things went quiet... too quiet. Thunder clouds built up along the coastline and at 9:40 it broke against The Needles with a fury that sent the townspeople scurrying for home. Drew, against his fear for Thomas, was forced to move the boat into shelter further inland.

"We can see the light from here," he told the frantic Charlie. "But the boat would be his only chance if we needed to get him away, or, God forbid, he fell into the water. We can't afford to lose it against the rocks."

Up on the rock face Thomas huddled against the storm folded in upon himself, trying to keep from being blown into the sea below. Lightning struck again and again terrifyingly close at times. His helmet was metal and metal attracted lightning. He unfastened it and flung it out over the sea. As it fell a bolt struck it full on and shattered. He breathed a silent prayer and pulled the hood of his jacket over his head... it was soaked, but it gave a modicum of protection.

The fury of the storm increased, the sheer noise of it adding pressure to the tightly strung nerves of the man flattened against the stone. It was time to call on some help. At 11:00 Thomas dug deep inside himself and summoned the first of his promised respites. He forced himself to stand erect against the wind and spread his arms out. With his head high he took a breath, and raised his arms above his head... and pronounced the Word of Power, Paralda had given him.

The wind dropped in strength in a gradual slide over ten very long minutes, then stopped altogether and Thomas slumped down breathing in short gulps of air, and wished desperately for something hot and sweet to drink. Leaning against the cold rock he asked himself if all this was worth it. But he knew the answer would be yes... The outcome was never to be about him, but about The Blessed Isles and those who lived and breathed in its four corners. Meanwhile he tried to ease his cramped muscles and prepare himself for the next bout.

It began with Voices. From the past, his grandmother pleading with him to give up and go home. When he didn't answer, it changed to repeating stories told to him as a child. When that had no effect it was Grim's bark he heard. It changed to yelps of pain as if the animal was being tortured. He found it hard to disregard, but did the best he could.

He heard Charlie's voice talking to Drew, telling lies about his conduct at university. Drinking, nights spent with prostitutes, and the lies he spread about his friends. He listened and dismissed them. Those who had known him since he was fourteen, would never listen to that.

At Midnight the sea below became rougher, it swelled up in wave after wave almost reaching where he stood. Shouts, screams, calls for help in Drew's voice battered his ears. He struggled to dismiss them but wept hearing his father's voice begging him to come home... that he was ill and needed him.

He sang songs in his head, repeated poems he knew by heart... shouted prayers into the wind carrying the false insidious accusations, threats, and lies. An image of little

Jess lying lifeless in her mother's arms, almost broke him. The power of air was so real... preying on his love for those around him, hoping he would give up and fail.

In desperation he used his second time of rest, and a deep quietness descended on him. The sea became calmer, the wind less vicious. The voices dropped, and became silent, then a few minutes later he heard them again, but this time they sang to him, soft crooning notes that soothed his mind and eased his spirit. The awesome presence of Paralda touched his body, mind, and soul with a breeze that carried the scent of spring flowers and an inner voice chanted a mantra...

'Om Tare Tu-Tare Tare Sohar'.

He repeated it to himself until he felt a lessening of the tension within.

At 2:30 am the sea came at him again, wave upon wave drenching him with ice cold water. An image of the boat below being dashed against the rocks made him retch with fear. The wind returned, this time peppered with hailstones that stung his face and hands. More voices, telling it was useless to continue, that his friends below were tired, cold and wet.

Then at 4:00 am the voices suggested he could give up now and the time already spent would be credited and he could finish the rest when he was stronger. That actually made him laugh for the first time. But he was tired and felt helpless, worthless, as if he had already been judged a failure. At that moment things changed. The third respite came of its own accord. Though it was not yet light and far too early for them to wake... the gulls rose in a flock of white wings and began to circle his tiny fortress. They called to him and in their voices he heard their recognition of his courage and his thoughtful provision of food.

When they tired they went back to roost, but a second

group arose and took up the task of keeping him awake and aware. From their calls he realised that this was a colony from further along the coast. Word had gone round that the soon to be Merlin had need of them.

The sky began to take on the promise of morning and Thomas made a discovery. He was, The Merlin not just for the people of The Blessed Isles, but of the land itself and the life it sustained. He reached out mentally and thanked the birds and blessed them. The sea, now calm and still, swelled up almost to his feet as if in homage, then dropped again. The wind, now gently blew on his wet clothes and they began to dry on his body. All this was his domain, his to love and cherish, to bless, defend, and honour. He stood and held out his hands and blessed the sea, turning he sent a blessing throughout the land.

He became aware of a tiny plant in the apartment of Ap Gryffdd, and its part in helping to protect him and re-cognise him as The Merlin. He reached out to it and healed its damage, then touched the mind of the butler who, waking early made a decision. He got up, packed his belongings and quietly left the apartment with the plant. Thomas filled his mind with the address of one of his hotels. There he would find work and a place to live with his plants.

Then he turned his attention to himself and dried his clothes as the first rays of the sun reached out from the east. He drew strength from the air around him and absorbed it, drinking it in like rare wine, and revelled in the strength and vitality it provided, then shared what he received with the gulls, blessed them and gave thanks.

The sound of an engine got his attention and he saw the boat below with Drew and Charlie waving. He waved back and shifted to Gull form to fly down to the deck. They hugged him, fed him, and warmed him, but did not ask about the Test. He would tell them in his own time. But both

194

recognised a change in him. A new strength and a new self-awareness. The Power of Air had tested him and he had not been found wanting...

As he guided the boat ashore Drew thought over the events of the night and drew his own conclusions. The last of the "boy" had gone. The "man" had taken his place.

# Chapter Twenty-Two

**From the Journal of Thomas Greystone-Carrick:**

**March 1st 11:15 am.**

**I thought I** would have more time between these darned trials. Instead Cormac turned up just four days ago to tell me the next one would be on the 21st of this month. I've hardly had time to draw breath, let alone think about how to cope with it. It's the Trial of Water and I just know it will be hard to deal with. There's this thing I have about being in tight places and unable to breathe. Just thinking about it makes me feel the walls are closing in on me.

Funny... as soon as I think about it I can see the faces of those three bastards and hear them laughing. I feel ashamed of the way I reacted then... I begged and pleaded and offered them my pocket money and fought as hard as I could. I remember the doors of the cupboard closing and hear the lock being turned. Then, when the police did come, I had wet myself out of sheer fright. My bike was all broken and dad couldn't afford another one. God, how I hated them... still do... I think. Cormac will come tomorrow and he will take me to where it will all happen.

**March 4th.**

3:00pm. Wow... that was some ride. Cormac took me from the Moor to... would you believe... Tintagel. I had been there before on a school trip but this time we explored Merlin's Cave. Then, just as we turned to go back to the beach, he... Nixsa... came up out of the water. There was no one around thank God! Mind you he was dressed in surfing gear and had a snorkel in his hand. He looked sort of normal, until you got closer... then you noticed or rather *felt* he was much more than who/how he was in his own Element. He said I would have help, but not until I really needed it. I had to rely on my own strength for as long as possible. Then he said a really weird thing... that "one day I would know his element much more deeply and in a different way".

**March 19th**

Charlie and I leave tomorrow for Tintagel, but I'm not looking forward to this. Charlie is in a right funk about it... so I have to pretend I'm OK with it. Can't have him going to pieces as well as me! I keep asking myself WHY ME... surely there's someone better at being a Merlin than me.

\* \* \*

**March 21st 3:35 pm. Tintagel**

"Oh my God," Charlie's awestruck whisper bounced off the dark damp walls surrounding them. "I've heard about it, and read about it, but never had the opportunity to actually be here. This is truly amazing." He turned in a circle trying to absorb the sheer magical power Merlin's Cave exuded. "But it's open at both ends, how does it fill up?"

Thomas turned from his examination of the roof. "The ceiling is quite low. At high tide the water fills it to the top and stays so for about six hours. That's how long I must survive. As the level rises there'll be pockets of air here and there as the roof shows some places deeper than others, I can use those to breathe for a while. But there'll be several hours when they'll be submerged. That's the hardest part of the test, the lack of air."

Charlie stared at him, for the first time realising what the Test involved. "Are you saying you'll be *without air* for HOURS! You didn't tell me that. When you said you'd be underwater I thought you'd have diving gear! Thomas, you don't intend to do this without anything to help you breathe do you... do you...? Thomas??"

Thomas probed a crack in the cave roof. "Charlie, that's the whole purpose of the tests. Each one holds a key to the power of the Element. The Trials must be endured on all levels, physical, astral, mental and spiritual. I have to attempt it or die trying."

Speechless, Charlie turned and walked out of the cave, away from the darkness and the threat of losing someone he regarded as the brother he'd always wanted but never had. Thomas followed him and laid a comforting hand on his shoulder.

"Charlie... you worried me through the last one so worry me through this one and we'll laugh about it afterwards. These trials have to be real or they don't achieve their purpose. In this case 'Power over the Element of Water'. Nixsa promised to help but didn't tell me how so I'll have to watch out for what it might be. I made it through the last trial, so there's more than a fair chance I'll make it through this one. Now lets get back to the hotel and see what's on the dinner menu."

Silently Charlie followed him up the winding path. At

the top he looked back at the dark opening of Merlin's Cave. Tomorrow Thomas would pit himself against a powerful Element in a bid to claim his right to be the Arch-Mage of Albion. A trial made more dangerous by the expected intervention of his enemy. With a sigh he headed for the hotel, dinner, and another sleepless night.

**March 22nd 4:15 am**

Thomas gave up trying to sleep. He thrust back the duvet and headed for the bathroom and the coffee machine in that order. He was tempted to add a splash of Scotch to the coffee, but decided against it. In a few hours he faced a life threatening situation and needed a clear head.

Slumped in the armchair he thought over the events since his Trial by Air. Somewhere in that Trial he'd been given a clue to the one he faced in a few hours time. Though he'd never admit it to Charlie, he had misgivings about this one but he had to go back over the last Trial and fathom out the clue he'd been given. He frowned at his choice of words. The synchronicity of the word fathom was too close.

He looked at his watch again, 4:45 am. He had to be in place by 6:30 pm when the incoming tide would have half filled the cave. That gave him time to prepare for the full tide at around 9:30 pm when the Trial would actually begin. Until now he'd kept his secret fear at bay, but with the moment almost upon him he had to face it. Mentally he travelled back to his school days where the memory and the fear were still buried deep.

There had been three of them, Dennis Haggard, Terry Williams, and Mick Fairclough. All were older and bigger and they wanted his bike. It had taken his father a year to save for it and it was his pride and joy. They beat him up, tore his shirt and ripped the pocket off his new blazer, then held him down, took his pants off and smeared him with dirt and dog faeces. Finally they locked him in a school cupboard, bent double and with little air coming in.

They took the bike, riding it in turns and finally dumped it broken and bent in a nearby garden. His frantic parents had spent hours looking for him. Finally the police thought to search the school. The constriction and lack of air had traumatised him for years. It was Father John who had gently and slowly taken him back through the experience bit by bit and shown him how to face the memory. He'd told no one, but when faced with the Trial of Water, it had reared its head again. It was this that kept him awake. The fear he would not be able to face similar conditions under water. Plus wondering what his opponent was planning. He wouldn't miss an opportunity to drown him. A tap on the communicating door roused him from his dark thoughts.

"Tom? are you up... your light is on."

"Yeah. Charlie, come on in. I've been going over things and trying to make some sort of plan. But my brain doesn't want to work." Charlie, red-eyed from lack of sleep, his hair on end from running his hands through it, edged through the door with a wad of paper, his iPad in his arms and still dressed.

"I've been doing some research," he announced, and gave an enormous yawn. His eyes lit up at the sound of the coffee machine bubbling. "Oh good, coffee, mine ran out a couple of hours ago." He dumped his burden, poured out a cup and loaded it with three heaped spoons of sugar. "I swear to God if I cut myself shaving I'll bleed pure coffee. To think I never drank the stuff until I met you. I've been looking at ways you can actually breathe underwater. It seems you can create bubbles of air and use them to stay under longer. It's part of training for a diving certificate and Pearl Divers use a similar trick. It looks pretty weird, but apparently it works.

I printed it off for you to read. It's better than nothing." He stood up and fixed Thomas with a pointed stare.

"No heroics Tom... understood? If it comes to a choice you get out quick. Keep close to the mouth of the cave. Before you go in I'll put an air tank and mouthpiece close to the area and if you get into trouble... promise me, promise me Thomas, that you'll use it. Maybe we could rig up some sort of alarm signal. Oh God... I should have thought of that."

"Charlie, stop... I really appreciate what you are doing... and have done, but I'll be OK... honest. I trust Nixsa. I'll have help down there. But I have to keep to the rules if I am to win through. All I need you to do is to be there with a thermos of coffee, dry clothes, a blanket and something alcoholic in a bottle. I'll need it. As soon as the cave mouth is open the test will be over. Then I'll have a hot bath and get some sleep. I don't plan to lose out on this test. But to keep you from worrying I'll read this stuff you've printed off and if I need it... I'll use it. I promise. Now get some sleep while I read these papers."

He bustled him through the door and closed it after him, then leaned against it. For the first time he allowed himself to wonder if he would make it through. Then he shrugged... too late to back out now... nor would he. He picked up the papers and began to read. They were surprisingly informative and offered advice it would be stupid to ignore. He drank the last of the coffee and, his former fatigue forgotten, settled down to read.

* * *

The day passed slowly as the Sun dipped towards the horizon, but over the ruins of Tintagel castle The Spirit of Albion waited with eternal patience. To human eyes it was just a build-up of evening mist, but its true composition was made from centuries of deeds of courage, of blood shed with no thought of self, and a deep rooted love of The Land. The energy of every deed, every life offered, every tear shed, every wound sustained finds its place in The Heart of Albion. Today was no exception. It had no idea of the outcome, it simply waited to gather into itself the energy of the offering soon to take place.

As the light grew stronger, Paralda riding on the last of the March winds, came to rest beside Nixsa. The Elemental Lords of Air and Water waited silently for the outcome of the Trial, with thoughts passing between them.

*"There is great fear in him, yet he shows it not."*

*"It is always so, but these human forms are truly remarkable."*

*"Will you aid him?"*

*"If the need is there and willingness is shown, my people are ready."*

*"The one who stands with him is of the same mind. Time and again they have stood together. And always will."*

*"It is part of what makes them important to The Creator."*

\* \* \*

### 6:00 pm

The last of the tourists had gone, only the two men stacking diving gear were left. The wind dropped but held the promise of rain. Charlie had placed an air tank and mouthpiece inside the cave where it could be found easily if needed, plus an underwater torch. He spoke quietly, "I'll be up in the ledge over there Tom, I've got dry clothes, a blanket, towel, coffee, and brandy." He didn't mention the mobile with the Lifeboat's number ready to hand, or the second tank and mouthpiece in case he had to go in himself. He was not a strong swimmer but he felt happier knowing he was prepared.

The tide surged more strongly, the wind was colder and Thomas shivered. He'd finally agreed a wet suit was not cheating and gave a modicum of protection, but he began the Tibetan breathing technique that would boost his internal heating system. The Cave was filling quickly, it was time. He turned to Charlie and smiled, clapped a hand to his shoulder and dived in before anything more could be said and headed for the entrance of the cave with a fast crawl. Charlie looked away, not wanting to see him go and cursed the wind that made his eyes water. He climbed up the rock face and huddled into the wind break. He had promised himself he would not panic (like… yeah!) and tried to get interested in a lecture on Roman Warfare recorded on his mobile.

## 7:30 pm

Thomas had signalled twice… he was still there, but the cave was now fully underwater and Thomas would be moving from one tiny breathing space to another. It was time to worry. Charlie sat huddled in his blanket and held an internal conversation with himself.

Q? Why had he let Thomas take on this test?

A. Because he couldn't stop him!

Q? Should he have locked him in his room and told "them" to get stuffed?

A. No, It was something Thomas, had to do.

Q? Would he make it through the test?

A. He'd better or he would find a way to make **"them"** rue it.

He picked up a pebble and threw it with all his bottled fury into the tide that filled the cave below. A tide that could,

203

maybe already had... kill his friend. The first real friend he had ever had, at least in this life. Each day had deepened the bonds of trust between them.

He dropped his head into his hands. Who was he kidding? He had no hope in hell of preventing what was happening down there, in the cold darkness, to someone he cared about. What use could he be? Nothing, he could do nothing but wait. He reached for the thermos, then drew back. No, Thomas would need all of it to combat the cold when he came out of the cave, that and the dry clothes, the blanket, the scotch... and the...

"... and the love, the tenderness, the caring... the support you have always offered him. The knowledge that you believed in him, and his destiny." Charlie jumped as Cormac appeared and sat down beside him, "Cormac, What are you doing here?"

The Sidhe laid a gentle hand on his shoulder. "The same as you my friend, worrying about Thomas. The difference is, I know what he is capable of enduring, and achieving. But I also came for your sake. I am aware of your love for him, it is something we share."

Charlie nodded. "I've learned a lot since he and I met. I've also learned from you Cormac. You've helped me to understand, to grow, to know, see, and feel things on different levels. For that I thank you and revere you as a friend and teacher."

"You honour me Charles, more than you know, for it is long since the Sidhe have been seen as teachers. It is not just Thomas who takes these trials. You think you have no power... but you do and in the coming time you have a part to play, as will the Guardians. The Stones will soon need to sing again. The effect of these Trials is far reaching and there are battles yet to be fought."

They sat silently for a while then Charlie asked quietly, "How far has he got?" "The last cache of air ran out a while ago. Now he is relying on his own, as yet, untapped power and courage, and the promised help of Nixsa." Charlie turned to face Cormac, "Albion can't do without him, but that bastard Gryffdd will use this time to strike, I know it."

Cormac produced a silver flask and unscrewed the top and handed it over with a sly grin. "It is time to introduce you to the wine of Tyr nan Og, but sip it slowly and take very little for it is powerful." Charlie looked at it doubtfully.

"Is this the stuff you gave to Thomas? He said it could knock out a Komodo Dragon, and I don't do too well with spirits." He took a cautious sip and swallowed. The effect was immediate. His eyes bulged, his skin flushed bright pink and his hands flapped as he tried, unsuccessfully, to remain standing, and even to breathe. He made an unsuccessful attempt to speak.

Cormac sniggered and took back the flask, taking a mouthful of it himself. "This holds the secret of immortality and eternal youth," he said, smacking his lips. "And it certainly seems to work. Don't worry Charles... you will live." Charlie slowly heaved himself into a sitting position and held his head in his hands. "Thank God they don't serve that in this world. You can keep the immortality and eternal youth. I'll settle for growing old and dying... just so I never have to touch that demon brew again. What the hell is in that stuff?"

Cormac took another swig. "A mixture of rare herbs, water from a spring far below a mountain called K2. Water that has never reached the surface. Then there is powdered seed from the original Apple tree, which by the way still lives and produces apples, and the final ingredient is the rarest of all, three drops of Dragon Sperm."

Charlie sprang to his feet, his face ashen white, his voice as high pitched as a bat call. "Dragon's WHAT... you mean I've drunk... That had... it was full of... oh God, I need to be sick... I mean what will it do... can it... oh God... I'm dead... Cormac... you faery bastard... what have you done?"

Cormac was all but rolling on the ground holding his sides with laughter... "Oh Charles, Charles, did you think I'd poison you? It is the name of a herb, a very rare herb which is why it is called Dragon Sperm, because Dragons mate only once every five hundred years. But it gives warmth and extra energy. I thought to halt your worries about Thomas for a while and succeeded. Have faith in him *Fae Friend*. He will win through." He got to his feet and enveloped Charlie in an embrace.

Charlie stopped in his tracks and stared at Cormac. Had he heard right. Had he just been named Fae Friend. A title that meant he could call on the Sidhe for aid, that they would know and trust him, and give him entrance to Tyr nan Og. He dropped on one knee and bowed his head.

"Son of Midir, grandson of Aengus Og, thank you for this gift. You have my word of honour it will never be misused." Cormac took on his true Princely form and the landscape around them wore its ancient shape. Tintagel Castle rose on the hill top and for one eternal moment Charles Naughton was clad in armour and wore the Deep Blue mantle of the Table Round.

**10:40 pm**

Far below in the numbing cold of Merlin's Cave Thomas struggled to hold on to the last breath of air. Creating the air bubbles had been exhausting, and the wet suit was losing its ability to keep out the cold. He had sought out and used the small air pockets in the roof and was beginning to feel the first ripples of panic. Frantically he mentally reached out to Nixsa, but got the calm voice of Paralda in his ear.

*"The Cave is old and there are cracks through which air can be drawn down. Above you, there is one such point. Place your mouth over it and command the air from above to flow down to you, three times you can do this."*

Obediently Thomas reached up a hand and felt for the tiny crack. There was a definite flow of air. He fastened his mouth to it and drew in a lungful of cold sweet air. He held it as long as he could, then used it a second time and a third. Then felt a touch on his leg, a Seal gently nudged him with its nose, then placed its mouth over his and blew cool air into his lungs. Then it returned to the surface, and seconds later brought him another mouthful of air. The third time it had a human head, a girl with long hair streaming behind her. She sent him an image and his heart leapt. She was a Selkie.

He tried to shift but he was weak from lack of air and his ability to hold images was weak. The Selkie disappeared again as he sank down, the last of the air leaving his lungs. He thought of his father and reached for his presence, as the Selkie re-appeared. But now she was fully human in form. She took his head in her hands and her mouth on his offered the kiss of life... Air... but the battle was not yet over. As he sank down into the cave he found himself trapped in a box with no way out. *Gryffdd was making his attack.* He was back in the school cupboard... no way out, no air. Hanging in the water before him he saw a vision of his three tormentors, laughing at his fear and pain. The old panic rose up, he was choking, no air, only water, no way out... Again the Selkie came with the gift of air on her lips.

With a last effort he kissed her back and they rose through the dark water. The Selkie's thoughts touched his,

*"Till we meet again…"* He formed the seal image in his receding consciousness and felt the wrench as the shift to a Seal took place. His companion pushed him to the surface. There he took in the air he needed and plunged again into the cave. The water was warmer now. All he had to do was relax into the form, no need to fight. Like the first life forms that emerged from the ancient sea and learned to breathe air, he was going back into the past, becoming what life had been before. Water and Air. He was in school, listening to the teacher.

*"The human form is 80 percent water. Early life learned to amalgamate the two elements and evolve into a form that needs and uses both air and water."*

That early form was still in his genes, he could go back. He could become Air… he held that Power. He could become Water, it was his to claim. THAT was what having the POWER of the Elements meant. It meant knowing, understanding, feeling and using them as they really were, a part of himself. He did not FEAR himself… so how could he fear what was a part of him. HE WAS WATER, it was part of him, to command, use, and wield. All four of the elements were part of him, and he would soon know know how to claim and use them all.

Cormac and Charlie turned as they heard the scream of rage, fear, and despair fill the air. The twisted form of Ap Gryffdd erupted from the water and fled into the vanishing dark clouds. Then came another sound. A column of water rose into the air and from it emerged another form that slowly took on the form of Thomas. He raised his arm and his voice echoed across the now receding tide.

*"I hold the Power of Air, I hold the Power of Water. They are mine to use and to wield in the Service of Albion."*

The first ray of sun clothed him with light, and those who watched in awe knelt and bowed their heads.

A few minutes later they dragged his unconscious body from the water and set about bringing him round The bloody fool never does anything by halves," complained Charlie, as they wrapped him in a blanket and poured Cormac's brew down his throat.

## From The Journal of Thomas Greystone-Carrick:

### March 31st

Posy came today with new seedlings to plant in the herb garden. It's been some time since her last visit, which is surprising as she usually comes at least once a week. She says she draws strength from working with the earth. I went out to help her, and at first she said she didn't need any... then she called me back and said she needed to talk. She then she threw down the trowel and faced me. It seems she was really frightened by the attack on the Carrick Arms by the Dark Side. Posy is very aware of the hidden side of things, it's what makes her so good at her work. Her fear is that Jessica was the one threatened by the attack and she is thinking of moving away from Deepdale. This would mean losing Drew as well.

I know, through talking to Cormac, what the attack was about and Posy is right. "They" needed Jessica for something... but, they were faced by Forces they couldn't deal with. First, the fact that Excalibur rested for a day and night in the Carrick Arms, and, far more important, Jessica had been held, actually held, touched and blessed by the Four Greatest Angelic Forces of the spiritual world. She can never be harmed by the Dark Forces. Posy herself saw that happen, she was there. She saw her daughter held in the arms of a Power that had once held the Babe of Bethlehem. Hell itself cannot harm Jessica. I shared what I know with Posy and she finally understood and cried in my arms; then she went to sit in the chapel for a time to allow the peace there to fill her up. The Dark Side will always try to hit the weakest, but they'll have to go through me first... correction... through me, Charlie, and Four Archangels.

## April 9th

Cormac was waiting for me on the Tor, sitting at his ease in the chair of dreams.. There was no preamble and he seemed unusually nervous (a Fae nervous?) "The First of May," he said and handed me a map. "This is where you must be, it's a small town in Wales. Llyddstep Cliffs is the name. The trial will take place in a sea cave, difficult to find. Djinn will meet with you before you get there and instruct you how to find the place. It is deep underground." He paused... "I thought they would give you more time... but your opponent has made a pact with the Dark Lords... so it was decided to bring it closer. The Dark Ones are moving quickly.

"Take note of what Djinn says; you will be facing something very old and not seen for many thousands of years. Djinn can be mischievous to deal with, I often think he is a son of Hermes! Also he is fond of using different forms, so make sure it is him. May 1st is an ancient celebration when fires were lit on high hills and sacrifices were offered. So take care." Then he was gone.

I went back to the Manor to look up ancient Fire Festivals!

# Chapter Twenty-Three

## THE TRIAL OF FIRE

**Thomas peered through** the window of the camper to make out the name on the signpost: Llyddstep Cliffs. Wales was a beautiful country, but deciphering its language was something else. But this was where he needed to be according to instructions. He drove into the main street of the little town and looked for a space to park the Camper he'd hired for the trip. It was less hassle than explaining why he would not be sleeping in a room for which he was paying.

During the drive down he had fallen in love with the beauty of the land and its music. In turn it welcomed and acknowledged him. In the Llanberis Pass he'd paused to admire the view, when an elderly shepherd driving a flock of sheep had stopped and stared at him. He then approached and, taking off his battered hat, he bowed.

*"Mae'r Tir yn eich croesawu chi Guardian, a oes angen lle arnoch i orffwys y noson hon?"* ("The Land welcomes you Merlin, do you need food and a place to rest this night?")

Instantly Rhys ap Hoel was with him, offering a knowledge of his native tongue. To Thomas' amazement the language he needed was in his mind and on his tongue. *"Bendith arnoch chi a'ch un chi, ond na ffrind, rydw i ar genhadaeth ac mae'n rhaid i mi fynd ymlaen."* ("A blessing on you and yours friend, but no, I am on a mission and must go on.")

The old man knelt before him and asked for a blessing. *"Maen hir ers ichi gerdded daear Cwmri Myrddin. Mae hwn yn ddiwrnod da."* ("It is long since you walked the earth of Wales Merlin, this is a good day.") Thomas laid a hand on his grey head and felt the power flow into him. *"Bendith ar eich gorffwys y noson hon."* ("A blessing on your rest this night.").The Shepherd rose and bowed and without looking back, walked on with his sheep, and Thomas drove on through the April afternoon to Llyddstep Cliffs on the coast.

It was late afternoon when he found a parking space in the small town. It was Charlie's idea to drive down a day before the Trial to rest, get his bearings and search for the Cave. In Deepdale, the Guardians were standing by if he needed help. But with two Trials behind him Thomas felt able to face the Trial of Fire with confidence.

It felt strange not to have Charlie with him, sharing the driving and the comradeship that grew deeper day by day. Since the Trial of Water he was less inclined to worry and had decided to take a year out before returning to Cambridge for a Master's Degree, his excuse being to get Thomas through his trials. After a long argument he also accepted the offer of a retainer but grumbled it was too much. Right now his father was undergoing surgery on his knees that, hopefully, would enable him to walk without pain. His mother was nervous about being alone in London, so Thomas pulled rank and ordered him to stay with his mother in one of the King Stag Hotels close to the hospital.

Ap Gryffdd remained a threat, but nothing had been heard from or about him, which in itself was worrying. All they knew about the Trial of Fire was the need to find a particular cave in this area. One deeply hidden and known simply as Ogof Dubh (The Black Cave). He was to spend the night there to claim the power and obtain the blessing of the present holder for his own use. He had not been told the nature of the Holder, only that it would test his deepest emotions.

He'd searched the first two Trials for a clue but found nothing to help or explain. Nor had a brief meeting with The Lord of the Element been helpful. Djinn had met him in a car park, casually leaning against a Mercedes Benz, wearing a superbly tailored Tuxedo and smoking a cigar. With a wicked grin the Elemental King told him that something vital would be made available to him, and that the greatest gift is bought with Sorrow. These comments gave little idea of what lay before him. He then gave him a set of instructions to be followed exactly. Then he stubbed out the cigar and simply vanished.

He ate dinner at a small café but left half the meal, too restless to enjoy it. Instead he walked out to the headland and looked out to sea wondering why this ordinary place, could hold the Power of Fire. A workman wearily making his way home passed him on the narrow coastal path and stopped to exchange a friendly, "Nos Da." ("Good night.") The man offered a cigarette, but Thomas politely refused. The man lit his own and before leaving warned Thomas of the dangerous condition of the path, then went on his way. Left to himself Thomas recalled his instructions from Djinn, Lord of Fire.

*"Tomorrow at this time bring a torch and follow the path until it begins to slope downward, and then turn towards the sea. Fifty steps will bring you to a place with a seat looking over the bay. Step to the edge and look over. Below are remains of a path once used by smugglers. Now overgrown and barely visible, it is still strong enough to take your weight. Lower yourself over the edge and seek out the old path. Here and there you will find metal rods hammered into the rock but they are old so do not trust your full weight to them.*

"*Keep going down but carefully, for the cliff face is covered with plant growth too weak to offer a hold. Follow the shape of the cliff with your hand until you come to a small, narrow entrance that to the eye seems like a fold in the cliff face. This is the way you must follow. It leads into the cliff itself and descends steeply for quite a way. Soon you will hear the sound of the sea, but keep on until you come to a much larger space with three tunnels leading from it. Two are fairly large; the furthest one is small and narrow.*

"*The first leads to a cave where you will find many ancient artefacts of great value, but do not touch them. The second opening leads to another cave much deeper into the cliff. This is filled with human remains so respect their rest and leave them. Before you enter the third tunnel, leave your torch behind. You will not want to do this for the way is dark. But trust is required of you from this time on. Feel with your hands and trust with your heart. To hold the power of fire needs courage, prove your worthiness to me.*

"*The way before you leads down steeply at first, but you can hear the sea through fissures in the rock. Now the way will turn inward and take you into the very heart of the earth, but the air is sweet and cool and flows direct from the sea. The whole area is filled with caves, passages and hidden paths, many have lost their way here and their remains lie hidden. But remember you are on Trial and trust in me. Now repeat my instructions*"

It took several tries, but finally Thomas repeated it word for word. The Lord of Fire had some last advice. "*Remember the reason for these Trials and hold true to it. Until we meet again, rest well this night.*" Then Thomas was alone. Night had closed in and the town lights were his only guide as he made his way back. On the way his foot struck something on the path. He stooped and picked up a lighter the workman had dropped when he lit his cigarette. He put it in his pocket planning to leave it at the Police station.

He slept well and rose the next morning feeling ready to face the day. After breakfast he called Charlie and was relieved to know Jim Naughton's surgery had been very successful. Filming on his father's new book was due to begin in a month's time, and Grim was courting a flirty little terrier in the village. Things were in hand in Deepdale so he could rest easy.

He spent the day exploring the town. In an antique shop, bordering on the disreputable, he found a carving of a dragon curled around a china egg. As an example of local handicraft it was not good, the dragon had lost a bit of its tail, and one eye was missing, plus the egg was cracked, but it *"called"* to him so he bought it for a few pounds. At a local gift shop he looked for a print of the bay as a reminder, but nothing appealed to him. However, he recalled seeing a print in the antique shop and retraced his steps, but though he searched for an hour he couldn't find the shop again, so he returned to the Camper to rest knowing he'd be awake all night.

As evening approached he put on a pair of worn jeans and an old but warm sweater over a cotton shirt. He added woollen socks and comfortable hiking boots that had seen a lot of wear. He filled the pockets of his denim jacket with leather gloves, a torch with an extra battery, the Swiss Army knife he always carried in situations like this, and a pocket sized first aid kit. He added a folded plastic mac. Djinn had spoken of damp tunnels so it might be useful.

He recalled something about human remains and instructions to leave them in situ. With that in mind he added a bottle of Chalice Well water. Finally he added a length of rope that he slung over his shoulder. Lastly he checked he had the vial of Sidhe wine Cormac had given him. He called Charlie to tell him where to find the Camper if things went wrong. Then left the parking lot to find the smugglers trail before the light grew too dim. He made his way to the coastal path with a sense of purpose he had not felt with either of the first two Trials. Perhaps he felt closer to Merlyn here in Wales but he felt almost happy as he walked.

It took a while to find the old path, and some careful judgement to swing himself over the edge without falling the rest of the way. But once he found the first foot places it was fairly easy to follow though it twisted and turned and went back on itself time and again. Those who had made the path centuries before had hidden it well. Slowly and carefully he made his way downward until, just as Djinn had promised, he found the fold in the cliff face. Using the torch he saw that it hid a dark narrow entrance leading deeper into the cliff. He took a deep breath and squeezed in.

Some forty minutes later drenched with sweat and covered in dust and dirt he was facing the three entrances. He rested for a while still battling with his fear of tight places and a lack of fresh air. Then using the torch he entered the first tunnel and found the cave in a few minutes. It was an antique dealer's dream come true, filled with swords, helmets, shields and bits and pieces of armour, jewellery and personal ornaments. His time with Charlie had not been in vain and he knew he was looking at weaponry salvaged from the wrecks of the storm battered Armada. Its value was beyond price, but he had been told to leave everything as it was. Charlie would have had a field day.

The second cave was sombre for it held the remains of those who may have worn that armour. Though they had come to conquer, they had shown courage, so he bowed his head in honour of their sacrifice and blessed their bones in memory of their last hours and turned to go. Then stopped. He took his Swiss Army knife from his pocket and placed it in the bony hand of one of the fallen warriors as his tribute to the fallen.

The third and last tunnel made him pause. He remembered the Trial of Water and his fear of tight places and lack of air. He straitened his shoulders... he'd gotten through that trial... he'd get through this one. Giving up the torch was the hardest thing to do, feeling the darkness close around him and knowing that it would get tighter.

It got worse. The tunnel became narrower and the ceiling lower. He went to his hands and knees, and then to his stomach and finally had to inch his way forward, trusting as he had never trusted before, that this was the way he had to go. He paused, fighting back a wave of fear that he would be stuck here, one of the lost forgotten ones who had never been found. What aspect of Fire could be down here, so deep, without air, or light? Could it be a ruse of Ap Gryffdd to win the Battle as Arch-Mage? He fought down his doubts, and reached out for the next handhold and dragged himself forward another few feet.

A faint glow appeared ahead and he sensed an opening. The air was fresher and smelt of the sea. A final burst of strength and he broke through into a much larger space. Another push and he was able to stand upright, but with a sick feeling in his stomach that he had to return the same way... if he could find the outlet again without a torch, and, if there was more than one outlet... it would be guesswork to find the right one.

But for the moment there was space to stand, air to breathe, and the sound of the sea around him. With luck he might find a way out that way. A scratching sound made him turn round. In the farthest corner of what he now saw was an enormous cave, a reddish glow appeared. It moved, slithered, and slowly narrowed the space between them. He was not alone!

A massive head covered with red/gold scales bent down to him, and an eye fully three feet across blinked slowly.

Thomas stood rooted to the spot. In the past ten years he had met, spoken to, and shared experiences with life forms of many kinds, but this took his breath away. He had seen the Sidhe in their true forms, he was on drinking terms with Leprechauns, Centaurs, Gnomes and Shifters. He'd shared a fish dinner with a Seagull, swum with Selkies and kissed a mermaid on her salty lips. He had spoken with Elemental Lords, and been touched by arch-angels. But this was something he had never given more than passing thought to. This was Legend... alive and real.

He cleared his throat, took a deep breath and made an attempt to speak... "You... You're a... I mean... I think you're a... but there aren't any... I mean... there... isn't any... weren't ever any..." He paused took a breath and tried again... "Are you really a..."

The huge jaws opened, baring a triple set of very white, shiny teeth... "A Dragon...? Yes. I am indeed, I am also the last of my kind, and you, Thomas of Carrick... are here to kill me." The voice in his head was warm, melodious, and very feminine.

Thomas froze, whatever this was, it was nothing that belonged in this time. It was big beyond imagining and covered in scales that gleamed red gold. Each scale fitted over the one before it so that it appeared to be clothed in delicate armour of a kind that had not known the skies of Earth for over 10,000 years. Something that had not breathed its native atmosphere for fifty times that long, not since its own star had died in the gaping mouth of a black hole.

Thomas sank to his knees in awe at the sheer impossibility of what he was seeing. "Dear God in Heaven, you ARE a Dragon, you're Real, you're... Beautiful. How have you not been discovered until now?" The massive head bent close and the sweetness of its breath filled his lungs. A tendril of thought reached out, sought, found, touched and gently, filled his mind with words.

"Your 'Calling' is Thomas? My 'Calling' is (a series of musical notes filled his head) in your vocalising it would mean something close to *A memory of Love*'."

"I can't pronounce that… but would it be alright to call you Bella? It means beautiful in my language."

"I can see from your mental pattern that 'Bella' is a Calling I would be pleased to accept. Are you not afraid of me 'Thomas Calling'?"

"Well, I suppose I should be, you're enormous and those claws look sharp. In legend Dragons are supposed to breathe fire, and hate human beings, but I don't sense that in you. You *could* be dangerous… but no, I'm not afraid of you. Did you say I was here to kill you? Why would I do that? Why would anyone want to kill something so beautiful, so magical, so… so awesome?"

"Djinn told me you would not be afraid and I am happy you like me. I am not here to harm you Thomas Calling, you are here to set me free and in doing so you will receive my Gift of Fire. We have much to talk about and every moment must be used to its fullest. Come I have a place of resting that will be more comfortable for us both."

Bella backed away and turned, her movements graceful and fluid as she led the way deeper into the cave. The radiance of her internal fire was dim, but it was enough to show him an area that was her "Nest". Leaves, dried seaweed and grasses were piled high and a small waterfall flowed from a fissure high up in the roof.

Watching her arrange her coils Thomas estimated her length to be some 50 feet and her height from head to claw maybe 35. He also saw she had lost part of her tail, and one eye had been damaged its lid drooping over the retina. He realised the carving he had bought in the antique shop had been a representation of Bella. For a fleeting instant he felt the mind touch of the Lord of Fire who was obviously watching…

*"I wanted you to be able to recognise Her."*

Thomas shivered in the chill of the Sea Cave and tried to pull his jacket closer. But his crawl through the tunnel had shredded it. Bella bent her head and with her forked tongue gently laved his face and hands, cleansing them of dirt and dust. Her musical voice filled his head. "Come close Thomas Calling, rest in the circle of my coils, the fire in me will keep you warm while we talk. There is much to tell you and the night lies before us."

Eagerly Thomas climbed over her coils until he could rest against her body. As her warmth filled his chilled bones he remembered lying in his mother's arms when he was ill. It was years since he'd thought of her in gentle terms and felt her grief at his present coldness towards her. Bella filled his head with images stored in his memory giving him time to adjust to the intimacy telepathy invoked.

For a while there was silence as both adjusted to the differences in their mental powers. Then Thomas asked, "If you are the last Dragon, how did the former Merlins pass their Fire Test?"

"Every Merlin is different in their strengths and weaknesses so their hardest trials are adapted to put pressure on the weakest point. Yours was Water. But you are different Thomas Calling. You are the only Merlin to be given the one sword that can free me."

"Bella, tell me about your kind and why you are no longer seen. Where did you come from and why I am supposed to kill you?"

Her coils gently increased their pressure. "I will explain it all, but first tell me do you have anything that can give a flame? I long to see and taste fire not of my own making. It has been many of your timings. Once there were others of your kind who came and they made fire that tasted so sweet. They were friendly and unafraid. But then they no longer came, your kind have such short lives." She sounded wistful.

Thomas remembered picking up the fallen lighter. He reached into his pocket and brought it out, and struck it. Bella's whole form lit up with happiness, she was as she had been when young. Thomas was the first human being in thousands of years to see a Dragon in Glory.

Bella sang her joy, music poured out of her and filled the cavern with song. Thomas was entranced, as he listened he gathered together some of the bedding and pieces of wood from ancient wrecks and built a small fire. Bella wept as she sang, for so long she had had only her own internal fire to keep her alive. Then, her song ended, and she drew Thomas close to her again and began to tell him of her own kind. The Naghareem, the Keepers of Wisdom.

As she talked she built images of her home world in his head. A world of volcanic landscapes, high mountains and deep gorges. But life evolved in the fiery heart centre of the planet. The Naghareem were telepathic and developed language via musical notation. Their throats evolved into something like musical instruments. The Males ranging from the deep bassoon, to the lighter trumpet, while the females were more like the woodwinds and stringed instruments of humans. Music was their religion. With it they communicated with each other and with their Creator — *The Eternal Flame*. Bella explained:

"As we were gifted with long lifetimes, we explored the planets close to ours. Through such contacts we became aware of the variety of life forms and shared their information, ideas, and music. Then came disaster. The galaxy was engulfed by a Black Hole. Of the many life forms of that galaxy only the Naghareem survived, but few in number."

Bella was silent for a while then resumed her story.

"As Beings of pure Energy we were impervious to the cold of space so we looked for a new home. After centuries of searching we found Earth. A place with volcanoes for us to nest in. But Life had already staked a claim. A life different to ours, and who looked on us as Gods.

"We shared our knowledge with them. Showed them how to shape the planet to their needs and there was trust between us. We discovered humans had the gift of speech. They did not use it mentally, but made pleasant sounds with their mouths and breath. So we, the Nagas, as the humans called us taught them to sing, and to make music.

"In the beginning there was a sharing of skills, know-ledge, and artistry. But soon the closeness died, clouded by jealousy of things humans could never have. *Flight, and the length of life, the knowledge and memory of a million years of learning.* Closeness turned to envy, envy to fear, fear to hatred.

"But, though seemingly immortal Nagas can die if they so wish. The Supreme Gift of the Eternal Flame is to become one with IT. To that end we are born with one scale in contact with the Inner Fire Centre. If that is pierced, the Inner Fire reduces the Naga to ash and frees it to be one with the Eternal Flame.

"Humanity learned of the Death-scale and built a wall of fear and distrust. Lies were told of our intent to kill humans, that we ate human flesh and wanted Earth for our-selves. They used our love of gold to tell of caves filled with it, all stolen from Humans. Slowly the fear grew. We were driven from our Volcanic Nests, left without access to the fires that fed us. One by one we were killed. We hid where we could. There were a few, who trusted us, and to them we passed the last of our knowledge. They were the Priests, the Merlins of the Drowned Land, of which you will soon be one. It is time Thomas Calling. The dawn is close, soon I will give you my gift of Fire with a blessing. This is the scale." She touched her breast with a clawed foot. There, shielding the pulsing heart and as large as a man's hand was a single scale made of pure gold.

"Remember I go of my own free will. Keep the scale to remind you of me. When I lift the scale you must thrust the sword with all your strength straight and true. Then, pull the sword out and you will find on its tip a single drop of Dragon's blood. This you must drink and quickly for if you hesitate it will be lost and you will lose my Gift. It will burn as you swallow it but keep your lips closed tightly. It will find a place to rest within you."

"What about you Bella?"

"My form will become ash, but the Essence of my Fire will return to The Eternal Flame. I will be with my own kind once more. When our work has been assessed we will be given a new form and a new task. But all we have been, all we have learned, all we have done will be contained in the blood you have ingested. It will be available to you as and when it is needed. You Thomas Calling will be the Keeper of Fire."

A scream of defiance and hatred lanced through the cave and a figure in diving gear emerged from the shadows.

"NO. NO, it will NOT be so. I will kill the Naga and take her Power. I will become The Merlin and the Dragon hoards will be mine." Ap Gryffdd cast off his diving mask and brandished a sword stolen from the Death Chamber. He was beside himself with rage and the fear of losing for the third time. The long and demanding swim through the sea cave had drained even his enhanced Sidhe strength. He had been so sure he would reach the Naga before Thomas but had been distracted by the treasure of the hidden chambers. His greed had delayed him.

He grabbed Thomas and held the edge to his throat. "You will watch me become the Keeper of the Sacred Flame.

The most powerful of all the Merlins. It will be the last thing you see... you will die knowing I have won." His laughter rang through the Sea cave and it held the touch of madness within it. "With Her power I can defy even The Dark Ones. The Eternal Flame is the Shaper of Life. It IS the Universal Creator and I will wield its power." The Naga rose to her full height and with one swipe of her claw sent him sprawling.

"His mind has gone, he looked upon the faces of The Dark Ones and his reason died within him. Time is short Thomas Calling, already the first rays of the sun come towards us, do not delay. STRIKE, Now!"

Thomas lurched to his feet, his head spinning, The Naga turned to him, She sang out her name and lifted the scale to show a brilliant point of light that pulsed furiously and emitted a note so high it threatened his very sanity.

"Now, Thomas Calling, NOW!!!"

He lifted his hand and in that moment realised why he had chosen the Art of Swordplay. His voice rang out loud and clear...

### *"REMISSIO!"*

The hilt smacked into his hand, the power of the name vibrated through him as he thrust hard and deep, and with every ounce of his strength, into the Heart of the Naga. She flung back her golden head and screamed aloud her in her ancient tongue:

"I come, I come O Eternal and ancient Flame, receive me."

Her whole form became incandescent within and of Itself, lighting up the entire cave with searing light... then it was gone. But in his head Thomas heard the 'Song of Welcome' as the Naghareem welcomed back its last daughter.

The Cave shook the floor rose and began to crack, the roof sagged, rock and debris showered down on him as he withdrew the sword. On its tip glowed a single brilliant drop of blood red liquid. He touched his tongue to it and licked it clean. Fire raced through his veins, his whole body began to burn, not with fire but with the burden of centuries of knowledge. He would never use all of it, but would share what he could, with those who could accept it. What he could not use he would pass on to the next Merlin.

He became aware of the ash that now covered the floor and still fell, covering him with all that was left of his Fire Mother who had birthed him into the Teacher he would become. At his feet lay the Golden Scale. He picked it up and slipped it into his pants pocket. He thought of the artefacts, and the bones that this place had guarded for so long. He looked at the sword in his hand and remembered receiving it from the hand of Michael. There was a burning in his solar plexus and he felt a faint pulsation there. The Power of Fire had settled in place. It was time to go home. He went to where the unconscious Ap Gryffdd lay and with no effort lifted the inert form over his shoulder. He followed the trail of discarded diving gear down a long, half flooded passage way leading to a small cove. He laid his burden down and looked round.

Half the cliff had given way. Boulders, rocks, foliage and debris were scattered everywhere. The final moments of the Naga's passing had caused an enormous landside. Overhead a helicopter scouted the area assessing the damage. The pilot saw Thomas waving and dropped low enough to shout a promise of help coming then soared away. Thomas made sure Ap Gryffdd was breathing and sat down to wait.

He felt different, quiet but different. He reached out to Charlie and touched his sleeping mind. Without waking him he inserted what had happened into his mind, as if it was a dream. Charlie stirred, woke and sat up. "Tom? Is it you... are you... are you... I mean... you're not..."

"No Charlie, I'm alive and kicking. I want you to get

in touch with the others. Let them know I am OK, but there's been a huge landslide. I'm waiting for a helicopter to pick me up. Ap Gryffdd is with me but he's unconscious. There's bound to be a lot of panic and newspaper interest… but as far as anyone one knows I was just caught in the landslide and found this guy unconscious and got us both to safety. With luck I'll be home again in a day or two. Don't worry, Charlie… The Power of Fire is with me. All is well. Let them know."

"But how did you… I mean how can you reach me like this…"

"It's a long story… over 100,000 years long… but it can keep. I'll be back as soon as I can. We need to get the Guardians together."

Charlie rolled out of bed and reached for his mobile.

"Betty, I'm sorry to call you so early, I need to get to Thomas in Wales, but don't want to leave mum alone. Would it be possible for you to get down here and stay with her? Dad's due to go home next week and Frank was due to come down and drive them both back home. If he can drive you down today he can have four days in London with you and mum, then take you all back together. It's a lot to ask but I need to be with Tom. No, no, he's OK, honest… I've just spoken with him, I know, but he got caught in a landslide and is a bit shaken. I don't want him to drive in that state. Yes, honest, he's fine just shaken. Thanks Betty, you're a star, see you in a few hours."

He looked at his watch 06:59 and raced for the shower. By 07:15 he was shaved and dressed and ordering an early breakfast to be delivered to the suite. Packing was easy, everything got thrown into the case. At 07:30 he gently woke his sleeping Mother and gave her a watered down version of what had happened and that Betty was in her way down with

Frank. They would stay with her until Jim was discharged then all four would go back together. Comforted to know she would not be alone Maisie got dressed and sat down to her breakfast. Charlie went down to see about hiring a car. He explained the situation to the manager.

"Has Sir Thomas been injured?"

"No Mr Hastings, but he is shaken up and I don't want him driving up to Derbyshire in that state. I need a car to get down there and I'll drive him back."

"No need for a car Mr Naughton, there's a Helipad on the roof. I'll call the firm Sir Thomas uses. It can get you down there in an hour. It will be less tiring than several hours driving. I'll see to it right away… and please give Sir Thomas our best wishes." He bustled off leaving a bemused Charlie facing his first flight in a helicopter. Hell's Teeth, he didn't know there was a Pad on the hotel roof.

The 'copter took off just after 09:30 with a petrified Charlie doing his best to behave as if he was used to this form of travel. The pilot had radioed ahead and arranged a landing point, and a car would be ready to take him the last 20 miles to Llyddstep Cliffs. Betty and Frank were on their way down to London, so he began to relax. A warm feeling spread over him as he remembered shyly asking Thomas if they could train back to the north together. Was it really a year ago? His life had changed beyond belief, and not just his life. HE himself had changed. Between that fateful first journey and now, here, in a private helicopter, he was a thousand miles away from the painfully shy person who had marvelled at travelling home in a chauffeur driven car.

He had been befriended by a Fairy Prince, had watched his friend shape shift into a stag, a wolf, and a bird, and he had dealt with it all. He leaned back and closed his eyes, Tom was safe, he had won through the third Trial, maybe they could have a break before the last one, in the meantime a nap sounded good.

\* \* \*

Llyddstep was crowded with reporters, TV crews, local dignitaries and sightseers. The coastal path had been cordoned off and, to Thomas' relief, the inner cave system had not been laid bare. The hidden treasure and the human remains were safe from discovery and would remain so. Thomas sported a shoulder brace, the effort of carrying Ap Gryffdd over a mile of twisting tunnels had pulled a couple of muscles. He also had several stitches in his head and along his arms. The nurse had been intrigued by the "tattoo" of a sword in his right palm. Thomas explained it away as being part of the family Coat of Arms. Unfortunately that led to her looking up his family name. Hence the headline of:

### Millionaire Baronet injured in Massive Coastal Collapse!

Followed by the later editions with...

### Oscar winning author's son injured in rescue attempt.

Tom binned them both. "Let's get the Hell out of here Charlie, I want to go home and, away from all this. Thank God you came when you did I'm too tense to drive. I'm not safe to be behind a wheel yet.

He had moved from the Camper into the local Inn to avoid being kept in the small local hospital overnight. Gryffdd was still there, booked in as Professor Justin Thorndyke. A broken arm, various lacerations and concussion would keep him there for some days. Thomas denied knowing him, explaining they met on the path, and had only exchanged a few words when the landslide occurred.

Charlie's Yorkshire common-sense kicked in, "You're not going anywhere except to bed until tomorrow at least. You're wound tight as a flywheel and need to get some sleep." Between common-sense and outright bullying he got him showered and into bed with a hefty shot of rum disguised as Hot Chocolate inside him.

"You can give me all the details tomorrow. I'll drive us home, I thought about using the 'copter again, but a slow drive through the countryside will be better. You can talk, I'll drive and listen. From what little I've heard it'll take you some time to process it all. This has been really tough on you Tom. Let me take over for a while." But Tom was already asleep.

* * *

Two days later Charlie eased the camper out of the Inn's parking lot and onto the main road. Thomas sat silent... all talked out. During the last 48 hours he had slowly and painfully taken Charlie through his experience. In doing so he had finally absorbed and accepted the multi-layered emotions that had all but torn him apart. He realised that of all the Trials, Fire would always be the most influential.

He explained to a stunned Charlie that in every human being one of the Elements was paramount. In some it needed to be tightly controlled in others it was a basis for the work of that lifetime. But because of the Law of Duality much depended on how it was used... Good or Bad. He also told him of the Armada weaponry and the remains of the dead. Charlie was silent for a while... then said quietly, "I have never envied you before Thomas... But to have seen what you have seen does make me envious. I would have given so much to have seen those weapons." Then they drove on in silence.

Some twenty miles outside of town a man stood by the road smoking a cigarette, by his side a sack. He waved a hand and as they drew up walked over to them. Thomas knew him at once and got out of the car...

"You were the one I met on the coast path, you dropped the lighter. Well met Djinn, Lord of Fire, a blessing upon you and those in your care." He handed over the lighter.

The stranger accepted both the lighter and the blessing. "Your blessing is gratefully accepted and will be shared among those in my care. In turn I offer gifts for each of you. Charles, you did not see the cave of weapons, but I have something for you as a reward for your care of The Merlin." From the sack he took a Spanish Helmet, and a beautifully crafted poniard. Both bore an ornate Heraldic crest.

"They belonged to a Commander of the Armada fleet, a man of high degree. Juan Martinez de Recalde, Marquise de Sedonia... and for you Thomas of Carrick, I believe you were looking for this." He held out a delicate painting of the Bay, it was signed Edwin Landseer. "Then there is this." He held out a gold signet ring bearing the Royal Crest of Elizabeth the First. "It is inscribed 'To my loyal subject. ER'. She gave it to Drake after the demise of the Spanish fleet. As the soon to be declared Guardian of Albion it is fitting that you wear it. We will meet again under the Tor. Farewell." He stepped back dissolving into a beam of brilliant light.

Charlie's smile was almost as brilliant. "I didn't get to thank him." He caressed his gifts with a reverent hand. "These are magnificent."

Thomas slid the heavy ring onto his middle finger. "He will be aware of your feelings believe me. I am so pleased for you Charlie, it's about time 'They' realised and acknowledged your part in all this. Now let's get on, I'd like to reach Llanberis and stay overnight. From there we can get home by 2:00 at the latest. I'm still feeling a bit battered by all this."

Charlie shifted gear and glanced at him, "Take a nap and leave it to me. I'll get you home deartháir." Thomas groaned. "You're spending too much time with Cormac." He settled back and closed his eyes.

# Chapter Twenty-Four

**The Guardians monthly** meeting concluded as usual with a light supper and a good wine. The date of the June meeting at the Stones had been set, then both Thomas and Charlie had left earlier than usual. Drew lit a cigarette, but after a few draws stubbed it out on his plate, and turned to his companions. "This last test has changed him, it's as if he was wounded in some way. There's something he hasn't told us, something he experienced that made this trial different to the others. He's too quiet, too withdrawn, too… hurt."

Ian nodded, "I know what you mean. He's taken three trials in just under six months, it's too much. He's drained, exhausted physically and emotionally, and this fight against Thorndyke is not helping. It's as if he is fighting on two fronts. All that, plus the threat of The Dark Lords intervention it's eating him alive."

Marjory looked up from her coffee cup, "He needs a break from it all. You must tell him to take a holiday Ian, go fishing, lie on a beach somewhere warm, go trekking… anything but all these Trials. I know they're important, and have to be taken… but not one after the other."

Nurse Pym nodded. "I agree, and I would make a suggestion." The others gathered round to listen. She thought for a moment then spoke, "I suggest we go to the Stones and try to contact Merlyn. Tell him of our concern and ask for his help, or at least a suggestion of what we can do to help. It occurs to me that we always wait to be told or asked... But we have our own powers, powers we never really use. What if we put them together and call on Merlyn. I think there is a chance we can find an answer to the problem with his help."

The Guardians looked as each other. Then Posy said quietly, "It's true, we do have our own powers but we've not used them since the Battle against Mordred. Maybe because we always looked to Thomas, but never understood that we... each of us... have a power within us. If those powers were to be combined we might be able to do more than we ever thought possible. I know it's true of me." As she spoke she felt her own power awaken within her and realised that with it she could master her personal fears.

Stunned by the thought the Guardians looked at each other and for the first time realised that together they could be a force to reckon with. Then Drew rose to his feet, "Tomorrow is full moon, but there's already enough power to use now. Let's go. The van will take six, Posy you drive, I'll go on ahead with Ian and Marjory, we can travel faster in the Shift. Nurse Pym, you can take the rest, it will be a tight fit but you can get to the edge of the dales, and then shift. We meet at the Stones in 45 minutes. Let's Go." There was no hesitation, in minutes the room was empty.

* * *

The big stallion thundered over the moorland. On each side ran a sleek greyhound, ears flat and tongues lolling, but keeping up the relentless pace. Overhead the almost full moon lit up an unclouded sky and shone on the vehicles that ground to a halt within sight of the Stone Circle. They disgorged a grimly determined group of people that within seconds became a variety of equally determined animals. They set off for the Circle where Drew had already lit the lantern and Marjory was censing the centre Stone. They took their places and at Nurse Pym's suggestion resumed their own forms.

It was usually Thomas or Drew who opened the Circle, but this time, Drew acting on impulse asked Posy to do it. With no hesitation she accepted, and with a new born confidence she circled the gathering then, standing in her own place, she began the Calling.

"By the power of the Mother in me I call on the Spirit of the Stones to aid us in our time of need. We offer our human energy to enable Merlyn of Albion to cross time and space. We need your help and advice. Let us join together and bring him to us here in this sacred circle to be a Gate between our worlds. Merlyn, Merlyn of Albion, we call to thee, we summon thee to come to us. We have need of your wisdom. By the Power of The Stones we call, we call."

Twelve voices were raised in unison. "WE CALL! WE CALL! WE CALL!"

For a moment there was silence, then a rumbling sound began deep in the earth. Each Stone began to tremble and shake. The sound grew louder and louder and then burst from the earth in a peal of thunder that split the air and slowly died away into silence. Each of them sank to the ground, momentarily drained of energy. But before the centre Stone stood the figure of Merlyn as they had last seen him during the Great Battle. He gestured for them to stand.

"To offer your life energy for another, or for a cause, is a gift beyond price. What would you ask of me that is so important?"

Drew stepped forward and bowed. "Merlyn, we fear for Thomas, and for the toll these Trials take on him. What can we do to ease it, can we take some of the weight from him?"

Merlyn shook his head. "You cannot do the work for him. He has to prove himself strong enough to carry the burden he has taken on. The last was very demanding but he passed it, learned from it and, proved able to wield the Power of Fire at a level few Merlins have achieved. Yes, he has been drained physically, mentally and emotionally, but he has achieved more than we had hoped. I understand your care and your love for him and a respite will be offered. It will seem to you that he will take a rest. Do not ask where he will be. You will not see him for a short while but have no worries he will be safe. What else do you ask of me?"

Posy stepped forward. "Merlyn, I have greatly mis-judged him, because I feared for my child. How can I make it right between us?"

"Renew your trust in him. Your child was held in the arms of the Holy Ones, she will never be in danger from The Dark Lords. It is Thomas who must face and defeat those of The Dark Face. But not yet, he has the last trial to face. The power of your love and trust is his shield. Now I must go. The Blessing of Light be on all here." There was a peel of thunder from the Stones and Merlyn vanished. The Guardians drained by the sacrifice of their energy lay sleeping deeply. Their Stones supported them and drew heat from beneath the Earth to keep them warm. They sang to them in soft earthy voices filling their dreams with gentle healing.

\* \* \*

The dawn breeze kicked in and the sounds of a new day began to drift over the moors. Cattle and sheep turned out to their pastures. Lorries passed on their way north and the village began to wake. The everyday sounds woke the Guardians gently. For a few minutes they stood shivering in the cool morning air and remembering the experience they had shared.

Silently they crammed themselves into the van and the car. Once in the village they dispersed expecting to be worn out, but to their surprise found their energy levels on high. But, mentally they had changed. From now on they would live, work, think and understand as empowered individuals and even more so as a group.

* * *

Posy went about her work with Jessica playing beside her when a thought came to her that they were now much more than Guardians. They were a magical Lodge, a coven, a group working under spiritual guidance. Though a few went to church now and then, they were not regular attenders, but all were well versed in the old traditions. She paused, then quietly reached deep within herself and linked to her Stone. The surge of power was instant and the bucket of herbs she had intended to pick up, lifted itself and smacked into her hands. For a moment she stared at it... then put it down carefully and headed for the phone. Before she got there it rang and Marjory was yelling: "Posy, what is happening? My kitchen bin just floated outside and emptied itself into the garbage!"

Posy watched her range of Herbal pillows arrange themselves into neat piles according to type. "Welcome to the Club," she said.

# Chapter Twenty-Five

**In the library** Charlie was translating a medieval book of military tactics into modern English that would be the basis of his work when he returned to Cambridge. Thomas looked out of the window and debated whether or not to go for a run on The Second Road.

Charlie sighed and looked up from his papers, "Thomas I don't suppose by any miraculous chance you have a copy of *'Marvels of Milan'* by Bonvesin de la Riva published in 1288. There are only 200 copies in the world, but I sure could use one at the moment." Thomas looked along the top shelf of ancient books. One detached itself from the shelf and floated down to land in front of Charlie. He stared at it, then buried his head in his hands. "Why do I bother to ask let alone have it delivered. The weird thing is I'm getting used to it."

Thomas hitched a hip on the desk top and ruffled Charlie's hair, "Charlie let's do something utterly normal." Charlie didn't look up from the book. "Like what?"

"Take a holiday. Your parents are in Portugal, Dad's in LA, Adam's in Paris, and no one has mentioned the Trial of Earth so we're free to do whatever we want. We can go anywhere, and do anything for a few days. Charlie it would be great, just the two of us. What do you say? If you don't want to travel we could go fishing. I know a cottage we could rent up in the Lake District and the fishing there is really good."

"I've never done any fishing."

"I'll teach you or you can laze around on the bank and watch me. BUT, you have to promise NOT to bring any work with you. Books to read as long as they are nothing to do with history. Have you ever read any of P.G. Wodehouse? No? Then you have a treat coming, we'll take a set with us. What do you say?" He slapped Charlie on the back and stood up, looking at him eagerly.

His companion looked at him and noted the weariness behind his eyes, remembered the state he'd been in when he collected him in Wales. He really did need a break, and... he thought with surprise, so did he. "OK you're on. But don't expect me to put worms on hooks."

"No problem... its Fly Fishing. Today is Friday. I'll book us in for a week. We'll leave early on Sunday, take our time driving up, and be there by 6 pm. Go and pack... old clothes. We won't be going anywhere posh, I'll get on the phone now. This is going to be great." He made for the door which opened obligingly, then it waited for Charlie. It had never done that before. Charlie automatically said thank you as he left. The door hesitated, then closed slowly as if it was thinking.

By dinner time friends and family had been informed, the cottage was booked and would be stocked with food for their arrival. Frank and Betty were delighted and Grim was used to being with them when Thomas was away. Charlie drove home to pack and close up the house and Thomas settled into bed with a sigh of happiness. A whole week of peace and quiet lay ahead. He turned over and closed his eyes.

\* \* \*

In Tyr nan Og, Cormac smiled and began to make his plans. Thomas would have the break he needed. But not in a cottage on the edge of the Lake. A week in his world was much longer than a week in the human world and would be a great deal more interesting.

\* \* \*

Charlie lay sprawled on the bank and watched Thomas delicately land a fly on the calm water. It was the third day of their holiday and he still hadn't caught anything. It didn't seem to matter, he was content to stand thigh deep in water and wave that damned rod around to no avail, but Charlie was bored to tears. He had no interest in fish unless they came with chips. He discovered he hated P.G. Wodehouse, and his books. A trip to the village shop offered nothing but fashion magazines, newspapers, and guide books.

In desperation he bought a note pad and pens and tried to rough out an idea for a book. But Thomas confiscated them and took him on a four hour hike that gave him blistered feet and an intense dislike of the Lake District. Now he lay sulking on the bank and counting the hours to the end of this so called holiday. He looked at his watch for the umpteenth time, it was only 15 minutes since he last looked. Would this so called holiday never end. He sat up and looked out over the water, it was totally calm, but a mist was gathering on the other side.

As he watched a boat emerged from the mist and headed towards the side of the lake. It was a strange shape almost old fashioned, with a sort of figurehead on the front, but there was no one in it. As it came nearer he made out the shape of a bird's head, like a swan… He stood up and called out to Thomas, who didn't seem to hear. The boat drew level with him and suddenly with no warning Thomas seemed to be lifted into the boat.

Charlie yelled a warning and ran to the water's edge. "Tom... get back here. it may be that Gryffdd guy. Tom..." There was no answer. He dashed into the water and with a strength he never knew he had he struck out for the boat. No one was going to kidnap his buddy. He reached the side of the boat and grabbed a hand hold. Another hand grasped his shirt and hauled him in. He heard a familiar voice laced with laughter, "I might have known you would follow him, there's no separating you two." Cormac looked down at him, "I suppose I'd better take you as well... Welcome to Tyr nan Og Charles Naughton."

* * *

Cormac considered the sleeping forms before him. The impulse to bring Charlie along with Thomas had complicated things but nothing too serious. He cast his mind back over the centuries to a mystery that still had human historians perplexed. In 97 AD, The 9th Legion of Roman soldiers along with their Commander Aulus Plautius, set out to march to the north and were never seen again. At least not by the human population. A strange alignment of planets had caused a disruption on the Inner Levels that opened The Second Road to the human world for a day and a night. The 9th Legion had marched into Tyr nan Og with military precision and set up camp for the night.

They drank the water, and enjoyed the trees full of ripe fruit and awoke to find themselves permanent citizens of Tyr nan Og. It took a while to convince them they had not been transported to either Olympus or Hades. Most had adapted, the few that didn't became the Wanderers that haunt The Second Road. A meeting between Aulus Plautius and Charlie would be something to see.

Cormac grinned mischievously at the thought. But first he had to make plans for Thomas. He reached out mentally to a shady pool where a young girl rose gracefully from the flower strewn water, her nude body gleaming in the sunlight.

"Faelinne?"

"Yes father, I am here, do you require my presence?"

"It would please me if you shared the evening meal with me. I will have a guest I would like you to meet."

"Of course father, it is always pleasant to share your company. I will be there at Moonrise."

* * *

Thomas opened his eyes and sat bolt upright, his last memory was seeing a small boat heading towards him on a collision course. The boat seemed to have a swan's head on the front. He dropped his rod and prepared to dive to avoid being run down. His memory cleared a bit more. Cormac, it had to have been Cormac in the boat and he was going to give him a bloody nose for scaring the shit out of him like that. He sat up and looked round. HE WAS NOT WHERE HE THOUGHT HE WAS.

He swung his legs off the couch, stood up and looked round. The room had a high ceiling and walls covered with tapestries. The beds were velvet couches and on the one next to him Charlie lay sleeping. He knew instantly where he was. This was Tyr nan Og. Dear God, Charlie is going to flip when he wakes.

"Oh he will enjoy his stay here, I have set up something special for him." Cormac rose from his chair by the curtained window and came to stand beside him. "Let him sleep a while longer. I hope you will also enjoy your time here Thomas, I confess I did not intend to bring Charlie along, but at the last moment it seemed the right thing to do. The Guardians called Merlyn from Avalon. They finally realised they also have powers both singly and together. They were worried for you and called on him for help. Now they are learning to cope with their new found powers." He took him by the arm and led him from the room and along a win-dowed corridor.

"When you take up the Mage-ship, they will be able to provide help when needed, as did the Guardians before them. You are here at Merlyn's request and with Midir's per-mission. The advantage is that the time you spend here will be but a few days in your own world. Here you can be healed and strengthened in ways not possible there. The last time you were in Tyr nan Og you were in the area ruled by Ober-on. Here you are under the rule of Midir. As in your world, we have what you call 'countries', though we refer to them as 'Courts'. I had the food from the cottage brought here, so you and Charlie may eat without fear of being trapped. Rooms have been prepared for you both. You will need to change, what you have on at present is unsuitable, and rather damp."

He stopped at a door and spoke Thomas' name. The door opened on to a room looking very like his own back home, with the exception of the curtained bed draped in blue velvet. On it lay a suit of clothing similar to that of Cormac. Close fitting trews, a full sleeved white linen shirt edged with fine lace, and an over-tunic in deep red embroid-ered in gold thread. Knee length boots in butter soft leather, and a belt of interlaced gold chains holding a leather purse completed the set.

Cormac pointed to another door, "That leads to a room where you can bathe and shave with the utensils humans need. Our needs are... somewhat different to yours. If there is anything you want ask Nazim." He pointed to a small slender figure that had just entered. "Nazim is a sylph, his name means 'breath of wind'." Nazim stepped forward and clasping his hands together bowed slightly. "Nazim knows you hold the Power of Air and regards it an honour to serve you. I'll leave you to change, all food and drink offered is from your own world, there's no trick to keep you here. When you are ready Nazim will take you to Midir. I must go and calm Charlie down, he is awake and very agitated." He turned and vanished.

Thomas and Nazim regarded each other, then Thomas held out his hand and said... "Please call me Thomas, and may I call you Nazim?" The sylph regarded his hand with wonder, then placed his own within it. When the human hand folded around his he looked up in wonder, then smiled and returned the pressure. "It is true what Midir has said... you are One with our world. I will learn much from you Thomas. Come I will prepare a bath for you."

\* \* \*

"Charlie, PLEASE... calm down. Thomas is safe, you are safe, and no, you are not dead, this is Tyr nan Og, not your supposed Hereafter. You are here with Thomas to rest. I'll take you to your room and you can bathe, change, and then you can go with Thomas to see Midir, whose Court this is. No, you can't share, you have your own suite, but you will be able to see Thomas every day I give you my word. But... By the Talking Head of Bran, can you just calm DOWN."

\* \* \*

Nazim guided Thomas along a series of bewildering

corridors and flights of stairs. He explained that the Court existed in several different dimensions and those who dwelt here moved in and out of them at will. "In actual fact the corridors are not needed as we simply shift from one dimension to the other as we have need. It was thought more comfortable for you this way, as moving between dimensions can be injurious to your human body. But we are now here." He stopped before a pair of elaborately carved doors.

Thomas, used to his own doors opening for him stood and waited. But these doors considered him for a few seconds then swung open slowly and with obvious reluctance. Thomas got the impression they did so because he was human and beneath their dignity. As he entered he sent them a thought, *"I am an invited guest so be quicker next time OK!"* The doors sent back the equivalent of an affronted sniff, and slammed shut behind him.

Midir rose to greet him holding out his hands and drew him into the Sidhe embrace of Fellowship. "My Son has spoken much of you and with great affection. You have acquitted yourself with distinction at the Trials. Consider my Court your home and be welcome. Come sit with me, we are awaiting your companion who is having some difficulty in adjusting I believe. Cormac will bring him soon. Some wine? I hope you won't think ill of us but Cormac brought it from your own wine cellar. A favourite of yours he said."

Thomas sat, accepting a glass of wine and two great wolf hounds rose from their Masters side and came to inspect him. Then having accepted him they lay at his side, one of them across his feet. The Doors opened again with an audible creak of indignation and Cormac entered with a visibly shaken Charlie who made a bee line for Thomas. "Are you alright? You didn't hit your head when you went under? You were not there when I woke up... I thought... I thought..."

"Charlie it's OK I'm fine, please. Remember where you are. This is Midir, Cormac's father and the Lord of this Court. We are here by his permission and generosity." Charlie stopped in mid flow and turned round. His eyes wide with wonder, then he bowed. "Lord Midir, your pardon sir, forgive my intrusion, this is my first time in your Court. It is a little overwhelming. I am an ordinary man and all this is…" His voice died away. Midir drew him to a chair and put a glass of wine in his hand.

"Charles Naughton, like Thomas you are Fae Friend and therefore welcome here." Charlie gulped his wine and sat down trying to resist pulling the Over-Tunic down over his tight fitting nether garments.

"I hope you will forgive me Lord Midir, I am unused to situations like this. I am not high born and for me this is similar to being in the presence of British Royalty." Midir laughed, and raised his glass to him. "I am not royalty in the sense you mean my friend. You are here as a guest and companion to the future Merlin of Albion. I believe my son has something special planned for you."

Cormac leaned forward with a smile and said, "Charlie, what do you know of the missing 9th Legion of the Roman Army?"

Charlie thought a moment… then said, "Well no one really knows what happened, there are ideas, but nothing specific. The most prevalent is that they were massacred by the Iceni tribe in a surprise attack but it seems unlikely to me. The Iceni had suffered a recent defeat and would still be recovering."

Cormac studied his wine glass, "Would you like to talk to Aulus Plautius its Commander?"

Charlie grinned… "That would be a difficult seeing he's been dead over 2000 years."

"Ah yes… but 2000 years in Tyr nan Og my friend

means very little." The speaker came from behind a painted screen. Of middle height and broad of shoulder, he carried himself with the air of a military man born and bred. His hair was cut to fit under a helmet and he wore the uniform of a Roman Commander. "Aulus Plautius at your service."

Cormac was beside himself with glee watching Charlie's face. "I thought it would be fitting for him to wear his old uniform to meet you Charlie. He is happy to discuss his former life with you. You will also meet those of his men who have adjusted to life in Tyr nan Og." Charlie clung to his sanity with grim determination. He would NOT disgrace Thomas or himself by passing out. He stood, and faced the warrior and gave the ancient Roman Salute. Arm extended, palm down, fingers closed. "Hail Caesar."

There was a moment's silence, then Aulus stepped forward and grasped Charlie's forearm, hand to elbow. A tear dropped on their clasped hands. "It is so long, so long, it feeds my heart to hear those words. Come my friend, let me take you to meet my men... they are eager to meet with you. Midir, may we leave your presence?"

"Go with my blessing Aulus, and Charles, enjoy yourself while you are here." They left together, Charlie sliding with little effort into classical Latin.

Thomas turned to Cormac, "There is nothing more wonderful to him than this gift. He may never want to leave here, but I need him with me. I'll have another glass of wine if I may... I feel the need of it."

* * *

Standing by the window and looking out onto a formal garden Thomas drew in a deep breath filled with a variety of scents. "It's as if the very air here is filled with all you need to exist. Why bother to eat when you can live on the air?" Cormac came to stand beside him and placed an arm over his shoulder. "That is why you are here, to rebuild your strength and prepare for the next trial. However it will not be as demanding as the three before it."

"Why is that?"

"Earth is what your physical body is made from, it is like a cup that contains and maintains the other three, air, water, and fire. In almost all humans those three vary in their amounts, strengths, and abilities. You have balanced the first three within yourself so they are all equal and in the proportions needed for the work you will do. The Earth Trial will bind them together in complete balance. That alone is a rare thing in humanity, tho' it will come to most eventually."

"Cormac, just what IS The Work? I mean I can't go around doing magical things in my world, very few people will even know about it… or about me."

"It will be little to do with what you call the real world. Your work will be to maintain the balance between the Racial Guardians, all four of them. To guard against the infiltration of those who would destroy or decimate their Unity. You will also be responsible for the Spiritual Guardianship of the Royal House. On the physical level, they have more than enough… but on the magical levels they have been vulnerable for many years. Your great-grandfather was the last Merlin. Your grandmother refused the post and so it came to you. You were too young to assay the Trials then, so we had to wait until your fourteenth year to approach you.

"The Blessed Isles have always held the Four Treasures of the West. The Stone of Kingship; The Cup of Healing; The Sword of Defence; and The Spear of Destiny. All Four will be brought together at your Ascendency to the Guardianship of Albion. But let us talk of other things, the table has been set for dinner and there is someone I would like you to meet." He drew Thomas back into the room.

"Thomas of Carrick may I present my daughter Faelinne."

Thomas caught his breath. His title, and his wealth, had brought him into contact with beautiful women both at Cambridge and the society in which he moved. He appreciated beauty and being young, healthy and male, he had had his share of liaisons, but always felt there would be one worth waiting for. Cormac's daughter was breathtakingly beautiful, and he felt an instant attraction, but she was not the one. However he knew there was a deeper reason for their meeting and thought back to meeting Cormac for the first time and his acceptance of "The Geas". Now he knew that Faelinne was a part of that pact. He took her hand and raised it to his lips, "It is an honour and a pleasure to meet you Lady Faelinne."

*　*　*

Charlie's ability to speak Latin was standing him in good stead with the Legionnaires, albeit they kept correcting his pronunciation. Aulus protested that he spoke it like a member of the Senate, but the men for the most part were not Roman born and used a bastardised version. By the time he had finished the lager Cormac had brought from the cottage he had learned at least six jokes he would never be able to tell in his own world and could sing the Legion marching song with the best of them. Aulus laughed so much he nearly choked.

Nor had the men neglected the nymphs who were their serving maids, though they were aghast to find him an innocent. They listened eagerly to him tell of the world as he knew it and compared it to what they remembered. Though they had adapted to life with the Sidhe they never revisited the human world. Aulus explained that it brought too many memories back, so they contented themselves with life in Tyr nan Og. He arranged a demonstration of Legionnaire close combat techniques the next day and promised to have a set of Roman armour made for him.

For the first time in his life Charlie was drunk and disorderly and loved it. He found himself in a world and with people he had dreamed of and read about all his life. Eventually Aulus and several of the men guided him (unsteadily) back to his own room and bid him a raucous goodnight then went on their way laughing. Charlie's servant, a three foot gnome named Alaric got him out of his Court clothing, after a tussle getting his boots off. Then he headed for his bed... to find it already occupied by two of the nymphs who took it upon themselves to complete his education.

# Chapter Twenty-Six

**In his elegant** apartment in London, Justine Thorndyke (Ap Gryffdd) sat nursing his still aching head and the injuries sustained in the Sea Cave. He had returned from a terrifying meeting with The Dark Lords on The Second Road and on his return found himself face to face with the shade of a screaming Morgana. The Dark Ones had made him fully aware of their displeasure at the outcome of the Trial of Fire. Due to his late intervention and unsuccessful attempt to kill Thomas before he received the Power, Morgana, in her maniacal fury at the loss of a new body (young Jessica) had unwisely defied them and suffered for it. She now languished in the cold darkness of her own inner space deprived of her senses, and beset by her memories of defeat.

He too had been punished being forced to endure facing his Masters in their true form. It had driven him to near insanity. He had been given one more chance, if he failed, it would mean an existence that made the medieval idea of Hell a summer holiday by comparison. He crouched in a corner huddled into himself, rocking back and forth in anguished fear. His dreams of power, wealth, adulation, and extended life were falling apart. He had been so sure he would win, so confident in his power to strike down the upstart who had defied him at every turn. His misery and fear cooked within him as he realised that he had failed and would fail again.

What he faced then would fragment his very sense of self.

Out of his fear grew a desire to lash out, if he couldn't win, he would at least make Carrick suffer. He would destroy something he loved... destroy it utterly, painfully. Yes, The Dark Ones would punish him as few humans had ever been punished... but he would take comfort in knowing he had destroyed something, someone he loved. He crouched in his temple and went through a list in his crippled mind. His father? ... no, one expected to lose one's parents sooner or later. Charlie? No, Charlie would die willingly because he loved Thomas as a brother, and a willing sacrifice died with a power that would counteract the whole thing and turn it into something Holy and Blessed. He needed to watch Thomas suffer. But there was one... yes, the child Morgana had planned to take over and live through. She would do nicely. He would draw her away from the house and out of its protection. He could infiltrate the brains of the village dogs and set them on the child... or... wait... he could do that himself... yes... that would be even better. He would shift into wolf form and tear her to pieces slowly. It would destroy Thomas to hear her scream and be unable to save her.

That would be good to see, but first he must rest, collect his thoughts and make plans. He would have only one chance. He needed to be strong in his power. For that he needed to take power from someone weaker than himself. Not too difficult, in London there were many who practiced on the dark side. He could gather strength from them. He felt stronger already, he had a plan, a goal, yes it would cost him many lives of retribution, but it would be worth it to see Carrick's pain. He felt stronger, and now with this in mind he began to plan how to achieve it.

# Chapter Twenty-Seven

**Charlie reined in** his horse and waited for Nerys to catch up. She came alongside him and halted, sliding a caressing hand over the silky neck of her mare. She looked around smiling, and said, "We always seem to end up here. What is it that draws you?" Charlie dismounted and went to the edge of the rise and stood looking out over a green moorland spiked here and there with weathered rocks.

"It reminds me of home. Tyr nan Og is beautiful and I have enjoyed my time here, but my own world calls to me. I have learned so much, and understand much more but... both Tom and I are needed back where we belong. We have work to do there, but..." He caught her hand and drew her to him, kissing her gently, "That does not mean I will forget you Nerys. Far from it, I will miss your sweetness and your gentle ways, and..." He twisted a lock of her hair in his hand... "the way you..." He whispered something in her ear that made her silver laughter fill the air. "You learn very quickly Charles." They remounted their steeds and Charlie cast one more look behind him, then set out for the Court. Nearly three weeks had passed in the world of the Sidhe, but now just a few more days and they would have to leave. To stay longer would begin an irrevocable change in their bodies. There was still a lot to be done and to be decided.

Thomas watched as they rode back into the Mews of

Midir's court. Charlie had changed so much both physically and mentally. He was a lot slimmer, and much fitter. Aulus and his men had seen to that. He could heft a sword and shield and had shown a surprising ability to throw a spear with telling effect. For someone who regarded horses as animals that pulled ploughs and were mostly seen in Westerns he now rode with confidence. In fact, he, Thomas, was seriously thinking of adding a couple of horses to his ménage at the Manor. A touch on his shoulder made him turn. Cormac looked out across Tyr nan Og and spoke quietly but with a depth of meaning unlike his usual self.

"Tonight Merlyn will come and with him those of the former Merlins who chose the road to Avalon. Midir, Oberon, Mabh, Aengus, and Gwidion plus myself will represent the world of the Sidhe. You will learn what the role of The Mage of Albion will entail and what the final Trial of Earth will offer you and what it will demand of you. At first this meeting was meant only for you, but Charles has proved himself worthy of inclusion. Plus when all have dispersed I will remind you of the promise you made when we first met. That will be between you and me… and one other. Come let us eat before the meeting… that is if we can coax Charles away from his lady."

Dinner was usually a time for talk, laughter, and the banter usual between friends, with music as a background. But tonight, with the prospect of the meeting ahead there was silence broken only by the odd remark or observation. Even the music was quieter as if trying to impress the moment on their memories. For Charlie this had been a time of personal growth and discovery. The shy, withdrawn and socially awkward youth he had been had gone forever. Now he was a man in every sense of the word. Mature, self-aware, sure of his strength physically, mentally and spiritually. Under Midir's gentle guidance his dormant abilities had begun to open and his role in the future had been made clearer.

Thomas and Cormac spoke little, and mostly of the future role of the Guardians of the Singing Stones. Faelinne and Nerys had not dined with them, knowing the importance of the meeting ahead and the need to strengthen the bond between their different worlds. Finally Midir rose. "They are on their way, let us go to the Meeting Hall." Silently they made their way along a corridor filled with portraits that turned to watch them pass. The Meeting Hall was central to the Court and used for the celebrations of the Sidhe. Its doors were guarded by Sidhe Warriors who came to attention as they approached. The huge doors swung open silently to allow entry.

Instead of a table, ten Chairs of State had been arranged in a circle, high backed and cushioned in red velvet. A standard stood behind each chair. Five bore the Lion Rampant of Camelot. Two the Four Stars of the Sidhe Courts centred by the Sigil of Eternity. One bore Thomas' Heraldic Crest. One was Blank. The Tenth displayed the Four Symbols of the Elements and the chair remained empty. Midir and Cormac took their seats, Thomas sat beneath his Crest, Charlie automatically took the blank Standard.

For a moment all was silent, then an unseen Trumpet sounded a muted Fanfare and they rose to their feet. Merlin Rhys Ap Hoel manifested in his place and bowed to Midir raising his hand in salute to the Lord of the Sidhe. Merlin Elias Ashmole came next and saluted, then Merlin Cuthbert of Lindisfarne. The fourth seat was filled by Merlin Dion Fortuna. All remained standing as the trumpet sounded again and Merlyn of Atlantis and Avalon took his seat. His presence was acknowledged with a bow.

"Midir, Cormac, my thanks for this welcome, may the stars shine upon you and your people. Thomas, it is good to see you and know you have won through three of your

Trials. The last now awaits. Charles Naughton you have earned your place here tonight, your strength and sense of duty will be needed in the future. Let us begin. Our purpose is to acquaint Thomas with the task of the Guardianship of Albion. To aid our explanation behold the Blessed Isles."

Before them on the polished floor of the Meeting Hall there appeared a contoured map of the Four Kingdoms, each depicted in colour with its main features outlined. Thomas and Charlie leaned forward, picking out the areas known to them. As they thought of each one, that area enlarged becoming clearer and more detailed. Merlyn smiled, knowing the deep love of the land that was inherent in all the Merlins. He gave a brief description of the demise of ancient Atlantis, the only time when The Lords of The Dark Face had been triumphant. It had taken thousands of years to re-group and strengthen The Forces of Light. He impressed the story on their minds so they could examine it at their leisure and with more attention to detail at a later time. Then he turned to Thomas.

"The task of a Merlin is to guard The Blessed Isles from the Powers of Darkness. This means a constant awareness of the boundaries and what is happening within them. Because of the Law of Balance the Dark cannot be banished completely, but only kept at bay. Occasionally IT attacks from without if IT can find a suitable focal point. This is the cause of Wars and Opposing Ideologies. Humanity has not as yet learned to accept that differences can be a strength rather than a division.

"There have been times when the Isles were without a Guardian because a suitable candidate was not found or as in your case, was not of an age for training. We waited until you were able to understand your destiny and if you would accept the burden it entails. Your grandmother refused to be The Merlin and chose an ordinary life. Her son, your father, showed creative powers, but not of the spirit. In you they are strong, and the Many Worlds sighed with relief at your birth. Your grandmother gave you the Crystal Sphere you still carry. It is the symbol of The Merlin. You showed power from the start so we made sure you had a teacher and protector, Father John. Then, when you saw through the anger and hurt Morgana had fostered, and relit the Light within Mordred's damaged spirit we knew we had a true Merlin. But let me show you what that title entails.

"The Blessed Isles have changed many times over the centuries, in the way they see themselves, govern themselves, and in their relationship to each other. They have fought each other and fought together against a common foe, they have died together on many foreign battlegrounds. But on the Inner Levels they remain and will always remain The Blessed Isles that uphold, protect, and sustain the Four Sacred Treasures of the West. The Stone, symbolising the Rulership of Earth, The Cup, symbol of the cradling Sea that surrounds and sustains them, The Sword of Fire with which you, Thomas, gave freedom to the last Dragon. And The Spear of Air that pierces the Darkness and lets in the Light."

He passed his hand over the Map of the Four Kingdoms and it became three dimensional. But around the edges and at certain points within there were clouds of swirling darkness. They came and went as some were cleared but reappeared elsewhere. Pin points of darkness occurred in the big cities, as cruel and unholy acts occurred. Sometimes the darkness was deep and pulsed with power, others were the actions of those unable to help themselves. Each Kingdom seemed to be engaged in an internal war, but over the Four shone a single star pouring light over them all. Over London one small cloud of darkness throbbed and roiled. Thomas took a deep breath and Charlie stepped protectively to his side…

"Ap Gryffdd," he said. Thomas nodded.

Merlyn waved a hand and the map disappeared. "Now you have seen, and understood a little of what lies before you and soon you, Thomas, will face the Trial of Earth. But, at this time you can still say NO and withdraw with no shame."

Thomas took a step forward. "I will take on the Guardianship of The Blessed Isles and shield it to best of my ability and my power." Charlie stepped to his side and behind him. "And I will stand with him as long as he has need of me."

Merlyn lifted his staff in Salute. "We will meet again tomorrow when the many worlds will come together for the final meeting. After the last Trial all will meet beneath the Great Tor. Charles Naughton, your crest will take its place beside that of The Merlin. You have earned this honour and have a part to play." (The Naughton crest filled the empty Standard). Each former Merlin came forward to bless their successor and his companion, then Merlyn himself laid hands upon them. "Until the Morrow."

Tomorrow, there would be a meeting of worlds. His own, that of Avalon, and the Courts of Tyr nan Og, and the mystical world that had overlaid Albion since the destruction of Atlantis. A meeting of a kind that had not been called since before the great flood when the Dark had almost taken possession. And… he would be part of it.

* * *

## The Last Full Day

The gardens of Midir's court existed on many levels and encompassed many different climates. Posy would

257

love to see this thought Thomas as he and Cormac strolled through the perfumed lushness. Cormac pointed out flowers, shrubs and herbs from different areas and explained their use in perfumes and elixirs. Then led the way to a secluded area where a carved bench overlooked a lake and they sat in silence for a while. Then Thomas turned to his companion.

"It's rare to find you at a loss for words Cormac, so let me help you. You have brought me to Tyr nan Og for more than a meeting with the Merlins, and it concerns Faelinne and the Geas we share, is that not the way of it?" Cormac laughed self-consciously.

"Your power grows stronger each day, but you are right." He paused gathering his thoughts, "Fohla, our Seer has spoken of the future for humanity. There are many changes, troubles, and new paths ahead for your kind. Soon you will begin the greatest adventure of all. The discovery of what lies beyond what you call the Solar system. You humans have always looked outwards, and soon you will venture beyond the earth. The Sidhe have neither the desire or ability to go where you are headed. We are of the earth and must remain here.

"But... it was my dream that one of my kind would be part of that adventure. The make-up of our form is unable to go beyond physical Earth. All we know, can ever know, is here on the many levels open to us. But I hoped that a way might be found to enable my kind to go with you. Someone of both human and Sidhe descent. I searched long for someone who might understand.

"Centuries ago there were matings between our species, indeed in your own line there have been at least two. But in this age there is no belief in our kind. I hoped..." his voice tailed off... "You were so easy to be with, so open to all that I... we... are... Maybe I asked... hoped... too much. I will take back the Geas I made with you. I realise now it was too much to ask. Faelinne is willing, we are less... insistent than humans on keeping to one mate. But I realise it is not your way... I also know, so Fohla told me, that the one meant for you is coming closer. Forgive me Thomas. I just hoped that someone who is a part of both our worlds would be able to share that adventure. Forgive me." He hung his head and the light that played around his Sidhe form dimmed and lost lustre.

Thomas stood up and walked to the edge of the path and looked down at the lake. He saw Faelinne swimming and waved, she waved back. He thought of the welcome he had received and Charlie also, he could understand the eagerness and curiosity Cormac had for the future, something he shared. It was sad to think that the wondrous, laughing, magical people of the Sidhe were forever tied to earth. He turned.

"You and your people have given me so much, Charlie too, we have been made welcome and given recognition and honour. If Faelinne is willing let me give you what you desire Cormac. A changeling grandson who one day may take the Sidhe bloodline into space. I stand by the Geas, you will be his Guardian. I only ask that he may also know my world and my life." He held out his hand. Cormac stood and embraced him.

"You know Thomas... that the Sidhe cannot weep? I wish I could, it would show you what this means to me." Thomas linked to him mentally using the skill the Fire Dragon had given him. A tear rolled down his cheek, he took it on his finger and laid it on Cormac's face. "Let me give you my tear my brother in Light, we will share the moment together." As he spoke the Geas unwound and his hair fell free.

* * *

Beyond the multi-towered court of Midir in the forest of Llan Bedwyr, Time slowed down. It could never stop entirely, but if the need was great, it could slow its onward march and hold what had been, and what was to come in a space where the many worlds might come together. One world could step into another for a brief time only, but in the centre was a point of infinite stillness where a speaker could command attention. Around this centre gathered the world of Avalon. Its knights and leaders including past Merlins, stood armoured but with weapons at rest. Arthur, Merlyn, Guenevere, Launcelot, Galahad, and Mordred waited quietly.

The World of the Sidhe held Oberon, Titania, Mabh, Bobh, Midir, Aengus and Cormac. Behind them, stood Aulus, his Legion, and those who had chosen the Road to Tyr nan Og. The human group held Thomas, Charles Naughton, and the forms of those who held enough power to have been drawn here.

The Elemental Worlds stood silent, each King holding their power in check, and behind them their subjects. Silence reigned as they waited for the last world to take its place.

A trumpet note rang out, high and clear. A sound filled with a joyfulness that filled the Sacred Space with enormous power. It lifted the hearts of Human, Sidhe, Atlantean, and Elemental, filling them with a sense of love so pure and vital it held them in enthralled. The misty outline of Four Great Presences coalesced into being. One carried a Sword, one a Cup, the third held a flaming Spear and the fourth carried a silver Trumpet. Charlie, knew at once who that was, and excitedly called out, "Hey, Gabe, you brought the Horn with you." Then he realised. He moaned and dropped to his knees hanging his head in shame. One did not call the Archangel Gabriel "Gabe".

A stunned silence fell on the gathered worlds. Then gentle hands lifted the distraught man to his feet. "Charlie, it is good to see you, Do not fear, your love is as pure as the note of my horn and as true." Gabriel took his hand and drew him to his feet. A light flowed from the Presence, touched and filled him, loved him and shared Itself with him, then returned him to his place. The gathered Worlds breathed with relief and Merlyn of Avalon stepped forward, bowed and spoke.

"Albion has been without a Guardian for almost 100 years. A new Merlin has been found and has passed three of the Four Trials, he now faces the last. Then he will be called to the Temple beneath the Tor to take his rightful place as The Merlin of Albion. There is one who opposes him and has made a pact with The Lords of The Dark Face; they seek to harm him and those he loves. With the agreement of the World of the Sidhe he was brought here to rest and renew his power. As his proposer, I ask the Four Worlds to recognise Thomas of Carrick as a fitting candidate to carry the Staff of the Arch-Mage, to wear the Sword of the Reconciliation to support him in his Task and to grant him the Choice of the Three Paths." Merlyn turned to Thomas, "Thomas of Carrick, come and face the council of The Four Worlds."

Thomas took a deep breath, then walked forward to stand beside Merlyn who turned him to face the World of Avalon. "Avalon, how say you, will you accept Thomas of Carrick as the New Merlin of Albion?" Arthur and Mordred came either side of him and placed their hands on his shoulders. "We accept Thomas of Carrick as the new Merlin of Albion."

They stepped back a pace and Merlyn faced the world of the Sidhe. "Courts of the Sidhe, how say you, will you accept Thomas of Carrick as the New Merlin of Albion?" Midir, Oberon and Cormac came forward and placed their hands on his shoulders. "We accept Thomas of Carrick as the new Merlin of Albion."

They stepped back and Merlyn faced the world of Humanity. "World of Humanity, will you accept Thomas of Carrick as the new Merlin of Albion?" (To the surprise of Thomas, the faint forms of Drew, Ian, Betty, and Father John appeared beside him and placed their hands on his shoulders. "We accept Thomas of Carrick as the new Merlin of Albion." Their forms faded and were gone.

Merlyn now faced the four Elemental kings and Bowed. "Lords and Protectors of the Elements, Thomas of Carrick has faced and upheld the power of three of you, and has one yet to come, I accept him as The Merlin and offer my service. Do you accept Thomas of Carrick as the new Merlin of Albion? Paralda of Air?"

"He has dealt well with my Element, I accept him as The Merlin and offer my service."

"Nixsa of Water"?

"He faced my Element with courage and dealt with his fear. I accept him as The Merlin and offer my service."

"Djinn of Fire. Do you accept Thomas of Carrick as the new Merlin of Albion?

"He dealt exceptionally well with my Element and showed an ability to deal with my servant. It was hard for him, but I accept him as The Merlin and offer my service. Also I bring greetings from the Holder of the last Fire Breath. She spoke of him with affection."

"Ghob of Earth. He has yet to face your trial, but how say you at this moment?"

"I have watched how he dealt with my brethren. On that I make my judgement. I accept him as The Merlin and offer my service."

Merlyn came before the Angelic World and bowed. "Lords of Light, is the candidate I bring to you acceptable for your purpose?"

Raphael looked across at Thomas and his smile lit up the gathering. "We know of him, we have watched him grow in strength, knowledge, and acceptance of his destiny. He called to us in his need to protect those he loves. We tested him and he did not falter. We accept Thomas of Carrick as The Merlin and Arch-Mage of Albion. We offer the choice of the Three Roads when the time comes. The Road to Avalon, the Road to Tyr nan Og, or, the Road that leads to the Mystery of Humankind. BUT..." The Gathered Company held its breath. "We also offer that same choice to Charles Naughton, because of his loyalty, courage, devotion, and humility." Raphael turned his wondrous face to Charlie, who sank to his knees. He knew what the offer referred to and was speechless.

Raphael continued... "The time is not yet, but it will come and then... You can choose." Thomas turned to Charlie who was in tears, and gently raised him... Raphael continued, "The tears of such a man carry the power to heal." Merlyn produced a small crystal phial and caught the tears. He handed it to Charlie.

Gabriel spoke now: "Our time here runs out, we offer the Blessing of That which created all Life forms to those gathered and take our departure."

Avalon faded from view, followed by the Elemental Kings, The Angelic world faded leaving the scent of roses filling the air. Only Tyr nan Og remained and Midir led them back to the Court. Thomas and Charlie walked close together but silently. Cormac walked alone... There was still one more part of the plan to be accomplished. Tomorrow they would return to their own world... but there was still the night to come.

\* \* \*

The Stag stood silent and aloof at the edge of the forest clearing and looked out at the gleaming towers of Midir's Court in the distance. The fourteen points of his Rack, proclaiming him a "Royal", gleamed in the failing light. Soon the moon would rise and fill the mystical world of Tyr nan Og with its power. He could feel the answer to that power gathering strength within him and knew he was on the edge of something new; new and yet as old as Time.

Down there in the court, Charlie would be filling his mind and senses with information and knowledge of the Roman occupation of ancient Britain. He would take back with him the memories of those who had helped to create the Britain he had been born into, knowledge and understanding that he could pass on to others. The Stag blew out a deep breath and watched the far off windows fill with lights as the gloaming deepened.

But what of him, what would he take back with him? Renewed strength, a clearer sense of his destiny and its purpose, a firmer grasp on the three Elemental Powers he had fought for and a sense of the higher mystical purpose that lay behind the Guardianship of Albion. His role was not, and never had been or would be, either political or military. This had become much clearer during his time in the Court of Midir.

But there was something missing... What could he, Thomas, take back? The answer was simple, he could take nothing back, but he could and would leave something of himself here. Something that would be a part of each of both worlds. It was one of the reasons for all that had happened. The Doe stepped up beside him and touched his shoulder with her nose. She breathed over him with her warm perfumed breath.

The Stag turned and bent its great horned head towards her, catching her enticing scent. A silent question flowed between them and was answered. Then the Doe turned back to the forest, paused to look over her shoulder and disappeared into the shadows. The Stag looked at the far off Court now ablaze with light, and gave voice to a great bellow of sound.

Midir, Cormac, and Charles Naughton raised their heads. They listened, and understood. The Stag turned and followed the Doe deep into the forest where, under a shaft of Moonlight what was needed came into being.

# Chapter Twenty-Eight

**Thomas surfaced and** saw his rod floating away from him. He grabbed it and looked around. He was up to his neck in the river and his waders were full of water making it difficult to get to the bank. Charlie was already ashore, stretched out and alternately coughing up water and cursing Cormac in his newly acquired Legionnaires' Latin. Thomas struggled to the bank, kicked off the waders and crawled up to thump him on the back.

"That ****, **** ******, son of a *****." Charlie spat out the last mouthful of river weed and sat up. "Amen to that" was Thomas' response. "That's his idea of a joke, sending us back the way we went in, the Sidhe have a twisted sense of humour where humans are concerned. Let's go and get dry, then we'll go to the pub and have a hot meal and a gallon of tea, something the Sidhe never got round to using."

While Thomas showered Charlie went into kitchen intending to make the all-important first pot of tea. He stared at the table for a moment then went back to the bathroom and stuck his head round the shower door, "You'll never guess what I found," he said with a wide grin. "There's a pot of tea already made, a pile of sandwiches, and a note, saying he thought we might need it. For that I for one am ready to forgive and forget."

Thomas grabbed a towel and headed for the kitchen while Charlie took his place in the shower. "Don't eat all those bloody sandwiches," he yelled. Fifty minutes later having eaten their way through the sandwiches and downed three pots of tea they crawled into their beds. Charlie fell asleep with the Legion's marching song going through his head.

Thomas took longer but when he finally slept he dreamt of a quiet beach in the West Highlands and a girl with hair the colour of a polished chestnut sitting on a rock and looking out to sea. She was singing. He knew her, knew the song. Knew she was the one he was waiting for.

> *"Bheir me o, horo vano*
> *Bheir me o, horo van ee*
> *Bheir me o, ohooro*
> *Sad am I, without thee."*

He walked towards her, she turned, saw him and jumping from the rock she ran towards him. He caught her in his arms, lifting and swinging her round. "Laura Mo Gra." (my love) He bent to kiss her and the dream dissolved.

\* \* \*

The following day they slept late and after breakfast packed their gear into the Four Wheel Drive borrowed from the Manor's Work Force. Thomas disliked advertising his status and preferred to keep a low profile when possible. On waking they had found gifts from Tyr nan Og at the foot of their beds. For Charlie, The Helmet and Breastplate of a Roman commander, along with a sword. He was stunned to find out they were Aulus' own armour. For Thomas there was a box of sweet smelling sandalwood, within it a gold ring centred by an Alexandrite of deepest purple and supported on each side with a brilliant diamond. The note was from Faelinne and Cormac and said simply… "For the ONE".

With no need to hurry, after a quick lunch they took their time heading for home, changing drivers every hour or so. They stopped if something looked interesting, and talked over their time with Cormac and Midir. Just after 5:00 they came into the moorlands of the Wirral peninsular under a lowering sky that promised bad weather. Within minutes the expected storm hit them and in the heavy downpour they looked for somewhere to stay. Villages were few and far between and none had anything in the way of accommodation to offer. Then, after taking several wrong turns and getting completely lost they passed what looked like a dilapidated old mansion with a broken FOR SALE board hanging from a partly open iron gate.

Thomas braked… "You know this is getting us nowhere… at least this place has a roof and we have sleeping bags in the back and some food left over, let's do a bit of breaking and entering…" Charlie shook his head, "That's illegal Tom, what if we get caught?" Thomas grinned, "Then I'll buy the place. Can you get the gate open far enough to drive in?" Charlie heaved a sigh, zipped up his jacket, climbed out and was instantly soaked. He went over to the gate and shook it, testing to see how much effort it would take to open it wide. To his surprise it swung open with no trouble and he got back into the car.

A short tree lined drive took them up to the house where another surprise awaited them. The front door stood open to a large open area that was well lit, with a brightly burning fire giving a welcome warmth. Wondering what was going on but drawn to the idea of warmth and possible shelter they got out and walked into the house.

The hair of Thomas neck stood up, and every sense went on alert. He grabbed Charlie and pulled him back to the front door, but it slammed shut and its metal bolt slid into place. "Good Evening Sir Thomas, and you too Naughton, welcome to my home... a temporary acquisition of course, but it suits the purpose." Justin Thorndyke... aka Ap Gryff-dd rose from his place by the fire. "May I offer you a glass of wine... a sort of farewell drink between enemies so to speak."

Thomas took a deep breath and laid a restraining hand on Charlie's arm. "We must decline your kind offer Professor (or is it Dr?) Thorndyke. But I'm driving, and we must soon be on our way. However a few minutes can be spared before we have to leave."

Their opponent poured himself another glass and raised it in salute. "Oh I think you can assume your stay will be longer than that... quite a bit longer actually. I have two other guests who are anxious to meet you." He gestured towards the curving staircase. A man and a woman stood a few steps up. Both were of a beauty rarely found in humans, a beauty that hid, as Thomas was well aware, an ancient evil that was soul deep. The same evil that had brought fabled Atlantis to its end. His higher senses shifted into gear. He turned and bowed to The Lords of The Dark Face.

"Lady Negirani... Stealer of the First Breath of Newborns. Lord Amhurabah... Keeper of the Souls of Traitors. I am glad I refused the wine. To drink in such company would befoul my claim to be The Guardian of Albion. The demonic duo said nothing but Gryffdd smashed his glass into the flames and screamed defiance, spittle drooling down his chin.

"A Claim you will never take on, only I, Iorwyth Ap Gryffdd will have the right to hold that title, and I will extend its power over the whole world. I will live forever and the world will be at my feet."

Charlie laughed... the sound broke the tension and

everyone looked at him. He doubled up and laughed until he cried. "If only you knew how daft you look... and you sound like something out of a really bad movie." He laughed again as he turned away, then suddenly grabbed a heavy carved chair and with a strength he never thought he had, he lifted it and swung it at Gryffdd's head. His opponent waved a hand and uttered a single word of power. The chair crashed down on Charlie's head and knocked him semi-conscious to the ground.

Thomas grabbed a heavy brass candlestick and went for Gryffdd like a man possessed. The Dark Lords simply waited, allowing the two to fight it out, knowing they could bide their time. With Charlie down Thomas fought with every bit of strength he could muster. His foe was strong and well versed in battle, so Thomas switched to his inner powers and summoned his Power of Air. The door flew open and off its hinges. The force of a wind gust slammed Gryffdd up against the wall and momentarily took his breath away. But he retaliated by causing the bottle of wine to shatter and the shards of glass to aim for the eyes and face of his opponent. Another gust of wind deflected them and sent them back full force. Thomas was now aware that all this had been carefully set up and it would be a fight to the finish. Even if he managed to win against Gryffdd he would still have to face The Dark Lords. He was on his own.

Charlie staggered to his feet and tried to tackle their crazed opponent to the floor, but got his ribs kicked in retaliation and collapsed in agony. The two would-be Magi faced each other. Thomas leapt on to the table and reached for the heavy iron candelabra above, grabbed it and swung with his full force at the other man's head. Gryffdd reached for his feet to pull him down, but Charlie, with his last ounce of strength twisted to his side, gasping as his broken ribs protested, grabbed Gryffdd's foot and pulled hard. Gryffdd fell forward his head connecting with Thomas full weight and was thrown back into the fireplace.

Thomas dropped to the floor and pulled on the Power of Fire. He reached for the memory of Belle and sang out the musical phrase that had been Her Dragon Name. The flames reached out like so many eager hands of fire. Intense heat far greater than normal engulfed Gryffdd and his screams rang through the house. Within seconds what had been a seemingly unbeatable enemy was just ashes on a dusty floor. But the battle was not over.

Thomas turned to those who watched and waited. Charlie, had lapsed back into semi-consciousness. The pain of his broken ribs taking him out of the battle. Amhurabah raised a hand and aimed a bolt of energy at Thomas who erected a curved wall of Light before himself. The energy swept into the curve and roared back to the sender who re-absorbed it. His companion wove a net of dark power and flung it over Thomas who used his Power of Air to rip it apart.

Amhurabah then shifted to a point behind him and reached for his heart centre with a hand of ice intending to freeze with its power. Thomas gasped as the coldness hit him, then, realising what it was he called up a memory of Father John and his love for him. The ice hit the memory and melted in its warmth. Negirani's form began to change becoming something no human mind could accept and Thomas realised he had to call on higher Powers than his own if he was going to win.

The two Dark Powers now held him between them. Negirani half way between semi-human and demonic smiled and licked her lips in anticipation of absorbing her share of such a prize. She extruded a long thin black tongue and fastened it to his Solar Plexus and began to draw on its sweetness. Her companion, now behind him in a many armed nightmare elongated a tentacle of utter Darkness and fastened it to the back of his neck and began to suck Power from him.

Thomas felt it like a red hot point of pain that threatened to eat him alive. Caught between the two Dark Lords he was now danger of losing the battle and Albion would fall to the Dark. In desperation he sent out a call for help to the Guardians as he felt his strength beginning to fail. "Albion, Albion, It must not fall into the hands of The Dark Lords."

Far away in Deepdale little Jessica woke from her afternoon nap. She climbed out of her warm bed and toddled to her play desk where she had drawn pictures of her favourite subject... the Angels her mother said looked after her. She picked up her favourite 'Angel Gabby' who always carried his trumpet with him and kissed him. Then it was the turn of Micky Angel who got a cuddle, Raffi angel got a kiss as well because he always got rid of her colds and coughs, finally it was the turn of Angel OOly... she never quite managed to say Uriel. She gathered them all together and went back to bed. She wondered what Nunkle Tom was doing and if he would bring her something back from his holiday. She fell asleep holding her angels and thinking of him, but the purity of her intent answered the call for help.

Thomas felt a sudden surge of energy rise in him. The attached adhesions fell away and he staggered back against the wall and slid down to the floor to catch his breath. His opponents, suddenly aware of a massive flow of high level energy halted their advance towards him. Feeling the touch of Angelic power they began to change to their full demonic forms, knowing the battle had taken a different turn.

Thomas backed away turning his head from their true faces. He crawled into a corner by a broken cupboard and put out a hand feeling for something he could use as a weapon, knowing it would be futile against what was facing him.

He felt something small and round under his hand and looked down. It looked like a brooch, but it was something far more precious. He was holding a reliquary bearing the Papal Seal. A piece of bone from the body of St John of the Cross. The power in it brought him to his feet. Leaning against the wall he held it up towards The Dark Lords and stopped them in their tracks. He recalled the Four Holy Ones manifesting in the chapel back home and knew the medallion could act as a clarion call.

Suddenly he was surrounded by four immense figures radiating light and power. Raphael, Uriel, Gabriel and Michael stood two each side of him. Between them for a brief moment he saw little Jessica and knew she had called them to his aid. The Dark Ones halted and cringed back from the purity of light that faced them. They turned to escape only to find the Lords of the Elements behind them. Paralda, Nixsa, Djinn, and Ghob. Caught between the Warriors of Light, and the Four Creative Powers of Earth, Water, Fire and Air they were slowly diminished, shrivelled, disempowered, and bound for all time into the darkness from which they had emerged. Weary to the point of collapse Thomas held the unconscious form of Charlie in his arms, and asked Raphael, "Can you help him, he's in great pain." The Response was gentle and immediate. "Sleep now, let us do what must be done." Then the whole site was cleansed.

Thomas slept. It was morning when he woke up. For a moment he couldn't remember where he was. Then realised he was in the car. Charlie was asleep in the passenger seat. He looked peaceful and pain free. They were outside the gate and the house was a total ruin. A vendor's notice fixed to the gate said:

**FOR SALE.**

**CONTACT HEYWARD AND SONS.
112 WHITFIELD ROAD.
PENSBY.**

A weathered notice board lay in the bushes by the gate, it read. **Monastery of St John of the Cross.** Thomas switched on the engine and let in the clutch, it was time to go home.

# Chapter Twenty-Nine

**May came in** with a flurry of action. On the 15th Betty and Frank celebrated their silver wedding with a memorable party at the Royal Stag Hotel in London. Thomas hired a bus to take 35 people down and booked the entire place. The worn out staff, who ended up as part of the whole celebration, managed to get them all up, dressed, and more or less sober the next morning. They got back in the bus to make a noisy journey down to Southampton where they waved the happy pair off. Then Steven, Thomas, Charlie and Adam went back to the hotel to sleep and recover. Drew however took over from the worn out bus driver and drove the rest of them back north, via Stonehenge, the Westbury White Horse, The Cerne Abbas Giant, and the ancient Rollright Stone Circle!!! The bus driver eventually recovered.

Steven returned to Hollywood a day later and took Adam with him. Left to themselves Thomas and Charlie booked into a Spa and spent three days being massaged, pummelled, baked in the Sauna, dunked in ice-baths, shaved, trimmed, detoxified and returned to the world squeaky clean but worn out. "Let's go home," said Charlie with a pleading look. "I need to put on old clothes, go without shaving for a few days, and eat Mum's Cottage pie and chips and with two helpings of creamy rice pudding. Plus, do NOT EVER suggest doing this again." Thomas laughed and slapped him on the back… "Bloody good idea… let's go home."

The Full Moon fell on the 5th and as usual the Guardians gathered at the Stones. Thomas in Stag Form took his usual place, remembering as he did so the last time Father John had led the Rite. Drew had then held it until Thomas' 18th birthday when it was formally handed over. As each Stone's Guardian answered their summoning the Stones themselves rumbled and trembled sending small shock waves round the circle. All except the one Stone that still remained empty.

Edna's place had never been refilled and as she had no descendants it was accepted that it would remain so. But as the Cup was passed around, a drop of wine was always given to the Stone in remembrance. Tonight however as the usual Rite was played out when it came to that one place the Stone gave forth a cry, it shook and trembled, the moonlight gathered strength and a single beam bathed it and grew brighter and took on form, indistinct but growing stronger until Merlyn stood before them smiling and holding out his staff in blessing. They greeted him with joy and an outpouring of love and respect. He held out a hand to silence them and spoke.

"Guardians, I ask you to loan me your strength and energy that I may bring an old friend into the circle. Will you give me permission to draw from you?" There was no hesitation, so he circled the stones, touching each of them with the staff. On returning to his place he struck the earth with the staff and a column of brilliant light rose from the ground and took a form they all knew. Thomas cried out… "Father John." He would have run to him, but Merlyn raised a restraining hand.

"No Thomas, do not touch him, it will disrupt the energy and he will disappear." Father John raised his hand in greeting and his well-remembered voice filled the silence.

*"I am here by the gift of your energy and the permission of the One to whom I owe allegiance. I come to offer a new Guardian to complete the Circle… but you must all agree and accept the one proposed. Without complete acceptance the place will remain empty until another suitable one can be found. The one offered as a companion is known to you, but is not born to it as you were born. But he has offered himself in many ways to the Future Merlin. He has given love, strength, blood, companionship and proven himself to be worthy of what is offered. He has been a companion to The Merlin in many lives and in this life has already been his support and comfort.*

*"If you all agree, the Guardianship of this Stone will be offered to him… BUT, he must ALSO agree to accept it and all it entails. Only then will he be given the Power of Change. If he will not accept, memory of this time will be taken from him and it will be as if it was never offered. Guardians, the one offered to you is Charles Naughton who has proven himself worthy to be one of you. If you accept lay your hand upon your stone and let it answer for you."*

Silence fell upon the Circle as each searched within themselves for the answer. Thomas held his breath, of all the gifts that could be given to Charlie, this was the greatest , and the most demanding.

Drew lifted his hand and laid it against his Stone. The Stone gave a deep resonant rumble. Posy followed suit, Ian and Marjory hit their stones together, the stones answered with their deep deep voices. Stan and Les, Nurse Pym, Wally, Ben, all followed one after the other. Not one refused. Each time the stones answered. Finally it was the turn of Thomas. He turned and laid his hand against the King Stone and it answered, sending a full throated roar into the night sky.

Merlyn and Father John looked at each other and smiled. Then Merlyn spoke, "Meet here on the eve of the coming New Moon and bring Charles Naughton with you, it will be left to him to say Yeah or Nay. Thomas you may prepare him at your discretion." Thomas bowed and turning to Father John, sent him a thought full of love, thanks, and honour. He smiled and touched a hand to his heart in acceptance. Both Forms melded together and were gathered up into the full moon above them. Behind them a stunned but elated group of Guardians came together to celebrate becoming a complete Circle once again.

# Chapter Thirty

**Thomas stood at** the open window looking out on to the windswept moorland. In the distance he could see the top of the Tor and the weathered stone outcrop known as the Dream Chair. The whole Tor was a place of dreams, and he thought back to the countless times he'd sat there and thought about his life. In the Dream Chair he had cried for Father John. At fourteen he had sat with Bald Bessie and little Grim and listened to her tales of Camelot. At seventeen he had raged and screamed every swear word he knew when his mother demanded a divorce and left Deepdale for good. He'd sat there the night before leaving for Cambridge. Here he'd met Cormac for the first time. The Hill of Dreams and the Ring of Singing Stones at its foot were a living part of his Life and always would be.

Tomorrow he would take Charlie there and no matter what his answer was, his life, and their comradeship would change.

"Father John, if you can hear me, please help Charlie make the decision that is right for him. I don't want him to take on something he'll regret or be unable to fulfil. For myself, I regret nothing, I am content with my life and its demands. I know which of the Three Roads you took, a decision I have yet to make, and one Charlie will also face."

He sighed and went to close the curtains, then paused.

No… tonight they need to be open so the moors can fill the room with their strength and power. He got into bed and was asleep in minutes. As he slept the mossy, earthy scent of the moors stole into and filled the room with the perfumed essence of Ancient Albion.

* * *

The Gates to the Manor swung open and Charlie drove his Toyota RAV into the courtyard. The early morning call from Thomas had sounded a bit confused, and he'd been insistent on him staying overnight. Not a problem, he'd had his own room and study there for months, dividing his time between his parents' house and the Manor. Thomas had suggested they move into a new Barn conversion a mile or so down the road and on Thomas' land. A peppercorn rent had been offered, but Jim loved his allotment and wouldn't budge so Charlie split his time between them. He climbed out and stood for a moment drinking in the scent of flowers and trees, then the scent changed to home-cured bacon, eggs and fresh mushrooms. Connie, Betty's friend and their stand by cook/housekeeper until she and Frank returned, turned out to be almost as good a cook as Betty herself. He hurried in hoping Thomas had not eaten the lot. By good luck and quick thinking he managed to get what would have been Thomas' second helping.

"So what's all the urgency about? He asked scooping the last of the mushrooms onto his plate." I mean you don't usually call me at 6:30 am unless it's important. Thanks," he said to the sugar bowl politely offering itself to his spoon. It scuttled back to its place by Thomas. "Has something come up unexpectedly?"

"You could say that" was the reply as Thomas grabbed the sugar bowl from heading towards Connie. "She's not

Betty, he hissed…" The bowl hesitated then slid back to its place. Charlie grinned and reached for the toast rack. "You know living here is better than being in Disneyworld."

"Coming from someone who just said thank you to a sugar bowl that's beside the point. We'll be riding, so when you've finished stuffing your face go and get changed. Kevin's bringing the horses round after nine. Connie's packed us a lunch and we'll take a couple of bottles in the saddle-bags. The Horses can drink from the spring."

"You got me out of bed at 6 am on a Sunday to go riding…! Sunday morning lie-in is a sacred institution Thomas Greystone-Carrick." Thomas stood up, drained the last of his coffee and said, "Nine ten at the latest… this is not a joke Charlie after today you will look at life in a different way." Charlie groaned, "Oh God… we're going back to Tyr nan Og aren't we? I knew it was too good to be true."

"No Charlie… not this time, this time it's all about you, not me. Go and change." Charlie stared at him… "About me? Why should it be about me… have I done something wrong?" "No… in fact it's quite the opposite. Go and change… please."

Twenty minutes later Thomas watched Charlie swing himself into the saddle. "Three months ago you couldn't have done that!"

"Eighteen months ago I couldn't have done a lot of things. Ever since I was daft enough to suggest we took the train north together my life has been one hair-raising situation after another. Next life I'm going to be a woman and enter a nunnery at sixteen. What is this all about Thomas?"

"Wait until we get to the Stones. You have a surprise coming Charles Naughton, and you have a choice to make. Let's go. Thanks Kev… I would think we'll be back mid-afternoon." He bent over his horse's head, "Ok Barney Boy let's go." The horse took off like a rocket and cleared the gate leading on to the moor, Charlie followed more sedately going through the gate rather than over it. "Show off," he yelled and settled into the saddle for their usual race.

It was a dead heat and, as the horses slowed down, their riders settled into a gentle trot allowing them to cool down. Just after ten they arrived at the Stones and loosened the girths. The horses drank from the small spring and their riders shared a small beer. The day was still cool and Thomas took a walk round the Stone Circle. He reached one particular Stone and rested his hand on it. "Charlie, you never knew Edna but this was her stone. She inherited it from her mother. She had an older sister Alice but she was killed in a car accident. Her mother never really got over her loss but did her best to prepare Edna to take on her sister's task." Charlie came over to stand beside him.

"Though I never knew her personally Posy and Marjory often talk about her still. I have occasionally wondered about the empty Stone... and if it felt lonely. I know the Guardians meet every month, but I don't know what they do. I imagine it's got something to do with your destiny and they were or had been the Guardians of Arthur's Regalia. Perhaps one day they will find someone who can take on the Stone, then it won't be lonely anymore... I know you took the place of Father John. But Edna's Stone has been empty for a long time." Thomas ran his hand over the stone as if touching an old friend.

"You know Charlie, at the last meeting Merlyn and Father John both appeared. They suggested the name of one who could be offered Edna's Stone and given access to its powers. According to the rules all the Guardians have to accept the nominee. If one disagrees then it's off. That's what we were doing there. Merlyn and Father John offered a candidate. When it was put to the vote every single Guardian and their Stone agreed with the choice. Next New Moon that Guardian, if the chosen one agrees, will be joined with its Stone. They will spend the night communing with it, be privy to its memories and thoughts. They will be conscious of each other no matter how far apart they may be. The Stone will taste its Guardian's blood and a fragment of the stone will be sunk into the arm of the Guardian. They will be part of each other. The Stone will decide on form of shift best suited to their new Guardian."

"How does the Stone know what kind of shift is the right one?"

"It takes into consideration the strengths and weaknesses, shape and form of the physical and the 'feel' of the new Guardian. The following night we meet again and the Guardian is given the power to shift."

"You said someone has been chosen, might it be either Frank or Betty? I could see Frank's shift being a bull dog, strong and loyal. If it's Betty, maybe an otter, they are fantastic parents."

"It's neither Frank nor Betty, Charlie."

"I can't think who else it might be. They must be local to be near the Stones. Who do you think?"

Thomas turned to him and laid a hand on his shoulder, "They chose you Charlie, the Guardians AND the Stones. They chose you, if and only if, you accept." Charlie froze.

"ME, they chose me? But, I'm not magical, Thomas, I'm just plain me. I can't shift, I can't do the things you do, it's a tremendous honour, but how can someone like me take on something as big as that?"

"You were strong enough to help me defeat Gryffdd. Strong enough to stand by me when I needed it. You coped with Tyr nan Og, you can cope with this. Accept it and be a part of all that this is about. Your love of the land alone entitles you to this. Charlie, if ever anyone deserved this… you do. Accept the offer and become one with us in a way you have never felt before. I'll leave you with the Stone, talk to it, ask it if it will work with you." He turned and walked away to water the horses.

Charlie turned to the Stone and reached out to touch it, it warmed to his hand at once and a small, shy, inner thought reached out to him. It felt... lonely... outside of its fellow Stones and Charlie got the image of a small lost "being" desperately needing to be a part of The Whole again. Instinctively he put his arms around it as far as he could reach and he felt it move slightly as if it nestled again him. This was a small part of Albion and it needed to be loved, used and recognised.

"Do you really want to be MY stone and me to be YOUR Guardian?" From deep within the earth came a rumble that grew louder and louder and erupted into the air like a thunder clap. At the same time every Stone in the circle answered in the same way. Charlie clung to what was now HIS stone and always would be.

Thomas touched his shoulder... "Welcome to the heart of Albion," he said and held out a paper cup of wine.

# Chapter Thirty-One

**A few days later** Thomas entered his study, patting the obliging door as it opened for him. Inside Charlie was wading through a set of files. "What are you looking for?" he asked settling into his chair. "I need some info on Sacred Wells in the UK," said Charlie, "preferably within a reasonable distance." Thomas leaned back and asked, "…Thinking of writing a book… it's not your usual topic."

"No, it's something I'm working on at the moment. Thomas, would it be OK if I take off for a few days? I'll keep in touch in case you need me."

"Sure, you don't need to ask, just make certain you're back the day before New Moon, and keep your mobile with you in case we or your parents need you." He grinned. "Keep out of trouble. No trips to Soho with any of Cormac's brothers like last time." Charlie shook his head, "No way… this is just something I need to do… I'll be back on time. See you."

He headed for the door and when it took its time opening asked… "What's the matter Dennis? Am I out of favour today or are your hinges getting rusty." The door swung open slowly but as he walked through it suddenly slammed shut, sending him sprawling onto the landing. Thomas doubled up with laughter. "You know it hates being called Dennis, don't tease it." Charlie gave the door a light punch and ambled off rubbing his bruised hip.

* * *

Life was quiet in Deepdale for the next few days, Thomas caught up on his duties as Lord of the Manor and attended meetings, met up with Tenants, dealt with complaints and did the round of the older generation, making sure they had what was needed. Since the majority of Deepdale's housing belonged to him he was kept busy and it was only when Posy rang him three days before the New Moon that he realised Charlie had not contacted him for three days; the longest time they had been apart for almost two years.

"Posy... you don't think he got scared and did a runner do you?" There was a pause then Posy said, "Have you been to the Stones lately?"

"No, I've been up to my eyes in village stuff, tenants and suchlike. Why do you ask?"

"Because someone's been there... it's different and my Stone tells me it's Charlie, and there's just three days to New Moon. So where is he? I rang his parents but they've not heard from him either. I went up to the Circle this morning... to see if it was clean and tidy, you know what ramblers are like, they leave all sorts of rubbish around. It was absolutely clean, but something has been added. I think you should go and see. It's nothing bad, in fact the opposite, but it feels different. If you have time... I can meet you up there in an hour. OK!"

* * *

The sun set in a glory of reds, golds and soft purples that covered the moors from east to west. The shadows were lengthening as Thomas drove the jeep to the usual parking space, set well aside from the Circle. Posy was waiting for him. They walked together towards the Stones and even as they did so Thomas felt the touch of something new, the "feeling" had deepened and was waiting for the final touch. They walked into the circle then Thomas stopped, and drew in his breath.

The Stones had taken on a new lustre, a new depth, a new level of awareness. Watched by Posy he walked the circle. At the foot of each stone a small plant had been added, mostly wild flowers, but he also saw Violets, Anemones, Daisies, and even humble Dandelions, all adding colour, freshness and LIFE to the stones, each one ringed by growth and strength. Simple as it was, it lifted the entire Circle to a new level of awareness, and Edna's stone wore a wild rose.

Thomas turned and looked at Posy, she smiled. "It's his way of saying thank you to them, and allowing us to see that they need to be seen as more than Stones. They are part of Albion, the bones of the land if you like. We've never seen them in this way before, but Charlie did and when he takes on the power of his stone he will come into his own inner power. This will be a very special Meeting, let's go home."

\* \* \*

Charlie arrived back the day before the New Moon. He parked the car and transferred two large water containers from it to the all-purpose off-road vehicle the Manor used for rough work. Then he took off for the moors. Thomas arrived back from a town meeting and, seeing the Toyota parked outside assumed Charlie was in the house. He was not best pleased when he finally turned up an hour later.

"Charlie, where the hell have you been, we've been worried sick, not hearing from you. Then, when you finally get back you disappear again."

Charlie sank into an armchair and sighed, he looked as if he'd not slept well while he was away. "I've done a lot of driving, walking, thinking, and collecting. What I need is a solid meal, a couple of whiskies, and a good night sleep. Tomorrow is a big day for us and I need to rest. Please let me be and don't ask questions. I'll tell you about it later on. OK?"

Connie put her head round the door. "Dinner is ready in the kitchen… steak pie, roast potatoes, peas and asparagus. Plum pudding and custard to follow. I'll see you in the morning." She vanished.

Thomas poured two drinks and handed one to Charlie. "Get this down you and we'll eat, then you can take a long hot bath and sleep off whatever has you in knots. I won't ask questions." Charlie raised his glass to him, "Thanks."

True to his word Thomas kept the conversation to general gossip from the Village. Then, seeing Charlie's eyes glaze over he shooed him off to bed. At three am he woke and on impulse went to check on him. He slept soundly with smile on his face and the room was full of the scent of Lavender, Edna's favourite. Posy always made it for her on her birthday. Thomas pulled the coverlet closer around Charlie's shoulders and went back to bed.

# Chapter Thirty-Two

## New Moon

"**Tom... Tom... wake up**... what do we do about a robe... don't Guardians have to wear something like that. I don't have one. Where do you get them? Is there time? Oh God, what are we going to do...?"

Thomas sat up and tried to get his head around the panic in Charlie's voice. "Charlie... what are you talking about, it's only 7 am and you said you didn't want to be woken up too soon."

"Robes, robes... I don't have one for tonight..."

"Charlie we don't wear robes..." Charlie spun round to face him, his face the colour of wall paper paste. "What do you mean you don't wear robes... you mean... Oh God. Oh God... I have to be naked... naked in front of everyone... Oh God... I can't." He paced up and down wringing his hands. "It's too much to ask."

Thomas pushed back the bedcovers and got up. He took hold of Charlie's shoulders and shook him hard. "For the love of Heaven Charlie, you don't have to be naked, we don't wear robes, we wear ordinary clothes, something dark and comfortable. In Winter something warm and waterproof. We are not Wiccans... even they don't always go naked. This is England... it's too bloody cold most of the time to go bare arsed. Now sit down Jesus man, you're shaking like a leaf."

Charlie sat on the bed, his head in his hands, "I was dreaming about tonight and everyone was in long robes and I was there in my shorts. It was so real." Thomas grabbed a dressing gown and ran a hand through his hair. "Even if that happened by some remote chance no one would bat an eyelid. No one would think the worst of you, you are loved and held in high esteem, you are ONE OF US."

"I don't know what I have to do, no one has told me anything…"

"There's no script, this is not a film Charlie… you will be told what to do at each point. All you have to do is follow instructions. You have to give a drop of blood to your Stone, and a piece of stone will be inserted into your arm. Ian will do that. At that point you and the stone will be part of each other. You'll always be aware of it… and it of you. The only painful thing is the shift… for the first few times. It takes a bit of getting used to… but tomorrow we can practice. Be careful not to shift when others are around. Having four feet instead of two takes some getting used to. Also, remember animals don't wear clothes… as you may have noticed… Drew is by no means a gelding…" Charlie groaned.

"You'll get used to it. I'm awake now so let's get dressed and have an early breakfast. We'll have a lazy day and you can tell me what you have been up to while you were away. Go and get dressed… we'll meet up in the kitchen. Connie won't be there yet so you'll have to put up with my cooking."

\* \* \*

The day seemed to go past at great speed and Charlie got more and more nervous. So just before they set out for the Stones Thomas gave him a drop of Sidhe wine. An hour before Moonrise, the Guardians began to arrive in twos and threes in their shift form. The two Greyhounds came first, then the Hare loped in and sat before its stone, grooming its fur. The Badger ambled in and settled down, touching noses with the Hare, followed by the Ferret. A few minutes later the Ram arrived and playfully butted the Greyhounds before settling in its place. The sound of hooves heralded Drew's arrival with Posy's Deer form close by. On silent wings the Owl swept in and landed on its stone and began to preen. Last of all was the Boar who ambled in and took its place with a rumble of welcome. All showed surprise and pleasure at the decoration of their stones. Standing beside Charlie, Thomas moved into his Shift and took his place, the one empty stone stood alone. Now with all present The Royal Stag raised its head and sent a Bellow of greeting ringing into the darkening sky. The others answered in their fashion. He stamped his foreleg and as one, the Guardians dropped their shifts and stood before their stones in human form.

On the centre stone the Chalice of wine was ready. Tonight it was Nurse Pym's turn. She took the Chalice and raised it high to the four quarters.

"To the East, where Light enters the world, may we be Enlightened by its power. To the South, the time of High Noon. May we receive energy and strength for the work of the Day. To the West, where the Sun Sinks to its rest and we reflect upon the work of the Day. To the North and the rising of the Moon as she reflects the Hidden Light that lives within each one of us."

She then circled Stones and shared wine with each Guardian and exchanged the kiss of welcome. She kissed the empty Stone and left a drop of wine on it and returned to the centre. "I open the Power of the Circle to the presence of Merlyn of Atlantis, be welcome."

Charlie, standing beside Thomas could feel the slow

build-up of power as a flash of light sped round the circle outlining the forms of the Guardians. The voice of Merlyn vibrant with power was heard, "Charles Naughton, step forward and lay your right hand upon the centre Stone."

Charlie, jumped and looked at Thomas for support, who answered by pushing him forward. Holding his breath Charlie laid a trembling hand on the Centre Stone. The voice came again. "Do you Charles Naughton accept the Guardianship of the Stone and all that such a position implies?"

From somewhere deep within himself a new Charlie rose up, he felt another presence beside him, feminine, small and frail and he knew that Edna was with him. His voice was strong and firm... "I accept the Guardianship and all that position implies for my lifetime."

"Is this promise accepted by those present?" A unanimous YES thundered from the gathering.

"Is it also accepted by the Stones of this Circle?" Charlie had heard the Stones rumble and thunder before, but now he heard them actually Sing. Each note was true and followed a melodic phrase haunting and heart wrenching. A thousand years and more of the sound of trees in the wind, rain and storm, bird song and animal voices, children's laughter, and lovers sighs, the whistle of a farm-worker on his way home, the screech of a hawk, and the almost silent rustle of growing things. All was captured in the Song of the Stones.

Charlie stumbled towards Edna's Stone and threw his arms around it and for one never to be forgotten moment Edna herself stood in the circle of his arms. The silence was profound. Ian stepped forward and with a small scalpel made a slit in Charlie's arm and let the blood seep into the Earth supporting the stone, then a minute fragment of the Stone was taken and inserted into the wound that closed over it immediately. Silence fell on the group.

Charlie stepped back from the Stone and felt to the ground. He doubled up in pain and cried out; Thomas tried to reach him but could not move. The human form twisted, writhed and changed. For a few minutes it seemed to be covered with a black mist, then it cleared and a sleek black bull rose from the ground, its horns glistening in the moonlight. It stamped the ground with a polished hoof and lifting its head it sent a bellow echoing out into the night. A roar of approbation came from every throat and everyone shifted and crowded round their new comrade.

The release of energy was so great it enabled Merlyn to manifest long enough to give his blessing to the new guardian. With a bit of effort Charlie got back his own form and offered his gift to the circle. Water gathered from thirteen Sacred Wells from all Four Kingdoms and mixed together, was poured over each Stone in Blessing and the celebration lasted into the small hours. Then Charlie was bedded down by his stone to spend the night communing with it. The rest of the Guardians made their somewhat unsteady way home. Under the New Moon the Singing Stones rested, whole and entire once more.

# Chapter Thirty-Three

**A week later** and Charlie was still practising his Shift at odd moments. Sometimes the shift occurred without his say so... but he was slowly getting a grip on it, except for scaring Connie as she gathered vegetables in the Kitchen Garden. Her shriek had Thomas running outside... to find a bull happily munching the radishes... when it saw Thomas it stopped then turned and lumbered away, crashing through a fence as it did so. Thomas calmed Connie down and promised to get a stronger fence put up and "the bull" back to its owner. A sheepish Charlie apologised later. "Those radishes looked so good."

From then on he practised up on the moors, with Thomas and gradually got comfortable with his new skill. Cormac appeared during one session and added a few words, "You keep forgetting the tail," he said, "and don't forget the important parts under the tail. You forgot them last time. Nerys would be disappointed if you turn up in Tyr nan Og without them." He turned to Thomas... "The Trial of Earth has been set for August the First."

Thomas stopped with his beer halfway, "That's Lammas, the old Sacrificial Day. Isn't that risky? The old powers still have influence then." Cormac stroked the muscled back of the Bull slurping beer from a bowl. "That's just the time for this trial. The power of Life and Death come together and cancel each other out. What is dead takes on life, what is alive experiences death. That is why the Trial of Earth is always last. You must go to Scotland and meet with Ghob, the Elemental Lord of Earth. He will meet you on the Mag Moor of Kilmartin two days before the Trial.

"By the way Charlie, I have a present for you. I had the Sidhe Smiths make it to my design." He took two silver objects from his purse and fitted them over the tip of each horn. "If you need a weapon in addition to your horns, just a thought will cause change. Think of a weapon." The Bull lowered its head and the silver horn tips elongated into 6 inch steel blades. "They are made to lie within the horns so you do not need to carry them with you."

Charlie shifted to his own form, "Cormac, that is so kind of you, they will be useful in a tight corner." Cormac slapped him on the shoulder. "Glad you like them. By the way, the underwear is very colourful, though I confess I cannot understand why humans bother with them. Farewell."

* * *

The 26th of July dawned bright and sunny and Thomas pointed the nose of his Aston Martin to the north and waved goodbye to Connie. Charlie had already left to take his mother to the hospital. Since his father's sudden and unexpected stroke he had taken her every day. Jim Naughton was now in a private hospital room and being well looked after but his recovery was taking time. But it meant Thomas was on his own, as he had been for the Trial of Fire.

By heading for Kilmartin a few days early he hoped to familiarise himself with the area before meeting with the Elemental Lord of Earth. He had been reading up on the Kilmartin region and it was seen as one of the finest archaeological sites in the Blessed Islands. With luck and no hold ups he planned to make it to the border before stopping for the night in Carlisle. Halfway he stopped for a meal and a break and called Charlie. There had been no change in Jim's condition but neither had it worsened.

After lunch he took a walk to stretch his legs and breathe air untainted by petrol fumes. He sat for a while in one of the old squares and watched the people go by. Slowly he became aware of a non-human presence. Next to him sat an elderly man in a wheel chair. Thomas smiled at him, the old man smiled back and said, "You will be met at Kilmartin and taken to a place that has been prepared for you. Cormac was quite specific as to your preferences." Thomas thanked him and got up to leave, then hesitated and on an impulse said, "Is there a particular place for us to meet, Lord Gobh?"

The Elemental laughed; "My Brothers said you would know me. Thomas, you will be one of the strongest Merlins the Isles have ever had. Rest well tonight, tomorrow the way will be clear and you will make good time. I will meet you there with your instructions. Thomas took leave of him with courtly bow and returned to the car. He smiled as he headed for the Border. He was becoming fond of the Elemental Lords, Their presence was not as awe-inspiring and energy draining as the Angelic. It occurred to him that as The Merlin, he could interact with the Elemental Dimension as and when he wished, and he intended to do so.

Thomas return to the car and looked for a place to stay. If Gobh wanted him here tonight, there was a reason… He booked in to the nearest hotel and called home for any news.

* * *

That night in the hotel in Carlisle he slept fitfully,

waking several times. Finally he fell into a deep sleep and dreamt of walking down a long tunnel. The walls on either side were covered with pictures of his life, his boyhood, his grandmother, the grandfather he had never known, and the great-grandfather who had left him his land, inheritance, money, title, and... the inner power that one day would make him the Merlin of Albion.

He saw his mother and Adam, and his much loved father, Charlie and the Sidhe folk he had come to love. They were all part of his life past, present and future. Faelinne and beside her a boy with dark blonde hair and blue eyes... just the point to his ears hinting to his Fae blood. Beyond them was the girl with the chestnut coloured hair and eyes the colour of emeralds. Laura... her name was like a song to him. Beside her another boy holding a small dog and a girl, a little older, holding a crystal.

Someone was walking beside him... "They are all part of you, some in the past, some yet to come and all with a part to play in the task that lies ahead. The past must be faced and learned from, the future prepared for and planned. Albion is Sacred Earth, and I, Ghob, am the Ruler of that element. You must prove yourself worthy of the Guardianship offered to you." He woke with a start and the memory of Cormac saying... "Yes you will have two sons and a daughter also.

This trial would be the hardest of all... he had to face his greatest enemy... his own Dark Side.

The run up to Kilmartin on the 30th was as smooth as Ghob had promised and Thomas stopped to take in the whole area before going on. It was stunning, an expanse of moor and forest mixed, the village itself was small and cosy but... even just standing and looking round he could see Menhirs, Dolmens, partly demolished Stone Circles, and entrances to Barrow Graves all around him. The small guide book he'd bought informed him that within this small area there could be found nearly a hundred archaeological treasures. The very air was redolent with AGE.

As he entered the village a woman in a hand knitted shawl, tweed skirt and wellington boot hailed him. Her voice held the Highland lilt. "Ye'll be the laddie I'm to look out for. I'm Florrie Macmurty and ye'll be staying w' me. 'Tis a fine set o' wheels ye have there… but I'm thinking you'd be better with somethin' less fancy. The drivin' here is awfu' hard on the sort of thing ye have there."

She went round and climbed into the passenger seat. "The cottage is a wee bittie further on ye ken." She guided him through the village and on the farthest side stood a small cottage that could have dropped out of a painting by Constable. "Just park round by the wee fence there. T'will be quite safe. There's nay-one tae lay a hand on't. I'm the village Looker ye ken."

"Looker?" queried Thomas climbing out and reaching for his small case. "Aye…the Looker… the witch you folk would call it. Now I've a beef and ale pie that'll be ready in half of the hour wi' homemade bread and butter I churned meself. Apple pie and cream and a mug o' strong tea. Kyle'l show you to yer room. He's me son, a little slow but a good lad."

Inside the cottage was as magical as the outside… handcrafted furniture, and a table ready laid for dinner. His room in the attic was pin-clean and comfortable with a patchwork quilt any housewife would have been proud to own. He washed his hands and face in a basin of ready warmed water and, feeling as if he had walked into a fairy tale, he went down to a meal The Dorchester head chef would have given his finest knife set and his presentation "Whites" to have cooked.

Later, after a second helping of apple pie and cream Thomas and Florrie sat and watched the sun go down behind the hills and drank a whiskey older than the fabled Rabbie Burns. Kyle got his pipes and played "The Auld Folk" to sleep as he did every night. "The sleep of the Auld Folk is a long sleep and no one knows how long ago they were laid to rest," Florrie told him. "On the Morrow I'll take ye where y'll need to be when called. The High Folk have their ways and tis not fer us tae question them. This land has had many names. It was once a kingdom called Dariada and had its own king. Its other name is Moine Mhor.. The Great Glen. 'Tis an Ancient land that reaches back to the Great Cold. Much of the ancient ways, knowledge, and blood lines are still here."

"Florrie, who told you I was coming?"

"Why t'was the Auld Folk themselves Laddie, they ha' filled the air wi' their chunnerin' fer ower a full sailing of the moon. Fair keppit me awake they did. Then the Earth Lord himself came and made it clear, who ye were and why ye were here."

"Who do you think I am Florrie, and why I'm here? I'm curious to know about your powers and your work here with the Old Folk." Florrie re-filled the glasses. "Well now, you're the new Guardian o' The Blessed Isles, and on the morrow ye'll be treading the road all the Guardians take… The Death Road… but, unlike some Guardians… you'll return. You'll need strength Laddie and a strong belief in yer own destiny. Now, 'tis a long day tomorrow so get to bed. I'll see that ye sleep deeply and with no bother." Obediently Thomas went up to his attic room and slept as ordered, deeply and without bother.

## Lammas Eve: July 31st

He woke to the skirl of the pipes, muted as if needing to wake him gently. A pail of hot water stood outside the door, bringing memories of his childhood, when their tiny apartment had no bathroom and they had to go to the public bath two or three times a week. Breakfast was porridge but Florrie, mindful of him being English had provided both salt and honey, giving him a choice. Toast and tea followed. The sounds of the village as it came alive surrounded him and with Florrie he walked to the nearest of the ancient remains. He was surprised to find he was the only visitor there. Florrie laughed at his comment. "Did ye think I'd let the place be filled wi' strangers, with you needing the place to yerself? We've been expecting ye since way back laddie". They visited several of the Stones, Menhirs and half excavated Barrows and lunched in a little café on fresh trout and a sponge cake that almost floated off the plate. He tried to pay for the meal but was told it brought good luck to have him eat at their table. Florrie told him much of their ways but not what to expect the next day. He touched ancient stones and listened to their songs, connecting with them via his own Stone in Derbyshire. Throughout the day, he was treated with honour, respect, and awe. To one and all, He was The New Guardian, and children were brought to him to be blessed. It was as if a mantle had fallen on his shoulders. Now, as the gloaming slowly filled the streets he stood before the entrance of the Barrow he would enter tomorrow at dawn. To all intents and purposes its passage was barely fifteen long, but he knew with an utter certainty it was far, far deeper.

Florrie touched his shoulder, "Come Laddie, ye must eat and rest. 'Tis the last meal and the last sleep until ye return… whist ye now, tis all I may tell ye. Eat and drink yer fill tonight, but on the morrow and until ye return nothin' more may pass your lips. Now to home." They walked back to the cottage silently, there Florrie set before him a bowl of chicken soup thick with vegetables and herbs; two cups of tea and then bed. He didn't think he could sleep… there was so much to think about… But as soon as his head touched the pillow, it took him under and he slept dreamlessly.

## Lammas Day: August 1st

At three am Kyle woke him with water for washing and his shirt washed and ironed ready to wear. At three thirty Florrie gave him a small glass of water and made him drink it… it tasted terrible, but he knew it contained more herbs to settle him. Until now she had always worn a large knitted hat this morning she took it off and her hair, once dark brown, now streaked with grey fell to her hips. She took one hair and wound it around his finger and fastened it with a twist of Heather root. "If you get lost, this will guide you back," she told him, then opened the door.

The road between her door and the mouth of the Barrow was lined with villagers on either side. The men were hatless, the women had let their hair loose, all were silent. It was as if he was dreaming… Barefoot, coatless, carrying nothing in his pockets, he walked between those who were honouring the Lammas Sacrifice in the ancient way. At the open mouth of the Barrow a small boy offered him and cross of heather… "It's fra' the Laird o' the Land," he said and Thomas felt the touch of Ghob. "Thank you," he said… to both of them, and stepped down into the darkness of the Barrow.

\* \* \*

With a startling suddenness he was elsewhere. Still in darkness but with a sense of Time falling like dust all around him. Time he discovered, had weight, and it was crushing him into the earth with a relentless pressure that was close to pain. Time was a mixture of intense sadness and won-

301

drous joy. It had colour sound and taste and felt like being wrapped in velvet, a softness that turned to tight bonds, then to weightlessness.

A beat sounded in his head and he knew it was his mother's heartbeat. Intense light hit him from all directions, no breath, but pain radiating through him as his lungs filled with air, he used it to scream. Where was the warm darkness, where was that sound that made him feel safe. Noise, hands, touch, strange but comforting, a voice he knew. "A son... oh Steven... we have a son." Then darkness returned. He was back in Time and watching himself learning to walk, say his first words, the feel of his father's arms strong and secure and the love between them. His grandmother's voice telling him stories of how she changed shapes. He'd never realised she could.

Then she was beside him, "Of course I could, it's part of the inheritance. My shift was a wild cat, like me wild and impatient. But I wanted to explore the life my father's wealth could give me. I was uninterested in the fate of Albion and the privileges it offered. I wanted life, parties, dances, and David, your grandfather. He was very handsome, but shallow and uncaring of the things I could have shown him. I tried once, but he laughed and said I'd made it up so I shifted. He fainted and when he came round he was so afraid of me I lied, and told him he'd been drinking and had imagined it.

"I knew I had to make a choice. But I was carrying Steven so told my father I could not take on the task of Merlin. David's drinking had ruined his health, I couldn't look after him, bring up a child and take on the duty of a Merlin. My father was very bitter and disinherited me. I was given a small house and a smaller pension, for David never kept a job for long.

"When your father was born I had hopes, but his talent lay in writing, but when you arrived it all became possible. I arranged the move to Deepdale, closer to your great-grandfather. Then when Steven's book was a success, it became possible to place your education under the guidance of Father John. My father took new hope and made his will in your favour. You redeemed what he felt was a fall from grace. I am so proud of you Thomas." Suddenly Thomas was back in the tunnel tracing her picture with his hand. "Love you Gran."

The sound of running water made him turn. Now he stood by an underground river and a small boat with a grey bearded man sat ready at the oars. "There is a charge for the crossing." he said and held out a hand. Without hesitation Thomas passed him the cross of Heather the boy had given him and climbed into the boat. The boatman rowed in silence across the river and drew in before a line of seven steps leading to a double door. Three dogs sat before them. One bounded up to him and leapt up changing as it did so into Barney. No longer the dwarf companion of Bald Bessie or the skinny mongrel dog he had chosen to be in her exile, but the healthy young man he should have been.

"Barney!" He hugged him, "What are you doing here?"

"Repaying the biscuits, the understanding, the loving companionship you gave me." The form in his arms vanished, and it was his own beloved Grim licking his face and nipping his ear as he usually did. Then he too was gone. The third dog was a lean black hound wearing a gold collar. It stood up on its paws and became a human figure, but retained its canine head. "Anubis," said Thomas and bowed.

His courtesy was acknowledged, the door opened and the ancient Guide led him into a vast hall hung with rich tapestries and lit with candles as thick as a man's thigh. It was filled with familiar faces. At the far end was a throne like chair and on it a man in a dark red robe wearing a circlet of gold and a mask.

Thomas bowed, "Pluto, Lord of Hades I salute you and give you greeting." "Both are returned in kind," came the reply. Anubis stepped forward, "Thomas Steven Greystone Carrick comes before you to face judgement."

An absolute silence fell on the great hall and all turned to face the Throne. The masked head turned to him, "Will you accept my judgement and my decision?"

"I will accept it."

"Have you been a good man?"

"I have tried, but I accept I could have done more and better."

"Have you harmed another without cause?"

"I cannot recall having done so, if I have it was without intent, and I am willing to accept judgment."

"Is there one here who is glad that you were born?"

One man stepped forward from the crowd. "I am glad that he was born". The masked head turned to the speaker. "Who are you?"

"I was James Herbert Naughton and I have lately passed from life." Thomas gasped, and would have gone to him, but Anubis held him back. "Jim... oh Jim I am so sorry, I thought you were getting better and gaining strength. Don't worry about Maisie and Charlie... I'll take care of them." James Naughton faced the masked Judge.

"I owe this man so much, he and my son are like brothers. He has shown kindness and generosity not just to me but to those around him. He has not abused his wealth, but used it to help others. He has not taken advantage of his position, but counts himself as one among all. He has given love and time, unstintingly. He is destined to work on the spiritual level as The Merlin of Albion. I will stand witness for him."

Thomas eyes filled with tears, "Bless you Jim, your son

has made my life worthwhile. May you be blessed and rest in the light." The masked Judge turned to Anubis. "Guide of the Unliving. Who else will speak."

Abruptly they were within the Circle of the Singing Stones, their Guardians standing before them. Each spoke in turn of their love and friendship for the one standing before his Judge. They spoke of incidents that held memories for them. Posy spoke of her doubt, and her shame when the truth was known. All had reason in the past to rely on his help, given without question. Jessica in her mother's arms stretched out her hands and blew him a kiss.

The shade of Father John spoke of Thomas' pain at the hands of The Holy Four to bring about the safety of The Guardians. The image of a sleeping Charlie came forward; "He is my brother, I would die for him, and have done in lives past."

Anubis turned to the Judge, "When he was still a boy he re-united a father and son torn apart by lies and hatred. By offering friendship to one who was then an enemy he brought about a reconciliation that mended a kingdom."

The Butler of Ap Gryffdd stepped forward holding a small plant in a pot. "This is a child of Earth, he saw pain and damage inflicted upon it by one who had given himself to Evil. He gave it and me healing and safety. In return it spread news of the coming of the new Merlin among those of its own kind.

Cormac, stood tall and proud. "I am not of his kind, but I am honoured to stand beside him. He taught me to hope that one day Humanity may accept the Sidhe as part of their world." Others came forward, each with a memory of his help and gentleness. Finally there was silence. The Judge turned to Thomas.

"They have spoken for you. How do you speak of yourself?"

"As being unworthy of what I have heard. I am young and have made mistakes. But I will learn from them. I will do what I can, when I can, where I can and the best I can. No one can offer more. I love the land of my birth. Earth is what we are, we come from it, it feeds and nurtures us. I have seen beauty of many kinds. The strength of mountains, the majesty of plains of wheat. Hills and Valleys, Moors and Forests. From the Sidhe I learned to hear music in the sound of the sea and the call of the birds. I know the feel of age when touching an ancient oak, and have seen the willows dance in the wind. I watched the earth enclose someone I loved and knew it was taking her back into Itself.

"The Earth encloses us all eventually and holds us to its heart. It IS THE MOTHER. I will guard, protect, and uphold that part of Her placed in my care. The AIR is Her voice, the WATER is Her Blood, FIRE is her heartbeat. She is part of me, her breath, her blood, her warmth, her very Self. I am a child of Earth and therefore part of all Life." He paused and stood in silence. Then he said, "I understand now. This Trial is not about the Element, it's about me, because I am a representative of that Element. I've been brought here to judge myself. All this…" he waved a hand… "was to make me face myself but there's a part of me I have NOT faced.

"The final Judge is always YOU. To know oneself, the faults, sins, omissions, the doubts, fears, but also the joys, the love, the hopes, and the pain. It has always been so. In ancient Egypt, when the dead faced the 42 assessors they faced themselves… for we cannot avoid the truth that lies within. I still have something to face." Sure of his power he faced one wall and projected his thought image, it showed…..

A dismal two-roomed flat, with broken down furniture and two small children crouched over a meagre fire. A careworn woman was dishing tinned soup into four bowls four slices of bread lay beside each bowl. A man in a wheel chair was watching the children. His face was grey with pain and his breath was laboured. His wife wheeled him to the table and called the children, "I'll go and see if there's a cleaning job at the factory tomorrow," she said.

Thomas spoke. "That man is Dennis Haggard... he once caused me great pain and fear. I've hated him and his two friends for years. It's time to let it all go. They have suffered enough from my hatred. I can and will see to their help."

He changed the image: now it showed what had become of Mick Fairclough... Wrapped in newspaper and huddled in an alley that smelt of faeces, urine and total despair. An empty bottle of cheap wine... the remains of his "meal" lay nearby. "He needs help, food, and to regain his self-respect. For so many years I have blamed them... not realising that I was creating a Hell for them in my mind."

Now... Terry Williamson was in jail... drug dealer and addict. "He is my greatest challenge... but I will do my best." He turned to the Judge...

"I am responsible for what they have become... I wished them ill and this is the result. Now they will become my responsibility. Judge me... and I will accept it."

The Judge took off the mask and Thomas was facing his own image. The Higher Self spoke to the Lower, "The hardest test of all is to face yourself and take responsibility for your actions and desire for revenge. The true judge can only be the Higher Self. Like Orpheus, you descended in search of the Truth. Unlike Orpheus you took responsibility. Over a thousand years ago the man you were then was enclosed within this Barrow a willing sacrifice for your Tribe. Now you may claim your release. Return to the world above and do not look back."

He was curled in a foetal position and cold, bitterly cold, and very thirsty. With difficulty he got to his feet, a dim

307

light filtering through cracks in the ancient stones showed him he was back in the Barrow. Shivering with cold, dizzy with hunger and thirst, he crawled on hands and knees to the entrance. Florrie was there ready, with a blanket and hot tea with a drop of brandy in it. She wept as she wrapped the blanket round him as he slowly sipped and warmed up. Then four of the village men came with the carrying chair used for the procession of the May Queen, but now covered with wheat sheaves, and, after a hundred years, it would once again carry the Barrow King back from his descent into the Underworld.

Kyle in full Highland Regalia went before him, his pipes calling all to celebrate the ancient rite. They carpeted his way with flowers and ears of wheat and sang a song seldom heard for many long years…

## BRINGING HOME THE KING

Heigh Ho the reapers go, hear scythe blades sigh,
up and down the fields they mow with the gleaners moving nigh.
Heigh Ho the stooks they grow, and the wain is filling fast,
the horses strain with might and main and noon comes by at last.
Heigh Ho we bend down low, to bind the stooks full tight,
we lift and stack till bones do crack from morn to the last daylight.
Heigh Ho for those who sow, when the planting time comes round.
As the corn grows high then the king must die in the last stook he'll be bound.

Heigh Ho then the king must go, for he goes to feed us all.

when the corn is ground he'll be nowhere found but bread will be for all.

Heigh Ho for the harvest home, when all is gathered in

when the cold wind moans we will warm our bones and toast to the Lammas king.

(Traditional Lammas song)

At the cottage Florrie and Kyle bathed him like a small child and put him to bed where he slept for a full twelve hours.

\* \* \*

Two days later at 8:00 am Thomas left Kilmartin but promised to return. He had expressed his thanks to them all and, with the local council arranged a full Scholarship for three local children to attend the University of their choice. Kyle and Florrie would take nothing... but a few days later a gold watch arrived by special delivery for Kyle and a string of lustrous Pearls for Florrie.

A few miles out of the village he saw a sign for the Mull of Kintyre and stopped, feeling an impulse to turn off and explore it. But the pull of Charlie's grief at the loss of his father was stronger and he let in the clutch... Kintyre would have to wait, he was needed elsewhere.

# Chapter Thirty-Four

**It was close** to 10:00 pm when he reached The Manor, bone tired. Traffic had been fairly light most of the way, but earth works and road re-surfacing on the border had forced him to slow down. He climbed out of the car as Frank ran down the steps to greet him and collect his bag. Betty was ready to fix supper but he told her he had eaten en-route and needed only a shower and bed, but accepted a mug of tea.

As he drank and relaxed they filled him in on the events while he was gone. Betty was tearful as spoke of Charlie's urgent phone call early in the morning. Frank and Betty had dropped everything and gone straight to the hospital. Charlie and Maisie were at Jim's bedside.

"I wanted to call you Thomas... but Charlie said no, what you were doing was important and needed all your attention. So Frank and I sat with them and saw she had tea and water. Sometimes Jim opened his eyes and tried to speak, but couldn't. Maisie was so brave... she held his hand and talked to him. She went back over the years to special times, and told him how the allotment was doing. He'd smile and press her hand. Then just about dinner time... he opened his eyes and called your name... For a moment we thought he would be alright and then he said... he said..." She broke down and Frank took up the story.

"It seemed as if he was somewhere else, but you were

there as well... it was so strange... his voice was faint but quite clear... he said... 'I stand witness for him', then he smiled at Maisie and Charlie... it was such a brilliant smile... full of love and... and, a sort of joy... Then sighed and... he was gone."

Thomas got up from his chair and went to the window, looking out at the moonlit garden... then turned, "He came to me... where I was... and said that he had... passed... and he said those words to me... 'I stand witness for him.' I saw him, he looked younger and very happy. What happened next?"

Frank took up the story. "The next day the Funeral Directors came, then when... when... everything was done we brought him back here to rest in the chapel. We made sure his friends and what few relatives he had were able to come and spend time there. We knew you would want that... the funeral will be at 11 am, day after tomorrow. Charlie saw to everything and we helped where we could. Maisie stayed here with us, the others are at Drew's. They are both asleep upstairs... we didn't know what time you would be back... it's a fair old drive from the Highlands. You'd best get to bed... and see about other things tomorrow."

Thomas nodded and hugged them both. "My thanks to both of you for helping out. I'll pay my respects tomorrow. Betty if I'm not up... come and wake me 7 am please. It's been one hell of a four days, but I can tell you both... I SAW JIM and he told me himself he had passed... he was peaceful."

He left them and went upstairs, the door to his room opened quietly, and he patted it gently and said... "Thanks." For a moment he thought about a shower, then decided sleep was more important. He undressed letting things fall as they would and headed for the bed without noticing it quietly opened up for him. He was asleep as his head hit the pillow.

Cormac stepped from the shadows and passed a gentle hand over his head inducing a deep dreamless slumber.

**Three days later:**

James Naughton was laid to rest in his local church. It was full of neighbours, gardeners, dog-racing friends, his few relatives and everyone from The Manor. The vicar spoke of his cheery nature and willingness to help when needed. Charlie added his memories of growing up and his father's shock at having a son at Cambridge University... "He thought I would end up working for the local council, probably as a dustman! But I hope I made him proud. I am what he has made me."

The local Community Hall had been hired for the "wake", Betty and her friends provided all the refreshments, and Thomas provided a vintage Champagne for The Final Toast. But later, when everyone but the family has gone Maisie beckoned to Charlie and Thomas... "What can we do about the Others..." she whispered nodding over her shoulder. They looked toward the bank of flowers Betty and Frank had brought from The Manor to decorate the Hall. Small faces peeped out from the petals and leaves, looking anxious.

"They're the little folk from the allotment, you see. They miss him so much and they don't know if they'll be welcome to the new people taking it over. They've been so good to us and I worry about them." Charlie and Thomas looked at each other. She blushed and said, "Oh I know they're there, always have done... and I know both of you see them as well. Especially with Thomas being The Merlin and all."

"Maisie, how did you know about me." asked Thomas warily.

"The Gnomes of course... they heard it from the Flower Kin, and they got it from the really Big ones." Thomas took her by the hand and they walked over to the bank of flowers. Thomas cleared his throat and bowed.

"Good afternoon, children of Ghob. I have a very big garden and the moors are just behind it. There are many of your people in my gardens and I'm sure they would be happy to welcome you. Would you consider coming home with us and living there?" Suddenly the decorations were empty of vibrancy.

"Did you know the cars are now filled with an assortment of Gnomes and Flower Kin," said Cormac suddenly appearing. He bowed to Maisie, "They are ready to be transported to The Manor. It seems your invitation was taken up." For the first time in ten days Maisie's face lit up, "Thank you Thomas."

She turned and gave a shaky curtsy to Cormac. "Sir, I have seen you at The Manor and I know you are of the Other Folk, Thank you for coming." Cormac smiled and bowed again, then left.

Charlie wiped a suspicious wetness from his eye. "Let's go home," he said.

* * *

August passed quietly. Charlie and Maisie moved into the Barn cottage offered them before Jim's death. It had a garden front and back, and The Gnomes moved in with them to Maisie's delight. Less than a mile away it was nearer for Charlie, and his mother had access to Betty and Frank if needing company. Charlie bought her a mobility scooter and after a few mishaps she was soon enjoying the freedom it gave her.

Thomas took longer to recover from the Trial of

Earth, and spent time attending to the projects he had taken on. Summer lingered into September with no sign of the expected Summons. So Charlie took his mother on a trip to Ireland. Thomas obeying an impulse took off for Kilmartin meaning to surprise Florrie, but found himself taking the road to The Mull of Kintyre instead. He parked the car on the quayside and stood looking across the Irish sea to the distant hills on the horizon, It was breath taking, and the row of colourful little houses and shops behind him looked like a fairy tale come to life. He walked the length of the quay drinking in the flavour of it.

He booked into the first place with a vacancy sign. After an early dinner he made his way down to the unbroken sweep of sand running for miles. He walked slowly feeling an inner peace that soothed the raw emotional demands of the last Trial. Here and there rocky outcrops stood sentinel, guarding the town and its people from any danger coming from the sea. Then he heard it, and his heart nearly stopped. He had heard it so many times in dreams but now it was here, it was real. She was here, she was real, he could hear her voice, see her glorious hair, feel her presence as if it was a living part of him.

She sat on the rock looking out to the sea, her hair gleaming in the sunset,then she her clear soprano ringing like a bell in his head. She turned and looked at him as she sang:

> Bheir me o, horo van o
> Bheir me o, horo van ee
> Bheir me o, o hooro ho
> Sad am I, without thee
>
> Thou'rt the music of my heart
> Harp of joy, o cruit mo chruidh

Moon of guidance by night
Strength and light thou'rt to me

In the morning, when I go
To the white and shining sea
In the calling of the seals
Thy soft voice calls to me

When I'm lonely, dear white heart
Black the night and wild the sea
By love's light, my foot finds
The old pathway to thee

He held out his arms and stood there waiting. She jumped down and ran into his embrace. His thoughts cleared... It all came down to this moment in time. Everything that had happened in this life was a continuation of what had gone on long before. Then there had been separation, but with the promise that one day, in some time, they would be together. THEY had kept their promise.

"Laura," he said... "Laura, mo chruidh." He bent his head to hers.

# Chapter Thirty-Five

**From The Journal of Thomas Greystone-Carrick:**

**October 25th**

"**It is well over** a month since I wrote anything. Things happen and change so quickly it's hard to keep up with them. But the last five weeks have been crazy. My life went upside down. I have found her at last... No more empty dreams, no more wondering who and where she is... She's here, with me, a part of me and of my life. I used to wonder how I'd cope with someone who knows nothing about me or my life... I should have known 'They' would have it all worked out.

"I found her in Mull, waiting for me, just as I had seen her in dreams. She was sitting on the rocks and singing as I had always seen her in dreams. I knew her at once. Her wonderful hair, its colour, (like the conker my dad found and polished for me and I won all the conker fights at school with it). It's past her waist and so soft.

"It was so strange... we didn't need to explain to each other, we knew, I knew her, she knew me... She was the one who saved me during the Trial of Water by bringing me air. I saw the thin Gill scars on her throat... so faint you can hardly see them. She lives alone, has done since she was young... but she'll never be alone again... I worried about bringing her back to Deepdale, if she would miss the sea. But I'll enlarge the pool and enclose it so we can use it all year. She will miss the mountains but they are only a day's drive away.

"The Guardians loved her on sight, she and Posy specially, and she won Betty over right away, because she can make bread, the one thing Betty can't do. As for Charlie, I almost had to fight him for her, he runs around doing things for her!!!  As for ME, well... a Merlin and a Half-Selkie!!

"Dad, bless him, offered to get his own place, but she wouldn't hear of it. He spends much of his time away anyhow. The only one that worries me is Mother. They have yet to meet as she is on a world cruise at the moment. It will be an interesting moment.

"The other news is where it gets over the top strange. Cormac brought news while I was in Scotland. Faelinne gave birth to a son, my son, half human half Sidhe as Cormac longed for. He has been named Aidan and will be brought up in Tyr nan Og, but when the time is right, he'll also spend time in my world. It all sounds so ridiculous... I have, or will soon have, a wife who is half Selkie, and a Faerie/wife/ friend... who has just given me a son. Dear God... you couldn't make it up!!! But in some crazy way... it all works.

"The Summons has come and on Hallows Eve I will be installed as Merlin in the Heart of Albion under the Great Tor. The Trials are over and I will rebuild the Ancient Protection over the Blessed Isles. Laura and I will be married in The Manor chapel on Christmas Eve. But another, more magical ceremony will take place at the Singing Stones on New Year's Eve. As this year passes and all that has happened in it becomes established in fact, Laura and I will begin a new year, a new life, and a new Era for Albion.

"But something tells me I have one more battle to face. I have not mentioned it to anyone... but sooner or later... I know I will come face to face with Morgana. She may be imprisoned for now... but she is empowered by her hatred and desire for revenge. Plus the Dark Ones want pay back for those we destroyed. Morgana wants a human body to indwell, my instinct tell me it is Jessica. But that I will not, cannot, allow. I will bide my time until I come into full power after the inauguration. Then Morgana's destruction must be my first act as Merlin.

"At the next full moon Laura, and Charlie and I will travel to Tyr nan Og for the naming of Aidan, Cormac's grandson, and my son... Long ago Cormac said I would have two sons and a daughter... I have been blessed beyond imagining..."

Footnote: "Adam is planning to paint a portrait of Laura as a wedding present, with the Highland mountains as a background. It will hang in the hallway so she can greet all who come to our door."

I felt the presence of my grandmother the other day. She stood in the hall at the foot of the stairs looking up at the Arthurian window and smiling. Bless Her.

# Chapter Thirty-Six

**Hallow'een.**

**As darkness fell** the streets and lanes and alleyways of ancient Glastonbury began to fill with the excited shouts and laughter of children. Dressed in a variety of costumes, masks, and fanciful hats they thronged the town. The youngest accompanied by parents or older siblings carried baskets and bags, some already bulging with candy, sweets, chocolate and sundry small gifts. They ran, from house to house chanting their Mantra… "Trick or Treats, Trick or Treats, if you haven't got a penny then give us sweets."

Amid the swarms of children and their helpers no one noticed the many dark cloaked figures that moved quietly among them. Unlike the ghosts, witches, monsters, and other fanciful costumes, these moved with purpose, slowly wending their way through the excited crowds towards the Tor that dominated the whole town. In twos and threes, some alone, others in larger groups, but they moved in silence and un-noticed.

Ignoring the winding path that led to the tower they made for the darker side of the Tor. One rarely trodden, and hardly visible. A single sentry stood guard holding aloft a shrouded lantern. As the newcomers approached a question was asked, and the answer when given, led to the opening of a door that in daylight could not be seen.

The Guardians of The Singing Stones, and those invited, entered and followed a winding passage that led deep under the earth. It opened onto a Hall so vast it was hard to see where it ended. The ceiling reached up to touch the base of the Tower above it, and ended in a six pointed star. The frescoed walls showed the mark of ages from a far off time when the Tor bore on its topmost point a crystal pillar three times the height of a tall man, and the thickness of an ancient Oak. It had once crowned the city of Poseidonis on fabled Atlantis, and at noon, when touched by the Sun's rays, had flooded the city with light.

The pillar now stood in the centre of the Hall. Around it circles of robed figures sat quietly. Some were ancient, advanced souls who no longer needed human form. Others came from distant places and times and different belief systems. Some were not and never had been human. The Unseen of many countries were represented, the ancient Gods, the Nature spirits and the Sidhe, the smaller Fae and the Group Souls of the life forms of Earth and the small Folk that filled the moors and hedges. The Elven and the Tuatha, and those that guarded the ancient forests, mountains, seas, and timeless ruins built by hands long vanished. All were represented here.

The past Merlins and those who had held high office in forgotten Atlantis took their places. The Heroes and Warriors of Light, the courts of Camelot, and Tyr nan Og, Druids and Elementals began to fill the hall with colour and the shine of polished Armour. Opposite them by contrast were the delicate Rainbow Forms of the lesser Angelic levels.

The Guardians, and the family of Thomas and Charlie with Laura next to Steven were seated where the ceremony could best be seen, with a Fae close by if they should need anything. The Hall was now divided into four areas with paths separating them and a central pathway leading from a curtained entry to the foot of the Crystal Pillar.

Slowly, what little noise there was faded, and into the silence came music. Soft voices rose and fell in gentle harmonies bringing memories of different seasons. Then came the sound of a Horn, not strident but golden and mellow calling all to alertness.

The music began again but this time as if a drum was being beaten softly. The Curtains parted to admit the main procession. Maisie gave a little squeak of delight for proudly leading them were the Nature spirits from her own garden. As they drew level to the family seats they turned as one and bowed, then took their places in front of them, being considered part of the family.

Ghob, the Elemental Lord of Earth, was next. He walked slowly, his robes of green, russet, gold and snowy white echoing the seasons of the year and wearing a coronet of wheat. In his hands he held a crystal bowl filled with earth and nestled into its centre was a small green plant that had once alerted its fellow kind to the presence of the New Merlin and spread the need for his protection. After Ghob came Nixsa, Lord of Water, in robes of sea-green and moon-silver, crowned with Pearls and Coral and carrying a seal pup that rested quietly within the encircling arms, safe and contented. Now came Djinn, Lord of Fire, wreathed in smiles and clothed in living flames that rippled and flared and changed colour and shape from moment to moment. He wore no coronet but a helmet bearing the likeness of a Dragons Head. Last came Paralda, Lord of Air, here the robes were composed of feathers displaying every hue, shape and size, from the snowy whiteness of a Dove to the velvet darkness of a Raven. His coronet was from the spreading glory of a Peacock's plumage and at rest on his arm was the Leader of the

Seagull flock Thomas had befriended on his first Trial.

As they took their places the music changed again and now swelled with majestic overtones that heralded the next part of the procession. The Oversouls of the Four Kingdoms of the Blessed Isles walking behind their sacred emblems. Carried on a gold draped platform by six bearers in Highland Tartan came the Stone of Kingship followed by Cináed mac Ailpein the first King of Scotland in 843. Then came the Sword of Defence in its bejewelled Scabbard followed by Arthur of Britain wearing his Royal Regalia. Then strode a tall, proud Warrior, Cuchulain of the Isle of Erin who held aloft the Spear of Destiny. Last of all came a young girl cloaked in a mantle bearing the Red Dragon of Wales, she carried before her on a white cushion, a simple wooden cup, dark stained. From it emanated an influence that brought all to their feet with heads bowed as the Grail passed them.

The last to enter was the First Merlin, High Priest of Poseidinis in a mantle of dark green silk and wearing the Fish shaped mitre of his rank. He led the New Merlin by the hand and they stood together at the foot of the Crystal Pillar.

Silence fell on the gathering, a silence so deep, so full of expectation it was almost palpable. Standing behind Thomas, Merlyn turned him to face the North and spoke in a voice that held a Divine given authority.

"In the presence of this company, and facing the direction of the North Star, I offer this man to be the Merlin, the Defender of the Blessed Isles. Do you of the North accept my choice?"

The answer rolled back from hundreds of throats

WE ACCEPT

Merlyn turned Thomas to the West. "In the presence of this company, and facing the direction of the Setting Sun,    I offer this man to be the Merlin, the Defender of the Blessed Isles. Do you of the West accept my choice?"

WE ACCEPT

Merlyn turned him to the South. "In the presence of this company, and facing the direction of the South Cross I offer this man to be the Merlin, the Defender of the Blessed Isles. Do you of the South accept my choice?"

WE ACCEPT

Merlyn turned his charge to the East. "In the presence of this company, and facing the direction of the Rising Sun. I offer this man to be the Merlin, the Defender of the Blessed Isles. Do you of the East accept my choice?"

WE ACCEPT

By reason of my power, I summon the Holy Four who surround That which created and sustains this universe... are You willing to accept the candidate?

From the Crystal Pillar four beams of light emerged, lengthened took on colour and form. Four Archangelic Powers surrounded the trembling figure that stood between them. They reached out to touch him and Thomas, remembering the agony of their touch the last time, took a deep breath and prepared to endure what might come.

Instead, he was wrapped in warmth, love, and gentleness. Strength poured into him, power enveloped him, knowledge filled him, understanding became a living part of him.

Raphael touched his brow, Michael touched his heart,

Gabriel touched his genitals, Uriel touched his feet and he, for one infinitesimal moment became one with them. In that instant, the unspoken question was asked…

DO YOU ACCEPT?

"Yes… I accept…" The Stone was placed beneath his feet, the Sword was placed in his hand, The Spear pierced him and left its indelible mark on his breast, the Cup was held to his lips and he drank its bitter sweet contents.

The Light from the Star of Sirius crossed Time and Space and enveloped him, drawing him into the Crystal where it changed him, adjusted him, re-created him into what he needed to be. For one stark second he was all that had ever been, and held the knowledge of everything that would be. Then it was gone.

So was everything else… the Tor, the Crystal, the great Hall, and those who had filled it… The memory, the knowledge, the power was there… but the actuality was in another dimension. He was with his family in the sitting room of their hotel suite… He looked at them… and they shared the wonder of what had been and knew it for a reality they had all experienced. None of them would ever be the same. Least of all Thomas. Outside the sun rose over the horizon and a new day began.

# Chapter Thirty-Seven

**November 5th. Bonfire Night**

**The Manors usual** Bonfire Celebration, although the usual success, had been trying for everyone. Coming so soon after the ceremony under the Tor, the energy rush it had stimulated had run its course and left them all feeling badly drained.

Thomas had anticipated this. He had arranged all the Catering and Firework displays to be dealt with by an outside Firm. Leaving Frank and Betty and all of them free to relax and recover. The free pizza and hamburger stalls were kept busy, and there were clowns, balloons and sparklers for the young ones as well as the big display as a finale.

The Gates closed on the last stragglers in the small hours, leaving the weary professionals to douse the bonfire and make it safe before leaving. They would return in the morning to clear up and collect the generous fee they had undoubtedly earned.

Charlie and Maisie had already left, along with the other Guardians. Drew, Posy and a worn out Jessica were already asleep in their usual room. Steven had quietly opted out a couple of hours before, having just arrived back from the US that morning.

The sudden stillness after all the screams, shouts,

laughter and noise of the Fireworks was like stepping into another world. For Laura it was too much. She had never been to a celebration like that. The noise, the crowds, and the closeness of fire was scary. At the end of the evening Thomas had found her in Selkie form in a tub of cool water, crying with fright.

Coaxing her out and into her own form brought it home to him that she needed time. Time to be comfortable with lots of people around her. Time to understand that he was responsible for a lot of those people. Time to realise she needed to be in human form more often and a lot longer than she ever had before.

Finally, worn out with tears, and curled up close to him she slept, and dreamt of her lochs and mountains. But he lay awake and worried, and trying to find a way they could overcome the difficulties they both faced. In a few days they would be in Tyr nan Og, he would speak with Midir and Cormac, at some time in their immortal lives they must have had similar problems and setbacks. Their advice and knowledge would be helpful.

Laura stirred in his arms and murmured his name but did not wake fully. He drew her close and breathed in the slightly salty scent of her body. Whatever the cost, a way must be found.

The small group of four climbed slowly up the narrow track leading to the top of the Hill of Dreams. Though Steven was fairly agile for a 58 year old he was glad of Charlie's help on the way up, and sank down on the stone seat to catch his breath.

Thomas grinned and slapped him on the back, "Watch it Dad, sitting on that seat is what got me into all this trouble in the first place." Steven returned his grin, "If it can make me a faster typist... then bring it on."

Charlie stood taking in the view and in his historian's

inner eye trying to see it as it would have been a thousand years ago. "It can't have changed much over the last thousand years The village would have been much smaller and further away of course... but otherwise, not a lot of difference." Thomas and Laura stood hand in hand, that morning he had placed on her finger the ring made in Tyr nan Og and given to him by Cormac and Faelinne. The rays of the setting sun caught the Alexandrite and made it glow even brighter.

Thomas looked up at the slowly darkening sky. "Charlie and I have free entrance and can pass through on our own, but Laura and Dad, you will need to go through one by one with Cormac."

Charlie turned from his contemplation and placed a hand on Steven's shoulder. "I'll stay with Steven until Cormac returns and then go over myself. This place can be really weird at night." Steven stood and stretched... "Watch it you great Yorkshire Lummox... you're talking to someone who writes Weird books for a living."

"Speaking of weird..." said a new voice, "Steven... how about this." Cormac in full Sidhe regalia stood before them. "... and just to add to the occasion..." Two green and gold translucent wings sprang from his shoulders and swept to and fro creating a subtle scent that brought a low humming from the Stones below.

Laura gasped and reached out a tentative hand to touch them, "Ohhh, so beautiful..." Cormac took her hand and bent to kiss it. "Could I do anything less but appear in full Faerie mode to such a beautiful maiden." Thomas snorted and drew her back into his arms.

"Watch it you lecherous Elf... she's spoken for... and you can skip the maiden... I've seen to that."

Cormac grinned and Laura laughed and blushed. "But you do look splendid Cormac. Maybe I should have waited for you to come along... after all a lover with wings would be... useful."

"All is ready in Tyr nan Og my friends... Thomas, with your permission may I take your lady through?"

"Providing I go with you both." The pathway opened, silver and brilliant, Cormac lifted Laura into his arms and... with a flourish... spread his wings and took off, Thomas stepped onto the path and vanished.

Steven... for once open mouthed and speechless was left with Charlie who was enjoying the whole set up. In seconds Cormac was back. "Your son is getting very possessive Steven, he got quite bad tempered when I claimed a kiss as a transport fee."

Steven laughed and asked with a grin, "And do you expect the same from me?" Cormac stood back and bowed. "No indeed, but with full honour allow me to escort you." He took one arm, and Charlie took the other, all three stepped onto the silver path. Steven felt a fleeting moment of ice coldness, then he was bathed in the sunlight of Tyr nan Og, and clasping the hand of Midir. The Court was ablaze with colour and thronged with Fae from all the Courts.

In the next few hours Steven Greystone got to know a side of his son's magical life he had heard about but could never have envisaged. With his writer's eye and ear he drank it all in and stored it away, knowing he could never speak of it, but could draw on his memories to enhance his work. He took the chance to speak with Midir on an idea he had been hatching and asked how he could bring it about without endangering what needed to be kept secret.

When Thomas saw his son for the first time, tho' he expected it... he was taken aback to find himself facing what appeared to be a five year old. He knew time was different here, and the Sidhe grew in a different way and time scale to humanity. He knelt down and took his hands. Father and son communed silently and much passed between them. Then he took him into his arms and held him close. The link was made strong and true.

Steven and Charlie also made their links. Steven specially was moved to tears, something that was a wonder to the Sidhe. To them tears were something of a miracle. He tuned to Midir and asked softly, "Thomas said when he is older he will be able to come to my world and stay for a while, is that true?"

"Yes, he will. Have no fear Steven, you will not lose him, nor will we take him from you. Part of you lies within him. Now come, the naming ceremony is about to begin."

The Great Hall had been decorated with the banners of the Faerie Courts, and those belonging to that Court were lined up behind it. Their clothing was rich, varied and colourful. Jewellery flashed and gleamed in the Sunlight and music filled the air. Voices were raised in harmony and an outpouring of joy.

It was a special time. This child had been born with a purpose, to hopefully re-unite the Seen and the Unseen, the Human and the Fae, the Earthly and the Magical. He would, if successful, be the first of the Fae to go beyond the Earth and take his Race into the Unknown. The first of his kind to attend a human university, and, though his Fae blood would give him a much extended lifetime, there was a chance he might be the first of his kind to know the phenomenon of Death.

There was a stir among the guests as the time vortex shook announcing another arrival. Merlyn, Arthur and Guenevere with a smiling Mordred beside them headed the Camelot contingent. It made the day perfect for Thomas.

Faelinne had until now kept away, not wanting to embarrass either Thomas or Laura. But now she came forward shyly and offered her hand. Laura took it and drew her into an embrace.

"I know why and how it happened, Thomas told me, let us share him together. I may have his heart, you have his respect and his love in a different way. Let me share your son and I in turn and when the time comes will share my children with you. Let our children bring us together not tear us and the man we both love apart. We are strong enough to do this... and I, half Selkie as I am can join with you in this companionship."

Midir and Cormac came forward and embraced them both. Midir spoke low and with his heart. "That this man can inspire such an understanding between two female hearts makes me long for the gift of tears... but of joy, not sadness." He turned to the company, "LET THE NAMING CEREMONY BEGIN."

Midir, Cormac and Faelinne took their places. Aidan stood before them. Opposite them stood Thomas, Laura, Steven and Charlie.

A Herald standing between them read out from a scroll "The Lineage of the Mother". Then, from another scroll "The Lineage of the Father". Addressing Cormac He asked, "Cormac, son of Midir, scion of the ancient house of Aengus, do you accept this boy child as being of your House by reason of your daughter Faelinne being his mother?"

Cormac stepped forward and laid his hand on the boys head... "I do so claim this boy child as being of my House and of my Blood."

The Herald turned to Steven, "Steven Greystone, by reason of descent from your mother's line of the House of Carrick. Do you accept this boy child as being of your House by reason of your son Thomas being his father?"

Steven stepped forward and laid his hand on the boy's head... "I do so claim this child as being of my House and my Blood."

Both men came together and clasped hands over the boy's head. Then they clasped hands together.

The Herald spoke again. "Faelinne of the House of Midir, do you claim Thomas of the House of Carrick as the father of your Boy Child?" Faelinne came forward and laid her hand on the boy's head. "I do so claim him as the father of my son."

The Herald turned to Thomas. "Thomas of the House of Carrick do you claim Faelinne of the House of Midir as the mother of your Boy Child?"

Thomas came forward and laid his hand on the boy's head. "I do so claim her as the mother of my son." They clasped hands over his head and kissed.

The Parents and Grandparents now crossed hands over the boy's head. Cormac and Thomas, Faelinne and Steven. Then Cormac and Steven returned to their places. The Herald turned to the waiting crowd, "If there be one who would gainsay these claims. Speak now…"

No voice was raised. But Faelinne turned to Laura and beckoned her forward. Over the boy's head she took her hands and spoke.

"I Faelinne of the House of Midir, offer my friendship to you Laura of the Selkie Folk. I willingly share my son with you and he will be known among us as He of the Two Mothers."

Laura in turn spoke, "I Laura of the Selkie Folk, accept this offer of love and trust, in return I give you my own love and trust and pledge, that any child born of my body will look upon Faelinne of the House of Midir as their Mother and they will be known as the Children of Two Mothers. My children will be your children, as your son will be my son. This is pledged in the sight of this company." Silence fell as everyone realised the depths of trust these words involved. Then a cheer went up from every throat as the two women embraced.

The Herald spoke to the gathering, "As yet this Child is un-named. How shall he be named in the House of Midir?" Laura spoke strong and clear. "He will be named Aidan Aengus Mac Cormac."

The Herald turned to Faelinne and asked... "How shall he be named in the House of Carrick?" Faelinne smiled at Laura... they had planned this, "In the House of Carrick he will be named Aidan Steven Charles Greystone Carrick." Standing close to Steven, Charlie burst into tears.

A roar went up from the gathering. Even Thomas had not been told of the added name. He lifted the boy onto his shoulder and turned to the gathering his joy showing in his laughter. Now the celebrations began in earnest, as gifts were showered on the child. The music began, and the wine flowed, though for the human guests it came from Thomas' cellar. Aidan was passed from person to person and Tyr nan Og was filled with a rare joy, for births among them were very few. From the castle Tower the banners of the two families floated free.

Amid them all Steven filled his eyes, ears, and memory with all going on round him. He must remember this for it would soon be gone. He felt a hand in his arm and Midir drew him aside. "I know what is in your heart, and the struggle you fear, the loss will come... the loss of Aidan's presence... but I gave you a promise that you would be a part of his life." He turned and summoned those of his own kind to him. Those of the Tuatha, and of the Court of Oberon. He conferred with them briefly then came to Steven and laid a hand upon him and said quietly.

"Steven Greystone, I, Midir do name you Fae Friend. By doing so... you are granted access to Tyr nan Og and may cross the threshold that divides your world from mine at will. I do not give this lightly and it places our world at risk.

But I give you this so you may at any time visit your grandson here in Tyr nan Og. I rely upon your word to keep us safe."

For a moment Steven was unable to speak, awed beyond belief at the trust offered to him. Then he took Midir's hand and gave his promise. "I will never give you and your people cause to regret this gift, for which I thank you with all my heart."

The celebrations went on for three days. For the Fae it was a time of joy and hope, that it might be the beginning of renewal between their worlds. For the humans it was a "homecoming".

* * *

Once back in Deepdale Laura returned to Mull for a few days to visit with Florrie and Kyle and re-new her ties with her former way of life. Though Thomas had not asked about them, he knew she retained a few links with her mother's people and needed to keep in touch.

Christmas was looming and as usual there was a lot to prepare, including the fact that Thomas' mother had announced her intention to be there for the wedding on Christmas Eve. She was told it would be quiet, with just a few people. The "Society Event" she had planned was not going to happen. Her husband had not been invited; he was too busy with his new project.

The usual preparations for Christmas were well in hand. Posy planned to fill the Chapel with Holly and winter flowers and make the bridal bouquet of Scottish Heather from the hills of Kilmartin. Florrie and Kyle would be there to represent the Highlands. Florrie would give the Bride away and Kyle would pipe them down the aisle to a traditional song "She Moved Through the Fair". Drew offered them the hospitality of the Carrick Arms. Nora and Adam planned to arrive on the 23rd.

Betty opened up the Master Suite and planned the reception down to the last monogrammed napkin. Laura would spend the night before with Charlie and Maisie. Every house in the village showed a card of congratulations in the window and all households received a bottle of vintage Champagne to drink their health. Thomas planned a drive around the village in a festooned horse and cart immediately after the ceremony so everyone could cheer the new Lady Greystone-Carrick.

After the wedding dinner at the Manor, a helicopter would take them to Ireland for Laura longed to swim in the Lakes of Killarney. Thomas planned to spend some time alone in the Chapel the night before. It had seen so much of both joy and sorrow and he hoped in some way he might make contact with Father John. Here they would make their vows according to the law of the land. But on New Year's Eve, in the Circle of Singing Stones, they would make other vows and bind together not only two people, but two worlds, two life forms, and Four Elements.

Frank drove Posy and Laura down to London. Posy had strict instructions from Thomas to fit her out from head to toe. Until that moment Laura had not realised the wealth he commanded and was stunned to find herself seen as the future Lady Greystone-Carrick. Their suite at the King Stag hotel left her speechless, when she learned her future husband owned it.

Posy steered her out of Marks and Spencer's into the smaller select boutiques. With North Country common sense she began with the basics, underwear and nightwear, graduating to coats suits, dresses, evening wear, shoes and last of all The Dress. Along the way she added a matching set of Luggage.

Thomas meanwhile saw to mundane things like

passports, and adding Laura's name to documents, bank accounts, debit cards, his Will, and other legalities, including the wedding rings. Along the way he took from the Carrick vault the diamond necklace, unworn since the death of his great-grandmother, Deirdre.

On the morning of the 23rd Frank collected Nora and Adam from the Airport and Florrie and Kyle from the station. Florrie had balked at flying, but Kyle kept their carriage entranced playing Highland melodies to "make the journey shorter!" Thomas made his Christmas round of the farms and by mid-afternoon the Guardians, family, and assorted guests were gathering for the evening meal. But Thomas spent time alone in the chapel.

After a serious threat from Thomas, Betty allowed a catering firm to provide the dinner. At 8 pm, everyone gathered in the hallway and, to Kyle's "Gathering of the Clans" they walked in, headed by Steven and Florrie; Thomas and his soon to be bride coming last. In all thirty people sat down to a four course meal and the ancient hall rang to the sound of laughter and later to the clink of glasses and the skirl of the Pipes. If anyone noticed the glasses filling themselves from the crystal silver rimmed Punch Bowl (a Wedding Gift from the people of Deepdale) they thought it due to the champagne. The Bowl, surrounded by bottles, kept itself filled to the brim and once or twice was seen clinking itself gently against some of the elegant glasses!

Carol singers were brought in from the snowy driveway and plied with wine, mince pies, and Betty's Christmas cake. It was 3 am when the last light went out leaving the Punch Bowl empty but humming quietly to itself.

The 24th dawned with a snowfall. Posy and any Guardians on their feet finished off the Chapel decorations. Betty had the cases ready in the hall, while Frank made sure the landing space for the helicopter was clear.

Charlie and Steven got a surprisingly calm Thomas shaved, dressed, and ready. The gaily decorated horse and carriage stood ready and waiting outside Charlie's door, as Florrie and Posy got the bride ready. Little Jessica in her flower girl dress of red velvet with a lace collar played with Masie's new kittens.

By 11:15 the chapel was filling up and the Abbot from Thomas' old school was vested and praying quietly. 11:25 and the Guardians arrived and took their places, then the House staff headed by Betty (armed with a box of tissues) and Frank.

At 11.45 Steven escorted Nora in with Adam, and took his place beside her. As Laura had no family of her own Thomas had asked everyone to simply fill the chapel, and it was indeed filled to overflowing. The carriage could now be heard approaching and the Abbot took his place and motioned Thomas and Charlie to come to the altar. The carriage stopped and at 12 noon The strains of Kyle's pipes were heard playing "She Moved Through the Fair". The ancient tune filled the chapel and they all turned.

Resplendent in his full Highland regalia Kyle came slowly down the aisle; behind him a solemn eyed Jessica scattered autumn leaves before the bride. Maisie and Posy quietly slipped into their places. Florrie, in dark blue and, with the scarf of her clan tartan proudly displayed, led Laura down the aisle. Thomas looked with his heart in his eyes as she came towards him.

A simple unadorned dress of cream velvet with matching slippers. Swathed across from shoulder to waist was the proud Tartan of the Clan Buchanan fastened with a silver brooch. She brought with her the faint tang of the sea that was part of her heritage. She wore no veil, just a coronet of holly and mistletoe, and carried a bouquet of Heather. Around her neck she wore a circle of diamonds brought to her by Charlie as she woke. Her wedding present from Thomas.

Florrie stopped and let her take the last few steps alone as the pipes died away Thomas held out his hands and took hers to his lips. Then they turned as the Abbot began...

We are gathered together...

\* \* \*

As they left the chapel, The bells of Deepdale's Church rang out, sending their message of happiness to all within hearing. While those in the chapel headed for the Manor, Laura and Thomas climbed into the carriage, where he wrapped a cloak of pure wool around her and a blanket over their knees and they set off for the ride round the village.

Everyone who could was in the streets waving and cheering. Those who couldn't stood at their windows and waved. Thomas was well loved and respected and his bride would be a part of that. They were deluged by winter flowers, small gifts, miniature horseshoes, and gaily wrapped sweets as the carriage circled the market square and stopped so Thomas could stand to thank everyone and give the signal for every household to receive a bottle of champagne. Laura stood and held out her posy of Heather and, with a laugh she threw it high and wide. It sailed over the crowd and landed in the hands of a young woman, very obviously pregnant. She held up the posy and shouted out to Laura, "The Doctor told me yesterday... it's twins." The crowd roared with laughter and the carriage turned to make its way back to the Manor where the wedding lunch was waiting.

Right on time at five o'clock a helicopter, sporting a large bow of white satin, landed on the driveway. Frank passed in the cases and Thomas and Laura, now dressed for the journey came out and were cheered as they climbed into the passenger seats. The guests waved them off, then went back into the warmth of the house to continue their celebrations.

In the helicopter Thomas found something wrapped in silk and a note from Midir: "The Selkie Folk passed this to me saying it was their wedding gift to a "Daughter of the Wave." He handed it to Laura who uncovered a silver vase, inscribed with the words:

### The White Star Line, 1912
### Maiden Voyage of The Titanic

* * *

The 30th of December dawned bright and clear, though with a chill that promised snow later on. At midday, in cars, vans, on foot, and by motorcycle, the Guardians began to arrive. It was time to prepare the circle for the coming year. From Drew's van they took brushes, heated water, soaps and oils and the various tools that were needed.

First the grass in and around the outside of the circle was trimmed and weeded, along with the main pathway from the moorland proper. Extraneous growth was removed from around the stones, but along with the grass was kept in a bag. Charlie had brought a selection of small plants and seeds. Since he had decorated the stones just before his taking on of Edna's Stone, it had been agreed that this should be continued. But before the planting, the stones had to be cleaned.

Each Guardian attended to their own stone. They were washed down with blessed water, slightly warmed and mixed with a gentle cleanser. Since Thomas was away, Drew as next in line cleaned both stones. Loose gravel, from the wearing down by wind and rain, was removed with care and placed around the base of the stone. Then they were oiled and smoothed with one of Posy's special products that she made only for this purpose.

As they worked each Guardian communed with their stone passing on news of what had happened since the last cleansing. Even on a winter's day the stones warmed under the care of their Guardians and, as always, there was an exchange of energies. For Charlie this was the first time he had experienced a cleansing and his stone passed to him stories and memories of its past and of its former Guardian.

Then they planted the seeds and small plants for the spring, before finally coming together to attend to the King Stone. By now the evening shadows were gathering and it was time for the censing. This year Posy had created a new incense with herbs and oils gathered and distilled throughout the year. A friend had brought her a small bottle of Jordan Water from Israel, some ambergris, and frankincense from a temple garden in Ethiopia. With these as a base she had created an incense that was more powerful than any they had used before. Even Posy was shaken by its effect.

The centre stone hummed and throbbed and under its mental prodding Ian, acting as the Leader this time round, took the small bottle and anointed every stone in the circle, then returned to the centre. There was silence for a heartbeat... then every Stone gave voice. It was like a thunderclap. In unison they sent out a note of praise that sent birds flying, trees bending and dancing, and the small creatures of the moor came close to bathe in the power. But then the power centred itself in the King Stone and remained there. The message came to them all... tomorrow you will be told more. Then there was silence. Shaken they gathered their tools and returned home in silence.

## New Year's Eve, 11 am.

The helicopter landed with a gentle thud and its passengers, bending low to avoid being beheaded, scrambled out. Thomas thanked the pilot, wished him a Happy New Year, and slipped him an unexpected bonus before he took off again.

Betty and Frank came running to welcome them home, and hurried them in from the cold. Hot chocolate with a splash of rum soon warmed them and Frank relayed a message from Drew concerning what had happened at the circle. Thomas drank his chocolate then went off to see him and the other Guardians who were gathered at the Carrick Arms. Betty took Laura up to the Master Suite and helped her unpack.

The Master Suite of the Manor looked out over the moors and on a clear day, the top of the Hill of Dreams could be seen. A little overawed by the size and the ornate furnishings Laura moved around touching with gentle hands the old tapestries and the curtains of the massive Four Poster bed.

On the dressing table Betty had arranged the silver backed comb, brushes, and mirror that had belonged to generations of Carrick brides. Laura turned to Betty… "It's all so different to what I expected, I didn't know you see, Thomas said so little about… well… any of it… the Manor, the title, and all that money. I don't know how to cope with it."

"You don't have to dear, let Thomas do all that. He's good at it. But he never let it change him… and he won't let it change you."

"Who slept here before me?" asked Laura sitting on the bed.

Betty paused, then said, "No one since his great grandmother died in France over eighty years ago. Thomas wouldn't even let his mother sleep here. He said no-one would until he brought his bride home to Carrick Manor, and now he has, and you're here where you belong." She paused, "I've never seen him so happy as he's been since he found you. He's worked so hard to be as good to his people as his great grandfather was. I don't think there's anyone in Deepdale he's not helped in some way, since he took over." She paused to adjust the flowers in a big bowl on the window seat.

"It fair broke him when his mum and dad separated. She changed a lot when he came into the title and all that money. She thought it would be hers to spend and it wasn't. She thought she could use the title, being his mother, but she couldn't. He was just fourteen when he came into the title, and couldn't touch the money until he was eighteen. But she thought as his parents they would be able to dip into it. But Steven made sure she didn't get her hands on it." She paused, "But, it's all water under the bridge now. You are here and all is well. Now come along and I'll give you the keys and show what opens where…"

Laura stopped her… "No Betty, you keep them, you know this house better than I and if I need them for anything I'll ask you. But please, keep them with you."

Betty paused, then raised her head and wiped away a tear. "Thank you dear… I'll not say it wouldn't have been a wrench, but I'll show you where they are kept… so if you need them, you'll know where they are. Now, the girls from the village come in every other morning to do the cleaning… except for Mr Steven's office, and I do that once a week.. He hates it when things are dis-arranged and, like all writers he is untidy and forgetful. I have to call him on the house phone to let him know dinner is on the table. Even then he often forgets. Then I sometimes leave a tray outside the door and knock loudly. But there have been times when it's still there in the morning and him asleep at the desk."

Laura put her arm through Betty's, "Let's go and have lunch."

Over omelettes and fries Thomas shared his news concerning the Circle. "For Merlyn to expend the energy needed to cross worlds it must be important," he said, accepting the tomato sauce bottle as it nudged his hand. "I know he meant to be here for the hand-fasting, but to remain here longer to pass on information is very draining, unless he has help from somewhere."

"You always call him The Merlin, surely you're the Merlin now," said Laura sipping her tea. Thomas smiled at her, "He will always be the Merlin to me. He was and is the first of us. But I suggest we get some rest, it was an early start this morning, and it will be a long night as well."

Laura stood and began to gather the dishes. Betty shooed her off. "Get your head down Laura... you have a long night ahead." Frank grinned at Thomas... "You too lad... don't want you falling asleep in the middle of things."

Thomas gave an enormous yawn. "I didn't realise being married was so tiring," he said. "Or that Selkies seem to need less sleep than humans... but I'll take your advice." He bent suddenly and slung Laura over his shoulder. She gave a little shriek. Betty and Frank laughed as she was carried up the stairs.

Drew and Posy arrived just after eight thirty and sat talking until Laura and Thomas came down. Thick woollen cloaks and walking boots would be needed as a light snow fall began to cover the already frosted moor.

Betty fussed over Laura's hood, "Draw it tight dear, the wind can be fierce on the moor. Thomas, I'll leave a thermos and sandwiches on the table, you might need them later especially a hot drink. Now off you go."

Out on the moor dark clad figures began to gather

silently. Each taking their place before their stone. Most arrived in shift form, leaving their cars a distance away but returning to their own form once they arrived.

Laura looked around in wonder, she had seen Thomas and Charlie shift often, but to see so many, and in different forms was exciting for her. Her own shift could only be fully achieved once she was in the water, though she could retain the seal shape on land for an hour or so if she wished.

The moon began the long climb to her zenith and Posy and Marjory began to light the lanterns at the foot of each stone. Laura was instructed to stand outside the circle and wait until needed.

As the moon grew in power so did the circle. Each stone extruded its power enclosing its Guardian as it did so, then reaching out to its companion on either side making the entire ring a cauldron of power. Each stone emitted a deep hum on its particular note, this was picked up by the Guardians making a musical phrase that drew on the Earth power beneath and the Lunar power above.

Within minutes the entire circle had become a globe throbbed with power. Into its centre and drawing on the power to aid their manifestation came Arthur, Guenevere, Mordred and last of all Merlyn. The Circle as one bowed in reverence. Now the note changed, becoming higher in tone and lighter and the Guests from Tyr nan Og. Midir, Cormac, Aengus, Faelinne, and... to Thomas; delight, Aidan; no longer a child of five, but a bright eyed twelve year old who ran into his father's arms. Then he turned to Laura to be embraced by her also. The circle dimmed but the power remained and Faelinne ran to Laura and brought her into the circle.

Merlin beckoned to Thomas and placed him facing Laura across the centre stone. Then Aengus, the oldest of the Firstborn reached up into the moonlight and drew from its light a glowing crystal. "Into this shard of moonlight I place the power of strength."

He passed it to Midir. "Into this shard of moonlight I place the power of gentleness."

He passed it to Cormac. "Into this shard of moonlight I place the power of awareness."

He passed it to Faelinne. "Into this shard of moonlight I place the power of truthfulness."

She passed it to Merlyn. "Into this shard of moonlight I place the power of honesty."

He passed it to Mordred. "Into this shard of moonlight I place the power of dedication."

He passed it to Guenevere. "Into this shard of moonlight I place the power of love."

She passed it to Arthur. "Into this shard of moonlight I place the power of loyalty."

He passed it back to Aengus, who enclosed it within his hands and over his heart. Then he held them out and opened them. In his palm lay two rings fashioned from pure lunar power. He beckoned Laura forward and named her Fae Friend. He then beckoned Thomas forward and gave him one of the rings. He took it and placed it on her finger beside the gold one she already wore. Then on his instruction she took the second one and placed on Thomas' finger alongside his gold one.

Aengus blessed them both: "Thus do two worlds come together, two hearts beat to the same rhythm, Two bodies join in unison. Gold and silver together, the Sun and the Moon in harmony."

From the Stones came a thunder clap of sound.

Into the crystal cup on the centre stone was poured Fae-wine... Thomas offered it to Laura and she drank, then she offered to him and he drank and drained it. Then the cup was broken, never to be used again. And the shards placed beneath the stone.

Now Merlyn of Atlantis stepped forward and, with a sweep of his hand, enclosed the Circle of Stones within a sphere of Power. Within it, it became summer, warmth enveloped them, and the seedlings planted with such love blossomed. He invited all to sit and to listen.

"To all things, all life, all events, there is a time of action and a time of rest, but after the rest comes renewal, and with renewal comes change. So it is with this Sacred Circle and all in charge of it. From this time on, as each Guardian reaches their time of departure, no new Guardian will be appointed to their Stone. Charles was the last. The purpose of the circle has been accomplished, and to each Guardian the gift of choice will be offered at their time of departure. The three roads will open to you: The Road to Camelot, the Road to Tyr nan Og and the Road leading to the Mystery of Humankind. You will be free to choose.

"There are many such Circles throughout the world. The curious have always sought them out and wondered about their purpose. A few, a very few, have found what they sought. All such places are guarded, and often that guardianship passes from generation to generation who are blessed for their steadfastness. The time of this Circle draws to its close and with the passing of the last Guardian it will close down. The power it has generated will return to the Earth from where it came. There it will rest until needed once more; then it will rise again, renewed and ready to empower those who will seek out its secrets. This Circle has kept a secret for almost ten thousand years.

"As Thomas was told, in Atlantis twelve Swords of Power were forged. Six were given to the Kings of Atlantis, two were given to the Fae, of the Elder Race, four were given to the Lords of the Element. The Sword of Air, that governs the Power of Words, to Paralda — the human tongue is its symbol; the Sword of Water to Nixsa — the ice- cold stalactite that can freeze the blood, but preserve the form; the Sword of Fire, the first element to be tamed by humanity, was given to Djinn — it is fed by the emotions of the heart; the Sword of Earth, made from the matter of Earth, was given to Ghob — it lengthens the arm and strengthens the hand. But one more sword was made: the thirteenth, the sword that rules all the others. The first six were scattered throughout the world and many were found and used by the great warriors, but the thirteenth was hidden by its maker. It may only be used once by each warrior. It can call upon the strength, skill, power, and purpose of all the others. Whoever wields it must be sure of the intent and purpose. Such a warrior is always pre-chosen by a power far greater than any of us here can know or understand."

Merlyn looked towards Thomas for a brief moment, and the unspoken words "it is the Sword of Sacrifice" were fed into his mind. Then Merlyn struck the centre Stone with his staff and it rolled back to reveal the space beneath. They all craned forward, remembering the last time it was opened to reveal the Regalia of Arthur and his sword Excalibur.

From the darkness rose a sword, that shone with the power forged into it. Its hilt had been made of metal from the meteor that had wiped out the dinosaurs and opened the way for humankind. A single emerald had been set into the top of the hilt. A jewel that had once graced the brow of Samael/Lucifer the first of all great sacrifices. It floated away from the stone and hung breast high.

Thomas riveted by its beauty stepped forward to grasp it, but caught his foot in a knot of grass and fell. Charlie caught him and at the same time stretched out a hand to keep the sword from falling. It moved into his hand and he clasped it hard. Then he reversed it and held it out to Merlyn, who shook his head and pointed back to the opening. Charlie lifted the blade to his lips and kissed it, and for a brief moment saw inscribed on the blade a name. Then it floated back into its hiding place and the stone rolled back over it. Merlyn looked to the Fae…who nodded and stood back.

"Mummy, I'm cold… why are all these people here… is it a party?" Four-year old Jessica had woken from her makeshift bed in the van. She walked forward into the ring shivering.

Aidan came forward and wrapped his cloak around her and lifted her into his arms. "I'll keep you warm little one." Jessica reached up and touched his face, "Can I stay with you?" He smiled and nodded and held her close.

A shaft of moonlight fell on the two of them and the link was made hard and fast. Posy drew in her breath and Drew knew he was giving his daughter into safe hands; just as Thomas, weeping, knew the purpose of the Thirteenth Sword.

* * *

Way out in space a sudden Solar Flare of enormous proportions erupted causing a worldwide disruption of communication systems.

The papers are full of it over the next week as efforts are made to re-establish order.

In the utter darkness of a Withdrawn Dimension sudden cracks appeared on the surface. They widened and opened up an area where the Souls of the Unrepentant Lost await the end of Eternity. The Angelic Michaeline Guards were quick to catch those who had escaped and re-sealed them. But there were a few who evaded re-capture. Among them was Morgana, free to pursue her vendetta and her thwarted desire for vengeance against the newly elected

Merlin of Albion and those who had helped him.

Though aware of the continuing search for her, she set about looking for a suitable human body to take over and use. The indwelling soul needed to have the same internal greed, love of power, type of body, and the life situation she needed.

She spent several years searching worldwide, her insane desire for revenge feeding her slowly disintegrating personality… then, just when she was beginning to despair, she found the ideal host.

Michelle Muldoon had once been a promising film actress, but drink and drugs had pulled her down. The only work she had now, and infrequently, was as an extra. For over a year she had lived hand to mouth barely able to survive. Even porno films had fallen off as her looks deteriorated. Her hatred of those she blamed as the cause of her downfall grew, as life got harder. Selling her body on the street corners of LA late at night kept her in drugs, but with nowhere to take a client it was much harder, and her squalid room did not have a decent bed. Her heart, mind, and soul were wide open to what Morgana offered.

When a veiled stranger offered her a chance to regain her youth, beauty, and former position in life in return for the use of that body, doped up as she was… it seemed like a good idea, though she didn't really understand what it meant. But, when Morgana poured her essence into her, displacing the human soul and replacing it with her own, then, then, she realised in those final moments what she had given up. What had once been Michelle Muldoon fled screaming soundlessly into the void. In its place was a renewed version controlled by a vengeful fury.

Within a few weeks the new "Michelle" presented herself to her one-time agent and announced she had been rehabilitated and was ready to take on work. She looked fabulous, spoke with authority, and displayed a power of attraction that got her work almost immediately. Calling money to her was child's play. A new apartment, wardrobe, and hair style helped; and the power she commanded had renewed the worn out physical form. Within a few months she was back in circulation and being considered for a small but important part in a new film.

She had also re-acquainted herself with all that had happened in Britain. With Ap Gryffdd out of the situation and the Dark Lords licking their wounds, she revelled in the thought that she had the "field" of revenge to herself. She had plans for both Deepdale and Tyr nan Og.

Now, as she sat waiting for her call to the "set", a glossy magazine on the table caught her eye. Its cover picture was of a wealthy and titled Englishman and his wife who were visiting Hollywood.

"Sir Thomas and Lady Greystone-Carrick will be attending the Oscars, next week. Sir Thomas' father, author Steven Greystone, is expected to win his second Oscar for the screenplay of his prize-winning novel *'What Dreams May Come'*."

There came a knock on the dressing room door. "Miss Muldoon, they are waiting for you on set."

Michelle/Morgana rose and checked herself in the mirror... and smiled.

"I'm quite ready, let them know... **I AM COM-ING...**"

# The Thirteenth Sword

The final book of this trilogy will tell of the battle of Thomas and The Guardians to safeguard the Isles of the Blessed from the Fury of Morgana. It will take the combined powers of The Merlin, Camelot, and Tyr nan Og, to protect not just the Isles, but the human world. It is time for the Ancient Warriors to take up the twelve Swords of Light once more...

But *who* will carry the all-important thirteenth Sword? It can only be wielded by a Willing Sacrifice.